"Now I'm yours, too."

Those words reverberated within him, like an echo bouncing deep within endless caverns. He closed his eyes and forced out the words.

"You are mine, but I can never have you."

She twined her fingers tightly through his. "You *can* have me."

Those words crumbled him, sucking away his resistance. He felt the pieces of his heart fall away like shards of glass. He kissed her, let himself taste her, because he'd been living on the memory of that one kiss for too long. For a few seconds, he got lost in her, his fingers threading through her soft, long hair, breathing her in, feeling her tongue moving against his.

Too long.
Too late.

By Jaime Rush

BEYOND THE DARKNESS
BURNING DARKNESS
TOUCHING DARKNESS
OUT OF THE DARKNESS
A PERFECT DARKNESS

BEYOND THE
DARKNESS

JAIME RUSH

AVON

An Imprint of HarperCollins*Publishers*

This is a work of fiction. Names, characters, places, and incidents are products of the author's imagination or are used fictitiously and are not to be construed as real. Any resemblance to actual events, locales, organizations, or persons, living or dead, is entirely coincidental.

AVON BOOKS
An Imprint of HarperCollins*Publishers*
10 East 53rd Street
New York, New York 10022-5299

Copyright © 2011 by Tina Wainscott
ISBN 978-0-06-201891-5
www.avonromance.com

First Avon Books mass market printing: December 2011

Avon Trademark Reg. U.S. Pat. Off. and in Other Countries, Marca Registrada, Hecho en U.S.A.
HarperCollins® is a registered trademark of HarperCollins Publishers.

Printed in the U.S.A.

10 9 8 7 6 5 4 3 2 1

Dedicated to the Wainscotts and the Newtons,
and to R.J., the beautiful young man who gave
his life for his country.

Also dedicated to my awesome team of Rushkies:
Virginia Cantrell, Kelli Jo Calvert, Tina Wampler,
Nadine Bentivegna, Melanie Thomas,
Paula McDonald, Cynthia Hatfield-Garcia,
Marissa Montano, Carmen Rexford,
Christina Greenawalt, Chris Jones, Stephanie Russell,
Tammy Pruitt, Sharon Mostyn, and Ali E. Flores.
Thanks for spreading the love!

And to Kris Gilson and Regina Ross,
two wonderful readers
at Sue Grimshaw's Romance blog.

To My Readers:

If you've read my previous books, welcome back to the Off-spring series! If you're picking up one of my books for the first time, this is the fifth book in the pulse-pounding series that started with A Perfect Darkness *and continued with* Out of the Darkness, Touching Darkness *and* Burning Darkness. *Fear not! You'll get caught right up with what's going on, like jumping on a moving train. This book isn't directly tied into the story arc of the first three books. And I predict that you'll want to go back and read the rest of the books so you can experience all the excitement you've missed.*

Cheers,
Jaime Rush

BEYOND THE
DARKNESS

CHAPTER 1

Petra Aruda leaned back and surveyed the woman in front of her with a critical eye. "You are so going to knock 'em dead."

Sharla jumped out of the chair in the little cubby and surveyed herself in the mirror. "This is like one of those makeover shows. I'm amazing." She gestured to the outfit Petra had chosen, a professional suit and skirt from the adjoining thrift store. "You're amazing!"

Petra smiled as she finished jotting down makeup and skin care tips. "I enjoy it." Actually, she loved it. She handed the paper to Sharla and smoothed a stray lock of her hair.

Katy Perry's "Firework" trilled from Petra's big, plum bag.

"Go ahead, take that. Wish me luck with the interview!" Sharla gave her a quick hug and zipped off.

"You won't need luck! That job is yours." Petra pulled out her purple rhinestone phone; she didn't recognize the number. "Hello?"

A man's low, smooth voice said, "Petra?"

Her breath hitched for a second before she realized it wasn't *him*. "Yes?"

"It's Pope."

Pope. It took a moment to register. She'd only met him once, but the man had gone against the rules to save her and the lives of those she cared most about. They hadn't heard from him in three months, since he'd gone home to face the consequences—a home that happened to be in a parallel dimension.

"You're back? And all right?" she asked.

"I'm back." He didn't answer the second question. "Eric gave me your number. I need to meet with you as soon as possible."

Her heart plunged, taking her breath with it. *Not again. No more running for my life, getting shot at.* "There's not . . . we're not . . ." She couldn't even utter the words *in danger again*.

Post traumatic stress disorder had filled her dreams with nightmares and her days with paranoia. She couldn't even go to a therapist. Like he wouldn't escort her to the psych ward after she told him tales of being hunted by a Rogue CIA officer out to either use or kill her and her friends for their psychic abilities.

"Everything is fine," Pope said in his deadpan voice.

"No, it's not. Otherwise you wouldn't need to meet as soon as possible. That means urgent, and urgent means life-threatening. We're never going to be safe, are we? Every time we think it's over—"

"It's about Cheveyo."

Hearing his name halted her panicky flow of words. "Cheveyo?" She hadn't said his name in two months, when her friends stopped asking if she'd heard from him. Now the name slid over her tongue like honey, thick and sticky.

"I need an introduction. I'll explain more when I see you. Meet me for lunch, a noisy place where we can talk." Without being overheard. *Oh, boy.*

"Cleo's Café, in downtown Annapolis." She gave him the general location on Main Street, a touristy area by the harbor.

"I'll find it. See you in a few minutes."

Her throat tightened as she looked for the supervisor. The Women's Center for Independence helped those who were out of work and needed a makeover, job skills, and more importantly, self-confidence. She volunteered her time and skills as often as classes allowed.

"I've got a family issue," she told the woman in the office. "I'll try to get back before my afternoon class."

Why did Pope want to talk with her about Cheveyo? What was going on? The questions buzzed and crackled in her chest like a lightbulb about to burn out. She got into her bright yellow VW bug with its yellow silk flower in the holder, happy face charm dangling from her rearview mirror, everything bright and shiny to cover up those six weeks of Hell with a capital H.

Yeah, how's that working for you?

The fact that hearing Cheveyo's name twisted her all up inside said it all. He'd held her body against his, whispering in her ear, his hand tight on her waist. And that was their first meeting. He'd been locking her down to keep her from bolting, hand over her mouth so she couldn't scream. He'd come on business, to bring them someone who needed their help, but there was nothing businesslike about the way her

body came to life against his, how *she'd* come to life
when his gaze met hers. He'd known her in an intimate way, known her fears, her idiosyncrasies. She'd
felt every bit of the psychic connection he claimed
they had.

She was in full fidget mode by the time she walked
into the noisy seafood restaurant that overlooked the
docks. The seaside-ish decor fit its waterfront location,
with tables that looked like weathered wood, and
crab traps around the lights over each table. Tacky
quaint, but the food rocked. The scent of fried cala-
mari and fresh-squeezed lemon didn't begin to tweak
her appetite now, though. All she wanted was water
to moisten her dry mouth.

She spotted Pope sitting at a table near the window.
Her gaze was drawn to him as though he'd mentally
flagged her down. Maybe he had. He stood as she
approached the table, and people glanced over. At
six-foot-five, with a shaved head and dramatic, defined features, Pope was striking. He seemed to either
ignore or not notice the attention he got. He held out
her chair and waited for her to get situated before re-
taking his seat across from her.

"You're back in one piece," she said, taking a sip
of water from the glass on the table. "Does that mean
things went well over there?"

Please, please let things have gone well.

He shook his head and opened his mouth to
answer when the waitress arrived with a chirpy
greeting. He ordered iced tea; she ordered a latte, glad
for the waitress to depart so she could hear more. Her
brother, Eric, had pretty much squashed her nervous
habit of cracking her knuckles, but she'd picked up a
new one: braiding her hair.

Pope leaned forward on his elbows, long fingers

clasped together. "I stood before the C—the Collaborate—and had to explain why I used my deadly powers. Though we can't communicate when I'm in this dimension, my power usage is something they can track. They didn't believe me when I told them the truth, and they sensed my deception when I didn't."

Dread trickled through her veins like the slow drip of ice water at the thought of his facing the panel of leaders who resembled a powerful United Nations. "What did they do?"

"Neutralized my deadly abilities and scheduled a SCANE." His light violet eyes gave no clue as to the stress he'd gone through.

"A SCANE? That sounds freaky-scary. What is it?"

"A laser that probes your brain to extract your memories and knowledge. Unfortunately, the beam burns the tissues as it does so."

"But . . . you'd be brain damaged."

He nodded. "It's better when the recipient dies."

"That's barbaric. How did you escape?"

"I called in a favor from a comrade. Now I am a Scarlett."

Only then did she see a flicker of emotion, perhaps disappointment or shame. "An outlaw." She'd gotten the sense that he'd been a highly regarded officer for the Collaborate. Her hand went to her chest. "You saved our lives but put your own in danger. I'm sorry."

"I can live with that. Or . . . not." His mouth lifted at the corner in a smile tinged with resolve. "I do not regret my actions, so there is no reason for you to feel bad."

"Mostly I'm just grateful. But you're here, away from all that horribleness. You're now a permanent resident of our dimension. You need a life." Her gaze dropped to his shirt: boring, white cotton business attire. "And style advice."

"I need more than that, as you astutely surmised from our earlier conversation."

Her smile faded. "I was hoping advice was what you needed so badly. And maybe you just wanted to meet Cheveyo out of curiosity. It's all part of my bright shiny plan."

"Your what?"

"Never mind." She released a long breath. "Hit me. I mean, tell me what's going on."

"One of my roles while I worked as a Shine—an agent—for the C was Extractor. When a Shine went Scarlett and slipped through to this dimension, I brought him or her back. Or killed them if I couldn't. Now an Extractor has been sent for me. He is relentless, powerful, and ruthless. Apprehending me is preferable to killing me, as the C wants information. But killing me is the backup option. I have known him for many years. He used to come here illegally on independent business before he joined the C."

It seemed surreal, talking about lobotomies and hunters while all around people chatted and laughed about celebrity gossip or their baby's latest accomplishment.

The waitress brought their drinks, setting them on place mats that looked like fishnets. Petra hardly looked at her steaming mug. "Nothing else for me."

The waitress looked at Pope, who waved away any order he might have as well.

When she left, Petra leaned forward. "You need our help to get rid of this guy? Because we will. We owe you big-time." She pushed out those words like boulders from her throat. The ground shifted, threatening the tenuous hold she had on "normal."

He smiled. "You are brave, pretty one."

A laugh erupted. "Maybe with the rest of my peeps. But we can't include Amy, 'cause she's preggers. Or Lucas, because she's going to need him." She picked up her mug and lifted it to her mouth.

"I just need one of you. Cheveyo. I've heard you have a connection to him."

"You talked to Eric."

"Something about you being gooey and dewy whenever you saw Cheveyo. Can you explain this? Eric only laughed when I asked."

"He teased me because my eyes looked dewy, which means . . . Never mind that." She rolled her eyes. "Eric, who gave everybody a hard time about falling in love while we were in danger and then fell the hardest." The worst part was, she'd been the only one who wanted love, and now she was the only one who didn't have it.

Pope pressed a long finger against his mouth, regarding her with curiosity. "I'm getting anger from you."

"You can sense my feelings?"

"Since ours have been bred out of us over recent generations, they are much more apparent in humans. Like a loud sound in a quiet marsh."

She forced a smile. "It's not anger, only frustration." She waved it away and planted her elbows on the table. "I saw Cheveyo twice. Yeah, maybe I was a little gooey and dewy, but that's only because he's mysterious and sexy, and he saved my life. One of the enemy who could mind-control got into my head and made me start the car in the garage so I'd kill myself." She shuddered, still smelling the carbon dioxide. "Cheveyo swept in and got me out of the garage, breathed fresh air into me, breathing life into me." She shuddered again, this time for a totally different reason. His mouth on hers, his urgently whispered words, begging her to come back to him. "After I revived, he kissed me and the whole world spun on its axis." The memory still gripped her, just as it did every time she thought about the damned kiss, which was hardly ever.

When he saved her life, she'd hugged him, thanked him.

"I didn't do you a *favor*," he'd said. "If you died . . ." He couldn't even finish the sentence, but the fear of that thought was clear in his voice and expression. She'd seen his desire, too, when she pleaded with him to stay with her, and seen pain when he said, "I wish I could. You don't know how hard it is to stay away from you."

She squashed the way that made her feel. He had reasons for staying away, and she had accepted that. Well, pretty much.

"When two people kiss like that, it means something," she told Pope. "Three months have passed since the danger's been over and not even a lousy call." Okay, it hurt. She thought she'd shored herself better. "I'm not gooey and dewy anymore." She latched onto her braid again, unraveling it. "I'm so over him."

"I'm not sure if that is a good thing or not."

"It's a good thing. I no longer kick my couch or punch pillows." She gave him a forced smile because she'd said too much. "I've moved on. I'm taking a college program on esthetics, which is skin care and such. I have a date tonight with a guy who hopefully can't do amazing, crazy things with his mind, who hasn't killed anyone or been hunted by the government." She released a breath. "A nice, normal guy."

"A date: a social interaction with sexual motivation." He nodded.

"Wow, way to take the romance out of it. What'd you do, study our dimension?"

"Yes, we take extensive training to learn your ways. Our world is much like yours, but human emotions and social interactions are very different. So you have no troublesome feelings for Cheveyo?"

"None whatsoever. Just a lingering frustration, and only because I never found out why he couldn't contact me. It's like when you date someone once or twice and never hear from him again. You always wonder why." Had he ever fallen for someone and felt the ache of their loss? "Ever been on a date?"

"I have no desire to engage in that sort of activity, as I see the chaos it creates in humans."

She snorted. "Probably a good idea." *Look at me, and Cheveyo and I didn't even go out on a date.* "I can't tell you all that much about Cheveyo."

"I don't require information; I only need you to contact him. Your untroubled feelings will make that easier?"

"I suppose. But why do you need me? Can't you, like, teletransport to wherever or whoever? Or did you lose that ability?"

"My transport skills are still weak. Even when they were fully operational, I could not go to him. He's different."

"Yes, he is. Did you know he can turn into a panther? He did it in front of me once. It was freaky, sexy, cool, even if I am afraid of large animals with sharp teeth. He seems more advanced than any of us."

"Indeed. Since he trusts you, I want you to bring him to me."

Her chest tightened at the thought of contacting

him. She hadn't even tried, out of pure pride. If he couldn't be bothered to call her, why should she be the one to go knocking on his psychic door?

The sun slanted in through the window, lighting Pope's untouched iced tea to a deep amber. She pulled her gaze from the rich color. "What do you want me to tell him?"

"It would be better not to mention me until you get him to our meeting place. I've tried to find him over the years, and he may think I'm hunting him down." His mouth twitched again. "Use what you call here feminine wileys, if you must."

Now her mouth twitched in a smile. "Wiles, you mean. Yeah, well, I don't really have any of those." People seemed to think that just because she was pretty, she was (a) easy, (b) had tons of dates, or (c) was a man stealer.

A Mona Lisa smile stole across his features. "I think you'll be able to accomplish the goal."

His confidence buoyed her. Cheveyo had once told her she was stronger than she thought, and he'd been right.

"I'll try. That's all I can promise. Are you going to tell me why you're having me summon him?"

His smile faded. "Do you want to be involved?"

"No. Absolutely, positively not."

"Wise answer. Bring us together, and your part will be done."

"So the Rogues, we're okay?"

He blinked before saying, "Yes, your friends and brother are safe."

That blink spiked into her heart. She could hear the *for now* tacked onto the end of that sentence.

He stood and dropped a twenty on the table. His gaze scanned the restaurant. "You walk out first. In case the Extractor has found me, I do not want him to know we are linked in any way." His voice got lower. "You will need to be even more careful when we meet next."

She blinked as an image flashed in her mind.

"That is where we'll meet," he said. "Speak not of it to Cheveyo. Just bring him to the location."

She nodded, knowing where it was. "This is starting to sound scary again." Scary, but her heart was thrumming with adrenaline. Good God, she couldn't actually miss the danger, could she? That would be sick. And not sick in the good way, either.

Yurek watched a tall woman exit the restaurant where he'd tracked Pope. She headed to the right, unraveling her straight hair from its braid and shaking it out. The blond strands shimmered in the sunlight, falling to the middle of her back. Pope emerged a few seconds later, watching the woman for a moment. She looked back, and in that glance he saw a connection between them. He was close enough to pick up on the woman's emotions: an odd mix of excitement and trepidation. But he also picked up something from Pope. Was it *concern* that came from him? Yes, he cared about the girl. Interesting. They weren't supposed to have those feelings.

He picked up something even more interesting: the Geo Wave, an almost electric sense their kind got from each other. It shouldn't be coming from the human girl.

Intrigued, he followed her, making sure he wasn't picking up Pope's Wave. She looked as though she'd stepped out of one of the many advertisements that bombarded society here: tall, but not emaciated as many of the female models. Her body filled in her black pants and pink, knit tank top with luscious curves. Even though he saw humans as the lesser species, he found some of them attractive in their own way. Like this girl.

People streamed past them, many paying more attention to what was in the shop windows than where they were going. Some looked at him, at the handsome visage he had chosen for his visit here. Callorians, his species, took on a human guise when they visited this dimension. He could take that ability one step further.

The woman stopped at an intersecting road, and he bumped into her. She turned and looked at him without malice, and he apologized. She gave him a forgiving smile and turned forward again.

Yes, a beautiful woman . . . who was part Callorian. Then the pieces clicked together. Pope had been coming here for many years on various assignments. He had been an Elgin, a highly placed Shine, before he went Scarlett. He obviously broke the rules and had an assignation with a human. This lovely creature was the result. It explained why Pope cared about her.

The crowd surged forward again. Now that he worked for the Collaborate—the C, as it was referred to from within—his duties included eradicating anything troublesome in this dimension. This woman was troublesome, just by her very existence. It would disturb Pope if his daughter was killed, and that would distract him and further weaken his Essence. Yurek's smile wasn't all for show. The idea of bringing down the last vestiges of the once-powerful Pope was as luscious as the woman only inches in front of him.

CHAPTER 2

Petra walked down the sidewalk, her stomach churning with both excitement and annoyance. A sea breeze washed down Annapolis's main street, sending strands of her hair to tickle her face. The boutiques, restaurants, and novelty stores catered to tourists. She paused in front of a window full of baby items. With a sigh, she stepped inside, breathing in sweet smells, taking in all the soft squishy and squeaky things that would make a baby giggle. Not that she wanted a baby just yet.

She gasped at the sight of a Wizard of Oz crib set. The bumper depicted Dorothy and gang along the yellow brick road. She plucked out her iPhone and punched a speed dial number.

Amy answered. "Hey, Petra. What's up?"

"How about a Wizard of Oz crib set? It would work for a boy or girl, and it's *soooo* adorable!" They were waiting until birth before finding out the gender, which was so not fair for the rest of them. "No witch or scary monkeys in sight."

There was a—dare she think it?—pregnant pause

before Amy said, "I appreciate the thought, but Oz is your thing, not ours. Besides, we're already set on a jungle theme."

She pivoted to the right. "They have a huge giraffe—"

"You've bought enough stuff for the baby to fill the extra room already."

She hugged a stuffed Toto to her chest. "But I like buying the baby stuff."

Or did she like torturing herself? That Amy and Lucas were expecting a baby was stunning. Bittersweet. No, she wasn't jealous . . . exactly. She was thrilled that they'd found happiness. Amy had confided that the thought of having a baby was scarier than anything they'd gone through, but Petra knew they'd be great parents.

"No more, hon. You know what we'd rather have? You over for dinner. Every time we invite you, you have some excuse for not coming."

"I know, I'm sorry. Next time you invite me, I'll come. Promise."

"I'm holding you to it. Hey, you could buy something for Eric and Fonda's housewarming next month."

"Trying to distract me by throwing a different bone? Won't work. He's cut me off." They had a fully stocked apartment, and the barista machine was quite enough, thank you.

"How about something for Rand and Zoe's elopement?"

"Already bought them a gazillion things."

"Okay, then Nicholas and Olivia's wedding?"

Petra sighed. "The other half of my guest bedroom is filled with silver and white wrapped boxes."

"You know," Amy said, a teasing lilt in her voice,

"they say that shopaholics are substituting for something that's lacking in their lives."

"Like hip-grinding, sweaty sex," she said, catching the clerk's disdainful attention. Well, how did she think there came a need for all this stuff? Sheesh. Petra held up Toto. "Maybe you're right. I have a date tonight, but it's only a first date. Still, it could lead to . . ." Another glance at the clerk, whose petite nose was still wrinkled in disgust. " . . . crazy, screaming monkey sex."

The clerk *hmphed* and turned away.

Petra stroked the blue-checked ruffle on the mobile. "Are you sure about the Oz stuff?"

"Sorry."

"All right, I'll let you go." No need to tell them about Pope. They had their own lives now.

She walked up to the counter and bought Toto, ignoring the clerk's derisive *I'm only smiling at you because it's in my job description* smile.

Maybe it was the fear of Cheveyo's rejection, but an eerie feeling chilled her on the way back to the garage where she parked her car. She looked around. Only a few people in the area, and none were paying attention to her. *I don't like this feeling*. It wasn't like the pricklies she got when she was being psychically spied on during those six weeks of Hell, but it still raised a slew of chill bumps on her arms.

She felt some relief when she was locked in her car. She fished out the little foil-wrapped Dove chocolates she kept in her purse and tossed one in her mouth as she backed out of the spot. Back at the Center, she parked in the lot but remained in her car.

"You'd better not pretend you're not there," she muttered, closing her eyes and reaching out to Cheveyo. He had come to her, but she'd never gone to him. If they shared a connection, she should be able to talk to him, too.

She thought of his face, surprised at how easily she could conjure it in full detail, his thick, arched eyebrows, the curve of his mouth, his blue-gray eyes ablaze with a fierce protectiveness that squeezed her chest. Her heartbeat stepped up, a heavy, sensuous thudding that seemed to pump honey through her veins.

Cheveyo . . .

The connection was like two train cars locking onto each other. She felt him first. Then scenes flashed into her mind: a boy with blue-gray eyes and thick eyelashes staring pensively into the night sky; a dark alley, something moving in the shadows, and the flash of light on metal. The smell of blood. That same boy screaming in fear. Her body shuddered at those images.

The images went dark, and she saw him as he might appear in a dream, hazy and in a void. "Petra?"

She could hardly breathe. "Our connection goes both ways. I can reach you, too."

He didn't look particularly thrilled by that. "I heard you . . . felt you calling me."

"I need to see you. Not in a 'need to see you' way. I mean . . . I'm in trouble."

"What's going on? I haven't gotten any visions."

"I don't mean to sound all conspiracyish, but I have to tell you in person. And as soon as possible."

"Petra, unless this is life and death, now is not a good time."

She gripped the bottom of her steering wheel, quelling her irritation and the hurt that he would put her off. Was he with someone? Was she not important to him after all? "It's life and death. I wouldn't bother you otherwise." Okay, that had come out just a tiny bit snippy.

"All right. I'll meet you in an hour."

She gave him a location near the warehouse Pope had put in her mind. "See you soon."

She pulled out, feeling the loss of the connection tingle through her. *Take a deep breath. It was only Cheveyo. No big deal.* She called the number Pope had given her. "We're on, in an hour."

She went into the Center and spent twenty minutes hunting for makeup deals on eBay. Sometimes she could find brand-name product for a great price. Only Cheveyo could distract her from the joy of bargain hunting. She put in two bids and logged out of her account. A few minutes later she walked out to the parking lot.

As she reached for her door handle, a man standing by his car two spaces away caught her eye. She'd seen him earlier that day in downtown Annapolis. A normal person might think it was a coincidence and nothing more, given that he was nice looking, dressed in business attire. But after everything she'd been through, she'd developed a healthy respect for her sixth sense, and it was telling her something wasn't right. Their gazes met, and she held his for a moment, letting him know that if he had any devious thoughts, she was onto him.

He gave her a nod before getting into his car. She dropped into her seat and locked the doors, but waited until he backed out of his spot and left the lot.

Paranoid? Maybe, but deservedly so. She took the rear entrance out of the lot.

She pulled into the gas station and waited in her car for Cheveyo. She had a full five minutes before he was due. "Breathe." Her nerves felt like an army of ants marching inside her stomach. "Look, there's no point in getting excited or anything," she said aloud. "He only came because you fudged the truth. So seeing him means . . . nothing."

Still, she couldn't help but braid her hair, loosen it, and braid it again. The silky strands sliding around her fingers were comforting, even more so than cracking her knuckles had been. And she didn't have to see people grimace or hear lectures about developing arthritis later in life.

She glanced in the mirror, using her nail to scrape away a slight overlap in her lipstick. The only reason she'd taken the time to pretty up was because she wanted him to see what he was missing. Not that she went anywhere, even to the store, without going through her routine.

"So there, buddy. Too late now. I've got a date with a nice, normal guy tonight, to go along with my nice, normal life, which I love. Besides, who needs a guy that turns into a cat? Probably get cat hairs all over the furniture—"

A shadow fell across her lap and she jumped. Cheveyo leaned sideways in front of her windshield, his hand braced on the hood. Her heart jumped, too, because that's what looking into his eyes did to her. How had she missed hearing him ride up?

She pushed the door open and got out, cringing at the breathless quality of her voice when she said "Hi." Not helping at all were the high heels she was wobbling on.

Really not helping was how damned gorgeous he looked, his wavy dark hair tied back with a leather strap that matched the black bomber jacket he wore. It was unzipped, and beneath, a dark red shirt was unbuttoned enough to reveal a sprinkling of dark hair and a silver charm on a chain at his neck. Oh, jeez, she hoped she didn't look gooey and dewy.

He glanced in her car, his eyebrow arched. "Who were you talking to?"

"Uh . . . no one. The car. I was muttering to my car. It's temperamental sometimes."

He looked tense, his gaze shifting to his surroundings before returning to her. She'd seen that particular type of awareness before, when they were being hunted. Or maybe he suspected she was going to spring the Rogues on him, as adamant as he was that they not meet. Or spring herself on him. Fat chance.

His gaze softened as it swept over her, but it sharpened again, all business. "What's going on?"

She nodded toward the warehouses half a block away. The transportation company that had used these waterfront metal buildings had gone out of business, leaving the area abandoned. A sign had been promising an upscale shopping revitalization, but the economy probably put that on hold.

"Follow me over there."

He arched his eyebrow again, this time aiming his puzzled look at her. Then he shrugged and walked over to his black Harley. He had a smooth, powerful gait, efficient but not hurried. She was reminded of those wildlife shows where a lion walks his territory. In one move he got onto the bike and started it. When he looked at her, she realized she'd been too busy looking at him and not getting her car started.

He fell in behind her as she pulled through the tall fence that was opened just enough to let a car pass through. Otherwise, NO TRESPASSING signs made anyone think twice about entering. The artist's rendering for the future shopping area had faded beneath the graffiti.

She parked, and he pulled up beside her and dismounted. His black boots scraped on the faded asphalt as he walked beside her toward the door of the building she remembered. He smelled of fresh air and a smoky fragrance that wasn't tobacco. She remembered the images of the boy she'd seen, but the most vivid memories where when he'd held her in his arms and coaxed her back from death, whispering "Babe" in her ears, emotion in his voice when he—

"Why don't you look like you're in a life and death situation?" he asked, interrupting her thoughts.

"What do you mean? Oh, because I'm not freaking out?" He knew her well, which drove her crazy. *Babe, I know a lot*, he'd told her once, a ghost of a smile on his face.

"Yeah."

She took a breath at the door, not quite meeting his eyes. "Come in, and I'll explain everything."

She opened the door and stepped inside. His gaze scanned the interior of the large, empty building. Empty. Great, where was Pope?

She turned to Cheveyo. "Because it's not exactly my life and death."

His eyebrows furrowed. "You tricked me into meeting you?"

"No. Well, sort of. It's—"

At a sound behind her, he moved so fast he was a blur. He pushed her behind him, she saw a flash of metal, and before she could gain her footing, Cheveyo held a dagger at Pope's neck.

"What are you doing here, Otherling?" Cheveyo growled, his fingers gripping the blue handle so hard his knuckles were white. The knife was exotic, with a curved blade on one end and a hole for his thumb on the other.

Pope looked calm, his hands at his sides. His gaze flicked to her. "I gather you haven't had a chance to explain?"

She shook herself out of her shock, ran over and clamped her hands on Cheveyo's arm. "Stop! He's a friend."

His expression was fierce, transformed not into a panther but a warrior. His eyes were nearly black, and in their depths she saw death and destruction. He didn't even seem to see her. A cold feeling gripped her, but she didn't dare back down.

Cheveyo flicked a glance at her. "He's a *friend* of yours?"

"He saved my life, all of the Rogues' lives. Pull the knife back, Cheveyo. Now."

The knife was beautiful, the metal on the handle engraved with cat eyes, the blade reminding her of the tooth of a very large, vicious animal. She was close enough to see the details, including the deadly tip and blade edges sharp enough to shred the air. It was made to fit his hand, with grooves for his fingers.

She kept her grip on his arm, his muscles rock hard beneath her fingers. "Please put the knife down," she whispered, feeling as though she might be swallowed up in those dark eyes. Not the man who'd held her the day he saved her life. Not a man she knew at all.

By degrees he allowed her to pull his arm down. He kept those eyes on Pope, pinning him with a suspicious glare. Even when his arm was down, she kept hold of him, watching his eyes slowly lighten.

She could breathe again. "If you'd bothered to see me after we were almost killed down in the bomb shelter, you'd know about Pope."

Cheveyo's gaze hardened and he stared just past her. "I tried to go to you that day. I couldn't." He looked at Pope, then her. "By the time I could get away, it was over. You were all fine."

"Never mind. Pope risked his life to save us that day, and now he needs our help. Your help."

Cheveyo seemed to assess the situation. He looked at Pope. "Who are you, and why would you save them?"

Pope stepped closer. "The Offspring are family. My father's aircraft slipped through a crack between our dimension and this one. He died on impact. It was his Essence that was given to the parents of the Offspring, which they inherited. I've been watching over them while on missions here. I have sensed you during those missions, too, but you have always been elusive. I knew your father, what he was doing here. And I believe you have taken up his cause. An agent has been assigned to take me back to my dimension. I want to hire you to kill him. I'll pay you well."

So Pope thought—or knew—Cheveyo could kill this assassin. Having seen how quickly Cheveyo had that wicked knife against Pope's throat, she knew he could, too. He'd called Pope an Otherling.

Cheveyo's eyes, now back to their normal color, flicked to her, then back to Pope. "You saved their lives. I'll help you. But I won't accept payment."

Relief flooded through her. He was going to help. And he was doing it for her. Somehow she knew that's what that subtle flick of his glance meant. Because Pope had saved her. The thought of that tightened her stomach.

"You called Pope an Otherling. What's that?"

"My word for someone from the other dimension, a Callorian."

"And you just assumed he was evil?"

"Every one I've encountered has been. I have no reason to believe otherwise."

She wanted to say more about the injustice of that, but the first part snagged her. *"Every one* you've encountered?"

Pope stepped closer to her. "We have much to discuss."

Cheveyo touched Petra's forehead as though to brush away a stray lock of hair. His fingers remained, hot against her skin. "Leave now. There's no need for you to be involved in this."

His touch stole away her breath, her thoughts. She managed to shake her head. "I'm going." She remembered he could exert influence over her. He'd gotten her to come outside once, pulling her from a dream state. Her body wasn't moving, though. As if their bodies were magnetically drawn, she felt a force field holding her in place.

He dropped his hand and stepped back, breaking the hold. She inhaled, pulling her gaze to Pope. "Good luck. Please call me, let me know you're all right."

He nodded. "Thank you for your help. Have a good date. Be happy."

Cheveyo tilted his head. "Date?"

"Yes, a social interaction with sexual motivation." She turned and walked to the door, unable to stifle her grin. Had she imagined a flare of jealousy, of possession, in his eyes? She walked out, closing the door behind her, the screech of metal scratching across her nerves.

Walk away and go back to the normal, safe life you cherish. Whatever they're up to, you don't need to be involved. It's dangerous. He's dangerous. She conjured the memory of his eyes, black and deadly. *Stay out of this. It's not your business.*

She got as far as her car, bracing her hands against

the roof, pressing her forehead against the hot metal.

Don't do this.

Dangit. She closed her eyes and tuned her hearing in to their conversation. It was an ability she didn't use often, because it was invasive, and sometimes she didn't like what she heard.

Cheveyo's voice was all business. "Tell me what you know about the Otherling who's hunting you."

"He is called Yurek. Like you, he can manipulate the energy of his appearance, but his ability goes beyond that: he is gifted with mimicry. He can look like anyone, once he's been near that person, and worse, can also absorb and mimic the powers of others. He was what you would call a mercenary, hired privately to take care of matters in both my and this dimension. When I saw him yesterday, I was surprised to see the Collaborate ring on his finger: a diamond shape with a C in the middle. He's obviously working for them now. I'm sure he wants to take my place. He has been an assassin for a long time. He's good at it."

"So am I." Cheveyo's words chilled her. He meant them.

Okay, see, that's why it's a good idea not to be anywhere near him.

As she was about to pull out, Pope said, "That is why I wanted you for the job. When the Collaborate saw I was hiding something, they psychically handcuffed my abilities, intending to SCANE me. If they do, they will discover the existence of the Offspring."

Cheveyo's voice was tight. "And they will be killed."

Her eyes snapped open, her heart lurching in her chest. They *were* in danger! It thrummed through her, pulsing in dark waves, closing in the edges of her vision.

"Without my major abilities, I am no longer on equal ground with Yurek. Killing him will only temporarily solve my problem, however, as they'll only send another Extractor after me. I'm hoping my powers will return, and I will be able to handle future Extractors on my own. But I can never be taken back. Not only are the Offspring at risk, my brother would also be implicated, as it was his job to collect our father's Essence. Some of it was taken before he could get there. The C would view that as a failure."

"So you're only concerned about the Offspring . . ."

"I can't return to my home, my family. I am, in fact, a defector and criminal. My life now means nothing."

She was walking back to the door, one foot going automatically in front of the other.

"Which brings me to the other, more important part of my request for your services," Pope continued. "If I am captured, I want you to kill me."

"I can do that, but be absolutely sure."

"I am."

The door screeched when she yanked it open. "No!" She walked in and stalked toward the two men, her finger pointing at Cheveyo. "You are *not* killing Pope. I couldn't help overhear—okay, purposely hear—your conversation. I want to know and I don't want to know. Maybe that makes me crazy, but whatever. You can't just . . . just kill Pope! That's not a viable solution."

Pope shook his head. "You humans get so sentimental."

She could hardly utter the words, "Sentimental? *Sentimental?* We're talking about killing another person here! Killing you!"

Cheveyo said, "Death isn't that big of a deal. Our bodies die, not our souls." His voice went lower. "It's only hell when you lose someone and you have to live day after day without them. Dying is easy compared to that." His eyes sharpened. "You need to get away from us. This has nothing to do with you."

"That's not what I just heard. If he's taken back, we're all dead."

"And you as well," Pope said to Cheveyo. "You will be in my memories, too." He shifted his gaze to her. "I don't want any of you involved in this. Cheveyo can handle this situation, and you will be safe. Now, go."

She had been daydreaming about, yearning for a cold-blooded killer. He'd just agreed to commit two acts of murder without hesitation.

Cheveyo put his hand on her back and ushered her to the door. He opened it but turned her to face him before he might give her a shove through the opening. His hands settled on her lower arms, and his calluses felt like the light side of an emery board across her skin. He tilted his head down, eyeing her from beneath thick black lashes. "It's dangerous for you to be involved in this. Do you remember how it was when you were being hunted? When you were hiding in the old asylum, running through the woods with that man gunning for you?"

Those memories seized her. "How did you know?"

"I saw it, before it happened. I also saw Eric save you. Think about everything you went through."

"I'm trying to forget."

"Good. Forget it all. Forget what you heard today."

Logical advice. She looked into his eyes. "Am I supposed to forget you, too?"

"Yes." He let go of her and took a step back. "Go."

She lifted her chin. "I will forget you. Watch me." She started to walk but turned. "You'll let me know if . . . if something happens to Pope?"

"Of course. But that's not going to happen."

Another step. "Don't you dare kill Pope. Find a way."

"I will."

He looked confident. He sounded confident. She released a breath and continued walking. Everything she'd heard bombarded her as she reached her car. She never turned around again—good job on that—but felt him watching her. She wouldn't tell the others that danger loomed unless it became an imminent threat. She set the stuffed dog on her lap as she pulled out.

"Toto, we're still not in Kansas."

Cheveyo watched her leave. How many hells would he have to endure where she was concerned? Every time he left her, it tore a part of him. Watching her leave was no easier. *You think you'd be used to it by now.*

He closed the door and found Pope regarding him curiously. "What?" he growled, uncomfortable with being assessed.

"I find humans very interesting."

In other words, amusing. "Must be nice not having emotions. I wish I'd inherited that from my father."

"No, you don't. What I sense, the pain, joy, love and hate, all of it makes you alive."

Cheveyo glanced back at the door. "And it shreds you. She made me promise not to kill you."

He smile was bland. "She feels loyalty, a debt of gratitude. What she feels for you, however—"

"Isn't important. How will I know if you're captured? I may get a vision, but there are no guarantees."

"We bond. A replicate of the bond you share with her. You will see my capture, and I will let you know where I am. Yurek will have to take me to one of the finestras. There are two near here."

"Finestra?"

"What you call a portal. The first finestra to your dimension was found a hundred years ago in a tomb. We named it after the ventilation hole in case anyone overheard an insider talking about it. We can't let our population know about the finestras, which are guarded. It's bad enough that some know about the cracks between our dimensions."

"My father never spoke about the finestras, other than to say he'd come through a vortex a long time ago. What happens if a human finds one that leads to your dimension?"

"Humans feel them, like they feel the energy vortexes in certain areas. But their bodies won't respond to the finestra in a way that allows them to slip through. At least not the finestras we've observed humans encounter."

"What about my body?"

Pope considered that for a moment. "I would stay away from the actual finestra, just in case you have enough Callorian DNA to get you through in one piece. The guards on the other side would apprehend you immediately."

He thought about what it would be like on their end to have someone like him pop in. Not good. "So you'll telepathically let me know where you are."

"You'll have time to intercept us at the finestra, or possibly even catch up to us before we reach it. It's more important that I die than for you to kill Yurek. The danger to the Offspring exists as long as I do. I have even considered simply having you terminate me now to save us all the trouble."

Cheveyo shook his head. "I won't kill you unless I have to."

"Which is amusing, considering you had a knife to my throat minutes ago."

"Yeah, amusing. I didn't think Callorians had a sense of humor."

"I get twinges now and then. This is an entertaining dimension. Maybe it's rubbing off on me." Pope's pseudo smile faded. "If you do terminate me, know it is for the best. I have nothing."

"You have the Offspring. As you said, you're family."

He lowered his head. "But I pose them great danger. Being near them brings even more risk. I cannot do that." He met Cheveyo's gaze, his light eyes softening. "I believe you understand this."

He nodded, feeling a twist in his chest. "Too damned well."

CHAPTER 3

Petra had almost canceled her date, now that her mind was muddled with thoughts of Cheveyo and Pope. And Cheveyo. And Cheveyo. As she sat across from Greg Swenson, however, she was glad she hadn't. This was a distraction, and more importantly, a test to see if she could push all that away and pretend it never happened.

A mariachi band wended its way around Margarita's large, crowded dining room, taking requests at each table. She rolled her eyes as they launched into their next song. How many times would she have to hear the "One Ton Tomato" song? Piñatas hung from the high rafters, and the wait staff would bat them as they passed by so the twenty or so donkeys, parrots, and sombreros were always swinging.

This was a great place for a first date, filled with opportunities to people watch and chat about surface things. She took in Greg's blond hair, combed to one side, his bright, blue eyes and easy smile. They'd shared a couple of brief conversations as they crossed paths in the hallways at the Baltimore School of

Massage. She'd sensed that he'd had to build up his courage to ask her out, which she totally didn't understand. Was she that scary?

After the waitress brought another round of margaritas, he lifted his and said, "To having a salty margarita with a beautiful woman."

She touched her salt-rimmed glass to his and murmured a thank-you, but those kinds of compliments felt like empty peanut shells. What she looked like had nothing to do with who she was. Even though she was taking courses to learn skin care and makeup artistry, she didn't like being judged on her outer appearance. Confidence was key, and she was working on that from the inside out.

"Did I say something wrong?" he asked, his salt-crusted glass held aloft.

"No, not at all." She would rather have him say she was smart or funny, though she wasn't sure she was either. All her life people had said she was beautiful, but no one had ever made her *feel* beautiful.

She'd noticed a man sitting at a booth nearby. He was alone, and apparently the only people he was interested in watching were her and Greg. That he didn't avert his eyes when she looked over made her uncomfortable.

She turned back to Greg. "So, what's the craziest thing that's ever happened to you?"

He rolled his gaze up, chewing on his lower lip as he thought. "I fainted at my high school prom. In my defense, the air-conditioning wasn't working properly and I hadn't eaten much."

She gave him a genuine smile, though he couldn't have guessed exactly why. *See, that's what normal people experience.*

"How about you?" he asked.

"Uh . . . me?" *You should have seen that coming.*
"Let me think." Breaking into an abandoned insane
asylum to free a prisoner? Cheveyo turning into a
panther right before her eyes? She ran her finger
along the salty rim of her glass and stuck it in her
mouth to buy time. Of course, nothing normal came
to mind. "I saved my brother's life."

"Wow. What happened?"

Oh, shoot. She couldn't tell him Eric was shot. Nor
could she say that, actually, she'd saved the lives of
the two most important people in her life.

"CPR. He, uh, nearly drowned."

Greg's blue eyes lit up. "I'm impressed. What an
incredible feeling it must be to know you saved someone's life."

"Yeah." Her face flushed, warming to his admiration and the memories of how it felt. "When he
started breathing again, it was like the world shifted.
Not the ego thing of, like, 'I have the power to save a
life.' It's that I didn't lose them—him." Damn, she was
getting teary-eyed just thinking about it.

"I've never done anything heroic like that, other
than rushing my little sister's dog to the vet."

She smiled. Sweet. Nice looking. Couldn't dress
himself well, but that could be fixed. She liked Greg.
Except that compared to Cheveyo . . . *Forget Cheveyo.*

She waved her hand. "Other than that, nothing
weird ever happens to me."

"Petra."

She jerked her head to the right, where the breathless male voice had come from. Her heart leapfrogged
into her throat at the sight of Cheveyo standing there.
He still wore the red shirt and black leather jacket,
and was holding a helmet in his hand. His eyes were

wild, scanning the restaurant before locking onto her again. She could barely begin to grasp that he was there when he said, "You have to come with me. Now."

She lurched to her feet, sending her margarita glass tipping, and dousing the basket of chips. "Is it Pope?"

"No. It's you." Now she saw the fear that glowed in his eyes. She'd seen it before, when he'd come to her psychically with his vision of her and all the Rogues dying. She couldn't breathe. *Her. It was her.*

Greg stood, too, his blond eyebrows furrowing. "Is everything all right? Who is this guy?"

A bubble of hysterical laughter erupted. How did she identify him?

Cheveyo answered for her. "I'm a relative, and we have a family emergency. She has to go." He put his hand at the small of her back and guided her to the door.

"I'm sorry." She grabbed her purse, throwing Greg an apologetic look. She made the *I'll call you* sign as Cheveyo was escorting her out of the restaurant.

"Do you know how to ride on a bike?" he asked the moment they were outside.

"I've ridden a few times, but not in a miniskirt and high heels."

"There's a first for everything." He'd left his bike at the curb, and he wrenched the black helmet over her head and adjusted the strap. It had a plastic shield that went over her face and gave her a moment of claustrophobia.

She hitched up her skirt and felt the cool leather slide against her bare thighs as she got on.

The man who'd been watching her in the restaurant stepped out, his gaze on them.

"Hell." Cheveyo jumped on the bike, starting it in almost a simultaneous move, and tore away from the curb.

She turned to see the man running to his car. She tightened her body against Cheveyo's, squeezing her eyes shut, holding back the questions she wanted to scream out.

Breathe, she commanded herself, smelling the scents of nearby restaurants and the leather of Cheveyo's jacket. She wasn't crazy about riding on motorcycles, and going way fast was even worse.

A sense of exhilaration raced through her veins, as though some part of her had been waiting for this for a long time.

Which was just plain insane.

Maybe the thighs tight against his waist part, or him barging in on her date to steal her away part. Not the running for her life stuff again.

He looked back, and she followed his gaze. A sleek black car was trying to pull away from the curb but was blocked by the stream of traffic. The driver wailed on his horn, but traffic wasn't moving. They were, since Cheveyo could slip between cars and around the driver that was holding things up because he was waiting for a parking spot.

She wore his helmet. He'd sacrificed his own safety for hers. She could smell the scent of shampoo, crisp and clean, inside the helmet. He stopped at a light and turned to her. "We're going to your place. You'll need to pack your things."

"Pack? Like for a trip, an absence?"

"Exactly."

She had to push out the words. "I live—"

He turned right without hearing her directions.

He knew where she lived, had to, because he drove unerringly to her townhouse on one of the narrow roads in the downtown area. Buildings were stacked up right next to one another, two and three stories. He pulled into the narrow brick alley between buildings, past the two alabaster dog statues, and parked behind the white gate where they kept the garbage cans. The bike's engine echoed in the small space, and then suddenly it was quiet as he killed the engine.

"Get your keys ready. This has to be in and out. And pack *light*."

He was already scanning the area, simultaneously pushing her toward the door. She had the key ready as she always did. Stairs went directly up to her residence, the walls adorned with Wizard of Oz memorabilia.

She ascended, feeling him behind her.

"Is Pope all right? Who was that man at the restaurant?"

He steered her right to her bedroom. "Pope's at my place. He has limited power to teletransport. He's not sure how often he can actually do it. But my place is in the middle of nowhere, so he's got room to run if he needs to."

He glanced around her bedroom, the four-poster bed draped with gauzy material for the canopy, pink and yellow washed walls. It was startling having him in her sanctuary, his dark masculinity in her feminine space.

She faced him, gripping his leather sleeve. "Tell me what's going on. Because I'm only guessing that you didn't storm in on my date out of, say, wild jealousy. Though if you did . . ."

He walked to her closet and pulled a duffel bag

from the top shelf. "I had a vision of you and your boyfriend getting flayed by Yurek, the guy who's after Pope."

"F-Flayed?"

"Tonight, after you left the restaurant."

A chill prickled over her skin. "The man who followed us out."

"That's what he looks like tonight." Because he could change his looks, that's what Pope had said.

"What about Greg? Will he hurt him?"

"I doubt it. He wants you."

"M-Me? Why?"

"I don't know. Right now I'm only concerned with getting you out of here."

He was starting to pull down clothing. That had to stop. She stepped up beside him and took her clothes out of his hands. "I'll pack."

"Be practical. You may be running. Literally."

No, not again! She kicked off her heels and took in the array of clothing jammed in her closet. She had enough trouble choosing something when she didn't have a deadline and Cheveyo sending waves of urgency.

She started pulling things off hangers. "I saw a man in the parking lot earlier. Not the same guy—or maybe it was. He was just standing there looking at me. It didn't feel right, and I waited for him to leave. Then I left out the back way, so if he was waiting for me, I might have lost him. That was when I was on my way to meet you."

"Good job on trusting your instincts." He was taking the clothes from her and stuffing them into the bag, not even rolling them up to prevent wrinkles. "If he'd followed you to the warehouse, we'd probably be dead. So he picked up your trail again later. He probably knows where you live, which means we have to roll."

The tightness in her chest worsened with each word he spoke. This couldn't be happening again. But it was, and she didn't have time to wig out. She threw in pants and long-sleeved tops and two pairs of sneakers. He took out one pair with a roll of his eyes.

She ran to her dresser and grabbed a handful of lingerie. No time to be embarrassed at him seeing all of her lacy things. He closed up her duffel bag and slung it over his shoulder.

She ducked into the bathroom to scoop up some cosmetics, but he grabbed her hand and yanked her back out again.

"Forget all of that girly stuff. Deodorant is as fancy as you're going to have time to get."

She snatched up her deodorant. "Where are we going?"

"My place, to meet up with Pope." He took her in. "Our plan was for him to teletransport from one place to another to stay one step ahead of Yurek. I'd be right on his tail looking for an ambush opportunity. I hope Pope can take you with him."

"Wouldn't it be best if we all stick together? It worked for us before; the Rogues, I mean."

"Not this time." He stopped at the top of the steps, his body going rigid. "Hell. Get back, lock yourself in your bedroom," he whispered.

She heard a growling noise at the bottom of the steps and leaned around his shoulder. An ugly dog crouched between the base of the stairs and her door. Not a regular dog. It was bigger than a wolf but bulkier. Its narrowed eyes glowed red as it took them in, its teeth bared in what looked like a macabre smile, gums black and red. Those teeth were like sickles, curved inward to hook its prey, the tips going down to a needle point. And its eerie gaze shifted to her, its eyes glowing brighter, a string of drool dripping from its mouth.

"Is . . . that . . . Yurek?" she whispered, her hand tensing on his back.

"No. Its name is Baal. And it's not much fun either."

"There's *another* one?"

"Get in your room."

His body vibrated and heated so fast, she jerked her hand back and stepped away as he morphed into the black panther. She didn't need any more warning. She ran.

Could this really be happening? Her feet pounded into the plush carpet and slid as she turned into her bedroom and slammed the door shut. She pressed her back against it, listening to unholy growling sounds. She could barely pull a breath from her lungs. Fear pulsed in her chest.

She pinched herself, and oh, yeah, it hurt. Real, not a nightmare. Cheveyo, out there, fighting that creature, morphing into one himself. What if . . . what if he died? If that thing won, she'd be alone with it. The way it had looked at her, the predatory hunger in its eyes . . . oh, yeah, it would come for her. She needed to help Cheveyo.

She opened the door. The sound of claws scratching the wall electrified her spine. With a grimace, she pushed on, down the hall and to the kitchen. She yanked a knife from her butcher block set and followed the sound of a dog's high-pitched yelp of pain. Dog, not cat.

She slid along the wall to the entrance of the stairwell and peered around. Blood smeared the walls of the stairwell. Her Wizard of Oz memorabilia littered the stairs, picture glass in shards, a porcelain sculpture broken. Whatever Cheveyo had done to hurt the dog hadn't deterred it. Beast and beast crouched face-to-face, poised to kill, Cheveyo three stairs higher. His sleek black body was coiled tight, muscles defined beneath the shiny fur. Faint spots stood out in the blackness. His tail twitched.

Baal looked at her, its pointed ears flicking. Cheveyo took a second to look back, and that's when Baal moved. It flew past Cheveyo in a dark gray blur—right at her.

Cheveyo clawed the dog as it passed, a roar splitting the air. Blood and fur flew, but that didn't stop Baal. She gripped the knife in her hand and thrust it out. Baal ducked to the right, averting the knife and knocking her shoulder so hard she fell to the floor. The knife bounced on the carpet.

The hell dog leaped at her. She groped blindly for the knife. A black blur slammed the dog from the side, shooting it across the living room. It bounced against the wall and fell to the floor. Cheveyo flew through the air at it like a thrown knife. Baal rolled out of the way with a half second to spare.

Her fingers felt like an empty rubber glove, trying to grip the handle. She finally grabbed the knife and moved toward Baal, who was facing off with Cheveyo. It felt like slow motion, the blade coming down, *I'm about to stab a living creature, oh, God*, Baal snarling at Cheveyo, his back to her. The blade sank into the flesh of Baal's thigh and hit bone with a jarring thud. Blood squirted over her hand, stinging her nostrils with its coppery smell. Baal howled, and she screamed, jerking the knife out. A maw full of fangs slashed forward, closing in on her throat.

A second before those fangs would tear at her skin,

Baal jerked back, its bloodred eyes wide in surprise.
The panther's fangs clamped onto the back of its neck,
pulling it back. Baal threw himself backward into
Cheveyo. The two beasts rolled across the floor in a
flurry of claws. The heavy white chair tipped to the
side, blood smearing the leather.

She watched, breathless, frozen. She was in hell
with two demons.

The dog broke free, gasping for breath, and tore
toward her—too fast to pull up the knife she gripped
so hard her knuckles hurt. It knocked her to the side
and ran down the stairs. The door flew open. The
panther followed, pausing three steps down. She
ran to the top of the stairs, breaths heaving from her
chest, staring at the open door. No dog.

The panther shimmered. In a surreal moment the
man stood before her again, though his eyes were
still black for a few more seconds. He only looked at
her when they were blue-gray again. With the heat,
the adrenaline, the blood zinging through her body,
she felt the oddest sensation: arousal. *Are you flippin'
crazy?*

"You're bleeding," she said, the only words she
could manage to utter.

His arms were scratched, skin torn. Their gazes
locked, and she swore she saw a flare of the same
desire in his eyes.

"We go. Now," he said.

She nodded, only just then realizing she still held
the knife. She stared at the blood sliding down the
blade, gathering in a drop at the tip.

"Petra!"

The knife fell with a soft thud. She grabbed her bag
and purse and followed him down the stairs. On the

way she scooped up the stuffed Toto that had some-how ended up halfway down the stairs.

We're not in the real world anymore, Toto. God help me.

Cheveyo stepped out the door, looking both ways and even up before looking at her. She followed him to the bike, grabbed the helmet, and straddled the seat. He strapped the bag to the bike, made sure the helmet was snug, then got on. The sound of the engine exploded in the alleyway, and they were off. She held on tight to him. He was all man now, the only wild thing about him his loose hair in the wind.

He *was* different. Deadly. As much as she had longed to see him again, now . . . she wasn't so sure.

Yurek had used logic to track the woman to her abode, and he now stood in the narrow passage out-side her open door. He sensed the lingering energy of conflict, though the blood splashed on the stairs and bricks would have clued him in that something vio-lent had occurred here. Who was the man who had barged in and taken her from the restaurant? She had gone willingly with him.

He sensed a presence nearby, the Essence of a being from his own dimension. He followed a trail of blood toward where the alley came to a dead end. Something furry crouched behind a large urn where the light didn't quite reach. The dog rose to its paws and shuddered at the sight of him. In a blur, it became a man, lean and wiry, hair ragged and coarse. Blood glistened on his arm, and he held it tight against his side.

"You're a Glouk," Yurek said.

The man's eyes widened. "And you . . . you are

not human either." He sniffed, his nostrils flaring. "Callorian." Fear darkened his eyes, especially when his gaze dropped to the diamond-shaped ring on Yurek's finger. His authority. Pride. And for the Glouk, a reason to fear, since the creature was there illegally. "I have no quarrel with you. Are you after the woman?"

"No, the hunter. I tracked him here. I have not seen the woman until today." He flicked his glance to the door. "He was protective of her. But she fought with him, even as I sensed her fear. He had no fear."

"Who is he? What is he?" Yurek didn't like surprises, and the hunter, as this creature called him, was an unpleasant one. He sensed Callorian Essence in him, but like the girl, not wholly.

"I do not know. He tracked me in the woods north of here a few days ago. We have been hunter and prey since. I decided I must switch roles. I picked up his scent and followed him here, intending to put an end to his tyranny." A string of saliva dripped from the corner of his mouth. He swiped it away. "I would eat him. He is mine." His humanistic eyes, brown as dirt, glowed briefly.

Glouks were territorial, vicious, adept hunters. And perhaps useful. "As long as the hunter dies. And the woman. You can eat them both, for all I care. My prey is a Callorian named Pope. Do you know of him?"

"No."

"He was once an Extractor, someone who would have hunted you down." With three adversaries, Yurek was outnumbered. Not outpowered, but outnumbered. "We can help each other. You can track, yes?"

The man's nostrils flared again. "It is my nature."

Yurek nodded. "I will help you kill the hunter. And

you can help me with my prey. Does this partnership interest you?"

His eyes glittered. "Yes."

"This hunter . . . why does he want to kill you?"

"I eat humans. The hunter does not seem to like that."

CHAPTER 4

"You okay back there?" Cheveyo called as they rode west.

"Fine."

She reached up to brush a piece of hair that was tickling her chin but pulled back at the sight of blood crusted in the creases of her hands and nails. Her stomach lurched and she stared at the back of his head again. He'd secured his hair into a low ponytail when they stopped at a light.

Twenty minutes into the ride her body started shaking. She wanted to cry and scream. She held those back but couldn't stop the shaking.

"Do you need to stop for a minute?" He obviously felt her.

"No."

His body, solid and real, made her feel safe while they flew down the highway at speeds she didn't want to contemplate. She'd tucked her hair beneath the leather jacket he insisted she wear. It smelled of him, a sweet smell she couldn't place, and his own essence, and that made her feel safe, too. Safer, anyway. Questions and fears buffeted her more than the wind did.

He pulled down a gravel road that led into the woods, and a couple of minutes later they came upon an RV sitting in a small clearing. The back door flipped down to become a ramp that he rode up on and into a space that looked like a trailer. Tools, cabinets, and another helmet hung on the walls.

They got off, and he took her helmet and hung it on a hook. His expression was grim, his eyes still that smoky color that spoke to how close he was to his cat. Or at least she guessed that's what it meant. Even scarier was the fact that the edge was somehow arousing.

He turned the bike to face the rear door, ready for a quick exit, all in a practiced way. He unhooked her bag and speared her with those spooky eyes. "What the hell were you thinking back there, jumping into the fight? You could have been killed."

His sharp words were like a slap in the face. "What, I was supposed to hide in my room while you got chewed to death?"

He made a grunting sound as he secured the bike. "You were supposed to keep yourself safe. I have no intention of dying." He pulled the leather holder out of his hair and shook out dark waves that fell just past his shoulders. Like the way he'd positioned his bike for escape, it was a gesture so practiced, he probably did it without thinking.

"Good to know. But in my group, when one of us is in trouble, we help each other."

"I'm not part of your group."

"Believe me, you've made that perfectly clear."

He hit a button and the door slid closed, pitching them into darkness. She could smell the heat of him and something faintly musky. Cat.

"There's one thing you need to know when you pick up a knife: you're in it to kill, not fight."

"I was in it to disable that thing."

A door opened, sending light slicing into the space. He held it open for her.

"I've never seen an RV with a garage before." She ducked past him into what looked more like a normal RV: a narrow hallway, and two captains' seats at the front.

"It's called a toy hauler. The only downfall is that the bedroom doesn't have a lot of head room."

He took a few steps up and set her bag on the floor of a loft area above the garage. The mattress was on the floor, bed rumpled. She shrugged out of his jacket, and he took it from her and hung it over the short railing that separated the loft from the rest of the area. She passed a small bathroom and walked into the combined living area and kitchen, which was impeccably neat. He came up beside her and made to pass by.

She touched his arm, and he turned so fast, she instinctively snatched her hand back. "You're jumpy."

"I'm alert. On edge."

She put her hand on his arm again, only an inch from several gashes. "Let me heal these."

He pulled away. "I don't want you using your energy to heal superficial abrasions. Or anything more. I warned you about healing mortal wounds for awhile."

"I couldn't let Lucas or my brother die."

"Or Nicholas. Don't forget about him."

"If you'd seen him . . ." She shuddered at the

memory, then narrowed her eyes. "I guess you did see him. A vision?"

He nodded. "You nearly died that time. I could barely feel your essence." His mouth tightened. "No more, at least a year."

She crossed her arms in front of her. "And you're my boss now?"

His gaze sharpened, but at least his eyes didn't go dark. "Yes, I am, when it comes to this stuff. It's simple, Petra. Heal another mortal wound, your soul will fizzle out." He snapped his finger in front of her face.

"How do you know?"

"You're going to have to trust me. And obey me. I can't have you flying off the edge of your emotions. That will get you killed, too."

"And will you use that influence thing on me if I don't 'obey' you?"

His eyes sparked at her insolence. "If I have to."

"But you said it wouldn't work if you wanted me to do something that was against my will."

His eyebrow rose the slightest bit. "Maybe I was lying."

She narrowed her eyes at him, hoping he was bluffing. "Even though Eric was my younger brother, he bossed me around. And I let him. That was my bad. But I'm not letting anyone boss me anymore." She pressed her finger to his chest, which left her only inches from his face. She felt something hard beneath his loose shirt. "Especially some guy who flashes in and out of my life with no intention of staying in it."

He leaned a hair closer. "I admire your spunk, but you're in way over your head here, princess, and that 'guy' who flashes . . . is the only one who can save your life right now. So I suggest you save your spunk for your boyfriend and do what I say."

She huffed out a breath, because he was right, of course. "I need chocolate." She glanced at the cabinets. "I don't suppose you have any in here."

He paused for a moment, but she wasn't sure he recognized her retreat for what it was. Well, that was as good as he was going to get.

He turned and opened a cabinet. "I've got raw cocoa powder." He set a bag on the counter. "I mix it with maca, milk, and protein powder for a power shake. You didn't get to eat dinner. I'll make up one to tide you over."

"How do you know that?"

"No dirty dishes, and you were still eating chips. I make it a point to be observant," he added at her surprised look.

She liked watching his hands as they scooped out the powders, pouring in milk, all without measuring. Maca was some kind of Incan super food, according to the package. The blender whirred for a few seconds, and then he poured the light brown mixture into two glasses. She took the one he handed her, and he tipped his glass toward hers. "Cheers." He chugged it down in one gulp.

She tasted hers. Not bad. Her throat was so tight, though, that it felt like the liquid was squeezing down a straw. "Tell me what I'm involved in? What was that . . . beast dog thing?"

"That was a Glouk, an odd life-form from Surfacia." His expression darkened. "I've fought them before."

She leaned against the counter. "Surfacia? That's where Pope is from. The other dimension."

His eyebrows lifted. "You know about Surfacia?"

"Pope told us how the humans on the surface of the planet destroyed themselves, and that the Callorians—Pope's species—came up from their underground labyrinth to live there. But he never mentioned Glouks. You said they were an odd life-form?"

"Dogs in the other dimension are bigger and used in the way horses are here, and they had a special property: like a chameleon, they could change their appearance, only they changed their whole form. Callorians discovered that a human scientist had the warped idea of making the dogs more intelligent and less aggressive by inserting human DNA into them. The enhanced dogs, called Glouks, were employed for search and rescue missions and other high risk situations. There was an interesting side effect: the dogs could change into humans, though only for brief periods of time.

"Glouks survived the human decimation, maybe because there wasn't enough human DNA in their brains. The Callorians came to the surface many years later and didn't know what to do with these hybrid creatures. They tried to control them, using them like the humans had. Sometimes the Glouks reverted to their animal nature and attacked, the way so-called 'tamed' wild animals will sometimes attack their keepers. They are put to death then. Some escape to this dimension."

He leaned against the refrigerator across from her, hooking his fingers in the cabinet handles above his head, like a prisoner chained to the wall. The movement stretched his shirt tight across his chest, but she could see the faint indent of the hard thing she'd felt a few inches below the hollow of his throat. Not a gun. It was long, straight.

He set the glass in the sink. "Coyote attacks, wild dogs found in suburban areas—usually a Glouk. The wolf attacks northwest of Baltimore . . . Baal."

"That thing is what's been on the news, those horrible maulings?" Two hikers had been found, their bodies shredded. "But why?"

His expression turned grim, and she knew she wasn't going to like this. "They crave human flesh. The more they eat, the more it feeds the DNA they already have in them. It makes them more human and able to maintain the form longer."

She put her hand over her mouth, her stomach turning.

He ran his fingers through his hair, snagging on a couple of knots. His narrowed gaze was aimed just past her, his mind working. "Now Baal knows about you. How the hell did it track me so fast?"

"So you're, what, in a battle with this thing?"

He met her gaze. "I'm hunting it. But the thing about hunting prey—it sometimes hunts you back. Baal's the reason I told you that now wasn't a good time to meet. We'd better get moving."

He dropped into the driver's seat while pulling the keys out of his pocket.

She sat in the passenger seat, which was more like a chair with a high back. "You hunt these things."

He backed up at an angle without giving the surrounding trees much notice. Like he'd already calculated what it would take to leave quickly. She watched his hands, strong and capable, maneuvering the wheel. They were the hands of a man who used them. She could easily conjure the memory of how they felt on her arm, rough and firm. Unfortunately she could imagine how they'd feel on other parts of her body, too.

He didn't answer, and she realized she hadn't actually asked a question.

"Okay, so you hunt Glouks," she said again. "For fun?"

He slid her a *Are you kidding me?* glance, but focused on what he was doing. Since he was, after all, driving a large vehicle out of a forest, she supposed she'd let him concentrate on that.

As soon as they were on the highway, though, she continued. "You don't get paid for it, do you? Unless you're a secret government agent or something?"

Still, he only gave her a look that she supposed was an answer in the negative.

"Do you have a job?" she asked.

"I don't need a job."

He hunted Glouks, creatures that liked to kill humans and livestock. Then it hit her. Her eyes widened. "That's why you can't be around me—us. You said it was to protect us."

He kept his gaze on the road, his voice devoid of emotion. "Kind of hard to have a life when you're all over the country dealing with killer vermin."

Her body melted into the soft leather chair, the relief at finally knowing the truth softening her bones. It wasn't that he couldn't stand the sight of her, thought she was too flaky, or any other reason she'd thrown at the wall to see if it would stick.

It would be especially hard to have a woman with him who was a scaredy-cat. That he could turn into a panther scared the hell out of her, and he was the good guy. Now she'd seen the other side.

"So you think this Glouk will hurt me?"

"Yurek is the bigger problem. He's targeting you on purpose. Baal would only kill you because you're with me or in the way." He slid her a dark look. "Which you were."

"Well, excuse me for trying to help."

"You have no idea what you're dealing with. You don't have the skills or experience to throw yourself into my battles. Just because you survived Darkwell doesn't make you capable of handling either of these enemies."

"You told me I was stronger than I thought."

"You are. But you're not strong enough for this." He looked at her. "Have you ever killed someone? Something?"

"Flies." She shrugged. "I put out mousetraps last year when I found droppings." She wasn't about to tell him she'd begged Eric to take away the snapped traps.

Cheveyo chuckled, shaking his head. "Yeah, you've got a real killer instinct."

"I didn't think about how it would feel to stab a living creature. I just didn't want that thing to win." She pulled her legs close to her chest and wrapped her arms around them. "What now? You said we were going to your place to meet up with Pope. Where is your place?"

"Arizona."

That surprised her into silence for a moment. "How long will that take?"   .

"Day and a half."

She glanced back into the RV. "And we'll sleep here?"

"Yep."

She realized this was probably his home more often than not. She looked at him, still in disbelief that he was here, she was here, that they were to-gether. Temporarily. Good God, the last thing she needed was to be hung up on a guy who not only morphed into a black panther, but hunted things supernatural. He was the perfectly wrong guy. Perfectly gorgeous, intriguing, yummy, and totally, completely wrong.

Nice, normal life. Greg, with his easy smile and normalness, yes, that's what I need. Want. Desire. Lust for.

Except her gaze slid down Cheveyo's shoulders, wide and strong under his now wrinkled red shirt. He was lean but muscular, strong thighs encased in dark blue jeans. His gaze kept slipping to the monitor mounted above the rearview mirror, which showed what was behind them. Whenever a car passed, he surveyed the driver.

"Does the Glouk—Baal—know how to drive?"

"I don't think it does, but they're good at hitching rides, either as human or canine."

He picked up his cell phone and issued a command: "Call Pope."

She heard ringing, and then Pope's voice. "Hello."

"It's Cheveyo. Everything all right there?"

"I've been reading your survival manuals and studying the maps. It's very quiet out here, except at night. What kinds of creatures reside in the woodlands?"

His mouth quirked in a grin. "Wolves, bears, panthers—"

"Oh, my," she added with a grin.

He gave her a tolerant grin. "Nothing as dangerous as the Otherling. Or the Glouk that's tracking me."

"A Glouk?" she heard Pope say.

"I'll fill you in when we get there."

"We? Petra's with you?"

He looked at her, making it all too clear that he wasn't happy about it. "Yes. And she's going to stay with you. Yurek's targeted her."

Silence. "Not good."

His words tripped her heartbeat. Terrible. Awful. Much worse than not good.

"Not good at all. We'll be in morning after next. Call if you have any problems, and keep an eye out for big mangy dogs—or men. You may see my cleaning lady, Suza. Try not to startle her."

"If I see her, I shall depart from the house altogether."

He signed off, settling into silence. She was a burden on him, that's what he was thinking about, with those furrowed eyebrows and tightened mouth.

She used the bathroom, washed her face with the plain soap he had on the counter, and applied the powder and blush she kept in her purse. She pulled a brush through her tangled hair, reviving faint memories of a mother who used to brush her hair every night. She took the stuffed Toto from her bag and sat down again, catching Cheveyo's tug of a smile when he saw the dog on her lap.

"What happens to your clothes when you morph into a cat?" she asked. They were wrinkled but hadn't sustained any damage in the fight. The cat, of course, hadn't been wearing clothing.

"I change my energy, rearranging it into the form of the cat. Clothes, everything, is energy, and so it changes, too."

"Can you become any other animal?"

"No, just cat."

"Your father became a hawk. We learned that from the director of the psychic research place where he'd been working before he joined Darkwell's team."

Darkwell, the CIA hotshot who'd started a covert program to use first their parents' paranormal abilities, and twenty-some years later their offsprings' powers. He was dead now, the program dead and buried, too. Their parents had been terminated by Darkwell's silent partner to protect the program and his political career.

"My father only told them about becoming a hawk. He could morph into any animal he desired."

"How did you become a panther, then?"

"Actually, I become a black jaguar. My father took me out into the Sonoran Desert when I was a boy. He performed a ceremony. I wish I remembered more of it. I didn't understand all of this yet, and it was a bit unnerving as a kid to be out in the desert with a father who was chanting and dancing.

"We sat in the desert most of the night, a fire burning. Then a jaguar—a rare black jaguar—walked to within a few feet of us. He stood there for several minutes, and I thought he was looking into my soul with those golden eyes. Something shifted inside me. He turned and left, disappearing into the darkness. My father was elated. That night, while we slept in the desert, I dreamed of being the jaguar. Somehow, through my father, the jaguar chose to be my totem animal. We all have a totem animal, but because of who I am, I become my animal."

When she opened her mouth to ask more, he shook his head. "I need to concentrate."

"You don't like talking about yourself, do you?"

"I told you more than anyone else knows about me. That's enough."

Not really. But she did like being the only one who knew so much about him.

She looked around. "I need to stop at a store and pick up some magazines and face cleanser. That soap will dry out my skin big-time."

"Soap is soap."

"No, actually, it's not. Most soaps are made with animal fats, chemicals and synthetic detergents that rob your skin of the essential oils that keep it soft and smooth. And don't get me started on the artificial fragrances they put in there."

"Okay, I won't." He shot her a smile. "We can make a quick stop the next time we pass a populated exit."

"Thank you." She was already making a mental list of things she needed. Makeup. Hair spray. Chocolate. "Do you have disinfectant and antibiotic cream in here?"

"Yeah, in the bathroom cabinet." His eyes narrowed with concern. "You okay?"

"I'm thinking of you."

"Don't worry about me, babe. I've been taking care of myself for a long time."

She tilted her head. "Do you call every woman 'babe'? Is that just a word you throw out?"

His lips moved for a second without sound and then he said, "Yes. Don't take it personally."

"I'll try not to swoon." She got up and walked toward the back. "Do you have any books or magazines to read?" She opened a cabinet and her mouth dropped open at a display of knives like she'd never seen. Six knives of various kinds were mounted on a black velvet wall, their ornate leather sheaths beneath.

"Check the drawer by the table," he said, and she caught his gaze in the rearview mirror. "Be careful of the knives."

She quickly closed the cabinet door. "I will try to resist playing with them."

"Not just those. They're stashed all over the place. I need to be able to put my hand on one no matter where I am."

"Good to know." She found the drawer he'd mentioned. A couple of Harley magazines, an issue of *Money* magazine. Moments after resigning herself to *Money*, they slowed down. He was taking the exit ramp.

"You have ten minutes," he said.

"Only ten? Really?"

He spared her a glance. "You want either of those guys catching up to us?"

"Well, no."

"Then really. Don't make me come in there and get you."

"You're not coming in?"

"I'm going to take a quick shower. I've got enough water in the tank for two showers."

He was scanning the superstore's parking lot, the rearview monitor, and, she guessed, sensing for the presence of an Otherling. He dropped her off at the front entrance of the brightly lit store then grabbed his cell phone from a holder near his seat. "What's your cell number?"

She recited it, and he called. "Save that number. If you see or feel anything suspicious, call me. I'll be there in a flash."

She raised an eyebrow. "In a flash? You will put clothes on, right?"

Completely serious, he said, "Depends on how scared you are."

Oh, boy, the thought of a naked Cheveyo racing in to her rescue. She scrambled out before he could remind her how long—or not long—she had. She scouted out what she needed, including basic cosmetics—drugstore brands, *yuck*. Except, interestingly enough, there was a brand called Petra.

"Too cool," she said with a smile, choosing that, of course.

She grabbed up chocolate bars, three magazines, and a couple of paperbacks. She kept looking at her watch, eight minutes, nine minutes, waiting in the checkout line. Could she help it if the cashier was taking her ever-loving time?

Finally, at eleven minutes, she checked out. Her phone rang.

"I'm coming!"

But it was Eric's voice that said, "You are? To DC?"

"Sorry, I thought you were someone else." She exited and spotted the RV parked to the left. Cheveyo stepped outside, wearing only jeans, and walked to a garbage can. His gaze was on her.

"Is everything all right?" Eric asked. "Amy said she went by your place today and the door wasn't locked."

Uh-oh. "Oh. Did she . . . go in?"

"Yeah, when you didn't answer the doorbell. She was shocked."

"I can explain."

"Why are you still changing your decor around every other week? I thought you did that because you were restless being locked in the Tomb."

The Tomb was the name she'd given to the bomb shelter where they'd had to hide out. "I'm . . . bored." Was bored. Wait. Hadn't Amy seen blood all over? No, Eric would be freaking.

"It's not like you to forget to lock your door. Where are you?"

"I'm . . ." She looked at the man who was stuffing what she thought were the clothes he'd had on into the can. The sight of his broad bare back and narrow hips made her mouth water.

"You're . . ." Eric prompted.

"With Cheveyo. He came by to say hello."

"Oh, that explains it. Dewy and gooey."

"Yeah, that's what it is." She was standing next to him now, damp and smelling like a mixture of soap and pungency. "We're spending some time together. I've got to go."

"Don't do anything I wouldn't do," he chided.

She disconnected. "My brother, Eric. He was worried because my door was unlocked. Apparently, Amy went inside but didn't see anything that alarmed her . . . like *blood* smeared all over the walls, tufts of animal fur, furniture knocked over . . ." She took a deep breath, feeling hysteria rise.

"You didn't tell him what was going on. Nice job."

She tried not to beam like a sap at his compliment. "I don't want to drag him into this."

His expression hardened. "You weren't supposed to be dragged into this either." He touched her face, his fingers barely grazing her cheek before he dropped his hand. "I'm not pleased that Pope did that."

"He tried to protect me. We didn't go into or leave the restaurant at the same time, and we only talked for a few minutes. I don't understand how Yurek figured out we were connected."

"The bottom line is he did, and I hold Pope responsible." His words were edged in anger. "Always protect the innocent, that's the golden rule."

"That's why you stay away from me," she said.

"Yes."

"Maybe I'm not so innocent." He raised an eyebrow at her, and she shrugged. "Just saying." Time to divert the subject. "Would that hell dog have actually cleaned up my home to cover up?"

His eyes narrowed. "No. But Yurek might, if he'd

come by and found it like that. Last thing he wants is your face plastered all over the news as a missing and possibly endangered person. Make his job harder." He scanned the parking lot, then settled his gaze on the bags she carried. "We'd better hit the road."

He opened the door and gestured for her to go first. A gentleman.

"You kept it under twelve minutes," he said, closing the door behind her. "I thought for sure you'd take twenty."

"I had twenty minutes?"

"I might have given you fifteen."

"*Now* you tell me."

His dark wavy hair was still damp, and drops of water dripped down his chest. He wore a silver panther pendant on a chain that stood out against his olive skin. The cat was etched against a black background. What nearly stole her breath away was the scar that angled from his left shoulder across a well-defined chest, cutting across his nipple and extending two more inches.

"My God, what happened?" she couldn't help but whisper. It was all she could do to hold back her hand from touching the faded weal.

"My first battle with an Otherling. He was quicker than I was, knife-to-knife combat." He shrugged. "In my defense, I was twelve."

"*Twelve? As in twelve years old?*"

He walked to the driver's seat, grabbing a shirt he'd set on the counter. She followed, taking the shirt from him. He had other scars, too, faint lines and scratches across his back. He turned and held out his hand for his shirt.

"You were only a child." Her gaze went to his chest again, beautiful, yet marred so viciously. The thought of it . . . twelve. She had to swallow it down, get hold of herself.

"It was a long time ago," he said. "Stop looking so mortified."

She blinked, erasing the horror from her expression. "Let me put some antibiotic on your scratches. God knows what that thing had on its claws."

"I washed with tea tree oil soap. It kills germs."

So that's what she'd smelled on him. "Still, we should—"

He took both her hands and his shirt in his grip. "I'm not a child anymore."

No, he wasn't. If his broad shoulders and tensed biceps weren't sign enough, the hardness in his eyes was.

She released the shirt. "I'm a healer. It's what I do."

He picked up a black plastic thing on a cord and put it around his neck. That's what she'd felt earlier.

"What is that?"

"Knife sheath." He shrugged into the white cotton shirt with a swirling black design on the back. The white set off his skin and made it look darker in contrast. He pulled a belt from the kitchen table, along with what she guessed were two more sheaths.

"You're . . . well armed."

He looped the two sheaths and the belt through his loops. "I prefer working with knives, but in hand-to-hand combat, they can be knocked out of my grasp. So I have backups."

She put her hand to her chest. "God."

"We'd better go. It's not safe to stay in one place for long." He dropped into the driver's seat and started the engine.

They headed back onto the highway. He fiddled with the stereo and turned up a Green Day song.

She listened to the words to "Boulevard of Broken Dreams" and knew Cheveyo had turned it up on purpose. The lead singer sang of walking alone, his shadow the only one who walked beside him, his shallow heart the only thing beating.

She flicked on the overhead light, dug a *Cosmopolitan* from her bag of purchases, then opened it to the table of contents. A second later she closed it and laid it on her lap. "Cheveyo." His name floated on the air for a moment.

He glanced at her in acknowledgment but said nothing.

"You knew where I lived."

"Yes."

"You knew where my bedroom was."

A slight hesitation before, "Yes."

"You've been in my townhouse?"

"A few times."

She didn't know whether to be shocked, violated, or exasperated by his lack of both chagrin and further explanation. "And why would that be?"

His focus was on the traffic. "I check on you from time to time."

He would have just left it at that, too. She gave him almost a full minute to elaborate. But no.

"You break into my home?"

"If you want to be technical. I slip in, while you're sleeping, make sure you're all right."

The realization shivered through her, tingling down to her extremities. The image of him standing beside her bed, while she'd probably been thinking about him before she drifted off, mad, angry, frustrated. Gawd, had she said his name in her sleep?

She slapped her hand on the magazine. "Do you

get how wrong that is? You can't be bothered to pick up the phone and call me. No, you sneak in like a thief."

"There was no point in calling you. Now you know why staying away from all of you is in your best interest. I told you I would watch over you. That's all I was doing. I never checked on you while I was engaged, just so you know."

"Engaged? *You're engaged?*" Okay, her emotions were slipping into her voice, pitching it up a notch.

"In battle with an Otherling."

"Oh." *Duh.* She swiveled her chair to fully face him. "You once told me that we were psychically connected, like Amy and Lucas are. Lucas said he felt their connection since they were children. But they'd met as children, and that was why. How did we come to have this connection?"

"I have always felt connected to you. I saw visions of you, felt your pain, your loneliness, your joy. It was like some part of me was missing, and when I saw you, I realized you were it. Our connection is probably because Lucas and I share the same father. Through our DNA connection, I saw you."

She was his missing part. Did he realize how those words stabbed her heart? No, not a clue. For years she'd had a crush on Lucas, who'd come to live with them when his sole parent died. She never had the courage to tell him how she felt, and then Amy came along and it didn't matter anymore because they were clearly meant for each other. Now she wondered, had she transferred her innate feelings for Cheveyo onto Lucas? They had similar features. *Hm, interesting.*

"What are you going to tell your boyfriend?" he asked, pulling her from her thoughts.

Was he fishing for information about Greg? *Well, fish away, buddy.* She could play that noninformation game as well as he could. "What if you'd come sneaking into my home and found me in bed with a man?"

He kept his expression neutral, but his eyes darkened. "I wouldn't have stayed as long."

CHAPTER 5

Sometime in the middle of the night Petra felt the RV slow. She'd been lying on the bed dozing, as close to sleeping as she could get. Not easy since she could smell his scent on the sheets. Every time she drifted off, she dreamed of him lying next to her, touching her.

She sat up and pushed the curtain aside. A dead exit, only a closed gas station that hadn't seen a customer in years. She stumbled toward the front as Cheveyo pulled around to the back of that building and parked.

"What's going on?" she asked, hearing the fear in her voice. "Is someone following us? He found us, didn't he?"

He walked to the bedroom. "Calm down. Everything's fine."

She released a breath. "Sorry."

"I'm stopping to grab some sleep." Using his thumb, he pressed buttons on his cell phone. "The alarm will go off in two hours."

"Two hours? That's not enough. I can drive—at least I think I can—so you can get more sleep and we can keep going."

"I only need a couple of hours at a time, and never more than four or five."

He stripped out of his shirt as he walked back toward the stairs leading up to the loft. Stooping, he set his cell phone and shirt on the floor next to the mattress, leaving the knife around his neck in place.

"You threw away your clothes earlier," she said, following him.

"Bad energy, and for the Glouks, an even worse scent. You can never get it out."

Ah, the musky scent.

"Speaking of bad energy . . ." He opened a cabinet and pulled out a large shell that contained what looked like a fat joint but without the rolling paper. The flame of a lighter set the tip on fire briefly, leaving it in embers. He took a feather and used it to fan the musky smoke over himself and then her.

"What, exactly, are you doing?"

"Burning sage. It gets rid of bad energy." He pressed the tip into the shell to snuff out the embers and returned it to the drawer.

He cat-walked onto the bed, his hips swaying in liquid motion. Then he turned and dropped as though his bones had melted. Damn, he looked good, hair fanned out on the pillow, chest bare. The scar, though, reminded her of seeing him as a boy in the flashes of images. She liked the way the sleepy glaze in his eyes softened them, the way his features relaxed and made him look just a bit boyish.

He tapped his hand on the bed, inviting her to join him. "You weren't asleep for very long."

She knelt on the bed, her hand only a quarter inch from his. The urge to know him, to touch him, overwhelmed her. She held her breath to quell it, because she instinctively knew he would shut her out. To protect her. Because he hunted Otherlings.

Maybe he would let her in a little. "Your father was a Native American, right? That's where you got the sage burning from?"

"My mother is Hopi, but I only lived with her tribe for a couple of years."

"Why?"

He regarded her for a moment. "You ask a lot of questions."

"I've had too many unanswered questions rambling around in my head for a long time. They're like mice scurrying around, gnawing holes in my brain."

His mouth lifted in a brief smile before it faded. "But remember, when you bring in cats to get rid of the mice, they can end up being even more destructive."

She wrinkled her nose at him. Something bothered her, tiny shards sticking to her as though she'd brushed against a cactus. She picked at the crease in the rumpled sheets. "You told me your father communicates with you from beyond the grave. That's how you know so much."

He nodded.

"Your abilities go beyond ours. Besides the panther thing. You can freakin' change the weather. I mean, you brought on this terrific thunderstorm to camouflage our attempt to rescue Nicholas."

He shook his head. "My father did that."

"And the shield you put over the Tomb?"

"Tomb?"

"My affectionate term for the bomb shelter."

He settled his hands behind his head and closed his eyes. "That was me. It worked against the Offspring, but not against Otherlings."

Pope had been watching the Offspring, but he hadn't been watching over Cheveyo. Why? "You said something to Pope about your father and the mind scan."

He didn't respond. His chest rose and fell evenly, his body relaxed.

"Cheveyo," she whispered.

Either he was doing a good impression of sleeping or he was actually asleep. She looked at his face, his square chin with a slight dip, his thick lashes. Like the boy she'd seen. Her gaze drifted lower, to the dark hairs across his chest, the lean definition of his pecs and biceps. Definitely not a boy. Her hungry gaze took in the hard planes of his stomach, the ridges of his ribs. She moved closer to study the silver panther at the hollow of his throat. It was elegant in its artistry, catching the cat mid-leap. His only other piece of jewelry was a ring on his right hand. A gold band, not unlike a wedding band, that had a twist.

When she started to feel invasive about studying him, she remembered that he'd watched her sleep. *All's fair . . .*

She shivered at the thought of him standing by her bedside doing this to her. His eyes moved beneath his lids. Could he already be in REM sleep?

Studying his face for any signs of wakefulness, she moved her hand over his arm, healing the scratches that ran all the way to his shoulder. The old scars, though, wouldn't disappear, including the nasty one across his chest.

My warrior.

No, not hers. In a way, though, since he'd saved her life, held her in his arms and promised to watch over her, she considered him hers.

She waved her hand over the other cuts, briefly

feeling the pain of them tingle along her skin. He was definitely asleep, or he would have felt her healing him. Maybe he'd be angry at her for going against his wishes, but the hell with it. He'd saved her life; it was the least she could do.

She felt something else, too, and held her hand over his chest where she'd first picked it up. An energy that was deep and sad and lonely. It washed over her and made her eyes well with tears.

His fingers moved slightly. His toes flexed. She'd seen dogs and cats dreaming, their bodies twitching in sleep. What was he dreaming about? Fighting evil?

He was always wary, her warrior, ever watchful. Except for now. He trusted her enough to give himself over to the deepest of sleep in her presence. The thought warmed her. She carefully stretched out beside him, close enough to feel his body heat but not touching. Her eyes remained open for a while, facing the side of his arm, the dark thatch of hair at his armpit and the paler skin beneath it. She wanted to keep looking at him but finally her eyes drifted shut.

When she woke, sunlight slanted in through a crack in the curtains, and she was alone in the bed. The RV was rumbling along the highway. It was ten-thirty. That was pretty bad, that she hadn't even felt or heard him get out of bed.

She climbed off the bed and went down the steps to the bathroom. *"Ugh."* Being road weary didn't agree with her. Puffy eyes, pale skin. She dug into her purse and ran a brush through her hair. After smudging on some blush and lipstick, she made her way to the front.

" 'Morning, sleepyhead," he said as she approached from behind. He'd thrown on his shirt but left it unbuttoned. Which made him look juicy. The black sheath around his neck made him look juicily dangerous.

She dropped into the passenger seat, swiveling it toward him. " 'Morning, yourself. How long have we been on the road?"

He was scooping handfuls of Spanish peanuts from a can wedged into one of the drink holders. "Two hours after I dropped off. I woke before the alarm chirped." He held out the can to her.

She shook her head. "I don't like the crinkly shells around the peanuts."

"They're the best part. I like the way they crackle on my tongue."

She didn't want to think about things crackling on his tongue. Her gaze went to his ring. "I noticed your ring last night. It's pretty cool."

He took it off and handed it to her. "It's called a Mobius band."

It was warm as she turned it with her fingers. On the inner band the words ONE, ALL were inscribed. "What's the twist for?"

"It's what allows you to cross both sides of the band without going over the edge."

She traced the tip of her pinky finger on the inside of the band, and when she crossed the twist, she was on the outside. "That's what you do, isn't it? Walk on both sides without going over the edge."

She saw a spark of admiration in his eyes. "Perceptive."

She let herself warm to his compliment for a moment. "What does the inscription mean?"

"A diagram of the Mobius strip was found in an ancient manuscript, and that was the caption."

"Cool." She handed it back to him. "I'm going to take a shower."

"Ten minutes. Or you'll run out of water."

She pushed to her feet, rolling her eyes. "Is everything ten minutes with you? Never mind, do not answer that."

She'd grown up with two boys in the family. That was not a question she wanted to let hang in the air between them. Not helping was that Zoe, one of the Rogues, once confided to her that male Offspring could go on and on, staying hard and hungry long after they'd come. It had been so pitifully long since she had sex, thinking about it with Cheveyo around nearly did her in. She was thinking of it again now, watching the muscles in his arm as he grabbed a handful of peanuts. How would those hands feel on her? Calluses rough against her skin, hands possessive . . .

He held up a handful of peanuts to her. "Sure you don't want some? You look hungry."

Cheveyo timed her shower, and fifteen minutes later the water stopped and he heard, "Really? *Really?*"

He laughed, imagining her all full of soap. Then he stopped, because the mental sight of her tall, curvaceous body covered in bubbles zapped him in the groin.

Thank God he was getting rid of her the next day. He opened his glove compartment and took out a photograph tucked inside. Painful, looking at the face in that picture. A good reminder that people around him got killed. Innocents. He couldn't let it happen again. He tucked the photo away, feeling the familiar burn in his chest.

The bathroom door opened, and in the rearview mirror he saw Petra's head peer around it, bubble blobs on her hair. "That was so not ten minutes."

"You're right."

"I knew it!"

"It was fifteen. You were lucky you got as much water as you did. There are some bottles of water beneath the kitchen sink if you need to rinse off."

Since he was driving, he could hardly get them for her. She stepped out, wrapped in a towel. He saw her in his peripheral vision as he reached for another handful of peanuts. Long wet legs and soapy hair that hung halfway down her back. She knelt down, her knees cracking, and opened the cabinet. She grabbed two bottles and returned to the bathroom. A minute later he heard her howling.

"Cooooold!"

Served her right. She'd already taken over the Tank, his nickname for the RV, infiltrating it with her energy and her presence: chick magazines lying on her seat, the floor, and the table; beauty products filling every spare inch in the bathroom; and a bottle of aquamarine nail polish sitting in the cup holder. She was permeating his senses. Those few times he'd had a woman here, it wasn't for long. And no one like Petra.

She spent another twenty minutes drying her hair, and then longer doing who knew what. When she finally came out, she smelled good, she looked good, and suddenly she was way too close when she grabbed up her magazine and dropped into the seat next to him.

"That'll teach you to listen to me." Yeah, he'd sounded terse, and the fact that it stole the soft expression from her face meant he'd done the right thing.

Fire lit eyes the color of a mountain lake on a summer day. "I had no idea how much time had passed. There's no clock in the bathroom."

"Running out of water is the least of your problems. You weren't supposed to heal my wounds. I need to be able to count on you."

"You saved my life. Why can't I at least heal your scratches?"

"You need to conserve your strength. We don't know what we're going to encounter."

He'd felt her healing him last night. It was warm and loving, and if he'd surged to wakefulness, he might have done more than admonish her. He prided himself on his iron control, and it was all he could do to will his body not to respond in obvious ways. Inviting her to join him on the bed, bad idea. It was an innocent gesture. When he woke, he watched her sleep, as he had before. She was an angel, hugging her pillow, body curled up. He didn't feel the least bit innocent watching her, wanting her.

She pouted. "You sound like Eric, who forgets he's actually my *little* brother."

"That's a good way to see me, like a bossy big brother."

"Except my brother never kissed me the way you kissed me the night you saved my life." She was stroking the arm of the seat, a quick, nervous gesture.

"Forget that kiss. It didn't mean anything." That was an indulgence he shouldn't have allowed himself.

"Forgotten." She picked up her magazine and flicked the pages, reminding him of the way an agitated cat flicks its tail. "When I didn't hear from you, I realized it was just the whole saving-my-life thing that made it so powerful and magical. Sort of powerful and magical. I mean, it was *nice*. But, like LeAnn Rimes says in her song, 'life goes on.' I didn't sit around hoping you'd call or anything. I'm enrolled in college, learning to be an esthetician. Next I want to take massage school."

"It suits you." And her date, too, but he didn't want to know about the guy. As he'd walked up to their table, she had a glow on her face, smiling, happily unaware of her terrible fate. "The massage part of it, anyway. That jives with your healer."

She looked at him from above the top of her magazine. "My healer?"

"You're a healer. It's a strong part of your psyche."

She lowered the magazine, obviously forgetting that she was mad at him. "I remember how, whenever I would rub someone's shoulders, they'd make such a big deal out of how good it felt. I didn't know then that I was healing more than their tightened muscles. But I also felt uncomfortable touching people. Now I know it's because I was taking on their pain. I've been working on that, though, touching without absorbing. You told me to put a shield up, and it works. I know you probably think teaching people to take care of their skin and apply makeup is trivial—"

"I didn't say that—"

"—but it jives with my healing nature, too. You should see a woman's face when she sees herself in the mirror looking beautiful, maybe for the first time. I help her to see her beauty. So many women only see their flaws."

She had that glow now, her cheeks dimpled, her skin as smooth as the custom leather on the Tank's seats. She wore just a touch of makeup, her lush lips shiny pink, catching the light . . . and his breath. He turned back to the road.

The kiss had been a really bad idea. Almost losing her tore him apart, rupturing his iron control. He hadn't meant to lead her on. She was hurt because he'd never contacted her.

She continued to flip through those pages without looking at them. "You could have just told me why you had to stay away, instead of being so mysterious."

"I wasn't trying to be mysterious. You didn't need to know I fought otherworldly beings, didn't need to know that there *were* otherworldly beings."

"Living in ignorance isn't a bad thing, I suppose." He felt her energy change, from defensive to sad. She said, "You have a lot of scars. I couldn't heal those."

But she'd tried, that was what she implied.

"How many of these creatures have you killed?" she asked.

"I don't keep track."

"Have you ever killed a human?"

Maybe if she understood what he was, she would know she had to stay away from him. The bond they shared pulled at them, but he couldn't let it draw them together. "The men who hung my father were the first."

"But you didn't kill Steele, down in Key West. Zoe said you'd turned to a panther and had him on the ground."

He had saved Zoe's life from an assassin who was about to wipe her out. Then he'd taken her to the rest of the Rogues, and psychically summoned Petra so he could turn Zoe over to someone she'd feel safe with.

He checked the rearview monitor, an old habit. "I try not to kill humans, as a rule. And I didn't want to leave a mauled corpse for the police to investigate. A wild cat attack in Key West? And my DNA."

She set the magazine down. "You said something about not being able to come to me the day we all got infected by the crazy stuff."

"My father saw my death; I can't see my own

future. He knew I was going to try to stop it, even though I saw no way to save you. I don't know exactly what he did; he won't tell me. But he knocked me out. When I woke and checked on you, it was over."

His fingers tightened on the steering wheel. "And as soon as I take care of Yurek and Baal, you can go back to your life, your boyfriend." He remembered her question about what he'd do if she were with another man when he visited. To his credit, he hadn't gritted his teeth or clenched his jaw at the thought. Sure, he knew someday she'd take a lover, eventually get married. He told himself he'd be happy for her, while his cat yowled in rage and loneliness. She was his, yet he could never possess her. "And hopefully you can forget about all this."

"And you."

"Definitely me."

She picked up the magazine again. "I will."

He turned up the stereo. It was going to be a long day. The sooner he could hook her up with Pope, the better.

They'd been driving between towns, with little to see outside other than acres of forest on either side. She'd fixed them lunch from a recipe in her *Oprah* mag and a quick stop at a grocery store. She went through two magazines and stank up the RV with the acrid scent of nail polish, all the while rearranging herself in the leather seat a dozen different ways. All hard to ignore, with her long legs propped on the dash, feet pressed against the windshield, and now her legs dangling over the arm of the seat, freshly painted toes wiggling an inch from his elbow. The black, tight pants hugged her ass, of which he'd gotten way too good of a view when she bent down to fish a magazine that had fallen to the floor. Her white ruffled top hugged her waist and made nice work of her cleavage.

She'd tried to engage him by reading aloud articles about what guys were really thinking in certain situations. Thankfully not the "How to Achieve Ultimate Orgasms" story promised in bold print on the cover. "Here's a quiz. I *love* quizzes. Is your guy a keeper?" She eyed him playfully, raising her eyebrow. "Does he listen to you? Always, sometimes, or never. Do you listen?"

He ignored her.

"That'll be a never." She circled it. "Has he introduced you to his mother?" She tilted her head, studying him. "He hasn't even talked about his mother. Another never."

Honestly, he didn't know whether to be amused or annoyed. Annoyed was better, because he was no keeper.

"How often does your guy turn into a scary, wild animal?"

"Why don't you do the quiz for the boyfriend?" He hoped she hadn't heard the sharpness in his voice.

She lowered her chin, looking at him from beneath her eyelashes. "Because that was our first date, and since we'd only gotten about twenty minutes into it before I was hauled away, I can hardly judge him. You're all I have to work with."

He was even more annoyed by the relief that coursed through him at that revelation. He should want her in a nice, solid relationship with a guy who didn't turn into a scary animal.

The Geo Wave hit him at the same time as his father's voice warned, *Be careful. You're being closed in on.*

"We have trouble," he said, looking at the rearview monitor. "One of them has tracked us."

She studied the screen, too, her playful expression gone. "I don't see a car anywhere. H-How do you know?"

"Geo Wave. It's a cold wave of energy I feel when I'm near someone from Surfacia. I can't tell if it's Yurek or Baal. Either way, it's bad news. Hold on."

CHAPTER 6

Being bored was way better than feeling fear pulsing through her. The RV swerved as Cheveyo pulled off the road and into a gap in the woods. Now Petra knew why the thing had heavy-duty tires.

"Get your shoes on," he ordered. "Just in case."

She stuffed her feet into sneakers. "We are so going to die. I mean, how many times can I get lucky?"

"Surviving has nothing to do with luck. And don't throw around words like 'dying' and 'killing.'"

"They're just words."

"I take them literally because dying is always a real possibility in my life. And I don't think predicting our deaths is a good idea either."

Just out of sight of the highway he cut the engine. "I want to find him first and ambush him." He moved fast, launching out of his chair. "To the bike," he said, opening the door at the back of the RV that led to the garage.

The rear door was opening down into the ramp position, and he grabbed the helmets off the hooks. Her heart pounded, her hands already sweating as she took the one he thrust at her. She climbed on behind him before he could order her to. She was no stranger to having to move fast.

The engine started, and they shot out of the trailer. He turned sharply to the right and headed back to the highway. Any hair that wasn't beneath the helmet whipped all around her.

Another sound roared up behind them. She turned. The same black car she'd seen trying to follow them at the restaurant. Yurek.

"He's coming!"

Her grip tightened around Cheveyo's chest. His body was already tensed; he knew the car was behind them. Coming faster, closer, like a train aimed right for them. Cheveyo shot forward, staying ahead of the car. A few seconds later it closed the gap.

She couldn't take her eyes off the trident symbol in the grill. Closer. Sun glinted off the chrome in a blinding flash. About . . . to . . . hit—

Cheveyo swerved into the oncoming lane, tilting the bike with the movement. Only because she was holding on like a leech did she not fall off. She did scream, but her fright squeezed it into a guttural sound.

"Hold on, babe," he said, hitting the brakes as the car zoomed past. He turned the bike around and headed back in the direction from which they'd come.

Tires screeched, and she turned to see the rear end of the car swerving as Yurek spun the car around and propelled toward them.

Cheveyo glanced in the rearview mirror. "Playing 'tag, you're it' against a car is a bad idea. Keep holding tight. I'm going to lose him."

As if she could do anything but hold on tight.

He thrust ahead again. They rounded a bend in the

two-lane highway and came up on a semi. Her throat tightened. They were trapped!

Cars zoomed past them in the oncoming lane. Yurek was closing in. With what looked like about an inch to spare, Cheveyo pulled into the other lane a second after a car had passed. He sped around the semi and ducked back into their lane before a line of cars appeared over the slight rise in the road.

"Be ready to slow down fast," he said.

"Why does that sound dangerously scary?" And why wasn't he speeding ahead? Rather, he was staying right in front of the semi. The trucker blasted his horn at them, no doubt thinking them reckless.

In the rearview mirror she could see Yurek trying to pass the semi. Finally he got a break in oncoming traffic and started coming around.

"Hold on," Cheveyo called out.

He pulled onto a little turnoff that had a call box mounted on a pole. They were going too fast, though, and couldn't stop on the patch of asphalt. They bumped along on the grassy bank before slowing and turning in the opposite direction. Cheveyo watched the semi pass with another blast of his horn. No sign of the sports car that was on the other side.

"You're brilliant!" she screamed, her heart thudding so hard it hurt.

Yurek would get around the semi and see no sign of them. He'd speed ahead, getting farther away. Unless he looked in his right-side mirror.

They had to wait out traffic, though, to get back on the highway. How long before Yurek figured out they weren't on the road anymore?

Cheveyo slipped into a gap between cars that were coming and going. Everything went dark for a second, and then she realized she'd squeezed her eyes shut. *Hey, good idea. No, bad idea.* She wanted to know what was going on.

The car in front of them slowed before turning onto a side road. Cheveyo couldn't pass until the car was nearly at a crawl. He finally zipped around and hit the gas. Minutes later she heard the familiar sound of the engine behind her at the same time Cheveyo said, "Damn, that didn't take long."

She felt the bike jerk toward the left. The car bumped their back tire just before they moved out of reach, sending them skidding onto the shoulder. Fear froze her scream in her chest. *Trees. Don't hit the trees. Hitting trees, bad!*

Cheveyo turned the bike at an angle and twisted, his arm around her waist, pulling her off the bike as it slid to its side. She hit the ground, marginally cushioned by the overgrown grass and his body. The world spun. No, that was *her* spinning.

Brake lights burst into stars on the road nearby. She heard the car skid to a stop up ahead. She'd hardly stopped rolling when hands reached down and pulled her up. She wobbled as Cheveyo removed her helmet and set it down next to his in the grass. The car pulled off the road.

"You okay?" He was breathless. "Nod if you can run."

She nodded, sending the world rocking again.

"Go."

She hardly had time to gain her equilibrium before he grabbed her hand and hauled her into the woods. *No!* She swore she'd never go into the woods again.

The sounds of their feet pounding earth and her heartbeat obliterated anything else, even with her preternatural hearing. She dared to flick a glance back but didn't see anything. Except . . . that branch back there that was moving unnaturally.

Within a few minutes of jumping over dead trees and roots that grabbed at her shoelaces, they dead-ended at a wide river. Water tumbled over rocks that jutted out, foaming as though it too would devour them if given a chance. Cheveyo surveyed their options. He wasn't breathing as hard as she was, but his face was flushed with exertion.

"S-Something's back there," she managed, pulling her hair away from her damp face, feeling dried grass tangled in the strands. She pointed to where the branch had moved.

He nodded, his gaze behind them. He pulled the fanglike knife from inside his shirt.

Something else moved a few feet to the right of them. They swiveled to face the hell dog.

"What the—" Cheveyo narrowed his eyes at it. They were blackening.

"You said Glouks couldn't drive."

"That's not a Glouk. Doesn't feel like one. Which means—" He pivoted to the left, where another hell dog broke through the bushes. Spittle dripped from its black and red gums, unlike the first dog.

Yurek! They'd teamed up, and he'd taken the hell dog's form. "This is so not good." She wanted to blink and disappear.

Cheveyo's eyes darkened more, and she felt heat emanating from him. He shook his head. "I can't change. If I engage one, you're vulnerable."

I'm a vulnerability. Even, worse, a liability. No. After everything I've been through, I know I'm stronger than I thought I was. And I sure as hell am not going to be a handicap.

She reached out to him, keeping her eyes on the two dogs. "Cheveyo, give me one of your knives."

"Remember what I said earlier?"

"I remember." Knives were for killing. She could kill if she had to.

He extracted a knife from under his long shirt in one quick movement and handed it to her, handle out. She grabbed the smooth black handle, watching the two dogs moving closer. Panic warred with adrenaline, twisting her insides tight. But something else surged through her: anger. *That's where you'll find your strength. Draw from that.*

"What have I ever done to deserve being a target? Nothing. I'm sick and tired of these sons of bitches." She held the knife out, facing what she thought was the real dog. All she had to do was fend him off until Cheveyo could get rid of Yurek. "I've got this one. I do know what I'm dealing with now, so go, do your thing. You can fight a lot better as a cat."

She felt his heat and vibration as he morphed to jaguar. He leaped at Yurek, and the two creatures rolled into the cover of underbrush. She narrowed her eyes at the dog, her expression in a snarl. She swore it smiled, lifting its lips a little more, a long string of drool spilling to the ground. Fear stirred deep in her bones. It wanted to kill her. Hungered for it. It took a step closer. She fought the urge to step back. *Show it you're not afraid.* She gripped the knife harder, feeling it slip with her sweat.

Sounds of clacking teeth and growls tore through the air. A cat flew out from the brush toward her. She froze. *It's only Cheveyo.* Except its claws were extended, its enormous paw lifting as though to take a swipe of her.

Another black jaguar launched. Yurek had taken

the jaguar form. She thrust the knife forward. Cheveyo slammed into Yurek a second before he'd reach her, and the two tumbled to the side with a *thud*.

The hell dog took advantage of her distraction and leaped at her. She couldn't bring the knife around fast enough. It knocked her to the ground and landed on top of her. The knife slipped from her hand. The beast had to weigh at least a hundred fifty pounds. It crushed her against the hard ground, dripping saliva onto her throat, blunt claws jammed into her chest.

The smell of moldering leaves and earth filled her nostrils. And the smell Cheveyo had mentioned, an oily musk. The Glouk's eyes fired a brighter red as it lowered its mouth to her. Teeth, that's all she saw, sharp tips gleaming.

Wild cat growls behind her scrabbled up her spine.

Her fingers blindly groped for the knife. *Can't reach it.*

No!

She rammed her knee up into Baal's rear end, pushing it forward and off balance. It fell to the side as she rolled to her behind. Before it could regain its balance, she kicked it in the fleshy area beneath the rib cage. She kept kicking, her leg seemingly stuck in the pattern. Baal made a gurgling sound. Just when she thought she'd disabled it, it grabbed her foot and jerked her forward. She pitched forward as it reached for her with its paw, rolling out of its grasp.

She grabbed the knife, feeling dirt jam beneath her nails. The Glouk was the center of her focus, all she could see. It crept closer and she swiped; it backed up just far enough to avoid the blade and then lunged at her. She stumbled back a step and lashed at it. Missed. It was quick, a natural predator. She was a former

Hooters waitress-turned-facial technician in training. Yeah, even odds.

It doesn't matter. You're going to fight and fight.

The river roared behind her, cool air washing across her back. Her shoes sank into the dampened ground, making it harder to keep her balance. She didn't dare a glance to see exactly how close she was.

Behind the Glouk, one jaguar slammed another into the trunk of a tree. It leaped toward her, no, toward the dog. Cheveyo. His claws were extended, catching the dog's ear as the other cat, Yurek, hit him mid-leap. That threw Cheveyo into her, and she fell backward. For one second she whirled her arms, trying to right herself. She fell back anyway.

Ice cold water rushed up around her, sucking away her breath. She was rolling, spinning. No, she was rocketing downstream. A jaguar, a few feet from her, morphed back to man. Cheveyo reached for her hand, crushing her fingers with his grip. He pulled her toward him, against the current.

"Dammit," he muttered as they hit a rock just beneath the surface. He nearly lost his hold on her. She grabbed at him, clutching his arm as they rammed into another rock. It sent them spinning. He fastened his hand on her even tighter and looked back. Just a glimpse of dog and jaguar running along the river's edge.

"Glouks don't like water," he said just before a spray of water hit him in the face.

"Yurek's not coming in either."

"He's not going to take a chance of getting in this without knowing what his cat body can do."

He pulled them out of the path of a boulder that jutted out of the river. Eddies swirled around them, water spraying over rocks, getting in her eyes. With effort, they could steer clear of the visible rocks; the ones beneath the water were brutal on her body. The numbing cold helped, though.

"W-We have to g-get out of here. It's c-c-cold!" It was getting harder to hold onto him with her numb fingers.

"We'll swim to the other side and climb out over there."

Fat chance of that. The current took them where it would, following where the water was squeezed into one fast stream between the rocks.

The dog was keeping pace with them. Suddenly it sprinted ahead. She saw where it was headed: an outcropping of rock that would put it near where they would flow by. It studied the rocks, probably searching for a path closer to them. One flat rock put it even closer. Its haunches tightened, ready to lunge. She and Cheveyo tried to swim to the other side, fighting the current. Fighting fatigue and pain. God, her body ached.

Got to keep going. Can't let them win. Can't put Cheveyo in a position to have to save me.

Baal stuck out his neck, teeth gnashing inches away. Cheveyo pulled a rock from below and threw it. It hit the dog in the snout and made it jerk back just as they passed, only inches out of reach. Anger glowed in its eyes as it watched them tumble past. It jumped several boulders farther up, searching the fast moving water and rocks. Its body tightened. It was going to jump in! She tensed, ready to defend herself. Baal got into launch position, still searching for the best place to attack, and then its body sagged. It was smart enough to assess its chances of survival. It turned and continued to follow them on land.

An eddy spun her sideways. She saw Yurek some

ways back, the cat contorted as though it were made of black clay, a child stretching it into something else entirely. He was changing back to a man, she guessed.

The bank on Baal's side was getting steeper. Unfortunately, so was the other side, which meant having a bigger climb to get to shore. Her body wilted at the thought.

A change in sound farther down the river struck dread in her. "I hear something! The sound of the river is different." Her eyes widened. "Waterfall?"

"Probably rapids."

"Probably. Which means it could be a waterfall?"

He yanked her out of the way of a slab of rock jutting out of the middle of the river. "We need to get to the other side."

"See, you *do* think it's a waterfall!"

"Rapids aren't good either."

The current, however, had other ideas. And all along, Baal followed, climbing over the rocky shore above them, like a ravenous wolf tracking a mountain goat. The river was widening, though, which meant it was farther away. The rocks got bigger, too, making its trek harder. Small favors. It slipped, its foot getting caught between two rocks.

"I don't see Yurek," she said just before getting a mouthful of water. She coughed violently, feeling her stomach strain.

"Some beings have a harder time morphing. Let's hope he's one of them."

He struggled to latch onto something solid. She grabbed onto a smaller rock, but it was too slippery to hold. The shoreline was all rock now, cut steep by the river. Her hair clung to her face like octopus tentacles, and she couldn't spare a hand to push them out of the way. His hair, too, was plastered to his cheeks.

Baal had gotten free but was having a hard time picking its way across the rocks.

The sun reflected off the ripples of the water, blinding in its intensity. But warm. More small favors. Her body was chilled through.

"The water's flowing faster!" she said. "The fall's getting closer!" She imagined it plunging hundreds of feet down over treacherous rocks. "We'll escape those two but be crushed!"

They hit an underwater rock so hard their hands were wrenched apart. Panic roared inside her as loud as the coming waterfall. A large rock split the river, taking her in one direction, him in another. He lunged for her, and she gripped his hand.

"Calm down," he said, breathless. "Ahead, see those rocks that make an island? We're heading there. Hold your breath."

She could hardly see the dog now, though Yurek had caught up with it. The current sucked her down, dousing her in the cold water. No, not the current—Cheveyo. His hand on her arm, he'd pulled her under. She opened her eyes, seeing his hair floating wildly in the water. He pointed ahead, tugging her as he swam. She pushed through the water beside him and a few minutes later saw a large rock come into view. He pointed again. She kicked and flailed toward it.

He grabbed onto the edge and pulled them closer. Her fingers kept slipping on the slimy rocks, but she wedged them in a crack and was able to haul herself out of the current. She came to the surface when she had to breathe or else her lungs would burst. They were behind the lowest part of the formation. He put his finger over his mouth. *Shhh.*

The rocks formed a small cove on the back side of the island. She followed him behind the taller part of the formation and draped herself against the rocks, her body collapsing in relief. No fighting, no waves splashing into her face. Only a gentle swirl, and she could touch the ground. They were completely hidden from the shoreline now. Yurek and Baal would think they were still barreling along, maybe even drowned in the undertow.

He stripped out of his jeans, down to white briefs that clung to his tight derriere and, uh, other parts of his body. Wasn't cold water supposed to shrivel the male apparatus?

With a flick of his wrist Cheveyo pulled his tooth-like knife out of his pocket. He cut the legs of the jeans, which had to weigh a ton now that they were wet. His shirt came off next, and the sun glistened off his wet chest.

Could she really be turned on? Really? When her body was battered and worn-out? But she had felt something like this when they fought Baal back at her place.

Cheveyo was fully focused on his task, in survival mode. He yanked his shorts back on and surveyed their surroundings while squeezing the water from his shirt. Instead of putting it on, he tucked one end into the waistband of his shorts, letting it dangle at his side.

"Can you maneuver in those pants now that they're wet?"

She lifted her leg out of the water. "Not really."

He crooked his fingers at her. *Strip.*

Well, if he could do it without being self-conscious, so could she. It took some wriggling, but she managed to get out of her pants. He wasn't watching her, but he hadn't turned away either. He sliced and diced her pants and handed a pair of shorts back to her.

She slid them up and zipped them. "Much better."

He nodded toward the woods behind him. "No rest."

"For the wicked, I know. Except I'm not wicked," she added, hearing a little whine in her voice. "I'm a nice person."

"A very nice person." His eyes focused on her as she stepped up beside him, and she saw the fire of lust as his gaze swept down the length of her. "And still wicked all the same."

White shirt, now wet, thin bra beneath it . . . she didn't look but could well imagine. He pulled her hard enough that she fell against him. Her hands went to his bare shoulders to catch herself. His hands gripped her waist to steady her. The heat that blazed between their bodies, she'd felt it before when he held her.

He took a quick breath and set her away from him, yanking his gaze away to check for their enemies again. He flattened himself against the side of the rock and peered over the edge, his back stretching with his movement. Drops of water slid down his spine.

Even though the rushing water should cover their voices, he leaned close before saying, "They must have kept going forward, hoping to catch up with us. Which means we go back."

The river was narrower on this side of the island but ran harder. He took off his black boots and sent them flying toward the rocks at the shoreline. Socks went into a crevice between rocks. He probably didn't want them to tip off their pursuers down the river.

He took her hand and started walking across. "Follow my footsteps."

He positioned his feet in front of rocks so the current wouldn't knock him off balance, motioning for her to do the same. In bare feet, his balance was better. He'd obviously spent a lot of time barefooted, and probably in the wild. She stumbled, her legs as rubbery as blush-brush bristles. He pulled her back in balance and they reached the boulders at the edge. He took a big step up, turned, and pulled her up, too.

There wasn't much cover here. She scanned the area. Boulders interspersed with trees for as far as she could see. Miles of climbing, slipping, crevices. No, *hundreds* of miles. Millions! Her knees buckled, and his hands tightened on her waist.

"I can't do this," she said, still gulping air.

"You don't have a choice."

She nodded. *Not a liability. Not a burden.*

He grabbed his shoes and laced the strings together, looping them over his finger. He took her hand with his other hand and they headed back the way they'd come. He steered them away from the river, around a huge mound of boulders, finally out of sight of being spotted. She was dying. *Dying.* On top of the river beating her up, she'd been thrown from a motorcycle!

Finally they reached some fairly level ground, and wouldn't you know, that's where she stumbled again. He caught her, dropping the shoes in the process. She fell against him, her body plastered against his, looking at the hollow of his throat and the jaguar pendant. She couldn't move. Beneath her fingers, where she flattened her hands on his chest, his skin was hot. He wasn't helping her regain her footing. Her gaze met his. And her body wasn't dying anymore. It was more alive than it had ever felt.

The roar of lust consumed her like a fire out of control, licking at her senses—and her common sense. The answering lust in his eyes energized her body. His hands were on her shoulders and they slid down her back at the same time he covered her mouth with his.

"We have to get back to the Tank," he said between devouring kisses. He squeezed her butt in long, sensuous strokes.

"Tank? You have one of those hidden away, too?"

He chuckled. "No, that's just what I call the RV."

Her fingers threaded through his wet hair.

He stopped, blinked. "I must be crazy," he muttered, his eyes still simmering with heat.

She could only nod, her fingers tightening on his shoulders. "Definitely crazy."

"Not only should I not be doing this at all, I sure as hell shouldn't be doing it *now*."

She took a step back, steadying herself. "I know. So why do I want to keep doing it?"

"Beats the hell out of me." He turned to her. "You felt it, too?"

She nodded. "Even back at my place, when we fought Baal. I thought it was my imagination, because no way do I get *turned on* by fighting for my life. Why is it happening?"

"Adrenaline."

"You feel like this every time you fight?"

"No, not the lust part. Sometimes I want to puke or even cry. It's just an outgrowth of the overwhelming surge of adrenaline." He snagged his shoes, taking a look around while he did so. "We have to get out of here. And I've got to get rid of you."

"Me? This is *my* fault?"

"No, it's my fault. The fact that I want to throw you on the ground and tear off your clothes is obviously a volatile chemical reaction when mixing you and adrenaline. My weakness. And if I keep fighting with you around, we'll both end up dead."

Yurek caught up with the Glouk farther upstream. He had to learn to morph back to his previous form faster. It took longer to come back, and it felt damned uncomfortable being in animal form. Turning into the jaguar, though, had put him on even ground with the mysterious human who had even stronger Callorian DNA than the woman. She called him Cheveyo. The Glouks who came here were afraid of him. Some, like Baal, wanted to be heroes and slay him.

Yurek was beginning to feel the same way. He would be a hero to the Collaborate if he found and killed two people of unknown Callorian origin as well as extracting Pope back to Surfacia. Unfortunately, it was proving difficult.

Baal transformed to his human form so he could communicate. "You lost them?"

"It was your job to track them. I was busy."

"I can't track good if they're in water." His nostrils flared and his head jerked to the left. "They went back that way. Faint scent, coming off the breeze."

"Then we go. We don't want to lose their trail."

The Glouk lifted his chin. "I can track prey that's miles away." He transformed back to dog and bounded through the woods. The creature looked hideous, but it ran with speed and grace.

Yurek walked back along the river's edge until he came to the spot where they'd had the altercation. The underbrush was tamped down in places, broken in others. The dagger lay on the ground. He picked it up, running his finger along the edge, feeling it slice into his skin like a razor. Sharp. Deadly point. He had never met anyone like Cheveyo, who could transform into a beast but was not a Glouk. He'd only heard of them He liked being a jaguar better than the dog; made him feel powerful.

He ingested the energy imprint of the person he mimicked. Now that he possessed it, he could use it again. He would practice being the jaguar. The next time he encountered Cheveyo and the woman, he would be much better. Next time, he would kill them.

CHAPTER 7

She would be the death of him. Of them. Even though Cheveyo had taken the blame, his words prickled across Petra's skin.

They trudged through the woods back to the bike, which, thank goodness, started. It bore scrapes and dents, but landing in the grassy shoulder helped it, just as it made their tumble a little better.

A little.

Every muscle, bone, and hair on her body thrummed with pain, but it didn't feel as though anything was broken. She sucked in her groan of pain when she climbed on behind him. "I need chocolate. Like a mountain of it."

He flicked her an amused glance before heading onto the road. They went back to the RV—Tank—pulled the bike into the garage, and within minutes were back on the highway.

"They didn't see the Tank," she said, realizing that's why he'd stashed it right away. She pulled a Dove chocolate out the bag but paused and offered it to him. When he shook his head, she ripped into it.

"They'll be looking for a bike. It'll help, but eventually they'll track us down. How the hell did they come to work together? Glouks stick to themselves and don't generally trust anyone, not even their own kind."

"Isn't there a saying about common enemies making good allies?"

"The enemy of my enemy is my friend."

"Yeah, that worked with Eric and Fonda."

She changed into dry clothes and returned to the front. He'd jumped right into the driver's seat wearing his wet jean shorts and nothing else. She braced her hand on the back of his seat, remaining standing. She had to fight the urge to pull at the long string of denim that lay against his thigh.

"Want me to drive for a few minutes so you can change?" Not that she wanted him to change, because he looked juicy, but he had to be uncomfortable. "I know cats hate being wet." She gave him a smile to let him know she wasn't being mean.

He raised an eyebrow at her. "Do you, now?"

"And they love their chin scratched." She crooked her fingers.

"They also mount females from behind."

She narrowed her eyes at him. So much for light flirting. He was trying to cut her off. "I rescind my offer. Your behind can stay wet."

A smile tugged at his mouth, but he kept his gaze focused ahead. His hair was still damp, curling his waves. "Jags and tigers actually enjoy swimming. But not like what we just did."

She could imagine him, as jag, frolicking in a lake.

He was watching her expression, and she wiped the emerging grin from her face, still stung.

He nodded. "You did well back there."

"Something came over me, like I became someone else."

"Adrenaline and your survival instinct."

Bracing her hands on the arms of the chair, she slowly and painfully lowered herself into the chair. "Please tell me that you're hurting like you were trampled by a herd of water buffalo."

"I'm sore."

She rolled her eyes. Men. But he wasn't just any man.

A short while later he pulled into a home improvement store's parking lot, driving around to the far side. He put the RV into park and, engine running, walked to the back. She pushed to her feet and hobbled to the fridge to get a bottle of water. He hadn't bothered to close the door to the bathroom, so when he shucked out of his shorts, she saw just about everything in the mirror's reflection.

Of course, he glanced up while she was gaping. Without a blink, he dragged on a pair of jeans, replaced his belt, and then wriggled into a shirt as he walked to the front. The shirt was cool, red at the shoulders, beige at an angle at his midsection, and white on the bottom. He rested his fingertips on her shoulders as he eased by her.

He didn't seem the least bit bothered that she'd watched him, but *she* was. To cover her embarrassment, she said, "Don't you close doors?"

He dropped back into his seat and put the Tank back into gear. "I'm not used to having a woman in here. And when I do, I don't have to be modest."

"I see."

And she did, getting a mental picture of some sexy woman sprawled out on that bed with him. Not lying next to him as she had but wrapped around him, their bodies intimately joined.

Stop that!

She unwrapped another piece of chocolate and jammed it in her mouth.

He pulled out of the parking lot. "In a couple of hours we'll find a campground, dump the tanks, and fill the water tank. We can also grab a shower."

A hot shower sounded heavenly. She eased back into the chair, leaned her cheek against the back of the seat and drifted off, exhausted. In her disjointed dreams the river tumbled her and a jaguar ate her. She woke an hour later when she felt the Tank slow to a stop. A sign welcomed them to THE COZY PINES CAMPGROUND.

He obviously didn't know she was awake yet, because he winced when he got to his feet. He'd never give that away otherwise. He stretched, arching his back, then stepped out the door. She watched him walk to the office, noticing his gait was a bit stiffer than usual. That didn't detract from the view at all. His jeans weren't tight, yet they fit him just snug enough to show the solid body wearing them. They were unusual, with two waistbands and various zippers and pockets sewn on in places you wouldn't expect, like down the side of the legs.

A few minutes later he walked back, the stiffness gone. He had the confident gait of a soldier on a mission, his stride long, his movements economical. Two young boys raced across his path, so caught up in whatever game they were playing they didn't see Cheveyo. Instead of looking annoyed, though, he watched them run off, a wistful look on his face. Was he remembering himself at that age? Had he been able to play like that, free and fearless?

His expression turned grim again as he took in their surroundings, always checking. That was how he lived his life. Just like domestic cats she'd seen, never really relaxing or sleeping, always ready for either predator or prey. Sadness overwhelmed her, the need to heal his soul, to make him happy.

She wiped the expression from her face when he stepped inside, which was a good thing since his gaze went right to her. "One hot shower, coming up," he said.

She twined her fingers and sighed. "You know just what to say to a girl."

He dropped into the driver's seat. "Yeah, I'm a real charmer. Things like 'I've got to get rid of you' and calling you wicked." His mouth was quirked in a wry grin even as he maneuvered the Tank into the campground. He'd probably asked for a spot near the entrance, because he aimed for the second spot after the gate.

"You can sleep in the bedroom, you know," he said, tracing a line across her cheek. "You've got seat crease." He paused, his gaze holding hers for a breathless moment. He dropped his hand.

She rubbed at her cheek, checking the rearview mirror. Oh, jeez, it looked like a Frankenstein scar, with stitches and everything. "I like being up front. That way I don't miss anything." She honestly hadn't even thought about lying down on the bed, as much sense as that made.

Because you want to be near him.

He backed into the space and then went outside to hook up the water or whatever one did to these things. She got out, too, watching him move like he'd done this a lot. The word OUTLAW was painted on the side of the Tank. Appropriate model for Cheveyo. "Need any help?"

"Got it, thanks," he said absently.

He did, too, and she found herself following him back into the Tank. "How much of your life do you spend hunting?"

He walked to a small closet in the hallway and pulled out towels. "There's always something that needs to be taken care of. There are portals—what Pope calls finestras—all over the world." He held out a towel to her. "We'll use the common showers."

"Can I take longer than a ten minute shower?"

"As long as you want." The hint of a smile on his face warmed her. She'd never seen him full out smile. A desire to do anything, anything at all, to bring out that smile washed over her.

She shuffled over like a ninety-year-old, taking the towel from him. He stepped into the bathroom and grabbed shampoo and soap bottles. When she took them, he pulled out a black vinyl bag from the lower cabinet and threw clothes into a larger bag.

"Wait, need to get my razor and shaving cream." She was *not* going on the run with hairy legs.

He opened the door for her, and they walked to an old wooden building. People were friendly, nodding at them, obviously thinking they were a couple. As she headed toward the entrance marked WOMEN, he touched her arm.

"Uh-uh." He nodded toward another door with a sign that read FAMILIES. "We stick together until we get to my place. I'm not taking any chances with you."

With her. As though she were precious. Then it hit her: "We're showering together?"

"They have separate stalls. The guy was selling me on the fact that they had this family shower room so couples can bathe in the same space."

"Oh. After what happened today, do you think that's a good idea? I don't want to *kill* you or anything." She couldn't help the snippy tone in her voice, which he obviously picked up.

"Don't take it personally."

"How am I *not* supposed to take it personally? Especially knowing you don't throw words around like 'death' or 'killing' indiscriminately."

"What we feel is a jumble of neurotransmitters and hormones, probably increased by our connection. Biological and dangerous as hell when the enemy is in the vicinity." He opened the door. "But we're taking showers in the same general space. No big deal."

Easy for him to say.

He locked the door behind them, an ominous click that juxtaposed his words. She swallowed hard.

The room was softly lit and filled with the scent of soap and damp air. There were two stalls, each with a flimsy plastic curtain, and one dressing area with a sink and a bench. Perfect for shaving, since it had water and a drain around it. She turned on her shower and when it was good and hot stepped in. A long, guttural sigh escaped her throat. She let the hot water pound her back and neck, the most achy parts of her body.

Next door she heard the water hitting his body, and . . . a groan? She couldn't be sure and fine-tuned her hearing. Yes, another soft sound, because he hurt as much as she did. So he was human after all.

His shower cut out, and through the crack where the curtain didn't meet the wall she saw him step out and grab the towel on the hook. Steam wafted out with him like a magical mist. He dried his hair, his movements slow, languid. Or his thoughts were a million miles away, since he was staring off into space.

His back was to her, graceful lines dipping to

narrow hips and a butt that was so exquisite it hurt to look at. Even his palest skin was olive, and unmarred. Elsewhere, though, she saw faint scars. He bent over and rubbed the towel down his legs, muscled thighs finely dusted with dark hair. After wiping down the mirror above the sink, he wrapped the towel around his waist and started shaving.

Of course, she wasn't doing a bit of lathering while watching him. The sight of him and the hot water beating on her back were an alluring combination. She forced herself to turn and continue. As much as she wanted to linger, she realized he had no intention of leaving her in there by herself, which meant he would have to wait for her. That he was obviously willing to do that, well, it just warmed her heart. That he wasn't used to being around people made it all the more meaningful.

She turned off the water and blindly reached for the towel she'd hung on a hook. She yelped when she felt a hand instead of terry cloth. He was holding the towel for her.

"Oh, thanks."

It felt strangely intimate, him standing so close when she was wet and naked. She dried off, wrapped herself in the towel, and stepped out. He was dressed in the clothes he'd thrown on after their river dip. She grabbed her razor and cream and sat on the bench, squirting some on her legs and lathering them up.

After cutting herself badly early on, she always paid one hundred percent attention to the task. That wasn't easy with a sexy guy leaning against the sink watching her. She tried to ignore him, but that became impossible.

"Why are you watching me?" she asked as she rinsed the razor under the faucet.

"I've never seen a woman shave before. I'd think the knees would be tricky."

"Not usually." Of course, the blade nicked her, and blood poured out of the tiny cut.

He tore several paper towels from the dispenser and knelt down in front of her, pressing them against the cut.

"Can you heal yourself?" he asked.

"No, dangit."

"It's normal, you know, that people with abilities can't use them for their own benefit."

She met his gaze. "Does that mean my mother didn't purposely set herself on fire?" Her heart felt heavy, as it always did when she thought of that horrid scene.

He squeezed her hand. "No, she couldn't have." He quickly let go. "She probably just lost control. Many of them did."

She breathed that in, feeling something in her chest loosen.

"She died when she was my age. It's funny—well, not funny ha-ha—that when I was a kid, I thought I'd die at twenty-four. And I almost have, more than once."

He was looking at the wad of paper he held on her knee. "You'll live till you're eighty."

"How do you know?"

Now he met her gaze. "It's my job to make it so."

His job. She shivered at that, the straightforward way he'd said it, the fire in his eyes, kneeling in front of her like her knight-protector.

She turned her attention back to her legs, her heart taking a perilous dip. Once she was done, she took her clothes into the booth and got dressed. "Thanks for being patient," she said when she walked out.

"Is that what I'm doing?"

He didn't look the least bit annoyed. In fact, he was smiling just a little.

"Most guys would be pacing or complaining by now."

His smile disappeared. "Is that a fact?"

She ran that through her head, realizing how it sounded. "Not that I've been in this kind of situation a lot. Only Eric, who was totally impatient when he was waiting for the bathroom we had to share when we were teenagers. The problem was, he spent as much time getting ready as I did."

They walked back to the Tank, Cheveyo surveying their surroundings. It was late afternoon now, and the smell of BBQ wafted through the air.

"Hungry?" he asked.

"Why do you ask?"

"The way you were sniffing the air."

Her nose was tilted up to catch the scent. "Oh. Yeah, I guess I am." Her stomach gurgled just to make the point.

"The guy in the office said there was a good steak place down the road. We'll hit that."

They climbed on the bike and headed there. It was the first time she'd ridden with him that she hadn't had to hold on for dear life. Now she could enjoy holding onto him, leaning into the turns, feeling the freedom of being out in the open. She liked seeing their shadow on the asphalt, two people riding together. Together. Soon they'd have dinner like two normal people. And always, always, he would be watching for danger.

As they returned to the Tank, Cheveyo could see Petra's movements becoming stiffer. She was putting on a brave face, but he caught her wincing as she leaned against the kitchen counter. He latched the heavy duty locks he'd had installed on the door and stepped up beside her. Her hair smelled like cherry blossoms, and his fingers itched to unravel her long braid. He would resist the temptation.

Early evening light slanted into the dim space. They didn't have much time, and he needed to recharge. After taking care of one thing.

"Strip down to your bra and panties," he said. "And lie down on the bed."

She spun around, her mouth open in surprise.

"I have a special rub, made by the Navajo, that'll ease your bruises, cuts, and aching muscles."

She closed her mouth for a moment, though her blue eyes were filled with puzzlement. "Okay."

He was going to put his iron control to the test. He turned away so she could get undressed in private.

He'd glimpsed her in the shower earlier, through the gap in the curtain. If he'd been a lesser man, he would have shoved the curtain aside and taken her right there. She pushed his control to the fine edge, but he would master it.

He heard her pad upstairs to the loft, heard the *shush* of clothing fall away. His erection responded instantly, but he willed it down. He couldn't let her see his arousal. He went to the console at the front and turned on the seventies rock music channel on the stereo. Bad Company's "Ready for Love" flowed from the speakers.

"Okay," she said, a slight quiver in her voice.

He regulated his breathing when he got to the top of the steps and saw her lying facedown on the bed. He could lower his heart rate, and he needed to do that now. Her arms were up by the pillows, her head to the side. She was long, her body pale and gilded by the waning sunlight. Her back was elegant, curving in at the waist and flaring out at her hips, lush and curvy, not twig thin like most women starved to be. Her sweet ass was covered by silky pink panties edged in lace. All it would take was a flick of his fingers to break the thin ribbon at the side.

What he needed to focus on were the bruises and scratches that marred her creamy skin. None brutal, but the rocks had taken their toll on her. She'd suffered abuse that day. Unacceptable. He would do his best to make sure she never had to suffer it again.

She pushed her hair to the side, and he saw an eye looking at him from the back of her neck. It was roughly the size of a quarter, blue with slashes in the iris. "What's with the tattoo?"

"Zoe's a tattoo artist, and she'd drawn this eye. Said she had a dream about it. We deemed it the Rogues' symbol. She inked it on all of us. We decided the blue eye is for the program our parents were in; the O of the iris is for Offspring; and the R in the iris is for Rogues. Later we found out it's a symbol for elite Callorian spies and pilots, and Pope's father was a pilot. His DNA is in us, which is probably why Zoe dreamed about it."

He ran his finger over it, tracing the lines. Goose bumps popped up on her back wherever he touched, and he pulled his hand away. He lit the sage stick and used the hawk feather to clear their bodies of negative energy.

"That stuff smells like pot," she said, her voice muffled against the pillow. "Not that I've ever smoked it, but I was around it a couple of times."

He snugged it out in the abalone shell. "We should never use drugs or drink to the point of oblivion. Risks exposure. Or more."

"Like turning into a jaguar? Wouldn't that freak the weed heads out?" Her short laugh lit his soul like a flash of sunlight.

He dipped his fingers into the jar, a pungent cream that reminded him of the desert, and rubbed it into his palms. Earlier, touching her had put him in a state of delirium. He straddled her at her waist but positioned himself so only his inner thighs made contact with her. He felt the heat between them the moment his palms came down on her shoulders. She felt it, too, by her soft intake of breath. His hands kneaded her knotted muscles.

"Ouch, ouch, ouch . . ."

"Stop tensing." He worked the knot with his thumb, and it eased.

"Oh, God, that feels so much better."

He worked through several more and then ran his hands down the length of her back, stopping at her panty line. He closed his eyes, but his hands transmitted the torturous feel of her soft skin, indents on either side of her spine, even the mental image of her.

She let out breathy groans that just about drove him crazy. He scooted farther down, working the backs of her legs, and finally lavished her feet with attention. They were long, elegant, toenails expertly painted.

When he finished her other foot, she twisted her head around to look at him. "That was amazing. How did you learn to massage like that?"

He shrugged. "I don't think about it, I just follow my instinct."

"This is part of what I want to learn next," she

said. "I want to be able to help people like this." She grabbed a handful of sheets as she sat up. "Take off your shirt. I want to work your back."

He supposed that's how he'd worded it to her, but the order sounded provocative coming from her. "You don't have to do that."

"I know I don't 'have to.' I want to. And you'll let me, because you're sore, too. It's only fair." She pinned him with a stubborn gaze tinged with a smile that told him she was enjoying gaining her power and wasn't going to let him back out.

"If you insist."

"I do."

To give her privacy, he turned and pulled off his shirt. He could hear her putting on her clothes behind him and gave her a few extra seconds.

"You dress amazingly," she said when he turned around. "I love a guy who takes pride in his appearance. I mean, I love *when* a guy takes pride. Most seem to grab whatever they first come upon in a store and don't give much thought to putting an outfit together."

He wasn't sure what to make of that kind of compliment. Her expression, though, was sincere, as she knelt on the bed in front of him.

"You're not accusing me of being a metrosexual, are you?"

She laughed, again, that beautiful sound. "Not hardly. You don't use enough hair product."

He ran his hand across his forehead in feigned relief. "Whew."

She tilted her head. "You're way too . . . *primal*. Practical."

He raised an eyebrow at the way her voice had gone a little raw when she said "primal." He said, "I buy most of my clothing online. I'm not too primal to use one of those computer things."

"I didn't mean primate, silly. Primal, animal-istic . . ." Her gaze dropped to his bare chest. "Savage." She blinked. "I mean, it's hard to find time to preen when you've got some creature on your trail."

Why should it bother him what she thought, anyway? But the way she'd said "savage" with an ember in her eyes tightened him right down to his core.

"Okay, lay down." She took the jar of rub from the floor.

This was probably not a good idea. Bad enough, him touching her. For her to touch him . . . electric-ity zinged through his body at the thought. But he did ache, and he couldn't reach his back well enough to do a good job of working in the rub. *Sure, keep rational-izing when you should have refused.*

He held in his own intake of air when she ran her hands down his back. She sat beside him, her thigh touching his side, working his shoulders.

"Your knife got left behind in the woods."

"I've got others."

"I saw them. So many different kinds."

"I've been collecting them for a long time. And I in-herited my father's collection. They're not only func-tional, but artistic. Some are very old, from distant cultures and extinct tribes. I've traveled all over the world to hunt them down."

"You don't use a gun."

"I don't trust them. Sometimes they lose their effi-ciency when they morph with me. Knives are simple. They don't malfunction."

She worked in silence for a few minutes, running her hands down both sides of his spine, working out his aches. He let his arousal flare; she couldn't see it. Heaven and hell at the same time. It was a rare gift to be in a place where he could safely indulge his desires with a woman who wasn't looking for something permanent. He gave everything but his emotions. Now he was with the one woman he'd always had feelings for, and a back rub was all he could let himself do. When he was with her, he had to shut off those feelings in case she picked up on them.

She ran her hands down his arm, her fingers sliding between his. Desire coiled inside him. Her body leaned over his back, not close enough to feel physically, but he could feel her energy. The tip of her braid brushed his skin with her movements, leaving a tickly trail.

She worked his neck, a slow kneading motion. Her voice came from close to his ear. "You're not one of us, are you? An Offspring, I mean."

"Ah, I see. Get me all relaxed and then mind probe me."

"You got me figured out. Now that I have you right where I want you, you must answer my questions. And don't go to sleep again. I'm on to you."

He chuckled. He *had* dropped off to sleep to avert her questions. "What makes you ask?"

"A few things struck me as odd. Like when Pope talked about the Offspring being part of his family, he didn't include you. I don't know of any Offspring who can morph. And when Pope talked about the SCANE, you didn't ask what it was because you knew. I presume your father told you. And he knew Pope, but it didn't seem to be from here. I put the pieces together, and the only way they fit is that you're not an Offspring."

"Not exactly."

"You told us you were, that first time we met."

"It was easier than explaining, and it wasn't important. Still isn't."

"Yes, it is. I'm trying to make sense of it. Of you, I suppose."

He turned his head to meet her gaze. "Why?"

"I . . . I don't know." Her eyes narrowed. "I do know, actually. You know a lot about me. Heck, even about my crush on Lucas. It's not fair that you know so much and I know hardly anything about you."

He might have shut off her line of questioning, but he sensed her deep need to know more. He sensed so much from her, her own pleasure at touching him, her building desire and also her fear of him, though he wasn't sure if it was of his jaguar or his profession. Her fear was good. Her persistence was not.

She went on. "It drove me crazy not knowing why we couldn't be together, and even when I accepted that I wouldn't see you again, I still wanted to know who you were. I know some now, but not enough. I don't want to be part of your world of creatures, knives, living on edge . . . I tried forgetting about those weeks of hell." Defeat softened her words. "But I couldn't forget about you."

Her emotions twisted him. He understood that failing all too well, and he sat with it in silence. She was his greatest weakness. And his greatest love. He could tell her neither. But he could tell her what she needed to know. That would cost him little.

"I was born before the government program, so I didn't inherit the Essence of Pope's father."

She reclined next to him, face-to-face, her left hand still working his neck. "You said you didn't like to kill *humans*. As though you're not one. You're from Pope's dimension, aren't you?"

He shook his head. "No, but my father was."

"Pope said something about knowing what your father was doing here."

"Some Callorians have found ways to escape the oppressive world the Collaborate has created to come here. Many become corrupted once they are allowed to express their emotions and carnal lust. DNA testing could expose the other dimension, which would cause chaos and fear here."

She was listening intently, her blue eyes hardly blinking. So he continued.

"My father briefly worked for the C hunting down Scarletts, but found their rules stifling. It was the SCANE that pushed him beyond the edge of the law. He had a friend who underwent SCANE and survived, but with no memories of his loved ones or his past. He spent five years stumbling around reciting the law books until he mercifully died. My father wasn't an emotional man, but some things bothered him. It was why he became the very thing he was hunting.

"He made the mistake of joining the government program here, though, thinking he was helping mankind. He felt the Essence invading his psyche but didn't understand what it was. He already had tremendous powers, so it didn't enhance them. But the Essence affected him in other ways. It made him be unfaithful with Lucas's mother. He loved my mother too much for a casual dalliance."

"Your mother is a human."

"My father fell in love first with the Hopi, their beliefs and ways. He came through a portal near Sedona. The Hopi knew he was different, even though he'd taken on the human guise of one of them. But, of course, he wasn't one of them and had to keep his past a mystery. He and my mother had a bond like none I've ever seen in any other couple." He knew the bond well. "She knew what he was, what he did, before they married. She was willing to put up with all that it meant to be with him, but I saw what it cost her. In the end, it cost her her mate."

"He died when you were how old?"

"Seven. But he came to me, first in my dreams and then later in waking consciousness. He had already been teaching me the warrior ways during the times he was home. My mother didn't like it, so I didn't tell her he was still training me from beyond."

Her expression hardened. "Your father was training you to take his place?"

He nodded.

"That's just wrong. What kind of father wants his son to engage with deadly beings?"

"It was his purpose. Now it's mine."

He saw her struggle to push down her anger at his father. "You grew up with the Hopi people?" she asked.

"Not really. Though they came to accept my father, once he started killing they sensed the darkness in him. The Hopi are a peaceful people. When my father joined Darkwell's program, we moved to DC. My mother and I returned after he died, but the shame of a suicide taints the whole family. And I was different. I had the darkness, too. I didn't take well to being bullied by kids who felt threatened. Especially when I got good with knives. We moved to a cabin my father had built out in the forest. Now she's back with her people at Orayvi in the Third Mesa. She's a silversmith." He turned the pendant she'd made for him on his sixteenth birthday over to show her the back side.

"See the sun? That's her hallmark. Every artist stamps their hallmark on their work."

She touched it, and he released the pendant at the heat between their fingers. He felt every stroke of her fingers on the metal. "She does beautiful work."

His pride made him smile. "She's one of the best artisans in the tribe."

Her expression froze as she took him in. Then a smile transformed her face. "I've never seen you smile, really smile. It's . . . amazing."

He tamped it down. "Do you know enough now?"

She released the pendant, her own smile wilting. "I don't think I'll ever know enough, and I know you won't tell me what lies in the deepest places in your soul." She tilted her head. "Is there anyone who knows you so well? Your mother? No, you probably keep your distance from her to keep her safe. Your father, then?"

"My father is my teacher, my guide. Do you share confidences with your father?"

"No, but—"

"I need to decompress, clear my mind for a few minutes."

He rolled onto his back, staring at the ceiling. He felt the familiar dizziness that preceded his father's visits. He floated through the ethers, meeting him halfway.

"Did you get a warning?" he asked before Wayne could say anything, the two of them conversing as if they were indeed face-to-face.

He could see his father's stern face, mouth tight. "The woman with you, she will cause great trouble. You will be killed if you stay with her."

"I will be leaving her with Pope tomorrow."

"Good. She weakens you."

"Yes," he had to admit. "Do you see any danger coming to her?"

Now that Petra was with him, bonded to him, he probably wouldn't get warning visions about her future. Or about Pope's either, though he would know if something happened to either of them the moment it happened. But would it be too late then?

"I see nothing where she is concerned. Which, as you know, means neither good nor bad. I can feel that you care about her, but do not let your feelings put you, or her, in mortal danger. You have two worthy adversaries, and teamed up they are more than twice as dangerous. They cover each other's weaknesses. Be on your guard at all times."

Cheveyo heard his own weariness when he said, "I always am. But I must recharge now."

"Go. Be safe."

He disengaged, returning to his body. He didn't open his eyes for a few minutes more, trying to clear his mind. It was all he could do not to look at Petra, lying next to him. He could feel her breath softly pulsing on his shoulder, her gaze on him, and her tangled energy.

The only way they would be safe was to be apart. Now. Forever.

CHAPTER 8

Every time Cheveyo passed the turnoff to the Mesa where his mother lived, he felt a pang. He passed her road many more times than he turned down it.

He glanced at Petra, dozing on the seat next to him, an open magazine in her lap. He was a man at war, as much internally as externally, wanting to be with her and wanting to protect her by being away from her. Soon he would leave her with Pope and backtrack to find the enemy he was sure was on his trail.

She would have a crease on her cheek again. He would fight to not rub it away again.

He turned onto the unmarked road flanked by signs that warned about trespassing at the risk of imminent death. Petra woke when they hit a rough patch in the road.

"Are we there?" Her voice was husky with sleep.

"In time for lunch."

She scrubbed her fingers through her hair, slowly coming awake. Yep, a crease. "Sitting in a moving vehicle sure makes me sleepy."

"Rest is good. You've been through a lot lately."

"So have you, but you've hardly had any rest." She looked around at the dense forest of pines. "Where's the desert?"

"Flag is higher up in the mountains. Flagstaff," he added. The locals called it Flag. "The whole state isn't desert, you know."

"Oh."

"You've never been out West, have you?"

She shook her head, her hair brushing her shoulders. "I haven't really been anywhere. I went to New York City once." She took in their surroundings like a kid, her eyes wide, the haze of sleep still clinging to her eyes and voice. "Wow! Mountains!"

"Those are the San Francisco Peaks. No, not related to the California San Fran. Those are dormant volcanoes. The largest is Mount Humphrey. Great skiing."

"They're absolutely beautiful. It looks like God threw gold dust on green mountains."

They *were* beautiful, the aspens and ponderosa pines interspersed with the deciduous trees that were turning gold. He saw them through her eyes, fresh and vivid.

After passing Flag, civilization faded away again. She was still watching their surroundings. "The sand isn't all red either. Kind of a mix of red, dark gray, and rocks. I'm going to guess your place is in the middle of nowhere."

"Yeah. My father had it built before he met my mother. He used it as I do, as a respite between bouts." Acres of lonely, pine-covered land. "I called Pope, but he wasn't answering his cell phone."

She pulled out her iPhone. "I'm surprised there's service out here."

"I installed a personal cell tower. Unless he's out in the woods somewhere, he should get a clear signal. I left a message letting him know we're closing in."

"I remember hearing you talking. I thought it was a dream."

She'd stayed up through most of the night with him, though they hadn't spoken much. He was beginning to like having her there. Good thing he was dumping her off today.

She went into the back to gather her things. The passenger seat looked emptier than it had before. Toto sat wedged at the corner of the dash, staring at him.

When he finally pulled up to the cabin, he saw a bright blue Ford F10 parked out front. "My cleaning lady is here."

The dark wood house sat in a clearing, far enough from the trees for fire safety. The windows across the upstairs room, his bedroom, reflected the afternoon sun.

Petra came back up to the front. She took in his home, leaning forward and biting her lower lip. "I like it. Rustic but modern, blends in with the surroundings."

"By design."

He approached a large outbuilding that was connected to the house via a covered walkway and hit a button. The door opened and he pulled in. She met him by the side door a few minutes later and he took her bag.

"How long are we staying here?" she asked.

"I'm only staying long enough to get a game plan."

Her expression sagged. "Not long at all."

"You and Pope will hang here until I've taken care of Yurek and Baal, which hopefully will be sometime today. If there's trouble, Pope should be able to teletransport and take you with him. He said he was going to work on getting that ability back. Remember, you won't be able to bring anything but what you can fit in your pocket."

She pressed her iPhone to her chest. "I'm going to *wear* this thing."

The walkway led to a side entrance, but he continued around to the front door. "Pope's nearby," he said. "I can feel him."

Pope walked around the far corner of the porch that ran along the front of the house. Cheveyo started for his knife, a habit engrained in every cell of his body. Releasing the breath, and tension, he relaxed his fingers.

Pope noticed the movement and cracked a smile. "I come in peace."

She nudged him. "Pope made a joke."

"Humans are rubbing off on you," Cheveyo said, unable to help the wry grin on his face.

A board squeaked when Pope stepped on it. He stepped on it again, as though to verify where the sound had come from.

Cheveyo said, "It's an alarm. I was on a mission in Kyoto, Japan, and did some sightseeing after I was finished. At the Nijo Castle, I learned they'd installed these squeaky boards to alert the shoguns of intruders. I liked the idea."

Pope stepped on it one more time, nodding in approval. "Yes, primitive and yet timeless."

Cheveyo nodded toward the wrinkled map Pope was holding. "Been out exploring?"

"Studying the land in case I should have to flee on foot." He pressed the squeaky board one more time. "Like you, preparing for invasion."

They walked the final few feet to the front door. It was locked, just as Cheveyo had instructed Suza to do while she was there alone. He opened it and gestured for Petra and Pope to walk into the massive room. They stopped within a foot of the door. Maybe taking in the dark oak beams and the floor-to-ceiling rock fireplace. He stepped up beside them and saw that no one was looking at the fireplace. All eyes were on the woman posed on the back of the brown couch, wearing leopard-print panties and bra, black high heels, and nothing else. Her long black hair was artfully draped over her shoulder.

Her eyes popped when she saw the three of them. "Oh, hell in a coffee cup!" She fell backward, long legs flying, and landed on the other side of the couch. Her hand reached out and grabbed the discarded clothing on the floor.

Petra looked at Cheveyo, and he couldn't miss the edge in her voice. "I think you should have warned her you had company."

Suza rose from behind the couch fully dressed, embarrassment in deep blue eyes fringed with dark lashes and framed by bangs. "I am so sorry. Obviously I had no idea you had company or"—her gaze shifted briefly to Petra—"a girl. It's not what you think. Well, it is and it's not. It started that day a couple of months ago when you came back while I was still cleaning." She turned her attention back to Petra. "He looked ragged and worn, but it was what I felt from him . . ." She shook her head. "I know this'll sound a bit whoo-whoo, but I can feel people's emotions, and I felt this bone-deep loneliness and sadness. It about broke my heart."

She leaned back against the couch, her words still pouring out. Interesting that she was looking at Pope and Petra and not him. "When he interviewed me for the cleaning job, I felt something different than anything I've felt from a guy." She splayed her hand over the left side of her chest. "I could feel that he had a good soul. But that day his soul was hurting, and the need to take away the pain was overwhelming. He declined, told me he had a dangerous job and didn't want to jeopardize anyone. I couldn't get it out of my mind, though, so every time I came here, I put on my underpretties just in case."

Her gaze slid to Pope but came back to Petra. She blew out a breath hard enough to ruffle her thick bangs. "If you're his girl—and from what I'm picking up, you are—don't get your skivvies in a twist. He's innocent."

Well, innocent was not something he'd been called in a while.

"I'm going to stop babbling now and finish up." She finally looked at him. "Unless you're firing me." She waited for a second.

"I'm not going to fire you."

"You don't know what that means to me. I need these cleaning jobs till my shop gets established."

When he interviewed her a year ago, he'd felt her wild, frenetic energy. He also felt her attraction to him. She was a beautiful woman, but her need for love and loyalty ruled her out as someone he could get casually intimate with.

Suza asked, "Do you want me to freshen up the guest room? I haven't gotten to that part of the house yet."

Which was why she didn't know someone had been staying at the house. "We're fine," Cheveyo said. "Why don't you call it a day?"

Her smile wavered, but she revived it for Petra and Pope. "Have . . . a nice visit."

She grabbed the long handle on her container of

cleaning equipment and wheeled it to the door, her gaze still on Pope. Maybe because he was unusual looking. Then again, with that tiny smile, maybe it was more.

She paused in front of Pope and held a hand a few inches from his chest. "All of you have a buzzing energy I've never felt before, but you have it even more." She looked him right in the eyes. "You've got a good soul, too. And . . ."

Pope tilted his head, an expression of curiosity on his face. "And?"

Her eyebrows furrowed. "I'd better go."

With that, she walked out, closing the door behind her. Pope raised an eyebrow, and once the door closed, said, "Interesting. Me, a good soul? But she was right about our energy."

Cheveyo said, "I wonder what she picked up."

Petra was watching her through the front window. "She's not an Offspring, is she?"

Pope was watching her, too. "No, I didn't sense the Essence in her. But humans have innate psychic abilities, some more than others. She definitely has them."

Suza was halfway down the drive when Cheveyo realized he'd better have her wait a few weeks before coming back. He ducked out the door.

"Suza."

She was already at her truck, and she swiveled to face him, her expression tensing. "Shoot, you are going to fire me, aren't you? Not that I blame you. I probably got you into a sandstorm of trouble with your girlfriend."

"She's not my girlfriend."

"Yeah, right. Wait, you're serious." She pointed at her upper chest. "You're talking to a third gen empath. If she's not now, she will be. What I sense between you two is deeper than anything I've ever picked up before." Melancholy tempered her smile. "I'm happy for you. Gives me hope."

He wasn't going to correct her. "What did you sense from Pope?"

Her gaze flicked to the house, and a spark flared in her eyes. "I felt a deep yearning, but I didn't want to say that to him. Seemed a bit too personal and, well, we already got pretty damned personal already." She flashed a chagrined smile. "He's got the most gorgeous eyes I've ever seen, even if they are a bit freaky. There's something different about him."

Cheveyo nodded. "That there is."

She waited for him to elaborate. When he didn't, she said, "It's a good kind of different." She hefted the square plastic container of supplies into the bed of the truck and gave him a contrite look. "So, am I fired?"

"No. But I may have some trouble here in the next few days. I don't want you to get hurt. Call me before you come."

Her expression got serious. "It has something to do with the woman in there, doesn't it? I can sense your fear for her. Is everything all right?"

"We'll be fine. I'll be in touch."

She surprised him by giving him a hug. "Be careful." Just as quickly, she backed up and got into her truck.

He returned to the house. Petra had been looking out the front window but quickly turned as though to pretend she hadn't been. Suza's emotions were simple. In the house, things were more complicated.

Pope's head was tilted like a puppy who had heard an odd sound. "I've never sensed these emotions before. They're quite interesting. What are they?"

Petra's cheeks were pink. "What emotions? There

are no emotions here. We had an awkward little situation, but it's over," she added in a high-pitched voice.

Cheveyo leaned against the back of the overstuffed sofa, studying Pope. "You sense our emotions. How?"

"They come in pulses, like sound waves. I've sensed hatred and love and fear, but this woman caused emotions in both of you that I've never picked up before."

So Pope could pick up his emotions, even though he masked them. Interesting. "What do these emotions feel like?"

"Do we really have to go there?" Petra said, rolling her eyes. "Really?"

He hid his grin. These awkward situations were nothing in the scheme of things to him. He had to remember that Petra was a different person, with different perceptions and insecurities. "I've never met a Callorian that I didn't have to kill, so I'm curious, too."

She let out an endearing sigh and dropped down onto the deep red chair catty-corner to the couch, her arms crossed in front of her.

Pope narrowed his eyes in thought, violet blue eyes that some Callorians had when they didn't camouflage them with human colors. He hadn't taken on an ordinary visage for some reason.

Pope said, "From Petra I get a surge of pain and frustration. I felt this from her the first time I mentioned your name. But with the woman here, it was even sharper, like a laser beam. I had the sense that Petra wanted to leave this space but held her ground."

Cheveyo was watching her while Pope spoke, her face growing redder until she dropped it into her hands.

"It was a very curious emotion that surged in on

top of those two," Pope observed. "One that was even more powerful."

She looked up at them. "It was jealousy, all right?" She got to her feet, her hands fisted, keeping her gaze on Pope but jabbing her finger in Cheveyo's direction. "He told me we can't be together, and fine, we can't, but then there's obviously something between him and that woman, because he ran right out there to talk to her alone, which contradicts what he's told me."

Cheveyo couldn't help it. He liked her jealousy, even though he shouldn't, and didn't deserve the feelings it represented. Hadn't he felt the bite of it when he saw her with the guy at the restaurant?

Pope once again tilted his head, looking at Petra. "But you said you weren't gooey and dewy over him anymore."

She slapped her hand over her eyes. "Can I just disappear right now?"

"Gooey and dewy?"

"Can we not have this conversation?" she said, sliding her hands down her face.

Cheveyo grinned. "No, let's have it. What's gooey and dewy?"

Pope obliged, since Petra wasn't saying a word. "I believe it had something to do with how she felt after she was with you, a description given to her by her brother."

"I made you gooey and dewy?" Cheveyo asked. "And that's a bad thing?"

"It's a good thing that's a bad thing when it was about you."

Cheveyo could only nod, though he didn't get it at all. "Do you feel gooey and dewy about the other guy?"

"No."

Cheveyo leaned closer to her. "Can I see it? I confess that's an expression I've not heard of."

"No, but I'll be happy to show you annoyed." She made a face that only made him want to laugh more.

Pope was studying Petra's embarrassment. "Humans seem to be sensitive about some feelings, and yet others they lay right out there."

"Some feelings are private, Pope," she said.

"And so you hide them," he continued, pressing his finger to his cheek. "Or, as I've also seen, lie about them. Fascinating. In our dimension, the humans were overcome by them, sickened by them. They were their downfall. Here, humans both suppress them and get swamped by them. This doesn't seem healthy either." He looked at Cheveyo on those last words.

"Sometimes you have to suppress them to stay safe." He glanced at Petra. "Or to keep others safe."

Pope nodded toward her. "Her frustration was because you hadn't told her why you couldn't be together. But that apparently was in the past. She was pleased that she didn't feel the need to punch pillows over you anymore."

Ah, hell. He'd caused her a lot of frustration.

"He's explained that," she said, giving him a dismissive wave of her hand. "We're good."

"Now you will have to explain the woman," Pope went on, not picking up the tone of her voice, which said *end of conversation*. "She has a great curiosity mixed in with—" He took in her narrowed eyes. "—private feelings."

Cheveyo had to keep himself from laughing.

She turned, holding onto the arm of the chair, her gaze on Pope. "You laid out my feelings. What's he feeling?"

Uh oh. Now it wasn't so funny.

Pope studied him. "A deep sadness. Loneliness, like what the woman described. Something I can't identify. And great affection when he looks at you."

Damn. How had Pope picked up what he buried so deep inside? He held out a hand to Petra. "Let's go for a walk."

She hesitated a moment but then stood and took his hand.

Pope walked toward the front door with them, and Cheveyo added, "Alone."

"Oh, these are the private feelings you're going to discuss. We were schooled on human feelings, but I have had little direct experience with them. I only interact with humans as much as I need to blend in." He turned and walked back to the living room. "Clearly I need to study them more," he said to himself.

Cheveyo thought about the yearning Suza had picked up. Did Pope want to feel this mess of emotions deep down inside where all those repressed feelings hid?

He led Petra out onto the porch and down the stairs. There were no manicured lawns here, only brittle grass and pines scattered for miles. He led her over to his attempt at a garden, where dried up tomato plants testified to his neglect. Or, more precisely, to his illusion that he might have enough peace to grow a few tomatoes.

If he were a stronger man, he'd let her think he'd been banging the cleaning lady. He couldn't, because he knew it would hurt her. He'd done that enough.

She crossed her arms over her chest, staring at his plants. "You don't owe me an explanation."

"There's nothing to explain. I was just getting you out of there."

She looked up. "Oh. Well . . . thanks." She frowned. "How come *you* weren't embarrassed or thrown off?"

He smiled. "It takes a lot more than a half-naked woman on my couch to throw me off." Or to turn him on. "And she was telling the truth. There's nothing between us."

"I'm surprised. She's a hot chick, as my brother would call her. And she's obviously interested in you. You made a point to talk to her alone. And she hugged you."

"I needed to tell her to call me before she came to clean again. I don't want her coming out here and finding Yurek and Baal. The hug." He shrugged. "Nothing."

She nodded. "Why were you ragged and sad that day?"

He'd been feeling raw. He had killed a vicious Callorian the day before, and then gone to glimpse a bit of sunshine—Petra. So close, that if he'd shouted her name, she would have turned and walked over. "It was just a mood."

"I know that place, too."

He didn't need to hear that. He brushed a strand of her hair from her face. "When this is over, I want you to go find that guy. Greg." He had to push out the name. "I want you to have that normal life you want. Forget about me, this, everything. Promise me."

He didn't want that at all. She didn't either, by the hurt in her eyes. "I promise," she said, a bit too forcefully.

He stared at their linked hands, remembering Suza's words. She was right. Which was why he had to separate from Petra today. He slid his hand free of hers, slowly, feeling his reluctance.

She said, "The pillow thing . . ."

"You don't have to explain yourself."

"Yes, I do. I want to put it into context." She took a quick breath. "Do you know how hard it was being around people who were falling in love? Seeing the looks that burned, feeling the tension, watching them go to their room knowing they were going to have hot, sweaty sex. Of all the Rogues, I was the only one who actually wanted to fall in love with someone, but I'm the only one who didn't. Then there was you, us, and yet, no us. Not knowing was the worst part, but I understand now." She gave him a forced smile. "What I said to Pope was true; we're good."

Which wasn't true, but he wasn't about to refute it. "We'd better go in and make our plan. Time is running out."

They returned to the house in silence. They followed the sounds Pope was making in the kitchen. He was putting slices of smoked meat on pieces of frozen bread.

"I've developed a liking for the food here," he said, setting one completed sandwich on a plate. "Though I confess I've never actually made a meal."

Cheveyo stepped up to the stone counter. "Might help to defrost the bread first." He put several slices into the toaster oven. "I'm going to head back out tonight, backtrack and try to find Yurek and Baal. I don't want them coming here, but you have to be prepared if they do. Baal is tracking me, and even if I'm not physically here, my scent is."

Pope pulled out a gallon of orange juice and tried to pour it into three glasses he'd set out. He unscrewed the cap and tilted the carton. Nothing came out. "Two against one isn't good odds."

"This is frozen, too. Nothing keeps for as long as I'm gone, so I freeze everything." He put that in the microwave on defrost. "I've taken on three before. It's easier to do it alone."

"Not from what I saw," Petra said. "You engage one, the other can come up from behind."

"I've been doing this for a long time."

She leaned against the counter. "You should have a partner. Someone kick-ass who could have your back." She turned to Pope. "His father is the one who put him on this path. Trained him when he was a kid to kill these beings."

Cheveyo said, "It's my path. I'm here to protect the innocent."

She walked over to him, her eyes never leaving his. Her hand was warm against his cheek. "But you're an innocent, too."

He took her hand and lowered it, letting it go. "No, I'm not." He turned to Pope. "You'll sense them if they come near, right?"

"Yes, I can still do that."

"How are you with hand-to-hand combat?"

"I usually blew the enemy apart if I was tasked with that."

"Plan B is better, then: grab Petra, teletransport to somewhere else."

"One small problem: I don't know if I have the power to do that right now. Sometimes I can, sometimes I cannot. I can't guarantee that I'll be able to go, much less take her with me."

"Which would leave her here alone," Cheveyo said.

"And me possibly unable to come back to help her."

Fear seized his chest at the thought of that. Her, too, by the way her face paled.

"I'll have to fight them," she said. "I did pretty well back there at the river. You said so."

Just the memory of Petra fighting stirred his gut.

"Pretty well isn't going to cut it. As you said, two against one isn't the best of odds, especially when you haven't been dealing with these beings most of your life. There's something to be said about your natural instinct to survive, but it may not be enough against skilled killers."

Her veneer of bravery was wilting now that she was thinking it through. He felt her fear, too.

"I can hide even better," she said.

"Not well enough for these guys."

The toaster oven dinged. Pope swiveled around and took out the bread, setting two slices on each plate. "What do we do now?"

Cheveyo took a deep, heavy breath. "I'm going to have to take her with me."

CHAPTER 9

"Come at me with the knife like you mean it," Cheveyo said, facing Pope, who looked awkward holding one of the knives from the sacred weapons room.

Pope obliged, and Cheveyo grabbed his arm and had him on the ground in two seconds. "Now I'll show you how to do that."

Petra sat on the grass and watched them. The cool breeze caressed her as it whispered past, becoming a murmur in the pine forest that surrounded the cabin. She breathed in the scent of sun-heated pine and sap. On a black piece of felt next to her were several more of those knives so Pope could try different ones to see which worked best.

"What you need to do," Cheveyo said, "is disable his weapon hand and simultaneously go on the offensive."

He wore a pair of tan pants that clung to his body and allowed ease of movement. Or he was trying to torture her, but she doubted he knew what he was doing to her. He obviously wasn't self-conscious about his scars since he wore nothing else. She supposed he accepted them as he'd accepted being a warrior.

"The thing about knife fighting is that by default you have to get close to your opponent. It gives you a lot of flexibility but also puts you in proximity to whatever weapon he may have. If he has a knife, always know where it is and be ready to move your body out of the way of a slice. You want to keep moving; never be a stationary target. The best defense is to knock the weapon out of his hand."

"What if it's a gun?" she asked, feeling very much on the sidelines.

"You take it out from a distance." He threw the knife toward the edge of trees, slicing off a thin branch before the blade sank into the trunk of a tree just beyond it.

She didn't want to look impressed, but *holy hell* . . .
"I suppose you meant to cut that branch."

He merely lifted an eyebrow and then walked to the tree to retrieve his knife. "Your opponent may not expect you to use the knife as a distance weapon. If you throw it properly, you can disable him before he gets near you." He wrenched it from the tree and spun around to inflict a perfect slice through an imaginary opponent.

Pope looked at the knife in his hand and then a distant tree. "I should get used to handling the knife before I start throwing it."

"Definitely. Now, don't forget that you can use your body to both maneuver and to put strength behind your thrust, as well as evade."

He showed Pope a couple of moves that made Petra restless. What the hell was it about watching Cheveyo fight that got her so hot and bothered? She didn't even like fighting.

"Aim for soft, fleshy parts of the body, not places where the bone is close to the surface," Cheveyo was saying. "Remember, you're in it to kill. Callorians can take on a human appearance, which means they have human vulnerabilities. Go for the organs." He pointed to places on his body. "Heart, thrust up like this. Kidneys. Liver. If you thrust enough in this section, you'll hit something."

She relived the moment when she'd sunk her kitchen knife into the dog beast's leg. She'd felt the blade split through flesh and hit bone. Revulsion washed over her, but triumph followed. She'd been scared, but she took action. Maybe it was dangerous, but she helped in the fight and hadn't gotten killed. And again, by the river. She'd been an asset, hadn't she?

She picked up one of the smaller knives and felt the weight of it in her hand. Curled her fingers around the handle. Her teal-tipped nails looked good against the carved ivory handle. The ivory looked old and genuine and carved in perfection. The scene depicted in miniature was a man and tiger engaged in battle.

She stood, knife in her hand. "Teach me, too."

She was prepared to argue with him, but he nodded. His eyes flared. "You were amazing when we faced both of them at the river. Strong, confident, and fierce. *You* have to believe you're amazing, not that you did pretty well. The most important thing to remember is—" He grabbed her from behind, spun her, and dropped her to the ground. "—to never drop your knife."

Her gaze went to the knife, now lying a yard away. He hovered an inch above her.

"You have to be ready for anything. If you had your knife, you could still defend against me. Now you're defenseless."

She could only nod. *In so many ways.* "I dropped it during my fight with Baal, too. But I got it back."

He pushed to his feet and extended his hand to her. "You got lucky, but luck shouldn't play a part in surviving." He gave her a look that reminded her of the comment she'd made earlier.

She jumped to her feet without his help. Not to prove a point but to work on being agile, though she didn't do it as gracefully as he did. She swiped up the knife. "Teach us more."

He stepped easily into the role of teacher. "Imagine this common scenario: your opponent has a lock around your wrist and will either attempt to pry the knife out of your hand or squeeze so hard you'll have to drop the knife." His fingers clamped around her wrist. "Shake me off."

She brought her knee to his groin, but he blocked her with a swivel of his hips.

"Nice try," he said.

"I don't want to hurt you."

He tilted his head at her. "I've been through a lot more than this. Do what you have to do to get free. Let me see what you've got."

He was pressing at a point in her wrist that was weakening her hold, twisting her to the side so the knife would drop harmlessly to the ground. And dammit, it hurt. She shoved her body into his, tipping them off balance and sending them both to the ground. He was on the bottom, taking the brunt. She wasted not a second, taking advantage of his surprise and the momentary loosening of his grip to twist her hand free. She brought the knife down, but he grabbed her arm before the tip even got close to his chest. He flipped her over him, her legs flying in the air, and before she'd even landed, he had the knife out of her hand and pointed at her neck.

She was breathless, her back sore.

He didn't gloat, at least. He stood and this time didn't offer his hand. "You put up a good fight, but you're dead."

He turned back to Pope. "How do you usually fight?"

"My best weapon is—was harnessing my energy into a laser beam of destruction."

She jumped to her feet. "Eric said you incinerated the guy who was trying to kill us down in the Tomb."

Pope nodded. "I did." He held his hand out, palm angled toward the ground, his face a mask of concentration. "I feel a tingle, as though it is coming back." Another few seconds later he shook his head and leaned down to touch the ground. "Not enough to even warm the dirt." His mouth tightened, giving away his frustration.

Cheveyo said, "No matter how comfortable you are fighting with your skills, using a knife will be completely different. You have to be ready for that. You're sinking a knife into someone's flesh, and you'll be close enough to see them die." He included her in that warning.

They worked through a couple of scenarios, talking through his actions for both their sakes.

She thrust with the knife in her own imaginary scenarios, getting more used to it. Focused totally on her task, she didn't hear the footsteps coming up on her. Arms grabbed her and spun her to the ground. She rolled before Cheveyo could pounce on her, jumped to her feet and held up the knife, still clutched in her hand. She gave him a triumphant smile.

"Good job," he said. "Next time come up ready to attack."

Her smile sagged when she saw that the knife point was facing the ground. "Next time?"

"I'm going to jump you every chance I get."

She arched her eyebrow at him. "*Every* chance?"

He met her gaze, a playful glimmer in his eyes. "When you least expect it."

Pope walked up to them, his violet eyes shifting from him to her, his head tilted. "I'm picking up another new emotion."

They both looked at him and said simultaneously, "Forget about it."

For the next two hours, they worked on move after move, Cheveyo playing the opponent for her and Pope in turn. She didn't want to admit how exhausted and sore she was, bruises accumulating on top of the bruises from their last altercation. As the two men sparred, she dropped onto the scratchy grass and watched. The afternoon sun glistened on Cheveyo's damp skin. He had the grace of a ballet dancer but the fierce determination of a Native American warrior. And the patience of a saint.

Pope was getting the hang of it. Twice he had the knife within a few inches of Cheveyo's throat. Something sparked in those violet eyes as he fought. Pope was a warrior, too. Losing his skills had probably felt like castration to him.

A few minutes later Cheveyo wandered over and reclined beside her, shielding his eyes with his arm. He released a long breath, letting his body totally relax . . . for about a minute. Then he sat up, rolling up the cloth that held the knives so carefully she didn't hear the metal clank together once. "Let's grab showers. Does that knife work for you?"

She tilted it so the sun glinted off the blade. "Yeah. It's not too heavy. And it's pretty."

"Pretty." He rolled his eyes. "Keep it. I'll see if I've got a holster that works with it. You want to have it on you at all times."

"You think I've got a good handle on it?" Of course, she wanted to hear him praise her skills, amazed that she'd become proficient so fast.

"I hope so." He turned to her as he continued walking. "What do you think?"

"I think . . . I think I won't be a liability to you."

Pope said, "You looked capable to me."

She beamed. "Thank you."

Cheveyo tucked the bundle under his arm as they reached the front porch and held the door open for her. "Meet me in the Blade Room after your shower."

She went to the room where he'd put her things and took a shower. The floor above her creaked. His bedroom. She could well imagine him stripping out of his clothes and taking a shower, because she *had* seen him do both.

A half hour later she walked into the room he kept under triple lock. The cabinet in the RV was nothing compared to the scarily amazing room. Knives of all kinds were mounted on the walls in groupings, the corresponding sheath beneath each. The sheaths were often as elaborate as the knives. Three large cabinets probably held more.

Pope stood near one of the tables covered with an array of knives, holding a primitive looking knife with reverence.

Cheveyo was polishing one of the blades with a cloth, slow, thoughtful strokes. He slid an impatient gaze to her from beneath his eyelashes.

Pope took the two of them in. "I shall leave you to your task."

As soon as he left, Cheveyo set down the knife he'd been polishing. "Princess, you've got to cut your get-ready time by two-thirds." He took in her dried and brushed hair, made-up face, and probably the scent of her cherry blossom body lotion, since his nostrils flared. "For one thing, you don't need it. For a more important thing, we don't have time for glamour."

She leaned against the table next to him. "For one thing, I *do* need it. For a more important thing, I need to have control of something. Right now it's not my life, my surroundings, or much of anything." Especially her emotions. "But my getting ready process, which I enjoy, is something I can control." She tightened her hold on the knife she'd brought down. "And don't call me princess. My dad used to call me that."

"You don't like your dad?"

"No, it's not that. I love him, of course."

He regarded her. "But somewhere along the way he let you down."

She ran the flat edge of the blade along the thick velvet that covered the tabletop. "No. But if I'm a princess, then he's a king. He's not strong enough to be a king." She pushed away the hurt. "When he remarried, his wife wasn't thrilled to inherit three motherless teens. I know he was lonely, and it meant so much to have a woman in his life again. He didn't want to lose her."

"He sold you out?"

She met his gaze, seeing the hardness in his eyes at

the thought of that. "Not sold us out. But she chipped away at him, manipulating him into considering sending us off to a private school—one that was about two hundred miles away."

"Sounds like selling out to me."

"It wasn't like that. He was just . . ."

"It's okay to be angry about it. When you care about someone, you will do anything, sacrifice everything, to keep them safe and happy. Especially your children. He was being selfish, plain and simple."

She shook her head. "I don't want to be angry at him. I just have a hard time with his weaknesses. And when Darkwell was hunting us down, my dad called the police to report Eric. If I hadn't heard him, Eric would have been arrested—and killed. Dad didn't know the danger, and who would believe that kind of craziness anyway, but the man called the police on the boy he'd raised as his son."

He was still regarding her in that curious way. "In *Cinderella*, her father married the wicked stepmother. Didn't he abandon her or die, leaving her in the clutches of those awful women?"

Petra frowned. She'd never connected the story to her own life. "She was afraid to tell her father about the cruelty she suffered because he was too cowed to confront his new wife about it. Cinderella thought he might be angry at her instead."

"Then she became a princess. I saw the cartoon movie cel at your townhouse. And another of Snow White. Both princesses. Both orphans. As was Dorothy in the *Wizard of Oz*. Do you understand why you're drawn to them?"

She shrugged. "I like their stories. I always have."

"That's because you are a princess and an orphan." Before she could object, he added, "And you're also a healer. Those are part of your archetypes, which is what I meant when I said earlier that it was part of your psyche. We all have them, twelve archetypes who guide our journey here. There are almost ninety of them, like Victim, Queen, Knight, Avenger, Warrior."

"I suppose you're a warrior."

"And the hermit."

She picked up another knife, one with a blade half as long as a sword. "I also love the story of Aigiarm, an ancient Mongolian princess who challenged her many suitors. She put up her virginity to their horses if one could wrestle her to the ground. They say she ended up with ten thousand horses, and not one man won her virginity. I have a painting of her in my dining room."

"That's a good princess to focus on right now."

He grabbed her and spun her around. The knife dropped to the floor as he slammed her against the wall, his body pressed to hers. "Always be ready, princess. The big bad wolf is on the prowl."

It would be much more annoying if there wasn't an erotic undertone to the way he pressed her wrists to the wall at the sides of her head, the way he looked at her as though he would eat her up.

"Maybe I'm not afraid of the big bad wolf." She kneed him, gratified that he hadn't been ready for that. He grunted but didn't buckle.

"Better," he said on a tight voice, stepping back in a slow, deliberate manner.

She grimaced and wanted to apologize, but that sounded more princessish and not warriorish, so she didn't. "I don't want to be ready every second." She picked up the knife and set it back on the table, then picked up the one she'd been working with.

He walked stiffly toward the display table. "You have to be."

"What if I accidentally stab you? Or the knife drops and spears our feet?"

"I'm watching where it goes." He opened one of the drawers and pulled out a leather belt. "Most of my sheaths are made to be mounted horizontally on my belt. That's why I wear loose shirts that hang over my waistline." He wrapped the belt around her waist. "Too big. I'll take it into Flag and have the guy who made it put in another hole. I want it to fit tight." He surveyed what she was wearing, a form-fitting long-sleeved shirt. "Most of what I've seen you wear are tight shirts or sweaters, which look great but don't do much for disguising a weapon."

She was distracted by the feel of his hands on her waist. "What about an ankle holster? I've seen those in the movies."

"Imagine that you need to get your knife quick. You have to reach down, lift your pant leg, and then extract the knife. Takes too long. But I could have the sheath made into something you could wear around your neck. Either way, babe, you gotta wear something looser. Keep the knife in the sheath and go through the motions of pulling it from either location. See which feels best."

Baggy shirts and sweaters. Was there *no* justice in the world? On the upside, that meant she'd have to do some shopping. She watched him demonstrate pulling the knife from his belt and then beneath his shirt and copied the motions. "I think I like it around my neck."

"That's what we'll do, then."

"Thank you. For the knife."

"It's a gift I wish I didn't need to give you."

She nodded toward a display hanging on the wall. "Why are those knives displayed separately and on blue velvet?"

"Those are from my father's collection." He reached up and unhooked one with a wavy blade. "This was my first knife. He gave it to me when I was seven."

She shook her head. "Seven." The thing was a foot long.

"Right before he died. It was a big deal, that he trusted me with it. During the full moon he always took his knives outside to sanctify them. He dedicated them to the blood of the innocent. He would cut his hand to put his own blood on the blade and ask the gods to help him. That last time I saw him, we were living in DC but we came out West so my mother could visit her people. He and I stayed here for the weekend. That's when he showed me the Blade Room and gave me my first knife. He told me it would be mine someday.

"We walked outside to a fire pit, and we went through the ceremony, sanctifying the knife he'd given me with my blood." He was staring at his reflection in the blade, maybe standing with his father again. At seven.

She held the knife out on the palm of her hand. "I want to sanctify this knife."

He raised an eyebrow. "Do you even believe in that kind of thing?"

"I don't know what I believe anymore. I just know I want to sanctify this knife."

He met her gaze, and she saw something close to admiration in his eyes. "We'll do it tonight, before we leave."

She felt a strange trill go through her. At the prospect of being with Cheveyo in the moonlight, cutting her hand, or because of that admiration, she didn't know.

A short while later they reached Flag, parking in the historical area. It resembled an Old West type of town, with lots of shops and restaurants. Since it was a college town, she saw a lot of young people, and people her own age who enviably had nothing more to worry about than exams and studying.

Cheveyo parked along the curb in front of a bookstore. The streets were dusty and sprinkled with leaves that had fallen from the trees planted along the sidewalk.

She followed him into the leather shop next door. Cheveyo obviously knew the Native American man behind the counter well, as they exchanged warm greetings and a handshake. Maybe he was from his mother's tribe. Or, thinking of the many sheaths Cheveyo had, he was probably just a good customer.

"Petra, this is Vince Blackhawk, one of the best leathersmiths in the world. This is an associate of mine, Petra Aruda."

She nodded, and he gave her a slight bow. As Cheveyo described what he needed done, she looked around at the variety of leather items, from art to belts to boots. Associate, huh?

She breathed in the smell of leather. "Is it wrong to love the scent of dead cow?"

In a soft, reverent voice, Vince said, "Each cow that is used for my leather is honored in death and thanked for its contribution to my welfare, and to the enjoyment of those who buy my wares."

"Uh . . . that's great. Really."

Vince crooked a finger as tanned as his leather, beckoning her closer. When she hesitated, he said, "I need to measure you for length of cord."

"Oh." She released a breath and walked over.

After measuring the cord, Vince told them it would be ready in a short while.

They walked passed art galleries and shops that boasted turquoise, pottery, and silver jewelry. Lots of gorgeous Native American artwork. She kept pausing, taking in all the pretties. Gifts? Would Eric or Lucas like a silver pendant? Funny, she didn't feel that driving need to buy things for everyone. She looked at Cheveyo, who was watching her with amusement.

"Does your mom have a shop like this?" she asked.

"No, she works from a studio I had built for her at her home on the rez. Her work is in many of these shops, though."

"That must make you proud." She could tell that it did. She paused outside a clothing boutique. "Can I pop into this shop for a few minutes? I need to get some baggy shirts." It wasn't baggy shirts that had snagged her attention, but the cutest leatheresque fringe vest with turquoise beading in the window. She desperately needed to buy something fun.

Pope pointed to a shop three spaces down. "I am going into the pastry store. Perhaps it is a similar draw as yours I experience when I see éclairs in the window."

Cheveyo rolled his eyes. "Make it quick," he said, though she knew he didn't want either of them to wander off.

"I know, ten minutes," she said with a smile, breaking down the last remnant of his resistance, at least by the way his own mouth curved. "You can come in with me."

He leaned against a heavy wooden beam. "I'll wait here, thank you."

She walked in, dazzled by the upscale boutique and all of the pretty outfits. She sought out the rack with the vests and snagged one in her size. She wasn't as thin as the mannequin in the window, but she bet she'd rock the vest anyway. Turning to another rack, she picked out a couple of tops that fit the baggy bill. When she turned to ask the clerk where to try them on, she stopped, mouth half open. The woman behind the counter had the same expression, only hers was tinged with shame.

Suza the seductress cleaning lady's dark eyebrows furrowed. "Oh, shoot, you're not hunting me down, are you? I'm telling you, I never laid a finger on that man."

Petra stifled a smile. "I believe you."

Suza studied her. "Yeah, you're cool." She splayed her hand on her chest. "Whew. I know women can get crazy jealous, especially about a man as good-looking as that one. I should have known better. Not only is he hotter than the Sonoran Desert in July, I had a feeling his heart was elsewhere."

"We're not . . . you know, involved. I've only met him twice before now." She wasn't giving permission for the woman to continue to try to seduce him, was she? Hopefully not.

Suza was frowning in puzzlement. "That can't be true, not with what I picked up. You're very special to him."

Petra blinked at that. "How do you know that?"

She fiddled with her long black braid. "I felt it when he looked at you, right after I . . . well, you know. He was checking your reaction. And I just now realized the pictures in the china cabinet drawer, they're of you. He's known you for a long time, 'cause some of them are when you were younger."

"He has pictures . . . of me?"

"A bunch. Found them when I was polishing the silverware. I did wonder if you were his girl, but then, there were no signs of a woman living in that beautiful house, so I thought maybe you'd died or something. That would explain his sadness. Whether you're involved or not, that man adores you." Her gaze dropped to the hangers she was holding. "You want to try those on?"

"Oh. Yes."

The vest didn't seem all that exciting compared to what Suza had just told her. "You work here, too?"

"I own this place, opened it a couple of months ago. It took every penny I had, so I do cleaning on the side for extra cash."

Petra looked around the store, now seeing it as a woman's dream. "I like it. I hope you succeed beyond your wildest dreams."

"Thanks, sweetie. See, I don't do everything on impulse, though that part of me does get me into trouble sometimes. I need to tamp it down, for sure." Suza led her toward dressing rooms with wooden doors painted in southwestern colors in abstract designs.

Petra paused before going in the room. "You feel people's feelings?"

Suza was unlocking one of the rooms. "As does my mother and grandmother. A gift and a curse," she added with a wry smile.

"Don't I know it." At Suza's surprised expression, Petra said, "I mean, I've heard that psychic abilities can be a double-edged sword."

"Yes, but it's clued me in on three cheating bastards and one lying girlfriend." She opened the door for her and gave her a wry smile. "Once I got past being the Queen of Denial."

"I can see how that would come in handy." She liked Suza. Liked her even better because she hadn't slept with Cheveyo. She was a striking woman, with stormy-sky eyes, creamy skin, and hair that reminded her of Cheveyo's pitch-black jag fur.

Petra focused on trying on the clothing, the vest first. It showed off her cleavage and still maintained modesty, and the fringe danced with her movements. She was so buying it. She tried on the other shirts, shrugged, and put them in the keeper pile, too. No fun buying clothing she wasn't in love with.

A couple minutes later she took the clothing to the counter. Earrings that matched the turquoise beads caught her eye, and she held them up and surveyed her reflection in the oval mirror.

"All set?" Suza asked.

Petra nodded, and when given the total, handed her cash. "I don't think it's weird that you pick up people's feelings. You're an empathic."

"Yeah, that's what they say. Well, thanks for that. I'm not ashamed of it, but some people . . ." She waved a hand that sported two silver and turquoise rings. Her gaze went beyond Petra. Outside, Pope had joined Cheveyo, offering him something in the white bag as he ate an éclair. "What's his story?"

"Pope?" At Suza's nod, Petra had to stifle a laugh at the thought of trying to explain his story.

Suza's smile lit her face, her gaze still on him as she wrapped up her purchases like a gift. "He's got wild eyes. Is he involved with someone?"

"Ah, no. Hasn't ever been, actually. His job keeps him pretty busy."

"I was serious about feeling a good heart in him.

Don't feel that very often, let me tell you. There's something about him. He's different."

"Pope is . . . is . . ."

The bells on the door jangled, saving her from trying to come up with something, and both men stepped inside.

Pope licked his fingers as his gaze went right to Suza. "Uh-oh. This is—what is it called? Dejazoo?"

Cheveyo was obviously surprised to see Suza there, but he gave her a warm smile.

Suza spread her arms to encompass the store. "Welcome to my boutique, gentlemen. This is why I work so hard." She walked around the counter and closer to the two men, stopping in front of Pope. "You're not from around here, are you?"

He gave her a smile that Petra had never seen. A flirtatious smile. "You figured me out. I'm from a little town near Croatia." Probably his line to explain why he wasn't up on all nuances of American life and conversation.

Suza didn't look gooey and dewy; her eyes sparkled with interest. "I'd love to get you out of those clothes." His eyes widened, and she added, "And into something like this shirt that would bring out the gorgeous color of your eyes." Without taking her gaze from him, she snatched a shirt from a rack of men's clothes and held it up to him. She looked as guileless as could be, as though she hadn't tossed out that provocative line. "Not that you need to. They pop all on their own, but this would really maximize them."

Pope's expression was a mixture of wonder and pleasure. "Thank you." Without even looking at the shirt, he said, "I'll take it."

Suza looked at the tag and then at his upper body. "You'll need an extra large to fit those shoulders." She riffled through the hangers and produced a larger size. "You want to try it on?"

"No, I trust your judgment."

She held it against his chest, running her hands over the fabric to flatten it against him. "Yes, that should fit you just fine." She paused a moment, her hand still on his shoulder. Petra felt that pregnant pause between them, that beautiful moment when two people realize there's something going on between them, even deeper than surface flirting, that takes your breath away.

Suza blinked and dropped her hand. "I'll . . . I'll go ring you up."

Okay, *now* she looked gooey and dewy. It looked good on her, softening her eyes, curving her mouth into a misty smile.

Pope remained there for a second before snapping out of it. He stepped to the counter and pulled out his wallet. After he'd paid, Suza put all of her attention on wrapping the shirt in teal tissue paper and inserting it into an opaque plastic bag. She met his gaze as she handed it to him. "Come back and see me. I mean, come back and shop again. It was a business doing pleasure with you."

Pope's mouth twitched, and Petra saw the moment poor Suza realized she'd switched the words. Petra stepped up to the counter. "It was a pleasure doing business with you, too." She held out her hand. "Don't tamp down that impulsive side. It suits you. And thanks for . . . you know."

The moment they walked out of the store, Cheveyo asked, "Do I want to know why you're thanking her?"

She gave him a mysterious smile. "Probably not."

CHAPTER 10

Cheveyo spent a half hour stocking the Tank and readying it for the next trip. More than anything he did not want to share this small space with Petra again. But he couldn't think of one other place where she would be safer without bringing in the Offspring. Dangerous for them, and still maybe not enough to protect her. Hell, he wasn't sure he would even be able to keep her safe.

Back in the house, he caught her looking at something in the drawer of his china hutch. She held up a stack of pictures, a puzzled look on her face.

He walked up to her, gently took them from her hand and closed them back in the drawer.

"Why?" she asked, glancing toward the drawer. "Why do you have these pictures of me?"

"Because I'm a crazed stalker." He widened his eyes to make the point. Luckily, she hadn't gone deeper into the pile. He didn't want to explain anything else she might find in there. "Do you still want to do the ceremony? We have to leave soon."

"Yes, I do, but—"

"When I checked on you, I sometimes took a picture. No big deal."

She flicked a glance to the drawer. "No big deal. Right."

Pope was sitting on the couch, three different maps spread out on the coffee table that showed the surrounding area. Cheveyo caught his attention. "You want to come?"

Pope took them in, standing only a few inches apart, probably picking up the tension. "I'd better not. That Hotter'n a Bitch sauce you warned me about . . ." He pressed a fist against his stomach. "I should have believed you."

Was he really talking about the sauce?

Petra picked up the knife she'd set on the table and followed him out the kitchen door to the backyard. The night was alive with sound, crickets and a breeze whispering through the pines. Soon the crickets and katydids would go silent for the winter. The first snowfall could come in a couple more weeks. Cheveyo paused, sensing the surroundings. No sign of an unwanted presence.

A rustle of some animal startled by their exit from the house made Petra's body tighten. "What was that?" she asked from very close behind him, her fingers curling around his arm.

"Could be a raccoon or coyote. It's not a beast dog."

"That is only somewhat comforting."

"We don't have to do this." He turned, and she was walking so close she ran right into him. He automatically put out his hands to steady her, resting them on her shoulders.

"I want to. Let's just do it quickly."

He heard the apprehension in her voice, and yet she was determined to go through with it. He liked it better when she was the wigged out scaredy-cat than the determined woman with a knife gripped in her hand. The blade caught the moonlight, sending a flash across the ground with her movements. The moon wasn't full but bright enough to see by.

Her voice was soft in the darkness. "Did your father bring you out here in the middle of the night?"

"Yeah, but the moon was full." He stopped at the stone fire pit midway between the house and the forest but didn't sit on the circular bench.

She faced him, the light washing over her blond hair like silver, sharpening the planes of her face. "Were you afraid?"

"I was more afraid of screwing up the ceremony or doing something that would make him see I wasn't worthy."

She nodded. "Do you feel any anger toward *your* father?"

"Why would I?"

"Mm, let's see. He stole away your childhood, turned you into a warrior at seven, and has directed your life since then."

"He gave me a direction. When I saw other kids playing, sometimes I wished I could be like them, yeah. But I also felt special because I had a mission, a secret purpose."

"Do you still feel special?"

"That was a kid's ego. I can't let my ego play into what I do. I don't feel special. I just am."

She moved closer. "A warrior."

"And an exorcist, and shapeshifter."

She had been about to touch his face, but the reminder of his cat stilled her hand. "The archetypes. Is that from the Hopis?"

"I've studied many different religions and spiritual teachings. The question is there evil on earth and why, drove me down many paths."

"And what did you find out?"

He glanced up at the moon, feeling its rays as strongly as he felt the sun's. "The only evil is what we create in ourselves."

"So you don't believe Yurek or people who kill are evil?"

"They are beings who stray from their path. I kill. Am I evil?" Was he almost as bad as they?

"No." She stepped closer. "Are you happy doing what you do?"

"I don't think I'd use the word 'happy.' I do it because I feel a deep need to. It fulfills me. But I can't say I like killing anything, even if it deserves to die." He couldn't see her eyes, only shadows, orbs. She looked otherworldly with the moonlight kissing her hair in a halo. If he didn't start the ceremony now, he'd be kissing her, too. "Ready?"

She nodded, holding out her hands. "What do I do?"

"You have to make the cut yourself. Hold out your nondominant hand like this." He took her cool hand in his and held it faceup. With his finger he traced a line in the center of her palm. "Just a small cut, about here."

She placed the blade where his finger had just been and squeezed her eyes shut. "I don't even like getting shots. I look away." She took a breath and moved the blade. He knew how sharp it was; it would take nothing to slice her skin. She gasped but let out no other sound. He saw the line of blood form. He took his knife and sliced his palm, too.

Cupping her hands, he held them up to the moonlight. "We dedicate this knife to the protection of the blood of the innocent." After a pause, he added, "Let this knife become yours, Petra."

Looking at her gazing up at the moon, her expression so serious, took his breath away. She looked at him then, and he could feel the depth of her emotions. He felt her fingers graze his, and then she pressed their palms together. "Now I'm yours, too."

Those words reverberated within him, like an echo bouncing deep within endless caverns. He closed his eyes and forced out the words, "You are mine, but I can never have you."

She twined her fingers tightly through his. "You *can* have me."

Those words crumbled him, sucking away his resistance. He felt the pieces of his heart fall away like shards of glass. He kissed her, soft, completely in control, and yet . . . not completely, because then he wouldn't be kissing her at all. But he let himself taste her, because he'd been living on the memory of that one kiss for too long. For a few seconds he got lost in her, his fingers threading through her soft, long hair, breathing her in, feeling her tongue moving against his.

Too long. Too late.

He finished the kiss. No, not too late. He pressed his forehead against hers, listening to her breathing for several seconds.

"I didn't just imagine how spectacular that kiss was," she said on a breathy sigh. "I thought I'd built it up in my imagination because you were my mysterious savior. But . . . no. Dangit."

He stepped back enough to see her, pulling her fingers from his but keeping her hands in his grip. "And if we went further, it would be even harder to back away."

"Then don't back away."

She was killing him, and he didn't use that phrase lightly. "You see what my world is like. What kind of man would I be to bring you into this?"

She squeezed his hands. "Walk away. Stop living in the darkness."

"I can't do that."

"Because you can't go against your father's wishes?" Her voice had taken on an edge, her mouth tightening.

"Hell, Petra, I'm not doing this to please my daddy." He shook free of her.

"Then why? Why does it have to be you?"

"Who else is going to do this job? What do you think that classified ad would read like? 'Dangerous job fighting otherworldly beings, no pay, fame, or glory. Death possible. Slobber likely. Injuries always. Must distance yourself from family and friends for their protection.'"

She put her hands on either side of his face, and he smelled the copper of her blood. "When I was looking at those pictures, I wasn't thinking you were a deranged stalker. It hit me what you'd said earlier about planning to come to the Tomb to help even though your father had seen your death. You were going to take any chance that you could to save me, *knowing* you would probably die."

Her voice thickened with emotion. "That is a big deal. You don't do that for someone you only care about. You do that for someone you love." Her fingers stroked his face, weakening him as much as her words.

Still in control.

He brushed her hair from her face, feeling the wet tracks on her cheeks. He couldn't speak, couldn't deny or confirm what she was guessing.

She took a jagged breath. "I felt our connection that night you brought Zoe to us. When you grabbed me so I wouldn't scream and give you away. When you summoned me from my bed. I didn't understand what it was then."

It was the first time he'd touched her. Agony and pleasure at once.

"Then when you saved my life and kissed me, and said how hard it was to stay away . . ."

"Agony," he said, because the word was pounding inside his head. Her hands on him, her heart in her voice.

Her sigh was as soft as the breeze that whispered through the pines. "H-E-L-L. Sometimes I thought I'd dreamed you up. But it was all too vivid, too real, and Zoe had seen you, too. You were a terrible ache inside me, and I didn't understand why it hurt so much. Knowing the truth doesn't make it any better."

"That's why I stayed away from you, to keep you safe, to save you from feeling the ache I've felt most of my life."

"Too late. I'm here and you're here, and we're stuck together."

It was incredibly hard to pull her hands from his face. "We keep our heads so we keep you alive, and Pope alive, and then you go back to that safe, normal life you loved not long ago." He let go of her hands. "We have to go. I have two people to kill."

"And after that, you'll have more to kill. And more."

Weariness sank its claws into him. "Yes."

"I'm sorry I insinuated that you're the kind of man who would kowtow to your father's wishes. I know it's much more than that."

"I do what I do to protect the innocent, Petra. It's

what I live for. And someday it'll be what I die for."

Only then would he be free of the ache that consumed him, the losses he'd suffered, including when he sent her back to her life.

He walked to the house, hearing and feeling her beside him but keeping his gaze on his surroundings, as he always did. His night sight was exceptional, a carryover from his cat, but the trees hid much in their depth.

Pope was still studying the maps when they walked back inside. He looked up at them, his eyes narrowing as he homed in on Cheveyo. "You have blood on your cheek."

"Sorry, I tried to wipe it all off out there." Petra reached over, but he stilled her hand.

"I'll take care of it. Come here." He walked to a cabinet just outside the kitchen and opened it, pulling out a roll of gauze and a tube. He gestured for her to give him her hand, and he put a dab of tea tree oil on the slice and then wrapped the gauze around it. The strong scent, antiseptic and yet pleasant, opened his sinuses. He dabbed the oil on his cut, too. It was his imagination, he was sure, that made him feel their intermingled blood as it tingled through his body. "Get your things. It's time to go." He walked over to Pope, who was now standing. "Do you have a handle on the area?"

"Enough, I believe."

He hefted the backpack he'd readied and set it on the coffee table. "Survival supplies. Hopefully I can intercept them before they get here, but you must be ready. Signal me if you sense anything, and I'll be back."

"Don't you mean 'we'?" Pope nodded toward where Petra had gone.

The wood floor down the hall creaked as she walked out, pausing, it seemed, to hear his answer.

"We," he confirmed. "But me as much as possible." He turned to her. "I expect you to obey my every command, whether you agree or not. Understand? I can't have you running all over doing your own thing. If I'm worrying about you, I'm not paying attention to what's in front of me. Got it?"

She saluted him. "Got it, captain. Or sergeant. Or whatever."

He had a bad feeling that this was as obedient as she was going to get. To Pope he said, "I— We know what they're driving. They won't be looking for us in an RV, so we should have the advantage. I'll keep you informed."

He followed her through the side door to the outbuilding. A board on the walkway squeaked, too. As soon as they cleared the door, he grabbed her from behind, spinning her. She reached for the knife but he had her on the ground and pinned beneath him before she could get a grip on it.

"Dangit," she said, her fingers still flexing in vain.

"You're not ready."

"I think you just like tackling me."

He did, but that wasn't the point. He got to his feet and reached out to help her, but she jumped up on her own again. Very unprincesslike. A good sign. But not good enough.

CHAPTER 11

While Cheveyo drove back the way they'd come in, Petra worked on getting her knife out quickly. She could not cut her getting-ready time down, but she could work on her reaction time with the knife. When there were no cars to search, she saw him watching her from the corner of his eye.

He still had a speck of blood on his cheek. There was something intimate about *her* blood being on him, and maybe it was a little bit gross, but she wasn't going to tell him just yet.

"That's wrong," he said, making her wonder if he'd read her thoughts.

"What?"

"That you should have to practice pulling a knife out of your sheath. You should be having margaritas with your girlfriends or shopping or something. I hold Pope responsible for you having to become . . ."

She sat down, swiveling the chair to face him. "Become what?"

"A warrior."

"When I should just be a princess."

He shrugged. "I'm just saying."

She liked being a princess, loved shopping, and would like to have margaritas with girlfriends, if she had any besides the Offspring women who'd gone on with their lives. But as she flicked her hand down and came up with the knife, something thrummed through her body like the low beat of a distant tribal drum. Even the sting of the cut on her palm felt good, weird as that was.

Warrior.

Not a go-out-and-kill things warrior, but a protect-my-people warrior.

Cheveyo had sunk into his thoughts again, scanning the roadway.

She put the knife back in the holster. "When you've come to me, to summon me or whatever, have you ever seen images of my life?"

"Sometimes." Which meant always; she suspected he was playing it down.

"I saw things when I contacted you, like pieces of your life, even when you were a boy. Some were pretty scary." Just remembering it thickened her throat.

He didn't respond, but she saw his mouth tighten.

"And I can feel your loneliness, sadness, when you're sleeping and aren't blocking it." She leaned forward. "Do you have anyone to talk to? You can't hold all that in. Talk to me."

"I don't have time to get all touchy feely with my feelings."

"Actually, we do, until we find Yurek." She dug her elbows into her thighs, bracing her chin on her hands. "So unload on me."

"Let me think about it."

She waited as patiently as she could. Finally she said, "Well?"

"I'm thinking."

More silence. "You're not going to tell me anything, are you?"

"Nope." He turned at the next intersection and doubled back.

"I just want to help."

"You're a healer, Petra. I understand, that's who you are. But you cannot heal me. Just like you couldn't heal my scars, you can't heal the scars inside me. I don't want you in there trying. Right now we're together because we have to be. But after I squash these sons of bitches, you are going back to your life and I am going back to mine."

"Who are you trying to protect? Me or you?"

"Both of us."

Well, at least he wasn't going to try to sell it as something he was doing just to protect little ol' her. Which meant, she realized, he didn't want to hurt either.

She gave him a salute again, knowing he was right, the bastard. Look how much it hurt when he hadn't contacted her, and that was after only one kiss. "I get that we're not going to be together. And you know what? I don't want to be part of the world you seem hell-bound to. I just thought I could help—"

"You can't."

"Fine."

A few minutes later, when he stopped at another light, he blew out a breath of frustration. "This isn't working."

Trying to shut her out? "What isn't?"

"Driving around like this. It's too dark to see inside most of the vehicles on the desolate stretches of road. I could feel their Geo Wave, but that's only if they're close. I'm going back to the road leading to my place, stake out the entrance. I don't want them that close to Pope, but I can alert him when they arrive and cut them off before they reach the house."

He turned around. "I want you to stay in the Tank, out of the fray but close enough so you know what's going on. Be ready to face them if it comes to that, but don't put yourself out there in the battlefield."

She remembered well the scene at her townhouse and by the river. Fear clutched at her throat and squeezed her chest. "What happens if you're hurt?" She didn't want to think about the unspoken *or worse*.

Alarm sparked in his expression. "Take the bike. Best to run than engage. Have you ever driven a motorcycle before?"

"No."

"I need to give you some lessons."

Oh, boy.

He started giving her instructions, "In case we don't have a chance to do it hands-on."

Her phone rang. Amy's cell number appeared on the screen. Fear trilled through her. Was the baby all right? Had Yurek somehow found out about them?

"What's going on?" she answered, hearing the panic in her voice. She forced a smile that she hoped Amy could hear. "I mean, hey, how's it going?"

"You sound uptight. Things not going well with Mr. Gooey and Dewy?"

Petra laughed. "Things are going positively juicily."

"Snap a pic and send it to me. I want to see what this guy looks like."

As surreptitiously as possible, she angled her phone and took a picture. He glanced over at the phony camera click, narrowing his eye at her, but switched his attention back to the road.

"Ooh, yummy," Amy said a few seconds later. "I

can totally understand why you get gooey and dewy. Of course, I'm a little prejudiced since he looks like Lucas. Are you in an RV?"

"Yeah, he's showing me Arizona, where he lives."

"Hell of a first date. Maybe this will cure you of the buy-everything-for-everyone thing you've been going through."

"That's not a thing, it's just me."

"That's you buying stuff to fill a hole that things can't fill. But I think he has a lot to do with that hole, and it sounds like things are going great."

Great. Yeah, just great. And she was going to have to explain why they weren't together when this was over.

"Anyway," Amy said, "I sent you a picture, too."

She checked her in-box and gasped. "The sonogram! Does this mean . . . ?"

"No, we don't know the gender. The tech blocked it out at our request."

"Damn you." She stared, trying to spot telltale anatomy. Heck, she couldn't figure out where the baby was, much less the blacked-out part.

"It's a healthy baby, that's the important thing," Amy added, obviously taking pity on her curiosity.

"A healthy baby." Petra's voice had gotten all gooey and dewy on that. "Baby Vanderwyck. I'm so happy for you both."

And jealous, but mostly happy. She felt something else, though, building inside her, closing up her throat. "This tiny baby . . . so helpless. We have to keep her safe."

Amy clearly thought that was a strange thing to say at the moment. "Uh . . . well, sure. Feed him, change diapers, and keep him safe, that's what our jobs will be."

She imagined that tiny little fetus growing inside Amy's body, so fragile, and then Yurek hiding in some dark corner, waiting to kill them.

"She's just an innocent," she whispered at that terrifying picture. Cheveyo looked over at the use of that word in his golden rule.

"Yeah, for as long as we can manage it," Amy said, an unsure tone in her voice. "I knew you'd be excited, but you sound a little weird, actually."

"I am excited. Blown away. Seeing the baby . . . it's real. She's real." She touched the screen. "She's really real." And she would do everything in her power to protect her.

"Yeah, he is. We're calling it *he* for now, instead of *it*. I'm kinda hoping it's a boy. Less complicated. I'm freaking, but I've got a few more months to get used to the idea. Me, a mom. Lucas, a dad. It's mad bizarre."

She wasn't sure why she kept calling the baby *she*. "I hope it's a girl. Then I can buy her lots of clothes, oh, all the cute, frilly little—"

"Promise me you're not going to run out and buy a bunch of girl clothes till after the baby comes."

"Sure, take away all my joy."

"Promise me, Petra."

"Okay, okay, I promise." But she was already imagining matching hats and booties.

Cheveyo's head jerked to the right as they crossed paths with a car. "That was them."

"I've got to go," Petra said. "We're meeting some friends of Cheveyo's for drinks. He just saw them. Tell the baby hi for me."

She disconnected while he turned the Tank in a tight turn, considering its length. "I'm in."

"What?"

She got to her feet. "I'm in, one hundred percent. I won't let Yurek take Pope back and SCANE him. I won't let the Collaborate find out about the people in my life. I'm not about to let anyone hurt this precious baby." She held up her phone and pointed to the picture on the screen.

"Uh . . . that's me."

It had switched to the last photo she'd taken. She quickly flipped it back to Amy's e-mail. "This baby. Maybe Yurek finds out about us before Amy has the baby, and she never even gets born. Or maybe he finds out afterward, and the baby grows up without her mom." Her voice became soft. "She always wonders if her mom loved her, and what she was like. The baby girl grows up with an ache inside her that she can't even fathom, with a need that will never be filled."

"Is that what you felt?" he asked softly.

She shook her head. "I'm talking about the baby. And the golden rule, protect the innocent." She whipped the knife from her holster, spun it in her fingers, and readied it for a plunge. "Now I understand why you do this."

"I liked it better when you thought I was nuts. Get that gleam out of your eyes, like you want to do what I do."

"Well, not, like, for a living or anything. Just Yurek. And the Glouk. Then I go back to my life and date normal guys and forget all about you." *As if.*

She couldn't tell what he was thinking, but he sure didn't look pleased. His mouth tightened in a line and he looked ahead. She knelt beside him, her fingers lightly resting on his arm. "I've been afraid my whole life. My mom burned to death. Our house burned down when I was a teenager. Then there was my stepmother, who died in the fire. And thinking I'm going to die when I'm twenty-four, and *then* having people trying to kill me. So now people are trying to kill me again, and yes, I'm afraid. But I'm not too afraid to do something about it. If you're stuck with me anyway, I might as well make myself an asset instead of a liability. Could you say something?"

He kept his gaze straight ahead. "God help us all."

She wrinkled her nose at him.

He pulled up to a place blazing with lights and busy with cars and people, and yet it was in the middle of nowhere.

"What's this?" she asked as he pulled to the outer edge of the dirt parking area. Just beyond that were makeshift tent buildings, a whole city of them. She could hear two different kinds of music blasting from somewhere, and everywhere people wandered and danced and laughed.

A big banner rippled in the breeze: THE SECOND BURNING.

"Have you heard of the Burning Man festival? It's been going on annually for years now, out in the Nevada desert. From what I've heard, it's turned into a Mardi Gras for the earthy crowd." He was studying the lot. "There they are. The question is, what are they doing here?"

She watched the car that had run them off the road earlier as it idled in a parking spot, feeling some of her bravado trickle away. She breathed in the scents coming in through the vent. "Dinner? Smells delicious."

The aroma of charcoal, meat, and spices filled the air.

"Or they've tracked us to the area and think we're in there. So many people, keeping track of Yurek could be a nightmare."

As a group walked out to their cars, she realized what seemed odd about the people she could see in the distance. "But we could even up the score a bit. A lot of people are in costume."

His gaze found the group, dressed like desert nomads except for the vivid colors and makeup. One man wore a multicolored clown wig. A woman in the group wore tinsel hair. Many people, though, had given their costumes a lot of thought, obviously hand-making them.

The two men stepped out of the sports car. Baal was in human form, and looked homeless with his bedraggled clothing and sallow skin. She noticed that he walked without moving his body. It made her think of cartoon creatures when they tiptoed, their toes the only thing that moved.

Yurek looked like the man she'd seen in the parking garage back in Annapolis. Both scanned the area, but they weren't looking for an RV. Yurek's gaze scanned the dark interior of their vehicle. She held her breath, watching his body for any sign that he sensed them in there. She released it when his gaze kept moving.

"What are they up to?" Cheveyo asked, a rhetorical question. "We'll follow them, wait for a chance to get Baal alone. Getting rid of one of them will help."

She looked at the people all over. "Is hunting them down here the best idea?"

"No, but it's an opportunity I can't pass up. None of us can afford to make a spectacle. This is about subversive hunting. Find Baal, knife him, and get out. He'll revert to dog. People will think a wolf crept onto the grounds and someone panicked. These people don't want bad press. If they find a slaughtered wolf, they'll quickly dispose of it. Yurek would also revert to his Callorian form, which looks sort of but definitely not human. There would be an autopsy and investigation, and Roswell all over again. Too risky to hunt him in a public place."

She turned to Cheveyo. "Give me a second to grab my makeup. I can work up a sort of costume really fast."

"We don't want to lose them. As soon as they move, we move." He opened a small closet and extracted a long beige coat, handing it to her as he reached for the doorknob. "Tuck your hair inside the hood."

She smeared purple and teal eye shadow over his cheeks as he watched them from the window, hardly any light in which to work. He had great cheekbones, high and prominent.

"They're on the move," he said, ducking away from her ministrations.

She did hers on the fly and blind, her most challenging makeup session ever.

They stepped out and walked across the shadowy parking area. He led her to the first booth they came up on, his gaze on Yurek, and bought a burlap-type cape with a hood. He threw it over his shoulders, covering his head, and ducked behind the booth.

Looking like a desert nomad on an alien planet, Cheveyo paused at the rear corner of the booth. "He senses me here, but even Baal won't be able to pinpoint our exact location in this crowd."

Both men were on alert, so obviously not there to enjoy themselves. Their eyes searched the crowd, and they didn't even return the greetings of those they passed. They began moving apart as they worked through the area.

"That's a good boy," Cheveyo said under his breath. "Move away from the Callorian."

They closed in on Baal as Yurek moved farther away. She clutched her knife beneath the coat she'd draped over her shoulders for better movement. Cheveyo was steps behind her, his body in predator mode. Interestingly, he looked as casual as anyone else in the crowd. It was the gleam in his eyes, a shade darker, and the stealthy way he moved. She knew his knife was in hand, too.

Could she stab someone with intent to kill? Her fingers tightened on the handle. Yes, she could. For her friends and family. For baby Vanderwyck.

Yurek must have sensed their nearness. He spun around, raking the crowd with his gaze. She pulled Cheveyo toward her and planted a kiss on his mouth, putting both their faces at an angle Yurek couldn't see.

"He's looking this way," she whispered.

When she checked again, he melded with the crowd and . . . disappeared. No, he'd taken on the appearance of someone else. Her heart tumbled. In the blink of an eye they'd lost him.

"Where is he?" Cheveyo asked, shifting his gaze to search.

"Gone. Sorry."

They stepped apart, but he kept looking for Yurek.

"I think he shifted," she said. "One second he was there, and then he was gone. Do all Callorians shift?"

"No. Even fewer can mimic like Yurek."

Cheveyo was searching, too, without appearing to do so. His mouth tightened. "You watch Baal, I'll look for Yurek. They'll probably communicate. A nod, some kind of signal."

Knowing Yurek was out there, anywhere, scared the hell out of her. She'd had enough of unseen enemies. Baal was easier to keep an eye on, but they couldn't let their guard down. Whoever Yurek looked like now, his face would be tense, eyes searching.

They kept Baal in their sights, weaving in and out of the crowd. They neared one of the stages where an acoustic band was playing some kind of strange new age music, with one guy chanting or screaming, she wasn't sure which. Across the expanse of booths a rock band counteracted their sitar with heavy bass and drums.

Arms grabbed her and pulled her toward a sweaty, hard body. With a gasp she had the knife poised beneath her coat, ready to stab him. Except he reeked of alcohol and could hardly stand up.

"Hey, baby, I—"

Cheveyo knocked him to the side, keeping the man in sight as well as watching around them. "Stand back."

The man wobbled but kept his balance. He took in Cheveyo's stance. "S-Sorry, dude. I thought she was someone else." He ambled off.

"I almost stabbed him," she said, her eyes wide.

"But you didn't. Come on."

Now they'd lost Baal. He was easy to find again, hovering near one of the roasted meat stands. When the proprietor wasn't looking, he snatched one of the sandwiches. His eyes watched for them, and his canineness showed in the way he tore at the bread and shoved the pieces into his mouth.

"Didn't you say Glouks could only take on human form temporarily?" she asked.

"Yes, but I don't know time limits. He won't turn into a pumpkin at midnight, for instance. Or after twenty minutes."

Baal definitely sensed them. His eyes, beady even as a human, slid over the crowd. She and Cheveyo stayed at the edge of one of the booths, looking like a cozy couple picking out jewelry.

"Ooh, this would go great with the vest I just bought," she said.

"You're really thinking of buying a necklace? *Now?*"

"Just putting on the act. Sort of." It was a rockin' necklace.

Her hand was sweating where she held the knife, and she switched hands and wiped her palm on her pants. Her chest felt tight, body on edge. Yurek could be anyone, even a child, though he'd likely choose a form that would allow him to kill.

Baal was on the move again, and he led them on a slow-motion chase toward the other stage, where a band was playing Led Zeppelin classics. This time she definitely smelled marijuana, drifting in clouds above the clusters of people listening to the music.

Cheveyo moved closer. "Something's not right about this."

"I was thinking the same thing. It's like he's leading us into a trap."

Cheveyo spun around. "But I don't sense Yurek anywhere."

Baal drifted to another booth, pretending to watch the band.

"Go with your instinct. I'm sure that's what has kept you alive all these years."

Cheveyo snapped his fingers. "Baal *is* leading us, but not to anyplace in particular. See, he's not watching for anyone. He'd be communicating with Yurek like two predators working together would. So if he's not leading us *to* somewhere—"

"He's leading us away. We're at the rear of the grounds now."

He grabbed her hand and threaded through the crowd, still watching all around them. Her heartbeat thudded in her chest, tightening her breathing. Was this a setup? Would Yurek be waiting for them at the Tank?

They were nearly at a full run by the time they reached the parking lot. Yurek's snazzy sports car was gone.

"Hell," Cheveyo said. "He's gone after Pope. I've got to warn him."

"Could he have gotten to your place by now? I have no idea how far we are from there."

He glanced at his watch. "Possibly."

"You haven't been alerted by Pope through your connection." Because if Yurek got hold of him, Pope would have to die. That was their agreement. Her fingers tightened on her knife handle at that thought.

Cheveyo pulled out his phone. Something came at him from behind, shoving him to the ground and sending the phone flying. Baal was on Cheveyo's back, not quite man, and not dog either. He was trying to hold onto human form, but bloodlust fired his eyes red and his head was misshapen.

She lunged at him. He deflected her, but the blade sliced his arm. He snarled but turned his attention back to Cheveyo, pinned beneath him.

Cheveyo took advantage of Baal's momentary distraction, shoved up with his knee and then rolled so Baal was beneath him. Now this was the kind of two on one she wanted. Except as she approached, so did a group of people.

No way would Cheveyo change to cat at the risk of someone seeing him.

She said to the group of people, "They're blowing off some steam. Keep moving, nothing to see here."

"We're going to let security know," one man in the group said. "We're about peace and love here, man, not rage."

She stared them down and they slowly moved on. She turned back to Cheveyo. The two men, verging on beasts, wrestled for control. She kept her knife hidden from view as she approached the wriggling, grunting mass and searched for the phone. Hers was in the RV.

"Call Pope," Cheveyo said in a tight voice.

"I am. Or I'm trying to, anyway." She found the phone and pressed the speed dial for Pope. It rang. Rang. Rang. Then a generic message announced that the person being called wasn't available. Waiting for all the outgoing messages drove her nuts, but finally she was able to say in one breath, "Yurek may be on his way. Get out."

She shoved the phone in her pocket and angled in toward Baal's leg with her knife. Except the men were moving so much, she was afraid she'd stab Cheveyo instead. There were no lights here.

She saw two men approaching who, while not wearing uniforms, looked to be authority figures.

"Cops are coming!"

Baal lifted his head, his misshapen nostrils twitching. He didn't want to be caught. That was the one thing all beings from other dimensions had in common, Cheveyo had told her: the desire to stay hidden from the human race. Baal sprang away, and she saw him change to dog mid-leap, out of sight of the approaching group of people.

Cheveyo's eyes were nearly black as he got to his feet. His face was smeared with the dirt he'd been scrabbling in. He grabbed her hand and stalked to the Tank. "Did you get hold of Pope?"

"No answer. I left a message."

His expression became grimmer.

"How does this connection between you two work?" she asked. "You'll know if something happens to him?"

"I'll see it happen. And I'll be able to find him. His capture activates the connection, like one of those flashing lights on an emergency vest. Until then, I have nothing."

"So we know he hasn't been captured."

"Yet. We'd better get to the house before Yurek does."

Yurek made his way down the road where he'd picked up Pope's Essence, and where Baal had sensed Cheveyo's scent. Some creature cried out in alarm and scurried away. He broke out of the woods and into a clearing. The lights from a cabin at the center of it glowed, welcoming. He flexed his fingers.

His cell phone vibrated. The Glouk, given the number on the screen. Yurek had gotten the beast a pay-as-you-go phone when he'd come up with the plan to get the hunter and the woman out of the way. It clipped onto a collar.

"They're on to us," Baal said. "Be ready for them."

"I will come back for you when I'm done with Pope. Unless you can get here on your own."

He heard a low chuckle over the line. "I'm hitching a ride . . . on top of their large vehicle. Be there soon."

CHAPTER 12

Petra sensed someone behind her. She was in the Tank standing behind Cheveyo's seat, so no one should have been behind her. She spun and screamed before stopping the sound short.

"Pope!"

She couldn't help it; she gave Pope a hug. When he remained stiff and even a bit at a loss, she stepped back. "I'm . . . just glad to see you."

His mouth moved into something like a surprised smile. "Thank you."

He was growing on her. Of all the people who'd abandoned her, Pope never had. He'd certainly never meant to expose her to danger.

Cheveyo pulled off the side of the road and spun out of his seat. "Your skills are getting better?"

No doubt he was thinking she could stay with Pope if that was the case. That might have been her preference at one time, but not now.

"I wouldn't say that," Pope said. "It took several minutes to do so, and the process felt unsteady, as though my molecules might splinter. I'm not sure I could do it again." His eyebrows furrowed. "What has happened to your faces?"

"Oh, our makeup!" She rubbed her hand across her cheeks. Cheveyo's face was also streaked in dirt. "We were at a festival."

"A celebratory gathering of people? Now?"

"Not for fun. We—"

"No time to get into it," Cheveyo cut in. "Have you ever driven one of these?" He gestured to the Tank.

"No, but I'm proficient in automobile navigation and have been trained in all manner of vehicles."

"Good. You're going to drive this all over the place. They won't be able to zero in on you if you're constantly on the move." He pulled out a map from one of the overhead cabinets. After spreading it out on the small table, he pointed to a spot on the map. "We're here. See this triangular loop? Keep driving it. That'll keep you within reach of us. If you run into trouble, you can take one of these roads, but they're going to be pretty rough. They cut through the national forest. Petra and I are going to take the bike and head back to my place, see if we can catch Yurek there." He took out his wallet and handed Pope a credit card. "Use this for gas and whatever else you need."

Pope shook his head in a tight back and forth motion. "I have plenty of resources. It's my other resources that I'm lacking."

Cheveyo paused for a moment. "Maybe I'm feeling your Wave, but something's not right." He cut the lights. "Stay inside and away from the windows." He pulled his knife and slipped out the side door.

Her heart rose in her throat. She couldn't see anything out there, except for movement by the front window. Cheveyo? She angled herself so she could see out without getting close. Black fur glided by, too graceful to be the Glouk. It made sense that Cheveyo would stalk Baal in cat form. The Tank tilted slightly. Footsteps sounded on the roof. More movement.

The door opened and Cheveyo walked back in. "I didn't see anything, but I want to get out of here, drive a bit before we leave." He dropped into the seat and headed back on the road.

Pope remained standing, and so did she. No one talked for a few minutes, and the silence was driving her crazy. She touched his arm, feeling an odd vibration that made her pull back. "You knew Amy was pregnant long before anyone else did."

"I sensed life inside her. She is doing well?"

"Very." She pulled out her phone and her fingers flew over the icons as she held it up to him. "The baby."

His light eyebrows lifted. Of course, he probably couldn't tell what was what on the sonogram either.

"That's Cheveyo," he said after a moment.

She looked at the screen. *"Augh."*

"Why did you take my picture?" Cheveyo asked.

"To show Amy you're not a figment of my imagination." She pulled up the sono and held it up for Pope. "The baby."

"Yes, I see legs, head, arms. Ten fingers, ten toes."

She pulled the phone back, studying the blob. "No way. You can see all that?"

"More like sense it."

Which brought her to exactly what she'd wanted to ask him. "Can you tell whether it's a boy or girl?" Yeah, yeah, it was cheating. If Amy and Lucas wanted to wait, fine. She couldn't. And she'd never tell them, not even a hint.

"Girl. I felt the feminine energy when we were together."

"I knew it!" She spun, her hand on her heart, letting out a joyful squeal. "Frilly dresses, here I come." Had she promised Amy she wouldn't buy baby clothes? She couldn't remember. Either way, she would store them until B-day so as not to spoil their surprise.

Cheveyo said, "Now that we've taken care of the important things . . ."

"That was important." She slipped the phone back into her pocket and beamed a smile at Pope. "Thank you."

"It's nice to make you so happy with just a word. Funny how humans respond to something so simple." Pope looked genuinely pleased, and she felt an odd rush of affection for him.

"Words are powerful," she said. "Love, for example. Saying 'I love you' can change everything." She tried hard not to look at Cheveyo. "When you mean it. When I was a Hooters waitress, guys would tell me they loved me. They'd ask me out without even knowing a thing about me. It was so superficial."

Pope tilted his head. "What's a Hooters waitress?"

Cheveyo laughed. "Yeah, explain that one to him, why don't you?"

She sent a *hmph* his way before turning back to Pope. "Hooters is a restaurant that's named after a, uh, word for a woman's breasts." She made the universal motion. "Big breasts. Since men can't seem to call them that, they come up with all kinds of euphemisms for them, like boobs, jugs, and melons."

"And don't forget 'great mounds of joy,'" Cheveyo added, though she was pretty sure he was just kidding, given his wry tone of voice.

Pope said, "I find it interesting how humans use these odd words to describe the act of reproduction or the parts used therein. And yet, they use those words to describe each other and situations, too, mostly in a derogatory way. Once, in traffic, someone called me a 'dick.' I explained that my name was Pope, not Dick, and that seemed to stymie him. Later I found out 'dick' is another word for a man's penis, though I don't understand the meaning of calling someone a penis. It serves two vital functions in life, after all. By the same token, you also use words related to religion. God, Jesus Christ, and hell are used as exclamations, and yet humans are extraordinarily sensitive to the nature of religion. It's baffling."

Petra said, "I never thought about that, but you're right. When someone's being a jerk, you call them an ass, not a foot. Goofballs are called boobs. And yet, a woman's breasts also serve a vital function in life."

"As well as being beautiful and not the least bit goofy," Cheveyo added.

Pope's gaze drifted to her breasts, but not in a leering kind of way. "I have to admit, I am coming to appreciate the singular beauty of a human woman's body, at least what I've seen of them." He met her gaze again, a tiny spark in his eyes. "Like the woman in her underpretties."

Hm, this was getting interesting. But there was something she was curious about. "What do Callorians look like? Cheveyo said, sort of human."

"In form and general characteristics, yes, a lot like you. We have been conditioned to think of humans as a separate species, a disdained species. In truth, some scientists suspect we started out the same, all living on the surface. Many thousands of years ago, for an unknown reason, a large group descended to live beneath the surface. The theory is, because we lived so much closer to the Earth's magnetic field, it changed the characteristics of our energy, and thus our bodies. We lost the density of the human form, including the outer shell of skin. The meat suit, as it were.

"Because our energy vibration runs higher, some can change their form or use that energy in different ways." He held out his hand, probably thinking of the laser beam he used to harness. "Emotions were suppressed even back then."

"So you don't fall in love?" Petra asked. "Or marry?"

"We have unions based on common goals or other strategic reasons. Because of my service to the C, I never married."

"Or fell in love," Petra said, feeling both sad and envious for him.

"The words love and hate are also thrown around here, and yet they are supposed to signify deep emotions."

She slid a glance at Cheveyo. "Unfortunately, love and hate are baffling to all of us."

Cheveyo's mouth twitched, but he gave away nothing more on his thoughts about love and hate. Several minutes later he pulled off the road again and looked at Pope. "She's all yours. Once you hear the bike leave, get out of here."

He probably wouldn't take the time to jump her, but she was ready anyway as they made their way toward the back.

It hit her, that this was how Cheveyo had to be all the time when he was on the hunt. Living on edge. Ready to kill. Ready to die.

She jumped on the back of the bike, gripping his chest as the gate lowered to make the ramp. He started the bike and gunned it out. When she expected him to continue on, he spun around and watched the gate go up. Once it latched closed, he rode next to the Tank as Pope pulled away, speeding ahead, turning, and coming back toward it. No sign of anything unusual.

They took off in the opposite direction, hoping to catch Yurek.

Baal held tight, tucked into the tight spaces of the undercarriage, the pads of his paws protecting him only slightly from the heat. He had quickly learned that the two pipes got very hot and had to reposition himself. When the RV had stopped, he suspected the hunter might have become suspicious. He'd jumped down and run into the woods.

What he'd wanted was to kill the hunter. Saliva pooled in his mouth at the thought of it, his primal instinct hungering to slice through flesh with his teeth, to consume him. But Yurek would not be pleased if he ruined this chance to capture Pope, especially now that the hunter had ridden away. He wanted to please the Callorian, an odd place to find himself. Yurek was the first Callorian to ever treat him with something other than disgust and hostility.

Yurek was a hunter, too, sanctioned by the Collaborate. If Baal didn't give in to his animal, he could show Yurek that he was valuable as a partner. Equal. Not even his own pack had treated him as such. Alphas ruled their packs with viciousness, and any member thought to be too submissive or too aggressive was expelled. Or killed.

He had found freedom in the Earth dimension. The pack part of his nature, though, was lonely. His pack nature wanted to please Yurek.

As soon as the RV slowed, he would jump down and climb back on top, where he could alert Yurek of their position, and his prize: Pope, all by himself.

Cheveyo parked the bike just out of sight off the road leading to his cabin. They ran parallel through the woods to his long driveway, and he cringed at their loud footsteps. Of course, Yurek would sense them anyway, but he didn't want to give away their exact location.

Crickets filled the air with noise, which helped. He tuned his senses to his surroundings but picked up no trace of another being. Yurek had to have come here. He wouldn't have set up the elaborate ruse if he didn't have a lead on Pope's location.

They reached the clearing, bathed in moonlight. One light shone inside the house, on a timer throughout the night to welcome him home if he returned after dark. He had no electronic security system, just as his father had none. His senses would alert him if trouble were near. Baal, however, didn't send off as much of a signal since he was both animal and human. Yurek would, but where was he?

Cheveyo leaned close to Petra, smelling her heat and fear. But he didn't need to say anything, he realized, didn't need to make a noise that might alert Yurek.

Petra, I'm going cat so I can see and hear better. Stay with me.

Her eyes widened at his sudden intrusion into her thoughts, but she only nodded.

He had communicated psychically with her before, when they were physically apart. He handed her his phone. Phones didn't take the change well either, and he had to replace them once a month.

He didn't like going cat in front of people. It wasn't embarrassment, but that it separated him from his humanity. Being cat was the edge he walked. He rubbed his ring, feeling the twist in his stomach, and then changed. His vision and hearing sharpened a hundredfold. He heard movement in the woods but knew the sounds belonged to real animals. Occasionally he let his cat free to roam the forest and hunt. The thought of eating raw flesh sickened his human side, but his cat craved the gamey taste, the blood that made his teeth slick. It was that base animal instinct that made him reign in his control even more.

Those hunts, though, made him intimately familiar with the sounds, scents, and habits of the creatures that belonged in his woods. That the raccoon hunted and the owl soared overhead meant they hadn't picked up an intruder, at least until they sensed Petra.

He circled the house, bracing his paws against the walls to peer through the windows. Nothing inside looked disturbed, and he picked up no change in the energy signaling that someone had gone into his territory.

Once he completed the circle, he felt sure Yurek wasn't there. Either he hadn't found this place or left once he figured out Pope wasn't there. This was different than how he'd felt earlier at the Tank.

He changed back to man. "It's clear."

She was staring at him, obviously having seen him morph. She didn't look horrified, which was a good thing. Or maybe not. She was apprehensive, though.

"Something's bothering me," he said. "I can't figure out what it is."

"But you just said it's clear. Being a cat, you'd know if something wasn't right here. So there's not, like, someone hiding in the edge of the woods or—"

He touched her shoulder, stilling her outpouring of panicked words. "It's clear."

"Sorry, I'm just jumpy. You're a beautiful cat, for a jaguar that can tear things apart with its teeth. I try to remember it's still you."

"It's me." His words felt heavy in his chest. Still him inside, still human.

"It's fascinating. Scary but fascinating. How does it feel when you morph?"

"Natural. I feel my essence stretch, pull, but not painfully." He liked that she was interested. Which was not good—her interest or his warm feeling over it. "I enjoy being in my cat body. I can swivel my ears to hear better, my senses are more alert, and my muscles have rubber band flexibility."

"When you changed to cat earlier, how did you climb up the ladder?"

The warm feeling vanished. "What do you mean, 'when I changed earlier'?"

"When you went out to check the Tank, I saw your black fur glide by."

In the moonlight he saw her eyes widen again at the same time he felt dread smack him in the chest.

"You didn't change to cat, did you?" she asked.

"No. You saw black fur?"

"Just a flash of it. I assumed it was you because it was so graceful, and how could that *thing* be graceful when it looks so ugly and—"

"Give me my phone." He was already walking back to the bike. "Pope, everything all right?" he asked as soon as Pope answered.

"I'm following your route and getting acclimated with the way the vehicle handles. Something is wrong?"

"I think Baal hitched a ride, probably back at the festival. Since Yurek's not here, I'm guessing he's on his way to wherever you are. You're going to turn around and go the opposite way." They synched up their locations and where they would rendezvous as he and Petra reached the bike.

"How can I get rid of him?" Pope asked. "Drive under the low branch of a tree? Swerve?"

"You watch too many movies. Just keep driving. I'll take care of Baal." He disconnected and swore. "I should have turned cat when I checked the Tank." He looked at her. "Are you ready to drive the bike?"

"By myself?"

"Yeah, but only after I've jumped off."

She gripped his arm. "You're going to jump off the bike *while it's running*?"

"I'm not actually going to jump."

She blew out a breath. "Thank gawd."

"Jumping would push the bike back. When we catch up to the Tank, I'm going to grab hold of the ladder and step off."

"You're not kidding, are you?"

They reached the bike. "I never kid about letting someone else drive my bike." He gave her a quick rundown on the mechanics of driving, then said, "Ready? We need to move out now."

She nodded and gunned the engine, sending them lurching forward. Her fear pulsed through him. Was she afraid to drive the bike, or afraid he'd get hurt?

They caught up with the Tank in ten minutes, which was why he had kept Pope in the general vicinity.

She shouted, "There he is!"

Baal was in human form, holding onto one of the

air vents attached to the slanted roof. Cheveyo hadn't taken time to grab their helmets when they hauled ass out of the Tank. If he was thrown off the roof and hit the pavement, he'd be a goner.

He called Pope. "We're right behind you. I can see Baal on the roof." A head lifted. "It sees us, too."

Petra turned to say into the phone, "The nut is going to jump on the Tank and fight it on the roof!"

"Just be aware that I'll be up there," he said and disconnected. "Ready?"

"No! But I'll do it if I have to."

He felt that stir again, the way he did whenever she grew into her strength. She was going to discover one of her other archetypes before long, and then she would be dangerous—most of all, to him. She pulled up to the rear corner of the Tank.

"Get closer," he said. He had to do this carefully so he didn't knock the bike off balance. Baal was already inching toward the rear, ready for him. "I'm going!" he told her, and a second before his muscles released, the roar of an engine made them both turn around. The trident, coming at them fast.

"Oh, hell," they both said in unison.

Cheveyo was already in midair. Couldn't stop. He latched onto the ladder at the rear, his eyes on her. She held onto the bike after his departure, though it wobbled. Her face was a mask of tension, lower lip clamped between her teeth. He knew she wouldn't be able to evade Yurek, who was aiming right at her.

"Give me your hand!" he called, reaching out. "Aim the bike toward the shoulder and let it go."

She reached toward his hand, her eyes scared-rabbit wide, and twisted the handlebars to the right. The car closed in just as the bike veered off the road. She shrieked, dangling, banging against the side of the RV. Their hands were locked together but her other hand slapped along the edge of the window, trying to find a hold.

He smelled the dog a second before he felt the swipe of its claws tear into his shoulder. Baal's face leered over the edge, its forelegs bent around the top handles of the ladder. It snarled, swiping again. Cheveyo instinctively ducked, which loosened his grip on Petra's hand.

He held on tighter. "Give me your other hand!"

She reached toward him. He'd have to pull her to bring her closer to the ladder.

Baal's claws raked his scalp this time, and blood poured down into his eyes, blinding him. Damn scalp wounds bled like a bitch. He could hear Baal's nails scrabbling as it tried to keep its balance.

She uttered a strangled gargle. He couldn't let go of her. Yurek was right behind them, headlights casting them in a fierce glow. If she survived the fall, he'd run her down. He blindly reached for her hand, grabbing onto her fingers. The blood made his hand slippery and he couldn't get a good grip.

She reached past him and grabbed the bar next to him. Her feet found the lower ladder rung and she banged into him as she brought herself close. She whispered his name, a whimper. Now that he didn't have to hang onto her, he wiped the blood from his face.

"Looks worse than it is," he said, trying to breathe through the stinging pain.

She reached down and in a second had her knife as Baal swiped down again. It yelped when she stabbed the blade into its paw and backed out of sight.

"Nice," he said in a strained voice.

The Tank jerked with the sound of a crash as Yurek

rammed his car into the rear of the vehicle. Luckily, the sports car he'd managed to procure was too low to inflict any damage on them or the RV, which had reinforced bumpers for this very reason.

Giving up on that, Yurek swerved to the left and came up beside them, slamming the car into it. He obviously didn't care much about the car or his furry buddy up on top, who skidded when the RV shifted.

From somewhere in his mind he heard, *Are you secure?*

Pope. He was going to do something.

Yes, he answered. "Hold on. Pope's got a plan."

Baal appeared above them again, but before it could try another swipe, the vehicle jerked to the left, ramming into the car. Tires screeched and the car zig-zagged across the asphalt in a jerky wobble, ending up behind them again. Thank God no one had come from the other direction. As much as he wanted Yurek dead, he didn't want some innocent killed in a head-on collision.

He saw human legs dangling off the side of the Tank. Baal had gone human. It was harder to hold on when you were a dog.

"Stay here," Cheveyo said. "It's the safest place to be." He wiped away the blood with his sleeve.

"Where are you going?"

"To get rid of the dog."

To call it a dog really wasn't fair to dogs.

"Let me heal you," she said.

"No, you need all your strength right now. I'll be fine."

He heard her words before the wind carried them away: "Obstinate, boneheaded male!" As soon as he got to the roof, he pulled out his knife. Baal twisted to his side, then morphed back to dog again, his only weapon. Cheveyo lunged at it and it backed off. The blood was getting in the way, though, making his hand slippery and forcing him to continually swipe it out of his eyes.

Yurek came around the side again. What the hell was that idiot doing? Oh, hell. Pope was going to do a sideways smash again. Cheveyo dropped to his knees and grabbed hold of the air compressor a second before the vehicle jammed into the car. This time Yurek lost control, overcorrecting and veering off the shoulder. The tires hit the rocks on the shoulder and the car rolled.

Cheveyo turned in time to see the Glouk lunging at him, teeth bared. He rolled to the side as Baal skidded on the slanted surface of the roof. Because of that surface, Cheveyo nearly kept rolling right off the side. He grabbed onto one of the air vents as the rest of his body slipped over the edge.

Baal approached, its teeth bared, red eyes focused on Cheveyo's hands where they clutched the unwieldy corners. He had no defense. All he could do was let go. He glanced behind him. He didn't like what he saw. On this side, the shoulder was edged in large rocks. He tried to pull himself up, but the blood loss was making him weak. The cold wind was sucking out his energy, too.

Baal edged closer, buffeted by the wind and slipping on Cheveyo's blood, trying to keep its balance as it readied for attack. Its teeth, bared as it approached his hands, were even sharper than its claws. Cheveyo was having a hard time gripping the plastic vent anyway. He would die by a hard landing on rocks either way, with shredded hands or without. What would happen to Petra? Pope? The questions were enough to overcome his pain and weakness. He glanced at the rocks going by in a blur. Maybe he'd survive.

One . . .

Two . . .

Baal roared with pain and jerked around to look at the knife handle sticking out of its flank. Petra's knife. It morphed to man again, pulling out the knife and searching for the perpetrator of its injury. Petra had climbed to the top of the ladder, and her upper body was above the roofline. She wouldn't be able to get out of Baal's line of sight fast enough. Baal shifted its grip on the knife, readying it to throw back at her, but its fingers fumbled on the slippery blood on the handle. The knife dropped on the roof and slid toward her. She grabbed it and, with narrowed eyes, made to throw it again.

Baal slid to the side, slowing its fall by grabbing onto one of the vents, and fell to the road on the other side. She scrambled across the roof toward Cheveyo, holding onto the vents for balance.

"I can't hold on anymore." His hands were slipping; he couldn't get a grip.

She pounded on the roof. "Stop! Stop, Pope!" She flattened herself and grabbed for his hands. Just like he'd held onto her, now she was holding onto him. The Tank was slowing. She grunted with the effort of pulling up his weight.

"Let me go!" he said. "You're going to end up falling over the edge with me."

He heard every ounce of emotion of her voice when she said, "I will *not* let you go! I will not let you die!"

"Petra, we're stopped! Let me drop to the ground."

With a start she looked around. "We are stopped."

"Yes. I'll be fine. But your devotion is appreciated."

With a hysterical little laugh/hiccup, she let him go. He landed on his feet, feeling every slice that son of a bitch had inflicted on him. The cuts on his scalp burned like fire, and now he could feel the warm, sticky blood flowing down his neck.

Pope came around the front. "Baal landed on the highway and rolled, then raced into the woods."

Cheveyo flexed his aching hands. "Let's go back for Yurek. If he's injured, we can take him easily."

She pointed at him. "You can't take anyone, not like that."

He looked down at himself, covered in blood, and then had to wipe it out of his eyes. "It's our best chance. Come on, let's get inside."

She dashed to the closet opposite the bathroom, pulled out towels, and returned to where he sank into the passenger seat while Pope put the Tank into gear again.

Cheveyo pointed ahead. "There's a turnaround coming up. We'll need to get my bike, too."

She knelt in front of him, carefully wrapping one of the towels around his head. A grimace warped her features. She grabbed a hand towel and ran to the bathroom, then returned. The wet towel was instantly bloodred.

"Let me heal you. These aren't mortal injuries, not yet. I won't be risking myself or your abilities."

"I'll be fine." Other than feeling a little light-headed.

"Stubborn, mule-headed . . ." She mumbled several other adjectives.

"Yep, every one of those and more," he said, his voice slurring a little.

Pope turned the Tank around and headed back. They came up on the wrecked car first.

"No, do not stop." She pointed at Cheveyo. "Look at him. Can he fight?"

"You should see the other guy," Cheveyo said with a chuckle. "He's not going to be in such good shape either." He got up, annoyed that he needed to use the arms of the chair to help. His knees buckled, and with one little poke from her finger, he was sitting down again.

"Keep going," she told Pope, taking charge. Damned unprincesslike, if you asked him. "Find the bike. *That* we can manage."

They all looked at the car, half buried in tall grasses.

"He's not in there," Pope said. "I don't feel him."

"Can he heal himself?" she asked. "The cretin who was trying to kill my brother and Fonda could."

"It's possible."

In a few minutes they spotted the bike lying just off the road. The chrome caught the headlights. Cheveyo started to get up again, but the damned woman poked him right back into the seat. "We'll handle it." She leaned down into his face, her expression stubborn, her gorgeous lips pursed. "And I'm healing you."

He opened his mouth to object but nothing came out. His vision narrowed to pinpoints. Then smaller. Then darkness.

He had no idea how long he'd been in the darkness when he came to the surface of consciousness. He'd fallen asleep, which was damned unwarriorlike. When he came to, they were driving down the road leading to his cabin. He heard her saying, "Even though they know what the RV looks like, I still think it's a good idea if you keep moving. We'll rest here for the night and start all over again tomorrow." She sounded weary.

He touched his scalp, his eyes still not cooperating enough to open completely. No towel, only stiff clumps of hair. No cuts. He shifted his shoulder. No pain. She'd healed him. Dammit.

He focused his eyes at last, her fine ass in view only a few feet in front of him. She stood between the seats. Woman knew how to fill out a pair of jeans, even if she couldn't follow directions worth a damn.

He felt drugged, woozy. She'd healed his cuts, but the blood loss would take longer.

"He lives," she said in a bright voice. She knelt in front of him, studying him. At least she wasn't wearing that stubborn expression, the last thing he'd taken with him into unconsciousness. "How do you feel?"

"Like playing a round of tennis." He pushed up to a sitting position.

"You'll be tired for a bit. We'll clean up here, rest for the night, and head out in the morning." Still bossing everyone around. "The wounds weren't terribly deep, but I could see the muscle in one cut on your shoulder. Which was pretty gross, actually. The bleeding had me the most worried, especially when you passed out."

How could she look so chirpy? Or was it chipper? "How come you're not wiped out?"

She smiled. "Because I didn't heal you. Pope did. I was going to, but he said he could try. Luckily he still has that ability. He doesn't get wiped out like I do. That way I'm still alert while you sleep."

"I'm not sleeping."

"Yes, you are."

He looked at Pope. "Did you encourage this bossy attitude?"

"I think it suits her. Don't you?"

The problem was, she was messing with him big-time, getting what little blood he had racing. The Tank came to a stop in front of the cabin.

He got to his feet, trying to look as steady as he could. "Pope, I think you should stay in the Tank, keep moving around. Hit the back roads."

Pope and Petra exchanged grins. "Splendid idea," he said with a nod.

She put her arms around Cheveyo's shoulders. "That's why he's in charge."

Oh brother, she was patronizing him. If he was just a little more delirious, he'd kiss her silly. Right now it was taking all his concentration to remain standing.

He walked unsteadily toward the door. Holding onto the lever, he paused, sniffing the air. "Do I smell . . . sage?"

She nodded. "I cleared the energy. Now all you have to do is clean yourself up." She gave him a sympathetic smile. "You're a mess."

He swiped at his cheek and looked at the teal eye shadow on his fingers. "The blood and dirt is fine. This makeup stuff . . . not cool."

CHAPTER 13

The car seemed to roll for a long time, though it was only for a few seconds. Yurek was thrown violently around, finally smashing against the door and crumpling in a heap. His body was twisted, battered, and he couldn't seem to move.

The sound of glass shattering and the thud of the car still echoed in his senses. He didn't know how long he remained there, but he heard thudding footsteps coming closer. The hunter? Pope? For a moment he didn't care, just wanted it over. The pain was overwhelming.

It was the Glouk's face that appeared through the broken window. "Are you alive?"

"Yes. Get me out of here."

After some jiggling sounds, the Glouk said, "I can't open the door. It's dented." He broke out the jagged bits of glass from the edges of the window frame, then reached in and pulled on Yurek's shoulders. Slowly, painfully, Baal inched him out the window. Glouks were strong, which was what made them so useful.

Yurek stumbled but caught his balance with the hood of the car. He was standing by sheer will. The will to live. To succeed. "We have to leave. They'll be back for us."

The car was smashed, the engine dead. He'd stolen it from a car lot. He would miss it. They loped toward the cover of forest. Baal was limping, and Yurek saw a shiny bloodstain on his pant leg.

They walked deep into the woods. "This is good," Yurek said, strain evident in his voice. He couldn't go another step. He collapsed on the floor of pine needles, his body wracked with pain. It would take a while to mend. "That did not go well."

Baal dropped beside him, wincing as he pressed his hand over the cut on his leg. He looked at Yurek. He had the tone of someone who had been scorned. "You could have thought about me being on top of the vehicle when you decided to ram it." He tore away the fabric to reveal what was obviously a knife wound on his thigh.

The Glouk morphed to canine form, his long tongue lashing the cut in slow, deliberate strokes.

Yurek had to look away, his stomach twisting. "I had faith that you'd hang on, skillful predator that you are."

Baal morphed back to human form, something he could do enviably fast. He thankfully brought the visage of clothing with him. His scowl disappeared and his shoulders lifted. "Next time I'll be prepared. For you and for her."

"Her?"

He pointed to the slit in his leg. "The female did this. She took me off guard. I would have killed the hunter if not for her."

Too bad the whole lot of them couldn't have been killed in one tidy accident. Except for Pope. Bringing him back alive had a much bigger reward. He, too, was curious as to what Pope was hiding. Likely it was his daughter, perhaps even the man with her. The man who was only part human. Yurek hoped to return to Surfacia with Pope in custody and a report on the deaths of the two rebels.

He tried to stand, grabbing the trunk of a tree for support. "I had picked up Pope's Essence near a road that went into the woods before you called to tell me where he'd transported to. Tomorrow morning, early, we'll return there. Maybe we'll get lucky." He collapsed to the ground again. Unless he died first.

He wasn't mad at her. Maybe was too tired to be mad, and that would come later. Petra helped Cheveyo into the house. He managed to walk on his own, but she put her hand on his back, just in case.

"Yurek may not have even gotten to the house," she said. "He may have just sensed Pope in the area and was homing in on him."

"Maybe."

He'd seemed a little tipsy in the Tank. She liked that side of him, even if she didn't like how he'd gotten that way. She knew he never got tipsy, would never lose control.

But he loses control when he's around you. And was none too happy about it. Bad timing, while they'd been running through the woods with their enemy in pursuit, but she wouldn't soon forget that kiss.

She'd felt it tonight, too, desire spiraling through her even while danger tore away at them.

"I'm taking a bath," he said, heading to the stairs.

"Let me help." At his raised eyebrow, she added, "Help you up the stairs and get the tub ready. You're still a little wobbly."

"I'm never wobbly." Then he wobbled. "Shi . . ." He let the word fade and accepted her presence behind him on the stairs as he made his way up.

His bedroom was spectacular, a large bed with tree trunk frame and headboard dominating the open, airy space with the wooden peak ceiling. A huge painting of a jaguar adorned one wall, and sketches that reminded her of perhaps Mayan artwork, all of jaguar gods, covered the other walls. A matching dresser ran along one wall, a desk and computer sat against the other. The curtains and bedspread were brown suede, very inviting. Too inviting.

The huge jetted tub in the bathroom was even more inviting. It had a blue window and European styling. She bent down inside it and pushed down the drain stopper, then ran the water. There was nothing feminine about the space, all done in a hunting lodge décor with twig-looking fixtures. Still, she loved it.

She poured some liquid body soap into the tub and watched the bubbles foam. At the sound of water running, she turned to find him naked, standing in the shower. "Aren't you going to take a bath?"

"Yeah, but I'm rinsing off the blood so I'm not soaking in it."

He cut the shower a minute later, walked over and up the steps to the tub, and sat down inside, even though it was only half full. Damn him, walking around naked and gorgeous, and her feeling all freaky aroused. She focused on his feet, propped up on the side of the tub.

She knew why getting sexually involved was a bad idea. Eric had warned the Rogues that it would put them at risk, distract them, and it had. But they'd survived. She was the only one who hadn't fallen, but now she could understand how, say, making suckface at the wrong time could be a tad dangerous. Mostly she knew how loving someone who was in constant danger would wear on her heart and soul. So she should go, leave him alone.

He tapped the ledge of the tub. "Sit, keep me company."

With a weary sigh, she did, even though she knew better.

His head was leaning against a built-in pillow. There was another one in the opposite corner, for a guest. The steam off the tub was nearly as inviting as the parts of his body she could still see, which was his chest and lower legs. Bubbles and waves of water washed up the ridges of his abdomen. She had noticed—okay, it was hard *not* to notice—that he'd been fully hard when he went from shower to tub. Was he feeling that freaky arousal, too?

"Let me wash your hair," she said, reaching for the shampoo bottle. She poured some into her cupped palm and gestured for him to turn around.

"You're going to torture me, aren't you?"

"You're healed. It won't hurt."

He turned anyway, sitting straight up in front of her. "Do you know how good it feels to have someone wash your hair?"

"Pretend I'm your hairdresser."

He grunted, whatever that meant.

She'd never dated a guy who had hair longer than midway down his neck. Cheveyo's fell past his shoulders in thick, lush waves. She scrubbed out some of the crusty spots of blood, trying to forget how lacerated his scalp looked before Pope healed him.

There was even a handheld sprayer in the tub, and she picked it up and turned it on, rinsing his hair. She thought, but wasn't sure, she heard him groan.

Be strong. Don't fall for him. He's totally right, you fall for him and he's going to leave or die, and you will be crushed.

"Did I tell you how effing fantastic you were back there?" He turned to face her, his expression wide-eyed with wonder. She liked this playful side of him, even if it was induced. Except it was making him even more juicy. "You threw the knife at Baal while hanging onto a moving vehicle. A *moving* vehicle. And hit him."

She settled into his praise, and then it hit her. She *had* thrown the knife and nailed her target. The rush of that! "I was pretty kick-ass, wasn't I?"

He had a lazy heat in his eyes that reminded her of when they'd fallen into lust by the river. "Very kick-ass." He held out his hand, and she reached out to shake it. Except he slid his wet fingers between hers and yanked her into the tub. "It's why I can't resist you."

She fell against him, her midsection instantly soaked. He was kissing her just as quickly, one hand at her cheek, the other at her back.

"It's just the adrenaline," she said, though her mouth was kissing him right back.

"The adrenaline, yes, you . . ." His mouth moved down her neck while his hands unbuttoned her blouse. "You were so strong and sexy and *fierce.*"

She moved against him, straining to feel his hands on her. He shoved her shirt back over her shoulders, and she unclasped her bra. "And when you pulled me off that bike and held onto my hand, kept me from falling . . ."

But he wasn't keeping her from falling now. In fact, he was pushing her right over the edge.

His mouth on her breast stole away her breath and words. She dug her fingers into his hair, tilting her head back.

"Have to . . . stop." But he didn't stop, thank gawd. He left a slick trail in the hollow between her breasts, lavishing attention on the other one now.

"You smell good, you taste good," he murmured. "I want to bury myself inside you."

She felt his erection pressed against her thigh, so close. "Me, too. I want that, too."

Her hand trailed down and touched him. He let out a delicious sound in his throat, and when she wrapped her fingers around the length of him, he shuddered. His teeth scraped her nipple and his hands tightened against her back.

The heat she felt wasn't from the hot tub. He filled her with it, his touch, his mouth moving against her skin. Her breath was coming in small gasps, the throbbing between her legs overwhelming. She ran her other hand down his back, her fingers splayed to feel as much of him as possible. To touch him, to finally touch him, and to feel him . . . heaven and hell.

"You are making me crazy," he whispered.

"I know, I know, I know."

"I mean, you . . . are . . . making . . . me . . . crazy."

Heat vibrated, and she was startled by the brush of fur against her stomach. She looked down to find an agitated jaguar leaping out of the tub. His black eyes glittered, his two fangs huge against the black fur. He shook off the water, his body rigid. Then he stalked toward her.

She backed up as far as she could go, sensing his on-edge energy. He came closer, his eyes sharp chunks of black ice, body trembling with pent-up restraint.

"Cheveyo . . ."

She leaned farther back. *Coward. You faced that hell dog but you're backing away from Cheveyo.*

But not Cheveyo exactly. He was barely in control, both when human and tearing off her clothes and in cat form. He turned and snarled, taking several steps away. Then he turned to man again, gloriously naked. He bowed his head, running his fingers through his hair. "I don't know what's happening to me. I *never* lose control."

She pulled her shirt together. "It's the blood loss. You're a little woozy."

He grabbed a towel from the bar and handed it to her without seeming to realize he was both wet and naked, dripping all over the tile floor. "It's not that. Look what happened at the river." He took her in as she wriggled out of her shirt and wrapped the towel around her. "And just now." He closed his eyes and shook his head. "Shameful. I had to turn cat just to regain control."

"And to put distance between us. You knew I was afraid and used that." Her lower lip pushed out in a pout. "You snarled at me."

"I'm sorry." He took another towel from a pile near the tub and wrapped it around his waist. "That was unacceptable." He met her eyes on that, and she could see regret.

He held out his hand again.

She eyed it speculatively. "Is it safe?"

He nodded, looking contrite. Because she couldn't stand for him to feel that way, she took his hand. He pulled her close, stroking her hair. In his arms, she knew what feeling complete was. She had hoped for a love, a man, to make her feel complete. Here he was, and he loved her, even if he'd never admit it. She doubted, with his life, that he'd loved any other woman. She could have stayed there forever, but he backed up far too soon.

Weariness saturated his expression. "Use the tub, now that you're all wet. I'll be in the bedroom. If I'm asleep, lie down with me. I don't want you all the way downstairs on the other side of the house."

She put her palm against his cheek. Words escaped her for a moment. He leaned into her touch before catching himself and moving away.

"Drain the water and run it fresh."

No, she wanted his water. "You rinsed first, so it's no big deal."

The bathroom felt big and lonely when he closed the door behind him. The tub, however, did look nice. After stripping out of her wet clothes, she sank into the hot water. She grabbed a washcloth from the top of a small stack and washed. She hadn't brought her bag into the bathroom, so she didn't have her favorite cherry blossom shampoo. His was nice, though, scented with manly spices. She ran her fingers down her leg and felt the beginnings of stubble. Better shave just in case they went out-of-control crazy again.

She could hear him talking out in the bedroom.

"Cheveyo?" she said. "Do you have extra razors and shaving cream?"

He cracked the door open. "Yeah. Want me to get them for you?"

"That would be great."

He walked in and opened one of the cabinets. Wearing cotton pants with a drawstring and nothing else, she could see the color of his skin through the thin material.

"Who were you talking to?" she asked, then added, "Sorry, it's none of my business."

He gave her a curious half smile. "Pope. I wanted to thank him for healing me. He said he put the bike in the outbuilding. Whether she works or not, we'll have to see."

He set the items on the shelf, and she propped her foot on the edge and reached for the can of shaving cream. Then he did something that surprised her. He sat on the edge of the tub, taking hold of her foot. "Can I do it?"

"You want to . . . shave my legs?"

He grinned. "I think it'd be interesting."

"I've never let a man shave my legs before. I've never had a man *ask* to shave my legs. But if you want to, just excuse my stubble."

He set her foot on his thighs, soaking the fabric. He studied it, as though he were gazing at a piece of art. And not ugly art.

"I hate my feet," she felt compelled to say, as though in apology.

"Why? They're beautiful." He ran his finger along her arch, tickling her.

"My toes are too spread apart, and too long."

"They're perfect. God doesn't make ugly, you know."

"Well, some parts of our bodies aren't exactly . . . pretty. The puzzle pieces."

He raised an eyebrow. "Puzzle pieces?"

She laughed. "That's how my dad described our sexual parts when I first asked how babies were made. Two pieces that fit together."

"Mother nature honors our . . . puzzle pieces. Our sexuality. Think about a half of a peach or pecan. Or some flowers. They resemble the flower of a woman."

"I do remember looking at an orchid once and thinking it looked like a woman's privates. But I haven't seen many penis-shaped flowers."

"There's a type of fungus that grows out of the ground and looks very phallic. And avocadoes resemble testicles. They grow in pairs, one lower than the other. We got their name from the Aztec word for testicle."

"*Mmmm.* Makes me think about, well, our parts differently." Unfortunately, it also got her thinking about *their* parts. His part and the way it felt smooth and hard in her hand.

His gaze was heated, too.

She cleared her throat. "Let's not talk about—"

"No, good idea."

He ran his fingers lightly along her leg, perhaps studying the contours, hopefully not the stubble. Then he squirted out shaving lotion and rubbed it down her leg in the same thoughtful way. She wasn't sure how to read him, his current mood in particular. Gone was the catlike edge or even the hunter. Here was not even the man who'd held her after saving her life.

He ran the razor across the top of her shin, focusing all of his attention on his movements. Stroke after stroke, rinsing the razor after each run. He was even more careful around her knee, especially where she'd cut herself last time. With each stroke, in that quiet stillness of the room, his tender care made parts of her crumble away. He looked up only after he'd rinsed her leg with his hands, a signal to change legs.

"Are you crying?" he asked.

She swiped at her eyes and realized she was.

"Am I hurting you?"

"No, you're perfect. I mean, you're doing perfect. It's just . . ."

He faced her now, waiting patiently for her to spill her heart.

"You shaving my legs is the most tender, beautiful thing a man has ever done for me. It's silly."

He leaned closer and wiped her tears with his thumb. "You're the princess. You are to be adored."

She sucked in a breath at that, because he'd put into words her deepest longing: to be adored. Cherished.

He touched her face as she'd done to him not long before. "I'm sorry I can't be that person." His thumb stroked her cheek, slow motions. "But right now, I can adore you."

She nodded, pushing back all the pain and regret at that, seeing it in his eyes. If she breathed, her tears would gush.

He dipped his hand into the water, bringing up her other foot. As he lovingly shaved that leg, she thought she knew what he was doing: living out a moment of a normal life, a normal relationship—with her. A life he could never have, and she saw that ache he'd spoken of before. The ache she once felt over not being able to have Lucas was nothing compared to how she felt now. Because Lucas had never been hers. Cheveyo was hers, in her heart, her soul. She had been oblivious while he checked on her, but when she first met him, she'd *known* him. Felt him. Loved him.

He rinsed her leg, then grabbed a towel and handed it to her. He held out his hand, and she let him pull her to her feet, the towel a shield and barrier between them. She wrapped it around her. This was when he should sweep her into his arms and carry her to bed. She stepped over the rim, and he leaned down to unstop the tub.

"There's a robe on the hook there. You can use that, and I'll bring up your bag. I remember seeing Pope carry it in."

He closed the door behind him, and she sagged down to the side of the tub, her hand to her chest. Now she understood why he'd stayed away from her. Not only to protect her from the danger that surrounded him, but to protect both of them from this. He knocked a minute later and handed her the bag.

He wasn't asleep when she finally left the bathroom, but he was lying on the bed. He'd changed into a dry pair of cotton pants, and she paused at the sight of him, his hair loose and tousled, expression somber. He'd left on a light for her, a child's lamp with a smiling bear.

She walked over to the chest of drawers it sat on. "Is it okay if I leave this light on?"

"I usually do."

To keep the shadows at bay? To see in the dark lest an enemy invade? So he'd know where he was, sleeping in the Tank so often?

She wore pajamas, silky blue ones with long lacy sleeves. She climbed onto the bed, and he pulled her against him. Her cheek pressed against his chest, and she ran her finger down that scar.

"Get some sleep," he said. "Tomorrow we get up early and hunt."

She thought that his gift of being able to slip so quickly into a deep sleep let his mind recharge faster than most. Her hand, lying on his bare chest, tingled. As soon as he reached the deepest sleep, she felt that ache again, his loneliness.

She had seen his soul when she'd connected with him. She wanted to see more of it, to know it as he knew hers. She closed her eyes and imagined walking into that darkness and pain.

The barrage of images hit her, the boy facing a terrifying creature who slashed at him with its claws, tearing that scar into his chest. Riding on his bike toward a sunset, his isolation a counterpoint to the beauty of the sky.

Then more horrifying scenes pounded at her. A woman's body on the floor, her throat slashed. A boy cowering between a dresser and the wall. When she thought it was Cheveyo, a creature tore the boy from his hiding place. The boy's screams cut right through her, but the creature's fangs silenced him, slicing through his throat. The boy fell limp in a pool of blood. Rage and grief swamped her, and then darkness.

In that darkness, a voice boomed, "What are you doing in there?"

She jerked out of the trance.

Cheveyo sat up, his eyes wide. They narrowed as he came fully awake. "You were inside me, weren't you?"

She sat up, too, still vibrating with the horror of what she'd seen. "I saw things, terrible things. I saw the boy who was killed, a boy who looked like you."

He sat up, planting his elbows on his bent knees. "Why did you do that?"

"Because I feel such sadness coming from you. The only time I can get to know who you are is when you sleep."

"You shouldn't have." He was closed to her now, his eyes shuttered.

"You know my soul. It's only fair that I know yours."

He pinched the bridge of his nose. He couldn't really argue with that, or at least he shouldn't. Finally he said, "You don't belong in the darkness of my soul. You'll get lost in the shadows."

She touched his arm. "Maybe I can pull you out of them."

"That would be impossible." He stared at nothing, his expression haunted.

"The boy . . . he was your son, wasn't he?"

His voice was soft when he said, "Cody."

The thought spun her. He had a son. "I'm so sorry." That seemed terribly inadequate. She looked at the bear lamp, seeing it with new meaning.

He remained closed, shielded. "Go to sleep, Petra."

"The thing that killed him, it was a Glouk, wasn't it?"

He nodded, his gaze blank and aimed past her.

"You were . . . married?"

"I was eighteen when I met Darcy. She said she was on birth control, but she wasn't. She got pregnant. I couldn't marry her because I could have no legal connection to her, to anyone. Nothing that would put her and the baby in harm's way. I didn't love her, but I planned to provide for them from a safe distance. Then the baby came, and I fell in love with him."

"How can you not fall in love with your child? Not even you can be that strong."

"No, but I was young and stupid enough to think I could have a normal life *and* fight demons. My father warned me, but I'd been raised to believe I was the unconquerable warrior. I never contacted them or went near our house when I was engaged with an enemy. I thought that would keep them safe." He laughed in a humorless way. "Darcy assumed I worked for the government or the police, and I let her believe it. I'd come back bruised, cut, and couldn't tell her a thing about it."

He went silent, and she gave him the time to process his thoughts. But not too much time. "And what happened?" she asked in a quiet voice.

"I don't know how the Glouk found out about them. It baffles me, even now. My father was the one who warned me there was trouble at home, since my visions don't work when it concerns my future. I raced home and found the Glouk there. Darcy was already dead. But Cody . . ." He took a deep breath.

"It's okay. I saw it."

"He was frozen, poor kid. I'd never worked with him. I didn't want him training to fight boogeymen, living his childhood in war mode like I did. I fought the Glouk for hours, but he was too damned powerful. I was exhausted, but he never tired. He threw me against the wall so hard, I heard bones crack in my body."

She winced, tightening her hold on his arm. "And you couldn't help Cody."

He shook his head, his expression a mask of grief. "I had to watch, unable to move. Even worse, I passed out, left him there to die alone." Self-incrimination saturated his voice. "When I woke, a whole day had passed. Everything was gone. Even their bodies. No blood, nothing. My injuries were healed, too. My father told me he'd pulled in other resources to heal me and clean the evidence. Having the police investigate would not be good. Darcy had been estranged from her family for years. I suspected that was why she'd wanted to trap me, so I could take care of her. She loved our son, though, and stayed home with him. There was no one to miss them."

She leaned forward and put her arms around him. He let her for exactly two seconds before moving away. The shadows in the room made his face look darker and more haunted.

She said, "I'm sorry I intruded into that very personal, painful place. Maybe it'll help to share it with someone."

"Sharing pain helps no one. It just makes two people sad."

Now she understood his steadfast refusal to allow anyone into his life, his heart. He blamed himself for his son's death. "It wasn't your fault that they died."

"Yes, it was. Somehow I led the Glouk to them."

She knew he wouldn't believe anything else. "Was that your voice booming at me?"

"That was my father. He sensed you inside me. It's what woke me up."

"That was Wayne Kee?" She rubbed her arms. "He's scary."

"He can be. Don't go poking into my psyche again. I won't poke into yours anymore either."

The truth was, now that she knew him better, she didn't mind so much. "What did you feel when you came into me?"

He stretched out flat on the bed again, but he was still looking at her. "Do you really want to know?"

She nodded. "Is it that bad?"

"No, but it's not always easy to see the shadows of your soul."

"Tell me." She had shadows?

"I felt your insecurity and how you cling to your outer beauty because that's all you think you have. You feel betrayed, but you're unwilling to acknowledge those feelings because they're ugly, so you tell yourself no one has hurt you."

She held up her hand. "Okay, that's enough."

"The only way to see the shadows is to aim the light at them. When you do, they go away."

"Then why do you hold onto your shadows?"

"Because they remind me to never let anyone into my life." He rolled onto his side, facing her, and closed his eyes. "Good night, Petra."

She stretched out beside him, watching the tension ease from his face. She wished she could escape into sleep so easily. It was her own fault, but she would be dreaming about those horrible moments that had changed him so irrevocably.

Some part of her heart challenged that. But as long as he was a warrior, he would never let her in. And that's how it had to be.

CHAPTER 14

Cheveyo woke at three in the morning. Moonlight streamed in through the window near the bed, spilling over them like liquid silver. He took a moment to look at Petra, lying on her side with her hand tucked beneath her cheek. She looked ethereal, like an angel. He'd watched her sleep before, but it was different.

She was different, because of what had happened in the last few days. She wasn't a vulnerable princess, wasn't just a distant dream to him either. He could touch her now, could let her wake and see him.

No, he couldn't touch her. He would never stop. He got out of bed with hardly a rustle of sheets.

She'd gone into his soul. He was angry about that, but he shouldn't be. He'd done it to her. The difference being, she never knew, and he never used what he'd found to prod old wounds.

He grabbed clothes out of a drawer and went downstairs to change. He stepped outside and filled his lungs with cool, clean air. The moon lit up the yard and house, like a silvery version of daylight. He smelled only pines, heard only the normal sounds of the night, and sensed only what should be there. He sat on the stone bench near the fire pit and caught the moonlight on the blade of the knife he carried.

The energy that preceded his father's visit tingled through him, washing him with a wave of dizziness. He closed his eyes, imagining a swirl of black clouds spiraling through him, taking him into the ether.

Wayne's voice and expression were harsh in his mind. *The woman has to go. I warned you that you will die because of her presence in your life. Is that not enough? That she violated your spirit is unforgivable.*

"I have done the same to her," he said aloud. "And I cannot send her away. There is no place safer for her to be than with me."

You risk your life for hers? A mere woman.

"Yes."

It is foolish. You risk not only your life but the lives you will save in the future.

"There is nothing I can do. I will not abandon her." He changed the subject. "How do I protect the Callorian?"

Your plan is a good one. I knew Pope back in Surfacia.

"He said he knew you, but I thought he meant in a surface way. Why didn't you tell me before?"

Have I taught you not to bring anything personal to your missions? Not that you listened. Pope is a good citizen. Worthy. But I think you already know that.

"He saved the lives of the Rogues. That gives him huge cred for me." And he meant something to Petra. "Was he ever tasked to track you down after you went Scarlett?"

Yes, but it was a mission he purposely failed to achieve. Failure is not something Pope takes lightly, but he suffered it for me. Will you be able to carry out the task he has asked of you, since you have allowed yourself to get personally involved?

Pope had saved his father. How could he kill the man? It would have been hard enough with the knowledge that he'd saved Petra and her people. "I don't want to, but I will. I hope to kill Yurek and the Glouk. It will at least buy me time to prepare for the next Extractor."

And what of the girl?

"If Yurek does not return to Surfacia to report our existence, the next Extractor will only come for Pope. I can send her away and know she'll be safe."

If she has not gotten you killed first. Love is a weakness that will destroy you. It is what destroyed me.

He opened his eyes at that. "What do you mean?"

I took the contract with the government because of your mother. I was able to fight the enemy in what was supposed to be a safe way so she would not worry.

He stood. "I can't stop loving her, father. I'm not strong enough for that. I'm only strong enough to send her away as soon as it's safe." And barely that.

You did not love the mother of your son this much. But you loved your son enough to consider giving up being a warrior for him.

"I would never have done that." He had only toyed with the idea of having a normal life, but he'd never communicated that to his father. His being away from Cody was hard for all of them.

Yes, you would have.

"You didn't give up the fight for me."

No, I did not.

He knew the loneliness of having his father gone most of the time. Of knowing he was in some dangerous situation, fearing he would simply never come back. Not unlike having a father in the military. "Do you know where the enemy is?" Wayne was often the one who directed him to the enemy, but he was not exact.

I pick up his Essence several miles east of the cabin. He has been severely injured.

"Dying?"

I sense no waning of his Essence, only much pain. You stabbed him?

"Injury by car wreck." He never knew exactly how much his father saw of life here but knew Wayne wasn't always around.

I will monitor him. Perhaps he will die on his own.

Nothing ever happened that easy.

Wayne's presence drifted away. Cheveyo took a few deep breaths, clearing away his father's disapproval. He pulled out his phone and called Pope. "How are you holding up?"

"I stopped for a couple of hours to sleep, but I'm on the wagon again, as the saying goes."

He smiled. "On the wagon means you've stopped drinking. You're back on the road."

"Your Earth dimension phrases are confusing. I'm getting rather fond of the Tank. A hotel room on wheels. Very interesting."

"It's a good home away from home." He looked at his real home. But not good enough. *That's because Petra's asleep in your bed.* He shook away the thought, his body's reaction. "My father talks to me from beyond. He told me what you did for him."

"He was a good man."

"You both seem to have a mutual appreciation society."

"A what?"

"Never mind. He senses that Yurek's been badly injured. When you were here on assignment, what happened if you were injured?"

"If we didn't feel we could heal ourselves, we returned to Surfacia to get healed in the Amber Tunnel. It's a chamber lined with amber and infused with psychic healing energy. It heals major wounds in twenty-four hours. I have never had to use it, but I understand it is so thorough it allows the Shine—the agent—to return to duty right away."

His chest tightened. "And if you returned to Surfacia, you would report your progress."

Pope's voice went low. "Of course, and Yurek would report yours and Petra's existences. He has no way to communicate with the C otherwise."

"Where is the nearest finestra?"

"I'll have to pull over and look at a map. I know there are two in this part of the country, because of the natural energy vortexes so abundant here."

"Check it out and call me back."

They couldn't let Yurek return to Surfacia. Cheveyo knew it would be his and Petra's death sentence.

The sound of metal clanging woke Petra. The sun was barely up, and it was an ungodly early hour—for her, anyway. She rolled over and was disappointed to see the other half of the bed empty. Then again, if he were there, then someone else would be making that sound.

She looked out the window and saw him working on the bike just outside the building. He was wearing jeans and a long-sleeved black shirt, his hair tied into an unruly ponytail, as though he'd done it in the dark. It looked as though he were pounding bent metal back into shape. The poor bike. Like them, it had taken a beating.

Poor Cheveyo. He had gone through so much in his lifetime, fighting since he was ten. Losing his father and then his son. She knew the hardest part for him was thinking he was responsible for Cody's and his mother's deaths.

He'd been a father. Was still a father in his heart. It made her see him in a different light. He was a man who could love deeply.

He glanced up, probably sensing her there, and waved. It would have been a sweet moment except he tapped on his watch. *Yeah yeah.*

She went through her morning routine, timing herself. How could she cut down the time? One swipe of blush instead of two or three, forgo the contouring? Skip outlining her lips? It was a lot to ask.

She went downstairs and found (or rather smelled) a pot of coffee in the carafe and a mug in front of it. She poured a cup, added sugar, which was also left out for her, and wandered to the china hutch. In the drawer were those pictures of her. She dug down through the pile, smiling at the candid, surveillance-type shots he'd obviously taken while keeping an eye on her. Beneath those were other pictures, the first of a baby. Not her. This one had dark hair, and besides, Cheveyo had been about four when she was born so he couldn't have taken a picture of her then.

Cody. It hit her, that this was his son's picture. There were others, of him growing up, playing ball, and then they stopped so pitifully soon. She looked at one of the last pictures of the boy, remembering the scene she'd witnessed. He must have been terrified.

She heard the front door snap shut and closed the drawer. She was back in the kitchen when Cheveyo walked in.

"If you want something to eat, I've got bacon and toast in the freezer."

Her heart tightened at the sight of him, rubbing his

hands with a blue paper towel. He smelled of grease, but she saw no smears on his face or hands.

"Just toast will be fine." She walked over to the freezer and pried one slice from the rest of the loaf. "Slice for you?"

"No, thanks."

"Do you have any peanut butter?"

"I have Spanish peanuts." He grinned. "I could peel the skins off and set them on the toast for you."

"That sounds, *mmm*, no. Butter will do."

He sipped on a cup of coffee he poured and watched her eat, an odd expression on his face. Sort of a melancholy grin, if that made any sense.

"Do I have crumbs on my face?" She wiped her cheeks.

"No, you're fine." He seemed to pull out of his thoughts, and the expression faded. "We'd better get going. I've already checked in with Pope. Poor guy, he's got to be road weary."

Poor Pope! Cheveyo was mirroring her thoughts. And poor Petra, too, for belonging to a man she couldn't have. She finished her coffee, washed out the mug and plate, and set them in the dish rack. "Let me brush my teeth and I'll be ready to go."

"Bring your bag. We won't be back here for a while."

She pushed on and was down again in ten minutes. Not bad. He grabbed a map from the drawer, pulled down two leather jackets, and opened the door for her. The bike was parked just outside.

She took one of the jackets he held out for her and slid into it. It was already cool without going sixty miles an hour on a bike. The jacket was too big, but it was warm and smelled of leather and Cheveyo. "Zoe said when she rode with you from Key West to

Annapolis, the helmet made her scalp feel like there were scorpions in her hair. And her butt was totally numb." Her breath hung like a mist in the air.

He slid into his jacket and zipped it up, then zipped up hers, too. "You're tough. You can handle it."

Did he really believe that? Yeah, he did. That filled her with a sense of strength. Everyone who knew her thought she'd freak out or wimp out, even her. Not Cheveyo.

He pulled out two pair of gloves from the bike's bags. "We may have a new problem. It's possible Yurek will return to the other dimension to heal."

"And that's a problem, how? Sounds good to me."

He told her why it was a very bad problem.

She bit her lip, fear darkening her heart. "Oh."

His cell phone rang. "Pope," he told her and answered. After listening for a few seconds, he opened the map and laid it out on the seat of the bike. "Found it. That's roughly three hours away. Where's the other one?" His finger moved over the map and stopped at the very top. "Near Mount Zion National Park. That'll be interesting. Petra and I are going to take off in a few minutes. We'll head in the direction of the closest finestra and remain in the vicinity just in case. We're also going to stay on the move, not too close and not too far from you. We might not have to worry about Yurek right now, since he's injured, but we still have the Glouk. And he's the tracker . . . No, I don't want you going to the other finestra. If you're that close, it'll be easy for Yurek to pull you in. Stay away from either one. We'll handle this. That's what you hired me for . . . It doesn't matter whether you're paying me or not, it's still my job."

He disconnected. "The closest finestra is near what barely passes for a town about three hours from here.

I'm guessing that's where he's going, considering his condition. Are you ready to roll?"

"Yes."

She climbed on behind him, and he started the bike. They'd hardly cleared the driveway when he pulled off to the side of the road and cut the engine. He didn't say anything, just stood there balancing the bike by planting his feet on the ground, his eyes closed. Her gaze darted around, looking for whatever had made him stop.

He turned to her, his face a taut mask. "My father just told me that Yurek is fading fast. I'll bet he's heading to the finestra. And we've got to stop him."

"Your job is to stop them should they show up before I go through the finestra." Yurek had spent the last twenty minutes teaching the Glouk how to hotwire a car, and the effort left him weak. Baal was beginning to get a handle on using his human hands.

It took all of Yurek's effort to make his voice sound strong and authoritative. "I will return in twenty-four hours to the second finestra, and you will guard that so I don't walk into a trap."

Coming in was always a vulnerable time. You couldn't see what was waiting for you. He'd chosen to return to a different location in case their enemy figured out where he had exited.

They had taken their new vehicle to a secluded location. Yurek leaned against the car door for support, feeling the warmth of the metal seep into his pain-wracked body. "If you do have to engage them at my exit finestra, I want you to retreat as soon as I'm gone, unless you're absolutely certain you can take them. Don't be foolish when making that decision."

"You want me to retreat? Like a coward?"

"I need you at my entry finestra."

"You need me." Baal's shoulders lifted at that, his mouth curling into a faint smile. "What if they find the second location? You said Pope knows about the healing procedure. He probably knows about the two finestras in this area."

"If they guess the plan, then you can try to take them out, but only if you feel confident that you can do so. Otherwise, lie low and wait for me to come in. That way, you'll immediately warn me, and it will be two on two."

Yurek winced as he unfolded the map they'd bought and pointed to its location. "Get in position nearby but don't go to the exact location until three hours before I'm to arrive, so the hunter doesn't track you there."

Yurek had heard about the Amber Tunnel, how claustrophobic the yellow tube in which he would have to lie still for twenty-four hours was. Though their emotions had been mostly bred out of them, he still felt a deep sense of failure and humiliation in having to return in such a way. He would have to explain that with Pope's allies he was outnumbered. He would also have to convince the Collaborate that he was capable of executing the two human/Callorians so the C wouldn't send backup or a replacement. He did not want to share the credit for Pope's capture.

Baal said, "You need me. And you trust me to protect you. We have been working as a team. We could continue to do so once you are successful in this mission."

"Perhaps."

Baal smiled at the prospect of that. "Maybe the Collaborate will see that Glouks are more than mindless soldiers and labor."

But Yurek didn't intend to tell the C about the Glouk.

Baal put his hand near the bandaged gash on his leg. "Can you bring healing drugs back for me? Black Lavender?"

Yurek nodded. "Get into the driver's seat, and I'll instruct you on how to operate the car. You'll be even more useful once you learn that."

He wouldn't tell the Glouk that he needed him to drive. He had to use the car like a big crutch to help him walk around to the passenger side. He was having trouble breathing. His body was weakening, the pain dulling his senses. If he didn't make it to the finestra soon, he would die. He had already waited too long, hoping he could heal on his own. His body had let him down.

Yurek eased himself into the seat, dropping the last few inches when his hands, holding onto the roof of the car, gave out. The jarring movement sent a fresh wave of excruciating pain through him. It would take more than three hours to get to the nearest finestra. He hoped he would make it.

CHAPTER 15

The drive through the mountains to the finestra was twisty, cold, and mostly through the middle of nowhere. Petra and Cheveyo stopped in one small town to fill the gas tank, and her butt was so sore and numb from sitting on the bike that she didn't care how she looked as she vigorously massaged the circulation back into it. As he gassed up, he watched her with barely suppressed mirth.

Zoe had been right about the scorpions-in-her-hair feeling. Petra scrubbed her fingers over her scalp as she headed toward the restroom.

"How much longer?" she asked when she returned to the bike.

He glanced at his watch. "We've been on the road for two hours."

"*Augh.* One more hour. And we don't even know what they're driving now."

He'd been watching the road that passed by the station. Not much traffic, but every vehicle could contain Yurek and Baal.

"Let's go," he said, and off they went again.

Two hours would have been bad enough, but after three, she felt as though she'd *walked* the damned road. The sun glared down at them, frying her eyes but at least warming her some.

Her physical discomfort was nothing compared to the tension inside. Were they ahead of Yurek and Baal or behind them? Would they stop Yurek before he went back and tattled to the C? Their lives hung on the edge of that one question.

What if the C sent back more Callorians to even the odds? Could they take her and Cheveyo back to Surfacia and SCANE them? They'd find out about the others, the baby.

She mentally screamed, trying to stop her runaway train thoughts. Problem number eight with riding a motorcycle: she couldn't read or otherwise distract herself. Problem seven was how vulnerable she felt out in the open. Yurek had sent them off the road with a nudge. Memories of the way he rammed his car into the RV came to mind. The Tank wasn't about to be pushed. This bike . . . no chance it would stay stable.

They made a left and headed toward their final destination, a narrow, barely asphalt road squeezed in between two mountain ranges. She was tired of seeing rocks, sand, and scrub, and nothing else. Ten minutes down the road she regretted that thought. There was something else, all right: several trucks blocking the road. To the right of the road the land dropped off steeply. To the left, two trucks were parked in the one portion that was flat, backed up to a mound of red rocks and sand. Three men were using some kind of a tractor to fill in where the road had caved away. All three workers looked up, their faces tightening in irritation.

Cheveyo surveyed the situation but couldn't see a way for the bike to get through to the other side. He cut the engine and removed his helmet as the bike drifted up to the one man within talking range. "What's going on here? We have to get past you, and fast."

"What the hell is going on out there?" The burly man jerked his head behind him.

Her heart froze. "Two other people came by here, too?" she asked.

"About ten minutes ago, saying it was urgent they get past. The one guy didn't look so hot, though what help he thought he was going to get thatta way is beyond me. The driver . . ." He shook his head. "Scary looking guy. We moved the trucks, big pain in the ass, and let 'em pass. You'll have to wait. We should have the hole filled in about thirty minutes."

Cheveyo met her gaze. They had no time to spare. "I'm afraid that's not going to do. Those two were fugitives. They're meeting others out here, and if we don't intercept them, they're gone."

The man looked skeptical. "Unless you got a badge, I'm not moving the tractor."

Cheveyo's voice was low, almost a growl. "It would be in your best interest to cooperate."

The man's scowl melted into a mix of puzzlement and wariness. He took a step back. "I'll see what I can do," he said, his voice soft and weak. He turned so fast he stumbled, then quickly walked over to the other men.

She looked at Cheveyo. His eyes were dark, as dark as the energy he was putting off. She shivered. "Did you do that influence thing on him?"

"No, that only works on you because of our connection. I used the cat energy thing. All he sensed was imminent danger."

An idling engine shifted into gear, and the tractor moved back. The man they'd spoken with jerked his arm toward the narrow space. They rode through it, and Cheveyo waved his thanks. She glanced back and saw the man staring at him for a moment and then pulling out something that looked like a phone.

"I think he might be calling the police," she said.

"Then we'd better eradicate Yurek and Baal before they come."

The man soon became lost in a cloud of dust. She squeezed her arms around Cheveyo. He was a spooky badass, but he was her spooky badass.

He tore down the dusty road. She looked around the side of him, seeing no sign of any vehicle up ahead. They'd gotten a good head start.

Sunlight glinted off glass in the near distance, about a half mile off the road. No chance of surprising Yurek and Baal; they would hear the bike's engine. A truck was parked next to a rise in the ground. It was the truck Yurek had obviously stolen, empty now, and they tore past it. The ground was covered in gray rocks and scrub brush. The bike climbed over and around them, but it slowed them down.

"Do we know what a finestra looks like?" she asked.

"I never saw one."

"Can it suck us in?"

"Don't know. But as Pope said, even if we survived the trip, we'd be captured on the other side. We'll feel it, I'm sure, so we stay clear of it."

In the same second that she saw Yurek, painfully walking toward a mound of rocks, Baal in dog-beast form leapt toward them. Cheveyo gunned the engine, and Baal sailed just behind her. She felt the brush of its fur against her jacket, smelled its musk. It tumbled to the ground but quickly gained its footing.

"We need to get on foot fast," Cheveyo said as he slowed to a stop.

She got off a second before him, and he laid the bike down so a rock kept it slightly upright. She already had her knife out as Baal came at them again, covering Cheveyo until he had time to get his out.

He lunged at Baal.

Petra glanced to the right, seeing Yurek far in the distance. "I'll go after Yurek," she said. "He won't be much of a threat right now."

She ran, fighting to keep her footing in the soft sand, and in a few minutes caught up to him. He struggled toward what she now saw was a shimmer in the air, different from the waves of heat. It vibrated through her being. His eyes darkened, and she saw an echo of black jaguar as he tried to change to cat, to Cheveyo's cat. But he couldn't hold onto it. Sink the knife into his heart, that's all she had to do to stop this. It would be mostly over, except for Baal.

Yurek picked up his pace, though he winced at every movement. She was breathless, the cold air searing her lungs as she gasped. She shed the jacket as she ran, wanting more mobility. The knife was gripped in her hand, damp from perspiration. Her leg muscles ached.

He was almost at the shimmer now. He was gasping, too, glancing back.

He was too close. *Have to stop him. Any way I can.*

She ran full out and threw herself at him, knife out. He fell into the shimmer. She sailed through it, landing hard on the rock-stubbled ground beyond it and coming to her feet, ready for anything. He was gone. The shimmer was gone, too.

Too late. No! Can't be.

Her chest ached, but Petra pulled herself up and made her way back to Cheveyo. She picked up her jacket on the way, relieved to find him in one piece. He was cat, sparring with his enemy. Magnificence and strength, black fur liquid indigo in the sunlight. She could clearly see the jaguar markings beneath the black. He spared her a glance, and Baal took advantage of that, slamming into Cheveyo and knocking him to the ground. Instead of pouncing, though, it fled, bounding over the rocks, favoring one leg.

"He's gone," she said on a whimper. "Yurek's gone. I couldn't stop him."

Cheveyo tore after Baal, all deadly grace. They'd get one, at least. She followed as fast as she could. As she reached the slight rise in the terrain, she saw Cheveyo studying the landscape. His tail flicked in agitation. All around, rock and mounds, and no sign of Baal.

"He could be anywhere," she said, catching her breath as she approached. She searched, as he did. His nose twitched, obviously trying to pick up the scent. The breeze blew her hair across her face. It was probably too windy.

Cheveyo morphed back to man then, his dark eyes still raking the area even as they slowly returned to their blue-gray shade.

She braided her hair, more to keep it under control than out of nervous habit. "Why did Baal run away? Did you injure him?"

"No, I think he's still feeling the wound you gave him. His instinct, his drive, is to attack, to eliminate the enemy. I don't know why he'd run away." He ran his hand back through his waves, still searching.

"Maybe he's afraid of us."

"I doubt it. I don't like it when Glouks don't act like they're supposed to. At the festival, he was setting us up instead of trying to eliminate us. He's up to something now, too, probably at Yurek's bequest. But I don't sense him anywhere near. If he's run off, he's not coming back. Show me where the finestra is."

"Was. I can't see it now that Yurek is gone." She led him back to where she remembered seeing the shimmer. "It was here, like a door, only taller and wider."

"Maybe it's triggered by Yurek's DNA, and we don't have enough Callorian in us to trigger it."

She rubbed her arms and then put on the jacket. "I'd be afraid to go to the other side."

"It doesn't sound like a place I'd want to live. We'd better get out of here, in case that yahoo back there did call the cops." He checked his phone. "No signal. Still, he may get a better signal than I do. A stolen truck, two missing men, and us—not something I want to explain."

They walked back to the bike, and Cheveyo pulled out the map. Then he surveyed the terrain. "I think we can go across that way to hook up with another road. It looks somewhat smooth. Hopefully it continues that way."

"Will we come back here in twenty-four hours?"

"Yurek knows we found this place, and he'll figure we know about the healing period. If he's the one coming back, he won't return here."

"Which means he'll probably come in at the other finestra."

"Which is where our furry buddy may be off to. I'll bet Yurek wants him to stay alive to guard the other finestra when he comes back in. It's a guess, but that may be why he didn't engage us. I'll stop when we get near the next town and call Pope."

They put on their helmets, got on the bike, and headed slowly across the crumbly terrain. She held onto him as the bike lurched and sometimes sank into the softer areas of dirt. It took a while, with the sun beating down on them. Thankfully, the air stayed in the sixties. They approached a more densely treed area, and she said, "Can we stop for a few minutes? I need to drink."

She'd been feeling a different kind of tension as she held onto his waist, mostly seeing his hair drifting in the breeze and his broad back. He'd stored his jacket, leaving the muscles of his back more visible beneath the black shirt.

Cheveyo cut the engine once they reached the shade, and she stretched and gulped down half a bottle of water in one swig. When she turned to face him, their gazes caught and jumped up her heartbeat. His eyes darkened, but not in that *I'm going to eat you up* way. More like an *I'm going to eat you* way that was far scarier. To her heart, anyway.

She opened her mouth, and for a second no words came out. His gaze went to her lips, and he instinctively licked his own.

Finally words came out of her mouth: "You . . . feel it again?"

He nodded.

"The irrational, inappropriate . . ."

"Lust," he finished, stalking closer, as deliberate as a cat eyeing its prey.

She was walking toward him, too, not even aware of it until this moment.

"Inappropriate," he echoed. "Extremely ill advised."

"*Mm-hm,*" she agreed, but couldn't tear her gaze from his. Her eyes felt heavy, as though she'd been drugged. "So we should . . ."

"Definitely." And he yanked her against his chest, his fingers threading into her hair, tilting her face to properly plunder her mouth.

She plundered back, her fingers curling against his chest. He pushed the jacket off her and it fell to the ground. She grabbed at the bottom hem of his shirt and pulled it up. He lifted his arms, widening his chest, flexing his muscles, and before it even cleared his head, she had buried her face against his chest. The dark, coarse hairs pressed against her mouth, and she breathed in the musky cat smell of him. She kissed across the expanse of hair and over to one nipple, gently tugging it between her teeth. He groaned, his fingers unraveling her braid. She kissed across to the other nipple, the scarred one, and ran her tongue down his scar.

A louder groan. She leaned forward and kissed him. He tilted his head back, surrendering. *Surrender, just for now.* She kissed the side of his neck below his ear, nibbling at his earlobe, and then over his collarbone and the hollow at the base of his throat. Then she picked up where she'd left off, circling his scarred nipple with the tip of her tongue.

When she reached the bottom of the scar, he pulled off her sweater. He unsnapped her bra with a flick of the fingers and pushed it back over her shoulders. Her knees buckled when he put his mouth on her neck, and then lower, and oh, how she hungered for him deep in her soul. She moved against him, and his tongue lathed her breasts. She felt the scrape of his teeth against her skin, then her nipple, and gasped.

He dropped to his knees, his hands on her behind, burrowing his face against her stomach. Then he unbuttoned her jeans and unzipped them, nuzzling the top edge of her pubic hair with his mouth. She let out a breathy sigh. So did he. His fingers started to pull at the top edge of her panties.

She dug her fingers through his soft hair. "Cheveyo . . ."

And then the brush of fur against her skin. She opened her eyes and saw him as jaguar. Pissed off jaguar, by the angry flicks of his tail and the fierce look in his eyes. She leaned back against the tree trunk, and he growled, showing gleaming white fangs, both upper and lower. He turned his back on her, taking slow, deliberate steps away.

She knew he was trying to intimidate her, push her away so he could control himself. But she couldn't be afraid of the jaguar anymore. She took a step closer, and he whirled, his growl even louder this time.

She knelt down to his level, her face only inches from his. Her voice was high and off-pitch when she sang the Tom Jones song, "What's up, pussy cat? Oh oh oh . . ."

She reached out to the cat's face. He flinched, making her flinch in return. *No, it's Cheveyo. Don't let him scare you.* She lifted her hands again and stroked his face. He let out a low, warning growl.

"I know you won't hurt me," she whispered, looking into his black eyes. "I know you're trying to control your humanity by becoming cat, but I'm not letting you scare me away." She kept stroking the cat's face as she spoke, and then she leaned forward and kissed his cheek, feeling whiskers against her lips.

"Hell."

In a blink she was kissing his face, skin, the faint scratchy stubble.

He surged to his feet, driving his fingers into his hair. "I liked you better when you were afraid. It was safer for both of us."

"You liked scaring me away?"

"No, I didn't like it. But it's better than getting distracted when an enemy is out there somewhere." He flung out his hand.

He was breathless, and it took her a second to catch her own breath as he shoved her bra and sweater at her. He kept his gaze on their surroundings as he spun in circles, even looking up at the trees. She pulled on her sweater and zipped up her jeans, stuffing her bra into the bags of the bike along with her water bottle.

Cheveyo started the bike then, and she held on tight as they moved toward what passed as a road. He paused once they were about to get onto a real road again and turned to her. "That crazy reaction we have, it's going to get us killed. When I'm in that space, I'm totally lost in you."

Lost in her. She inhaled those words. "Yeah, it's the same for me." Her voice had gone soft at that. "It's just some weird chemical reaction, us, the adrenaline."

"No, I just realized what it is, at least for me. It's watching you become strong. Even though I'm scared to death you'll get hurt, watching you fight, and fight well, it's a damned turn on. I don't know if that makes me a sick son of a bitch or—"

"Or human, maybe," she said, squeezing his chin. "Because that's what triggers it for me, too. Watching you, the way your muscles move, the fierceness of your face—"

"Even when I'm cat?"

"Yeah, even then." She touched his face as she had when he was cat. "You're a beautiful cat."

He sighed. "You're killing me, Petra."

Then he turned and continued on the road. She remembered that he didn't like when people used the words "death" and "kill" casually. A tremor rippled through her. So what did he mean by that?

Baal watched the humans through the binoculars, their hands sliding over each other's bodies. The woman was half naked, and the hunter's mouth was on her breasts, his hands on her ass. Baal could *feel* their hunger. Not a sustenance hunger. Not an animalistic hunger.

Human hunger mixed with emotions he couldn't identify.

Something was happening to him. As soon as he'd come upon them in this state, he had morphed into man without even thinking about it. The more he ate the flesh and drank the blood of humans, the more human he felt. And the longer he could stay in this form. He watched them hungrily touching and putting their mouths on each other. They didn't mate to procreate. They did it for pleasure. His body stirred, too, his penis becoming stiff and hot and uncomfortable. His humanness was mixing with his animal, melding, twisting inside him.

He was a direct descendant of one of the subjects of the experiments that combined Glouk and human DNA. He had only tapped into his humanity to perform tasks he was hired for. To be used but never appreciated or treated as an equal. Here, in the promised land, he could indulge his animal but still walk around as human without anyone knowing just how different he was.

Humans came in all shapes and sizes and degrees of beauty and ugliness. Yes, he was ugly in human terms, but no one gave him a second glance. He liked being human, and mostly, he liked being acceptable. He looked in wonder at the way his erection was pressing against the front of his pants. Sex for pleasure.

He liked this part of being human, the way hunger spiraled through him as he watched the two touching each other. Especially the way looking at the woman's body made him feel. He would touch her like that. He would have sex with her, filling her with his astonishing appendage. As soon as the hunter was dead, he would take her. Maybe he would even keep her around for a while.

CHAPTER 16

Petra noticed they'd passed the road with signs that read PARKS, where Cheveyo lived. He probably didn't want Baal tracking them to the cabin, but they had a day before they needed to be at the second finestra.

She leaned closer to him. "Where are we going?"

"Vegas."

Her heart tripped a beat. "As in 'Las'?"

He turned his head. "We're going to dinner and a show, and for a few hours pretend we're not facing the enemy tomorrow. Sound good?"

She leaned against his back, squeezing her eyes shut in gratitude and delight. Maybe he didn't hear her sigh or see her eyes well up, but she was pretty sure he got the message.

They were grimy and gritty by the time they reached Vegas. It was warmer there, low eighties, and she had shed her jacket. It was six o'clock, not dark enough for the lights to glow against a black sky like she'd seen in pictures. Who needed lights and neon when the sunset painted the sky in orange and purple slashes?

He cruised down Tropicana and turned onto Las Vegas Boulevard. At the corner was New York, with a roller coaster snaking around the buildings. She was spellbound by all of the huge casinos she'd only seen in movies: MGM Grand, the Monte Carlo, Paris, with its replica of the Eiffel Tower, Caesar's Palace, all the places and headliners she'd heard about. Elton John! Celine Dion! Cher! David Copperfield!

"Surreal, isn't it?" he asked, obviously sensing she was in awe. He was looking around, too, taking it in. "Pick a hotel, whatever tickles your fancy."

"We're going to stay at one of these places?" She was trying not to sound like a kid, but heck, the thought of staying at one of these magical places— and she got to pick!—was squeal producing. "Paris! I want to go to Paris."

He did a U-turn and pulled into the grand entrance, driving right by the Eiffel Tower. As soon as they stopped and got off the bike, a valet approached.

Cheveyo took a key from a compartment and handed it to the man, along with a folded bill. "I need this bike to stay here, where I can get to it quickly."

The valet's eyebrows rose, especially when he saw the hundred dollar bill. "Yes, sir."

Cheveyo pulled out their bags. "I've got them."

They walked into the lobby, so immense and glamorous she could hardly take it in. The marble floors had a ribbonlike decor. She trailed behind, nearly walking into someone because she wasn't paying attention. When she finally looked around, she didn't see Cheveyo for a second. She found him near the check-in desk, waiting for the next clerk.

He was watching her with a bemused expression. "Go ahead, wander around. I'll take care of this part."

She wondered if he'd get them separate rooms.

How far would their pretending go? Distracting herself from that thought, she wandered around. Everything was cream and gold, gaudy and wonderful at once. Huge chandeliers added to the elegance . . . or gaudiness, depending on how one looked at it. Still, it was all beautiful, and different than anything she'd seen.

One area looked like a miniature Paris street, with cafés and shops. She was entranced. A muscular blond man was wearing a skintight gold outfit and entertaining passersby.

She felt a hand on her shoulder and swiveled with a yelp.

Cheveyo smiled. "A bit jumpy, eh?"

"Can't imagine why."

He looped his arm through hers. "This way, mademoiselle. We'll get showered, then come down to the shops and pick out something for the evening. I've had the concierge make dinner reservations and get us tickets to a show."

She put her hand over her heart. "I get to shop for something pretty, *and* we're going to a show?" She hugged him, losing herself in the feel of him for a moment before stepping away.

He laughed—at her enthusiasm, no doubt—and she was stunned by how it transformed his face. He wasn't a creature hunter in that moment, wasn't haunted by darkness and loss. He was a man who found pleasure in her pleasure, and it made him breathtakingly gorgeous.

They stepped into the elevator, the only ones in it.

"This is the best date ever," she said, and then quickly added, "I know, it's not a date date." *Good move, there, Mademoiselle Dummy.*

He said, "It's a date. Our first and our last."

The first part made her heart soar; the second dashed it. They were only pretending to be normal. That didn't mean they could let all caution go to the wind. They got off on the tenth floor and she followed him to one of the doors.

He slid in the card and opened the door, then gestured for her to walk in first. "They don't have a two-bedroom suite, so we have connecting rooms. We'll keep the door between open."

She stepped into the luxury suite, too absorbed by his presence to notice much about the room. He let the door close behind him, set her bag down and unlocked the connecting door. "Get your shower." He glanced at his watch.

"I know, ten minutes!" Now, she took in the room. "Wow, this is gorgeous. Huge! Fit for a queen. Or at least a princess." She shot him a smile.

The suite had a living area that was separate from the bedroom. She picked up her bag and walked in. Yes, it all looked very Parisian, or what she thought Parisian might look like. A canopy set off the king-sized bed, both in matching upholstery. Immediately she pictured Cheveyo lying next to her on it, pillows flying, clothes, too.

The whimper came out louder than she'd anticipated.

"You okay?" he called.

"Fine. Just admiring the room." With a sigh, she pushed on to the bathroom. And gasped.

He chuckled. "Now what are you admiring? The view?"

"The bathroom. It's freaking wonderful, with a huge marble tub that reminds me of the one in your bathroom." Which reminded her of when he'd pulled her in. She had to get him drunk; there was no two ways about it. When he'd been in that blood deprived state, she saw a playful side of him that had to exist beneath his serious, ever-vigilant exterior.

She regretfully opted for the shower, using the hotel's shampoo and soap, and putting on the clothes she'd packed for fighting: knit pants, a blue sweater, and those god-awful dusty sneakers.

When she emerged, sans makeup because she didn't want it to rub off on the clothes she tried on, he was studying the map spread out on the coffee table.

"One bit of business," he said.

She sat down beside him. "Where are we going?"

"Here." He pointed to a place just outside Zion National Park, over the Utah border. "Pope's given me some orientation of where the finestra is. Obviously it's off the road, not where tourists would be. It'll take about three hours to get there, and we'll need extra time to locate it. He's psychically giving me landmarks to help us."

"Really? He remembers enough to help us find it? Oh." Just as Pope had put the image of the warehouse in her head, now she saw rocky landmarks to signal the finestra's location. One peak that looked like a witch's nose, complete with wart on the end. And steep drop-offs.

"See it?" he asked.

"Oh, yeah. Not fun. But I'm amazed he can remember such details."

Cheveyo leaned to the right and sketched out that same peak on a piece of paper. "He says he had to learn the subtleties of each finestra's surroundings as part of his training. If we leave at six tomorrow morning, we should be fine."

She jumped up, wrapped her arms around herself and spun. "We get a whole night here. I get to sleep in that big bed with all the pillows." Alone. Her gaze met his. She cleared her throat, sat down and looked at the map. "Doesn't look like a fun drive."

"I suspect it'll be like what we did today. Only not as long."

"Thank gawd." Her finger trailed across the map. "I love all the names of the mountains: Big Maria Mountains, Vulture Mountains . . . *Chocolate Mountains*? Really? I would love to live on the Chocolate Mountain range."

He raised an eyebrow. "You know they're not really made of chocolate, right?"

"Well, yeah. I just like the sound of it."

His soft chuckle trickled down her spine. He folded the map and put it in his bag. "Ready to shop?"

"Does lipstick come in different colors?" Though she could just as easily stay right there in that room, with him, too. The temptation of that was probably why he'd packed in dinner and a show. "What are we seeing?"

"One of the Cirque de Soleil shows."

"Juicy. One of them came to Baltimore but I had to work that night."

"At Hooters."

She swiveled to pin him with a gaze. "How . . . ? You came to the restaurant?"

He nodded. "You were bummed because you couldn't get the night off. It was a great way to check on you." He shrugged. "And the food's good, too."

"Thank you for not commenting on the scenery."

"Well, I did like one part of the scenery."

She felt her cheeks warm. "How many times did you come in?"

"A few."

"Did I wait on you? No, I would have remembered waiting on someone like you."

He held the door open for her. "What does that mean, 'someone like me'?"

"You're gorgeous, but not in a typical gorgeous guy way. You have exotic looks, plus you look a bit like Lucas, so that would have struck me right off the bat."

They walked down the hallway to the elevator. He punched the button. "I used to feel your ache when you thought about him."

"It's hard to love someone who doesn't love you back the same way."

"I know." He let those words hang for a moment, and before she could even think to ask if he meant her, he said, "Did you ever tell him you had a crush on him?"

"No! I'm so glad I didn't. He never saw me that way, and it would have strained our relationship." She leaned against the wall, her hands linked behind her. "Once I met you, what I thought I felt for him, romantically, all went away. Now I only feel toward him like a sister would. You said you connected to me through Lucas. I think I felt that and confused it for having those feelings for Lucas. It's kind of weird, I know, but nothing about us is normal."

The doors slid open and they walked inside. This time there were others in the elevator car with them. Too bad. Or maybe not, depending on how one looked at it. She wanted him, and she knew he wanted her, too. That had never been in question. She totally understood why they shouldn't go that next step, imprinting their bodies on one another's and leaving them hungry forevermore.

The problem was, she was hungry anyway.

They spilled out of the car along with the others and made their way to Le Boulevard, the ritzy shopping area. It wasn't as frilly here, but was still austere with a fountain and lots of marble. Big, glittering windows of clothing and jewelry would normally set her heart aflutter, but compared to having Cheveyo walking beside her . . . not so much. He paused outside the door of a woman's dress shop.

"I'll meet you here in about—"

"Ten minutes?"

"Take fifteen. I'm going to find a shirt. I'm treating you to tonight, so if you find something before I come back, leave it on the counter."

"You don't have to buy it for me," she said, touched that he would.

"Do you know how many times I've bought a dress for a woman? None. So let me."

If she didn't immediately walk into the store, she knew she would throw herself at him and start bawling. She nodded quickly and propelled herself in, wandering the various racks of clothing. Still, no excitement, not like before. No, what she'd felt before was a hunger, and buying things—for herself and others—had been her lame way of filling that hunger.

That's when Amy's words hit her: "That's you buying stuff to fill a hole that things can't fill. But I think he has a lot to do with that hole . . ."

She hadn't been ready to accept that truth then, but now it smacked her right in the face. Cheveyo was the man she was supposed to be with, her soulmate, and at a deep level she'd always known that. She'd tried to fit Lucas in that role, and at times other men, and when they didn't fill it, she went on to buy things that only temporarily sated her. Like an alcoholic, a drink to make her feel happy for a short time. Her credit card bills had been her hangover.

"Can I help you?" a soft female voice asked from beside her.

"No one can help me," she said on a long sigh, then realized she'd spoken aloud and turned to the petite blonde. "I need a dress, something pretty and simple."

"Famous little black dress?" the woman asked with a wink.

"Maybe."

Petra followed the clerk to a rack with several short dresses. She took three of them into the dressing room and came out three times, wearing two black-dresses and then a burgundy one. The third one fit over her curves, giving her cleavage without being trashy, flowing over her hips and ending with a ruffle just above her knees.

"I like that one."

Not the salesgirl's voice, but a low, masculine voice that tripped her heartbeat. She met Cheveyo's gaze in the mirror, where he leaned against one of the racks. He was wearing a burgundy long-sleeved shirt tight enough to show his physique. It was a match in color to her dress. He'd paired it with a tie, but was still wearing a crisp pair of jeans.

"Did you see the others?" she asked.

He nodded. "The first two from outside the window."

"You should have come in."

He gave her a bittersweet smile. "Watching you from afar is what I'm used to doing."

"I'm glad you came in."

He turned to the salesgirl, who was raptly watching them. "We'll take this one. She'll need shoes, too. Do you have anything that matches the dress?"

"I do."

He took her hand and followed the girl, who weighed about twenty-five pounds. She wore a black jumpsuit that showed off her trim body and tiny butt, but when Petra dared glance over at Cheveyo, he was looking to the left—at a mirror that showed her reflection.

They browsed fancy high-heeled shoes on glass pedestals, like Cinderella's slippers. He hooked his finger around a strap sprinkled with rhinestones. "How about this one?"

Something sparkly like that would normally swell her heart, but now she just said, "Sure."

"What size?" the girl asked.

"Nine."

She didn't have dainty little feet like the salesgirl, but then again, she had never been dainty. She was more embarrassed about her sneakers than her big feet. A few minutes later the girl returned with a box.

"May I?" he said to her, holding out his hands for the box.

Her heart in her throat, Petra sank into the red velvet chair and took off the sneakers and socks. He knelt before her and pulled one shoe out of the box. He gently took her foot and slid it into the shoe. With a spark in his eyes, he said, "It fits, Cinderella."

She *was* the princess just then, but she would not flee at midnight. Just as she had not fled at the growling jaguar.

He put on the other shoe, running his fingers up the length of her calf. His hands, olive-skinned and callused from years of working with knives, looked startling against the pale of her leg. They felt possessive, sensual, capable, and arousal warmed her right there in the store.

The salesgirl cleared her throat, then said, "I'll just be, uh, over at the register when you're ready."

She and Cheveyo shared the most wonderfully intimate smile. He stood and held out his hand to her. She took it, loving the way his rough hand felt on hers. She had calluses, too, she realized. Their gazes met for a moment, fire arcing between them.

"We'd better go," he said, his voice rough.

"Before we miss our reservation," she added.

"That, too."

He turned before she could see his expression on those words, but they shimmered through her body. He paid in cash and led her out of the store. When she looked back to thank the salesgirl, she was leaning on her palm with a longing expression on her face, watching them.

Petra leaned against him as they walked toward the front entrance. "No one has ever done that before, taken me to a store and bought me a beautiful outfit. Thank you."

His smile was warm and soft. "It was my pleasure."

He steered her toward a sign that announced the Eiffel Tower restaurant. "We're eating in the Tower?" she asked, once again giving away her excitement.

"Best views of the city, or so I'm told."

They ate dinner by the window overlooking the Bellagio across the street. The colored water light show entertained, the French food was delectable, but she most enjoyed talking about the mundane and deliciously normal things people who weren't in danger talked about: fave movies, music, other people.

Later, the show was magnificent, and she totally lost herself in the spectacle of it all. Of course, she was aware of Cheveyo next to her, and once in a while she slipped her gaze toward him. He always sensed it and looked over, but she suspected he was enjoying the show, too.

When they returned to the hotel, she felt the tightness in her belly, and lower, start again. Separate bedrooms. Good idea, that. And probably a good idea that he'd had no more than a glass of red wine with dinner, no chance of him getting drunk. She'd limited herself to the same, because all she needed to do was blab her feelings all over him. Yeah, she was one of those pour-out-your-heart drunks.

She'd slipped out of her shoes as soon as they exited the elevator, looping the straps over her finger. Lovely shoes, but comfortable they were not.

He locked the door of their room behind him. "Why don't you take a long, leisurely bath in that tub that enchanted you so?"

He hadn't said *Why don't we take* . . .

"Maybe I will. My body could sure use it." She walked up to him, feeling unsure and awkward, knowing he felt the same tension she did. "Thank you for tonight."

"When I said it was my pleasure, I meant it. I loved seeing you enjoy yourself." He brushed a stray strand of hair from her cheek. "You have a glow that made you the most beautiful woman in the whole city tonight. You looked sexy, but it was more than that. You have a beauty that comes from inside."

For the first time, she *felt* beautiful. The rush of joy took her breath away. Those weren't just shallow words based on nothing more than her appearance.

Her voice quavered when she said, "You could join me in that leisurely bath."

"No, I can't."

She knew the rejection had nothing to do with her personally, but it still stung. She forced a smile. "There's no adrenaline to make us crazy. You did say you had iron control."

"Not where you're concerned. A leisurely bath would be more dangerous than giving in to our lust."

Because it would be much more than lust. She nodded. "You're right. See, I'm the weak one." She dropped her gaze, stepping back. "Good night."

"We'll get up at five-thirty, go downstairs and have a good breakfast."

"Sounds good. The breakfast part, anyway."

She went into her room and closed the door. A strange, undulating glow was coming from the bathroom. Her throat tightened as she walked to the open doorway and peered in. Probably twenty candles flickered all around the tub, interspersed with vases of gerbera daisies. Either the flowers or the candles filled the room with a soft, sweet scent. The tub was up to the rim full, jets humming. This was why he'd ducked into the restroom on their way out of the show. She turned to go thank him but stopped. To go out there now, with her heart lodged firmly in her throat and eyes moist, would not be a good idea.

Accept the gift for what it is and thank him in the morning.

She swiped at her eyes and breathed in the whole scene before her. Fit for a princess. Tonight she had felt like a real princess, and he had been her knight. A man who loved her but couldn't let himself love her.

After slipping out of her dress and panties, she draped them over a chair at a small dressing table. She twisted her hair and reached for a hair clip. It would feel so wonderful to slip into that bubbling cauldron.

"He thought of everything but music," she whispered, taking a step toward the tub.

"I can sing if you want."

She spun around to find him standing in the

doorway, his hands resting on the upper frame. He wore only jeans, the top button undone. The candle-light made him look magnificent, washing out all the scars on his body but the long, deep one. She couldn't quite read his expression. Serious, sensu-ous, and more.

"Sing to me," she said.

She felt more naked than she'd ever felt, and more beautiful as his gaze softly dipped down over her and then back to her face. As though he were taking in the visage of a goddess.

His voice surprised her, low and smooth and right in tune. "'Ain't no sunshine when she's gone . . .'" He walked toward her as he sang, his gaze never leaving hers. " . . . 'It's not warm when she's away . . .'"

Her knees went to jelly. She'd heard Kris Allen sing the song on *American Idol*, and it touched her so deeply she'd downloaded the track onto her iPhone.

He walked closer, until he was standing in front of her. He cupped her face, his fingers barely grazing her skin. "' . . . Any time she goes away.'"

"You're always the one who went away," she whis-pered, her chin trembling.

He touched her chin, those blue-gray eyes nearly swallowing her soul. "I'm here now."

She pulled his face down to kiss him. He was kill-ing her, but this death was sweet. Their kisses weren't the frenzied, out-of-control ones they'd experienced lately, but deliberate and slow and sensuous. So much better, because he was here of his own volition, not being carried away.

He buried his face against her neck, holding her tight, and whispered, "Tell me again what you said to me in the yard, before the knife ceremony. Say the words."

She heard the plea in his hoarse voice, in the way his body was perfectly still. She remembered the pain in his words: *You are mine, but I can never have you.*

That he had claimed her like that shivered through her again. "You *can* have me."

She felt something unfurl in him as he released a small, agonized breath and claimed her mouth.

You do have me.

They kissed for long, sweet moments, but the sweet gave way to more.

She unzipped his jeans, and once she'd pushed them down his thighs, he stepped out of them. He hoisted her up, and she wrapped her legs around his waist. He grabbed a towel and laid it on the cold marble counter before setting her down on the surface. All the while he kept kissing her, hungry—no, starving—and it thrummed through her the same way it vibrated through him.

His hand skimmed down and over her breasts, then across her stomach to gently squeeze her inner thighs. His thumb slipped into her folds, slowly seducing instead of jabbing and hurried. He had all night to seduce her, that's what his movements told her. And he would take all night. She realized his tongue was moving in her mouth in the same motion, exploring, dipping, teasing. Her breath started coming in staccato gasps, an orgasm building.

She whispered between those gasps, "I'm already wet. You don't have to . . ."

"Only half the reason for doing this is to get you ready."

"What's the other half for?"

She felt his smile during their kiss. "You tell me."

"To . . . to drive me crazy."

He slid a finger inside her, easing in and then

stroking, brushing her swollen clitoris. He pushed her to the edge but not over.

"You are driving me crazy," she said, moving against him to push herself over. He moved slightly, his smile still in place.

"I'm not ready to let you go yet."

"You . . . are . . . s-so bad."

He withdrew his finger, and what he did next completely, totally took her breath away. He slid his finger into his mouth, sucking the essence of her, dark pleasure in his eyes as they locked onto hers.

"You taste good," he said, and those words alone, especially the thick way "good" had come out, without him even touching her, nearly sent her over the cliff.

Before she could respond—not that one word even came to mind—he hoisted her up and carried her down into the tub. It fit them both comfortably. He sat down first and pulled her onto his lap. His penis, hard and long and wet, slid against her thigh, and she pushed against him.

She felt adored and loved and desired. Desired for everything she was. Though he'd never said the words, she felt his love. In his heavy gazes, in the urgent way he ran his hands over her body, cherishing it with his eyes and touch. And wasn't she doing the same? Loving him back, hungrily allowing herself what she'd wanted for so long.

His mouth devoured her, tasting her, licking and nibbling. She dug her fingers through his thick hair, something she'd longed to do all evening. Heck, from the first time she'd seen him.

The heat between them seared deep into her body wherever they touched. Her breath came in long, deep waves, and she could hear his breathing, too. He came up to kiss her again, his hands bracing her face, his thumbs scraping across her cheeks.

So many words wanted to pour out of her, but she was afraid they would break the spell. She would not let him stop to protect her, would not let him second guess what they were about to do. She said his name instead, softly repeating it. He kissed her more fiercely.

Could they just stay there and do this until five-thirty in the morning? Who needed sleep, when every kiss, every touch, injected her with strength and energy?

They touched, explored, like in a dream, his every touch a reverence of her. He kissed her face, neck, over her shoulders, each soft kiss deliberate. As sexually hungry as she was, she relished this tender sensuality. She explored every part of him that was out of the water in the same way, memorizing each curve of his face, the dip in the middle of his chin, the edge of his jaw and the groove above his full mouth.

He leaned back, closing his eyes and sinking into the moment. Surrendering himself to her . . . the thought of it alone stirred deep in her soul. The way he'd urged her to repeat her words . . . he must have been holding onto them all this time.

She twirled her tongue through the hairs on his chest, blowing on them, sucking them into her mouth, loving the coarse texture of them. And when she had circled her tongue around his nipples, making them go tight and puckered, he let out a hoarse breath and opened his eyes. Languid pleasure changed to a fiery spark. He wanted her, and that hunger sparked in her, too.

She wrapped her legs around his waist, her arms around his shoulders. She moved her crevice against his erection, slowly, up and down. Two could play at the teasing game. His hands tightened on her back, fingers digging in. She put her hands on either side of his face. "No one has ever made love to me before. I want you to *make love* to me."

Love. Because it would be nothing less with him.

She could see, though, that he'd gone beyond surrender now. Neither would walk away before they sated their bodies and souls. That delicious knowledge tingled through her.

He lifted her onto the edge of the tub, clear of the candles, and spread her legs. His mouth trailed across her inner thigh and flicked her most intimate parts. It was the first time a man had put his mouth there, and as good as his finger had felt, his mouth felt infinitely better. Wet, soft, sucking and licking, his tongue dipping into every intimate fold. She arched and rocked her head back.

She let out ragged gasps as her orgasm claimed her. When she thought he would back off and let her catch her breath, he kept moving his tongue over her supersensitive nub until an even more stunning orgasm rocked her. When she dropped over the edge one more time, she was completely breathless and stunned.

"You're even beautiful down there."

He meant it, his gaze heated as he gave her one last kiss there.

He kissed her again, long and lingering, and then reached down to his jeans and pulled a packet from the pocket. Of course, he would be responsible. Even in this moment.

She ran her hands over his slick back and behind, small and tight and perfect. He leaned into her touch as he put on the condom. She pressed her body against his back and slid her arms around him, her hand splayed on his chest.

He turned and pulled her close, kissing her again before sinking into the tub and pulling her down with him. He sat, and she braced her hands on his shoulders and lowered herself, feeling the tip of him pushing against her entrance. She sucked in her breath as she eased onto him. He was big, she was tight. Her fingers squeezed his shoulders, from the tightness and her need to have him inside her.

Her eyes welled with tears at the completeness of him, filling all the holes inside her soul.

"Are you all right?" he asked, watching her.

"I am so all right."

He let her set the pace, his hands gripping her waist as she moved against him. She was still tingling from her earlier orgasms, and it didn't take much for the pressure to build inside her. When the explosion took her, this time inside, she gasped and held onto him. She'd only heard about internal orgasms or read about them in *Cosmo*. He held tight, letting it wash over her as she arched.

Once she'd caught her breath, she whispered, "You didn't . . ."

He was still hard inside her.

"I'm saving mine for the bed. I'm in no hurry, babe."

She smiled at the endearment. "You never called anyone else 'babe,' have you?"

He shook his head, then helped her to her feet. He dried her, lovingly running the soft terry cloth over her skin. She grabbed a fresh towel from the stack and did the same for him.

He swept her up in his arms and carried her to the bed, setting her down and joining her. They made love again, and a curious thing happened as she closed her eyes and lost herself in it: she shapeshifted into a jaguar. In her mind, her body was feline, her fingers claws that kneaded his skin. It was strange and wonderful, and she rode the sensation. She felt him come this time. Still, he moved inside her, as hard as ever, until she came again.

He continued to kiss her, holding his body above hers so as not to crush her. His hair fell down like a curtain around their faces.

He paused, considering her, his expression dark. "How am I going to walk away from you now?"

She touched his face. "You don't have to."

"Yes, I do. And instead of tearing out a piece of my heart, like it always does, it's going to tear the whole thing out."

Her chest tightened. "Walking away from me tore a piece of your heart out?"

He stretched out beside her, rubbing his hand over her arm. "I told myself I wasn't going to let this happen. I'd have the tub prepared for you and go to my room. I got half undressed, trying not to imagine you sinking into that tub . . . alone. But it wasn't that image that broke me down. It was the memory of those words you said to me."

She put her hand to his cheek. "You can have me. Heart, soul, everything."

She couldn't see his face that night when she'd first said those words. Now she could, and the impact was deep.

He took her hand, squeezing it. "I wasn't strong enough to stay away from you tonight. But for both our sakes, I have to be strong enough to walk away once we've killed Baal and Yurek."

She opened her mouth to protest, but he pressed

his finger to it. "I exposed my son and his mother to danger."

But the thought of living without him now, as he'd said, was unthinkable. She reached out to touch his cheek. "Then come into the light with me. You've been fighting for almost twenty years. That's enough."

"It's never enough."

"You'll never kill them all, you know."

She heard the weariness in his voice when he said, "I know." He covered her hand with his, squeezing for a moment and then setting it on the bed. "Protecting you is also my purpose, and I will never do anything to put you in danger."

No, he wouldn't. "I don't regret making love with you, even if it hurts more to say goodbye. I hope you don't either."

"I don't. Along with the pain, I will have the memory of tonight. It'll have to be enough."

No, it would never be enough, but as long as he lived for his mission, she could never have more.

CHAPTER 17

Yurek had been in the healing chamber several hours when Gaston, his superior, came into the room. Through the glass window in the chamber, Yurek watched Gaston consult with the technician on the healing process. He knew it was working; already he felt stronger.

Gaston walked up beside Yurek's head. "You are progressing well. Now you can tell me what happened."

This was not the conversation he wanted to be having, especially in the disadvantageous position of being on his back in the chamber. "Pope has unexpected allies." He told Gaston everything, excluding Baal. "I can handle them, sir. I need only a few more days," he added before Gaston could suggest sending someone else. "You must give me a chance to prove myself."

Gaston pressed his luminescent finger to his mouth. "Two half-Callorians. This is not good. But fortunate that you discovered them."

"Which means there may be more. I can find them,

hunt them down. I am glad to take on that mission once Pope has been extracted."

"Yes, Pope is our immediate concern. You feel you can complete your mission?"

"Without a doubt. I have been very close."

"We do not have a lot of time. The Collaborate is anxious to find out what Pope has been hiding. Your probationary period is contingent on your being able to complete a mission on your own."

"I know, sir." He could think of little else, especially lying in the chamber.

Gaston remained there for a full minute, perhaps deciding. Yurek would beg for another chance, but he knew that would demean him further.

Gaston looked at the ring given to Shines to prove their association with the C. It was sitting among Yurek's personal belongings on a table.

"I accepted your commission with us as a favor to Truxton. He assured me of your competence despite your family's unseemly past."

"I have long ago distanced myself from my family for that reason. I am nothing like them." Truxton was his friend, the only person he considered family. He was a Shine, from a long, distinguished line of Shines.

"No, I see that. You may return, but I can only give you two more days to accomplish both missions: eradicate the half-species and extract Pope. If you fail, you will come back here and be replaced. We will then have to consider a future assignment for you."

Something Yurek dared not acknowledge thrummed through him. He would not let someone take his place. If his probation was considered a failure, he would be dismissed or relegated to tracking down minor violators. He would have to quit and go back to being a mercenary, not much more prestigious than Pope now was.

"I will not fail." The words came on a knife's edge. "I promise you that."

Shines weren't allowed to bring weapons from their dimension, because they might be left behind and discovered. He knew it had once been Pope's brother's job to retrieve all such pieces, including fragments of aircraft that had slipped through dimension cracks. In recent years Shines had to rely on their inherent abilities when on missions to other dimensions. Yurek knew that his own power to mimic should have helped him achieve success, especially where the hunter was concerned. But thus far it had not been enough.

As a mercenary, he could bring whatever he wanted. He had to find a way to smuggle one of his weapons with him when he returned. He hated to admit he needed the edge. The C would never know.

"One more question," Yurek asked. "Is there a chance I can return to the Earth dimension early? Pope will expect me to be back in twenty-four hours. I'd like to surprise him."

Gaston nodded. "I'll consult with your medic."

Petra woke with a start, coming out of a dream—no, a nightmare—where she watched Cheveyo get slayed by Yurek. She pushed the images of the dream, and the terror and grief, aside, taking in the man lying next to her, whole, alive.

Right here, with her.

She hadn't moved, and he hadn't woken. He was in that deep sleep state, but she knew any movement or sound would wake him instantly. He was on his back, and she was tucked in beside him, her hand on his chest, leg slung over his. She felt the rise and fall of his breath.

Mine. And never mine.

Her heart ached at the thought of losing him. That he could be slayed as he had in her nightmare . . . the thought drove a nail into her heart. She lifted her head just enough to see the digital clock. It was four in the morning.

Go back to sleep.

She needed every second of sleep. But it didn't come easily. The nightmare clung to her. She had to remind herself she didn't have dreams that portended the future, but it still felt real, imminent.

If only he would give up his mission. It was all that stood between them, all that stood between him and a real life.

When his guard was down, she'd gone into his soul and seen that horrible memory. His father had sensed her there, and she pulled out like a scared rabbit. She wasn't scared of much anymore. She sank into Cheveyo, feeling his darkness, his isolation, and other feelings she couldn't identify.

"Wayne? Wayne Kee?"

This time she saw the man's face, in his human guise as a Native American, his expression a scowl. And she could converse with him as if he were actually in the room with her. "You dare to intrude in my son's soul again? And to summon me? You are either very foolish or very brave."

"A little of both, I suspect. I am here to beg you to release Cheveyo from this life mission you have assigned him. Can you not feel his loneliness? His need for love?"

Wayne's face tightened. "Feelings, as inconsequential as they are, only complicate, weaken, and endanger. Callorians evolved beyond them; unfortunately my son still has them."

"Yes, he does. Can you just dismiss them?"

"Feelings do not rid the world of dangerous beings. If he doesn't fight them, who will? Who will step up and protect the innocent?"

She thought of Amy's baby girl. They would protect her. "He's put in his time. Is it fair for him to never have love, a family . . . to sacrifice happiness for his entire life? You married and had a family, yet you deny him the same."

"I should have forgone love, though I would not have had my son. I should have been a lone warrior. Cheveyo will not make the same mistake."

"He has lost his son, and it hurts him badly. Surely you have felt this."

His voice softened. "That was indeed regretful. But necessary. The boy child was leading him astray. Softening him."

Anger unfurled inside her. "He was happy, dammit! You were displeased, I'm sure, that he was actually getting to have a real life. I could give him children, and love. I could make him happy. Don't you want that for him?"

"I want him to carry on the fight. It is in his soul. He could not live with himself if he let evil destroy his dimension."

"You're a selfish bastard."

She expected backlash, but instead he laughed. A bitter laugh, though.

"Interesting that you call *me* selfish. Didn't he tell you about my warning?"

"What warning?"

"I have seen his death, and that death is because he is with you. He will become distracted in battle when you are injured, and that will give the enemy a chance to strike. Still, he refuses to send you from him. In the end, your love for each other will destroy you both."

Cheveyo sat up, his body stiff, face rigid. He turned to her. "You were in my soul again." His eyes narrowed. "Talking to my *father*?"

She sat up, too, crossing her arms in front of her. "I asked him to release you of your duties."

"You what?" He got up, stalking into the bathroom. "You had no right to go rummaging around in my soul, Petra, especially after I asked you not to."

She surged up, following him in where he was shoving on his jeans. "You've been doing it my whole life. What makes it wrong when I do it?"

He spun on her, his mouth working but no sound coming out for a second. "I wasn't interfering with your life."

She grabbed a robe hanging on a hook nearby and pulled it on. Arguing naked was unnerving. "That's what you think I'm doing, interfering?"

He leaned into her face. "Yes."

"I'm trying to save you from living sad and alone the rest of your life."

He put on his shirt and buttoned it. "Don't try to save me from anything."

She knew he had a stronger motivation than even his father's directive. "You can't bring him back, you know. Kill a thousand Otherlings, but it won't bring your son back."

"Leave my son out of this," he growled, leaning in toward her face. "You think you know me because you've probed my soul a couple of times. You don't know me at all."

"I know enough about you. I know you're driven to protect the innocent but you long for love and a normal life. Like we had tonight." *And I know you love me.* But hell if she was going to throw that out there just now. Her voice softened. "And you deserve that."

He pulled back and ran his hand back through his hair, his gaze aimed past her. His mouth tightened.

She moved closer, touching his arm. "Cheveyo, you do deserve love."

He pulled away again, checking the time. "Let's get on the road."

He started to turn, but she grabbed his arm to stop him. "At least tell me why you don't believe you deserve love."

He still wasn't looking at her. "I kill monsters. I kill beings that become monsters." He turned to her finally, and she saw the darkness in his eyes. "And yet, I'm a monster, too."

He walked away.

"You are not that kind of monster!"

He was gathering his things in the living area. "What makes me different?"

"You kill to save lives."

The anger was gone from his face when he looked up at her again. "I am what I hunt. And I did not protect the most innocent person in my life. I did not protect his mother. Because of what I do, I caused their deaths. I will continue to hunt down beasts who prey on others. I will say this one more time: do not ever probe my soul again. When we're done here, I will find a way to sever our connection so we can both move on with our lives. You'd better get ready. You have ten minutes."

She remained there, hurt and vibrating. Their first argument. "Your father told me that he saw your death, because of me."

"Nine minutes," he said, flicking his wrist and pointing to his watch.

She stepped closer. "Is it true?"

"My father has never lied."

Her chest tightened. "You're willing to risk dying to save me. Why?"

"Because if you died and I could have done something to save you, I wouldn't want to live. I can't go through that again. Besides, what my father—or anyone who foretells the future—sees, is just one interpretation of it. I saw you dying in the Tomb, but even though I wasn't there to prevent it, you didn't die, because something extraordinary happened."

"Pope happened." She felt that swirl of gratitude and affection toward him. "Maybe he could save me again."

"Maybe, but I couldn't let you stay with him knowing he doesn't have the ability to protect you. I made my choice, and I'll live with it."

"Or die because of it."

"Eight minutes."

Once again he was putting his safety before hers. "I will not let you die."

"Yes, you will. Because if you try to save me, you'll die, and I'll be in the same place. You will revive me to live in a state of agony, because I will still have caused your death." He took her hand and pressed it against her heart, his hand covering hers. "Promise me you will not heal me if I'm mortally wounded. If you do, you'll never see Amy's baby. You'll never have one of your own. Promise." When she didn't, he ordered, "Promise."

She whispered, "I promise."

He narrowed his eyes. "And don't run off thinking

you're going to save me. You'll probably get me killed when I have to go after you."

She was pinned, by both his forced promise and her lack of choices. She spun around and went into her room to get ready.

Two hours later they were standing on the highway. Standing. Not riding or making forward progress. An accident had stopped traffic going both ways. An ambulance had raced north minutes earlier, and now they were waiting for the tow truck to move the wreckage out of the way. Those who were held up were lounging outside their cars, irritated, impatient, or making the best of it. She could hardly make the best of it. The sand here was too soft for the bike to navigate off road. Cheveyo had gone through the pacing phase, and now seemed to have resigned himself to the wait.

When they'd stopped, she said, "Good thing we left early, huh?" only to be answered by a grunt.

He'd wandered away from the people who were gathering and gawking.

She had handed him the perfect reason to cut her off. Well, maybe it was for the best. Wouldn't that make it easier when they parted? Because he was never going to give up his life's mission, and she wasn't going to live this kind of life with him. Not that he'd let her.

There was something that still bothered her. She walked toward him now, her hands stuffed into her back pockets. There was nothing for as far as she could see, other than red sand, scrub brush, and square-topped mountains. And Cheveyo, throwing small rocks at some unseen target. His hair was bound in a leather ponytail, tight at the back of his neck.

She knew the moment he heard her approach. His body tightened, but he didn't look her way.

"I heard someone say it would be clear in about twenty minutes," she said.

He threw another rock, as people did when they were trying to skip them across the water. The only water around here were the puddle mirages that were always just ahead on the highway, only to disappear when they got close.

She came up beside him, staring off into the distance. "You're not afraid of dying, are you?"

She thought he might not answer, but finally he said, "I don't like the idea of it, but no, I'm not afraid. It's much harder to lose someone than it is to die." He was still watching the rocks' trajectories.

"It's not because you have a death wish, or because you're reckless with life. You revere it. I'm terrified of dying, especially now that I'm the same age my mom died. How can you not be?"

"I know we never die. Our bodies, yes, but not our souls. Talking to my father helped me believe this. He's gone physically, but he's still here." He turned to her. "Why are you afraid?"

A breeze blew her hair across her cheek. "Because I don't know what's beyond this life. I believe in Heaven, but it's such a vague, surreal concept to me. And what if I screw up and go to Hell?"

She saw the hardness soften. He brushed her hair from her face, an amused smile on his lips. "Heaven and Hell are here, on Earth. The life you create. If you live in fear, you create Hell. If you let go of that fear and embrace what life is, then you're in Heaven. Do you believe in a God that is loving and merciful and created all of us and everything here on Earth?"

She nodded.

"Would He or She send you to eternal Hell because you 'screwed up'? Does that make sense? Or that you only get once chance to get it right?"

She thought about it. "No, now that you put it that way. You said 'or She.' I've heard women call God a Her and figured it was some feminist thing."

"That may be. God is neither a He or a She but encompasses both feminine and masculine energy. It's easier to consider God one or the other, but I've never seen Her as an old white man residing in the clouds watching us with a stern eye, granting some people wishes, punishing others for no good reason. Calling God *Her* breaks the illusion."

She nodded. "I always wondered about when a child dies. Oh, I'm sorry. I shouldn't have—"

"It's okay. Go on."

"I think it's totally unfair when a child or a baby dies. One chance here and it's gone, sometimes because of someone else's actions. And if the child wasn't baptized, did he or she go to Hell? A child? Really?"

"When a child dies, there's been an agreement before that child and his parents ever came here. The child is to teach them a lesson with his death. We come here to learn, in each lifetime, to become stronger and more enlightened. But our humanity leads us astray more often than not. Luckily we have many chances."

"You've given this a lot of thought."

"One of my archetypes is Seeker. When you live on the edge of death and life, you can't be afraid to look over that edge to either. But I have to stay on the edge without falling to either side." His fingers had unconsciously gone to his Mobius ring.

"You can't embrace life when death stalks you."

"I embrace it more." He met her gaze. "The next time you're afraid, I want you to think about your eternalness. Close your eyes."

She did.

"Hold out your hands. Without moving them, feel them. See them in your mind as energy fields."

"Wow, I *can* feel them, like a low, throbbing energy."

"That's who you really are. Not your body. That's your spirit. If you concentrate, you can feel your whole body. No one can hurt you, not who you really are."

She sat with the feeling for a few seconds. Maybe no one could kill her soul, but she sure did want to live in her body for a while longer. She opened her eyes and looked at him. "What did your son's death teach you?"

"That being part of a family is not my journey this time."

She met his gaze. "Then why do you want it so badly?"

She saw the denial of that on his lips, in his eyes, but he didn't say the words. "It's what I'm here to learn, to overcome."

"I don't believe that. I don't believe your purpose is to be alone in this world, eradicating evil."

"I'll never eradicate evil. They just keep coming. All I can hope for is to stay alive long enough to make a difference." Weariness saturated his words. He glanced over at the line of traffic when an engine started. The tow truck was pulling away, hauling the carcass of a wrecked car with it.

"Let's roll."

As they walked back, her iPhone rang. She pulled it out and looked at the display. "Greg."

"Your date?"

"Yeah." She answered. "Hey."

"Hi, it's Greg. I just wanted to check in, see how you were doing."

"That was really nice of you. Things are a bit . . . hectic." *Like you wouldn't believe.* "My grandmother broke her hip, and we're helping her out."

"If you want some company or moral support, I'd be glad to come out for a couple of days."

Her mouth turned into a frown. "That is so totally sweet to offer." She hated lying. "But not necessary. Listen, I—"

Cheveyo took the phone. "She should be done here in a couple of days, and she would love to go out with you again." He handed the phone back to her.

"Who's this?" Greg asked.

"That was, er, my cousin, Cheveyo. The one who hijacked me from our date."

"He's your cousin? I wasn't so sure. He's . . . different."

She eyed him. "That he is. Hold on for a second." She pressed the phone against her thigh. "What did you do that for?" she whispered fiercely.

"I want you to commit. You like the guy, right?"

He wanted to hook her up with someone else. "I want to marry him and have three kids and a dog with him," she hissed. "Well, not *have* a dog with him but get a dog." Then she looked down and saw that in her irritation she'd pulled the phone away from her thigh. With a grimace, she said, "Greg?"

"Uh . . . look, I'm not ready to get married anytime soon, and I'm allergic to animals."

Could she just die right there? She punched Cheveyo's arm. "Me either. I'm just annoyed at my brother and trying to rile him up."

"I thought he was your cousin."

"He's my cousin's brother."

"That would make him—"

They reached the bike, and Cheveyo climbed on.

"Never mind. I haven't been getting much sleep lately and life has been very stressful. Can I call you another day?" She climbed on, too.

"Sure. I hope everything's all right."

"Thanks, 'bye." She hung up, making sure she'd disconnected. Then she thumped Cheveyo's shoulder. "What'd you do that for?"

He started the engine. "I figured if you could interfere with my future, I could interfere with yours. Making plans is a good idea."

Traffic started to move, and the bike inched forward.

"Gee, thanks. I'm glad you care so much—about arranging a future for me without you. Do you think I'm going to cling to you once this is all over? Beg and plead for you to let me be your partner? You think because you're an incredible lover, that you risk your life to keep me safe, that we have some silly psychic connection, that I can't live without you?"

Uh-oh. Her voice was starting to break. She cleared her throat and waved him to go forward. "Keep moving. Traffic is picking up."

CHAPTER 18

Petra saw the Zion Park signs, relief coursing through her. "We still made it early, even with the traffic snag."

Cheveyo only nodded, riding on through the small dusty town. All around were the flat-topped mountains jutting up into clear skies. If she never saw a rock again, she'd be happy. It wasn't that they weren't beautiful, or at least interesting. Just that it was all she'd seen for days now.

He turned off onto a small shoulder area. "This is where we start hoofing it."

They got off the bike and she stretched. He pulled out the map from the bike's bags and moved his finger along the highway as he read Pope's notes.

She eyed the expanse of land that stretched for miles in either direction. Hoofing it was a cute way of saying they'd be walking in the glaring sun without a bathroom or a Starbucks to be had. No chair to sit down, and not a lot of shade either. She pulled out the hiking shoes they'd bought at a camping store, along with a backpack of food and water.

"We're not going far," he said, brightening her mood. "Unless we get lost."

"Thanks for that. Just when I was cheering up. Not that I'm complaining, mind you."

He met her gaze. "You're complaining."

"Only a teeny weeny bit." She changed into the clunky, butt-ugly shoes that didn't come in pretty colors. She called this color smashed bug-gut green. With as much driving as they'd been doing, she was way familiar with that particular shade. She, however, wasn't saying a word about the shoes' color.

Cheveyo's black shoes seemed capable of handling all kinds of terrain. He hefted the pack onto his back. During a lull between passing cars, he pushed the bike behind a large mound of boulders.

He consulted the map and notes again. "That way. Let's go. The less talk, the better. We don't know where Baal might be, but we have to assume he's out there. The terrain could be just as deadly. Pope said the ridge drops off into a steep ravine near the finestra. The ground is loose, and one misstep will send you falling to the rocks below."

"I know, I know. The mental pictures he showed us looked scary."

Thankfully it wasn't summer. It wasn't even eighty degrees, though the dry air felt like someone had stuck a hair dryer in her sinuses. Her skin felt dry and itchy.

He aimed for a low spot in the long ridge that turned out not to be that low when they reached it.

She groaned, staring up at the steep angle. "Okay, I'm complaining." She tapped her chest. "Right here."

Why didn't he look tired? He was hardly breaking a sweat. He rubbed the back of her neck as though sensing her frustration.

They climbed up and over. More mountains as far as she could see. She tried to remember the luxury suite back in Vegas, and tried not to remember what they'd done in that suite. No need for distractions like that.

The terrain got steeper as they went. Cheveyo kept stopping and looking at the sketches Pope had given him. "Over there."

"The witch's nose, wart and all." She found a smile inside her.

They reached four landmarks, and each one made him act more wary about their surroundings. She kept practicing whipping out her knife, ready to plunge it into an imaginary opponent. Every time Cheveyo looked at his watch, she looked at hers. Two hours before Yurek was due to return.

They climbed up another ridge, this one steeper. She stumbled, sending a cascade of pebbles and dirt down to the ground several yards below. Her feet slipped and she grabbed onto rocks, chipping two nails. He grabbed her arm, steadying her.

Okay? He asked psychically.

I forgot we can talk this way. I could have been loudly complaining all this time! At his chagrined look, she added, *Kidding.*

He motioned for her to remain low while he peered up over the ridge. After scanning it, he nodded for her to follow. They stepped up on the ridge, crouching low, and then down on the other side into a crevasse. Over there . . . the final landmark.

She felt the energy and saw the shimmer, as she had at the first finestra. He surveyed the area again, knife at the ready. As they'd planned, she went to the right and he to the left. They would wait until Yurek arrived.

The waiting was as bad as the walking, except it wasn't physically taxing. She was tucked into the shade, too, but in a place that left her two ways in which to run.

Ten minutes later movement caught her eye in the other direction. Cheveyo waved for her to come. Her heart clenched. He must have spotted Baal. She had been watching the finestra and didn't see Yurek come through. She made her way toward him, the boots clunky and awkward. He was watching something in the near distance, his gaze riveted there. She reached him, looking in the same direction.

Baal, in human form, leaning against an outcropping of rock, looking right at them. Then Cheveyo's arm came around her shoulder, pulling her against his chest. One hand came up hard against her mouth. She jerked her head toward him. *His eyes*. They weren't blue-gray, or black, but a muddy gray.

Yurek!

She kicked and tried to scream against his hand, but he'd locked her tight against him. Her fingers stretched but she couldn't begin to reach for her knife. Baal ambled over, a triumphant smile on his face. The two exchanged a nod, and Baal patted her down as Yurek held her, running his hands from her ankles all the way up, lingering on the roundness of her behind and even jabbing into the crack. She jerked, but he continued, finding her cell phone in her back pocket.

Baal put it in Yurek's pocket and continued to check her, not patting but rubbing up her sides, over her breasts, the bastard, and then finding the sheath. He pulled the collar of her shirt down, yanked the cord. It held, jerking her neck forward. She quickly stepped back. He pulled the cord over her head, removed the knife, and tucked it in his waistband. Then

Yurek pushed her toward Baal, who grabbed her just as tight. She had one second to scream before Baal's big hand slapped her mouth.

It hit her then that they had let her scream. To get Cheveyo to come over. Yurek crept up beneath the ledge, watching for him.

No, no, no!

She wriggled harder, kicking Baal's shin. Something shiny in Yurek's hand caught the sunlight. Wait! She could communicate with Cheveyo!

Don't come here! It's a trap!

Too late. He skidded to a stop at the edge.

Below you!

A white-yellow laser beam shot out of the small gold device Yurek held and hit Cheveyo in the chest. He staggered back. His body swayed when he stared at the blood pouring out of the hole. Breaking out of his shock, he jammed his hand over it, but blood kept gushing out between his fingers. He looked at her and dropped to his knees. Yurek was already crouching beside him as he fell to the side.

God, no! Cheveyo, don't die on me. Don't you dare die!

This was what his father had seen. Her fault, yes, her fault. Yurek, who still looked like Cheveyo, stood again, nodding toward Baal. "Get them to the car."

Baal dragged her across the dirt and rocks toward Yurek. For a few seconds all she could see was Cheveyo's legs, and then Baal brought her into full view of him. She gasped. Her stomach churned. The hole was two inches wide, a perfect circle, and the visible flesh and muscle meant it went deep.

He was looking at her, still there, though pain glazed his eyes. She saw fear pierce the glaze. Fear for her. His breaths came in short, choppy gasps.

Sorry . . . he got across to her.

No, I'm sorry. But this isn't over yet.

If they could get help—

Yurek nodded toward Cheveyo. "Get him, I'll take the girl."

In the exchange, she had a moment to let out a gut-wrenching cry. Cheveyo's eyes drifted closed against his will. Grief curdled her scream, sending her to her knees. She tried to crawl to him, but Yurek hauled her up and threw her over his shoulder as though she weighed nothing.

"He's still alive, but he won't be for long. Can I finish him?" Baal asked, looking at Cheveyo with a feral gleam.

"Let him suffer. He has been like the sandstorms that wreak havoc in Surfacia: unexpected, destructive, and creating a lot of work."

Baal struggled to pick him up. "Can't we just leave him here?"

"I cannot leave evidence."

She sobbed again, beating on Yurek's back. *Stop looking like him!*

He had her legs pinned against his chest, so she couldn't kick him. She went from beating to scratching, lifting his shirt so she could go deeper. Her broken nails left raw, red streaks across his back. He shifted but couldn't escape her claws.

With a quick twist to the left, he rammed her head against the side of the rock. Pain rocketed through her skull, followed by a wave of dizziness. She looked up to see Baal carrying Cheveyo in a similar way, but he wasn't moving. Blood continued to drip down the front of Baal's shirt.

Cheveyo's blood.

They reached a sedan that was covered in red dust, its tires caked with mud.

"Struggle, and I'll ram you into the car. It won't be pleasant," Yurek promised as he unlocked the hood. "For you, anyway."

She couldn't help the cry as Baal dumped Cheveyo into the trunk. She tried to see if he was still alive before the trunk lid slammed down, but he was lying on his side, facing away from her.

Baal opened the door to the backseat and pulled out several lengths of rope. "See, it was a good idea to pick this up. Just in case."

She felt the rope bind her ankles. She kicked, but her legs were still held tight. A few seconds later Baal's face peered from below, gazing up at her. She spit on him. He wiped it from his cheek, but instead of looking pissed, he licked it off his palm with a smile. Her stomach lurched.

Glouks ate humans. And the way he was looking at her, moving her saliva around in his mouth as though it was a sip of wine, he looked at though he would love to eat her, too.

He grabbed her hands, and though she fought him, he gripped her painfully hard and managed to tie her wrists tight. "Got her." He opened the back door of the car to dump her in.

"Put me in the trunk with him . . . please."

No one bothered to acknowledge her. Yurek dropped her onto the backseat, then slammed the door and morphed back to the guise she had seen before. She watched with morbid fascination despite herself. Bastard had tricked her; she hadn't even considered that he wasn't Cheveyo. Baal walked around to the driver's side while Yurek got into the passenger side.

They bumped along for several minutes. Cheveyo, in the trunk, was behind the leather seat Petra sat on.

She pressed her hand against the back of it. So close, and yet. . .

Are you there? Please answer me.

She thought she heard something, but it was too faint to understand. Tears streamed down her cheeks. *Cheveyo. Don't die. I love you. I'm sorry, so sorry. This is my fault.*

She felt the terrain go smooth as they got back on the paved road.

Yurek said, "Their motorcycle is somewhere along here, behind a rock. I'm sure he has the keys on his person."

They'd been watching at least since she and Cheveyo had arrived in the area. Yurek must have gotten back early. It still wasn't twenty-four hours yet.

They stopped and Yurek got out. He opened the trunk and a minute later slammed it shut. He walked over to the open driver's window. "I'll let you know the plan after I talk to Pope," he told Baal.

Pope?

Yurek held up her phone and looked at her, a smug smile on his face. "Won't he be surprised to hear we've got his daughter?"

"I'm not—" She held the words back. He thought she was Pope's daughter? Because he'd sensed Callorian in her. If she negated that, he would want to know how she'd gotten it.

"Not what?" Yurek asked, as though indulging her.

"I'm not going to talk to him, if you think you're going to use me to get him to come to you."

He smiled. "I won't need your cooperation." He held up her phone and took her picture. "Baal, get in back with her."

He was out his door in a second, hovering over her. "What should I do to her?"

"Just be in the picture. It's proof we have her. I'll take one of the hunter, too." Baal laid on top of her, swamping her with his odor. Yurek took another picture.

Pope would be devastated. She hoped he wouldn't turn himself in to save her. Her life for all the others, for the baby. No! If Yurek looked at her pictures, he'd see the sonogram.

Baal remained on her, his hot breath pulsing against her neck. She shoved at him. Yurek had gotten his damned pictures. He only pushed up and got to his feet after Yurek said, "We go now."

Baal was still looking at her. "I'll take her to the house."

Yurek held up the phone. "No signal, as I thought. Stay there until you hear from me. Don't let her loose, even for a second. We can't afford for her to get killed in an altercation. We can afford for her to escape even less."

She felt numb as she heard Cheveyo's bike start and then fade off in the distance. Numb even to the ache that permeated her.

Cheveyo?

No answer. Was he gone? She squeezed her eyes shut at that, tears spilling out. No, she would have felt it. Wouldn't she? She kept the sobs quiet so Baal wouldn't hear, wouldn't get the satisfaction. What house were they taking her to?

It was twenty minutes before they stopped. Baal got out. She hoped he would leave her there, but that was dashed when the door near her feet opened. Hands grabbed her ankles, pulling her across the seat. She didn't like the smile on Baal's face. It was predatory. Anticipatory.

She'd started thinking of him as *he*, because in that

rough face were human emotions. She could not treat him like a dumb animal.

He pulled her up, hitching her over his shoulder as Yurek had done. She struggled, but his strong hands just gripped her harder. With her feet and hands bound, she had no chance of escaping. She lifted her head, seeing nothing but more wilderness and a house that sat in a clearing. He walked toward the building, hardly thrown at all by her movements. She had stabbed him pretty badly, though he wasn't limping now. She stared at the car, the trunk, moving farther away.

Baal inserted a key into the lock. When he turned as he pushed open the door, she saw a sign that read WELCOME TO LUNA VILLA. They'd gotten a vacation rental. She got one last glimpse of the car before the door slammed shut.

Fight! the lizard part of her brain screamed. But her heart was so heavy inside her chest, like one of those huge boulders. It weighed her down. Not that it mattered. She was bound, and he was stronger.

He carried her through a nice living area and a doorway to what looked like the master bedroom. He deposited her onto the bed and climbed on top of her, pinning her down. He unwrapped some of the rope around her wrists. Would he release her? If she could get to Cheveyo . . .

He tied the rope, still around one wrist, to the iron headboard. One of the nightstand drawers held more rope. She fought him, because she should, but there was hardly any fight left. She was outweighed, outpowered, and Cheveyo . . . gone. Baal tied her other wrist to the headboard. He climbed off and stood by the bed looking at her, his head tilted. "Sadness has marked your face."

Marked . . . ? Probably tears had tracked through the dirt. He walked into the adjacent bathroom and ran water, then emerged with a washcloth. She expected him to be cruel, to gloat, maybe even hit her. This she didn't expect. It alarmed her even more than retaliatory violence.

"So pretty," he said as he wiped in gentle strokes.

The washcloth moved down her throat to the open collar of her shirt. It was the first time she'd seen him close up as a human. His features were blunt, mouth square, eyebrows thick slashes. His mouth and chin jutted out slightly, a faint resemblance to a dog's snout. He tossed aside the cloth and pulled her head forward. She felt him tugging at the band that held her braid. He tossed that aside, too, jerking his fingers through her hair to unravel it. She winced at his roughness but kept her expression stiff and neutral.

His gaze settled on her face. "Do not cry. It makes your nose red and eyes puffy."

He stroked her face. His fingers were weirdly smooth and soft, but the touch shot her heartbeat up into her throat. She said nothing, remaining absolutely motionless.

"I saw you and the hunter touching each other. Kissing. Humans enjoy the mating experience." He put his hand on her breast. "It woke something in me."

She shuddered, both from his touch and the knowledge that he'd seen them. Where? Obviously out in the open. She saw the flame of desire in his dark brown eyes. *Desire.* He wanted her, sexually.

Panic clawed through her. "When . . . when humans get involved physically, it's because they want to. Because they feel a deep desire for each other."

His smile grew wider. "I want to. I feel a . . . desire."

"I don't. Both parties have to be willing." She sure as hell wasn't going to explain rape to him.

He was still stroking her, his gaze on his hand as it moved to her other breast. "You will be willing. I saw the willingness grow between you and the hunter. It will grow for me, too."

The grief Cheveyo felt while bumping along in the hot trunk of the car was not for himself. Knowing that Petra was in harm's way and he couldn't do a damned thing to save her, it washed over him, searing him more than the heat that nearly suffocated him. Pain tore his thoughts to shreds. Hard to hold onto anything. Petra's voice? Calling out to him? Probably delirium.

Pain throbbed through his chest and then seemed to envelop him as much as the heat. It grew duller, though, but with the dullness came the inability to take a deep breath.

Dying.

The car stopped. He heard doors open and close, expected the trunk lid to open. Footsteps walking away, one pair. Was she still in the car?

He couldn't keep his eyes open anymore, though there was nothing to see other than a slash of light from a rusted-out hole near the rear wheel well. One last hope. He tried to speak, but his mouth wouldn't work.

Father? Are you there?

Wayne's face, wracked by sadness. *Son. It is as I saw. It is her fault—*

No, it's not. Can you save her?

I cannot intercede, cannot affect the physical world anymore.

You saved me once. Save me now so I can get her.

I had help then, help I do not have access to now. You will join me soon.

The disappointment in his father's voice was deeper than his grief. Wayne's face faded away.

No, I can't abandon her.

Cheveyo tried to move, but his body was too weak. He couldn't even connect to Petra. It took more energy than he had. He would die and leave her in the hands of the enemy. For the first time, he was afraid of dying.

CHAPTER 19

The numbness that had frozen Petra cracked apart into tiny, glasslike shards. Baal leaned closer, and his gross breath washed over her. "Humans kiss each other. I've seen it many times, sometimes a quick kiss"—he gave her a peck, his lips soft and mushy—"and sometimes a longer one, like what you and the hunter did. It went on for so looong," he said, drawing out the last word.

Her stomach curled even before his mouth touched hers again, rubbing back and forth against her lips. Thank God he didn't seem to know about French kissing. She would throw up if his tongue touched her mouth. He moved down her neck, leaving a smelly, wet line of saliva. His canineness came through as he lapped at her skin with a flat long tongue, down to her collarbone and the hollow of her throat.

Everything he'd seen her and Cheveyo do.

"He pulled up your sweater and removed the thing that binds these." He squeezed her breasts.

Her body was as stiff as a sheet of metal, muscles tensed so hard they hurt. She hardly breathed.

He yanked her shirt above her head, though it

wouldn't go farther than her bound hands. He left it there and studied the bra clasp. "He did something with his fingers. How does it work?"

"I can't explain it to you. When you do something every day, it becomes such a habit, you don't know exactly what you're doing."

It didn't deter him. He narrowed his eyes, tugging at the plastic clasp, twisting it, and finally tore the bra. A whimper escaped her throat at the bare vulnerability that ripped through her.

"Yes, I like the sounds you made. Make them with me."

"What you hear from me is terror and disgust. With him it was pleasure. You can't make me feel pleasure or desire."

He didn't seem put off. "I can and I will."

He leaned down. She could only see his bushy brown hair, and then his mouth clamped over her nipple. She screamed. He didn't stop, only left his slimy trail all over her, moving from one breast to the other. Tears slid down the sides of her face, the violation, the loss, everything. Cheveyo was in the trunk of the car, dying, or already—

No, don't think it.

He shook her. "Make more noises. And smile."

He moved his mouth across her stomach and down, and then she felt him fumbling with the button on her pants. He hadn't seen them make love. They'd done that in a private suite far from prying eyes.

"I can't," she said, her words a whimper.

Maybe he realized he couldn't remove her pants or spread her legs with her feet bound together.

He stripped off his shirt, revealing a mat of dark fur across his chest. "Kiss me, lick me like you did with the hunter."

His name is Cheveyo, dammit. But she didn't want to hear his name coming from this creature's lips. Bad enough that Yurek had looked like him.

"Do everything to me that you did with him," he said, his voice guttural.

"I can't, not when I'm tied up like this."

He leaned over her face, pressing his mouth on hers. Her eyes were squeezed shut, trying to close him out. She felt his nipple against her lips, surrounded by coarse fur. She curled her lips inward.

"Put your mouth on me!" His breath washed over her with his harsh words.

"I told you, you can't force what you saw between us!"

Frustration tinted his face red as he sat back. She could see his mind working, trying to figure out how to force her into submission.

An odd calmness stole through her, and with it, an idea. It was crazy, insane, but it was all she had. "I'll make you a deal. I'll . . . cooperate, the way you want, if you let me go out to see the hunter. I need to say goodbye to him. If I can do that, it will ease my pain."

He considered that, probably weighing the risks.

"You can keep me tied up," she added. "Carry me out."

"So you can't run away."

"Exactly." She felt her energy rise as her hopes did. "I love him. I just need to say goodbye, to touch him one last time."

What if he was already . . .

No, don't go there now. No way could she go through with the deal if he was. It wouldn't matter, none of this would matter.

Or maybe his father had healed him, and Cheveyo would leap out when the trunk was opened.

"Afterward, you'll make pleasurable noises, and kiss me? You'll do everything I saw. And more?"

"Yes, everything." Whatever *more* meant. She shuddered.

"All right. But I will kill you if you try anything."

He began to untie her hands from the headboard.

"I won't. You've won. There's nothing more I can do."

His mouth turned up at that. He wound the rope around her wrists again, pulled her to the edge of the bed, and slung her over his shoulder.

He opened the door and looked outside, leaning to the side to make sure the trunk was still closed probably. Nothing had changed.

She watched the ground bob up and down as he walked. He used the key to unlock the trunk and popped the lid.

Blood. So much blood. It pooled in the bottom of the trunk, but wasn't flowing anymore. She noticed that before the heat that billowed out. Cheveyo was still lying on his side. Was he breathing? Dammit, she couldn't tell.

Baal set her on the rim, his hands tight on her shoulders. "Do what you came to do."

She twisted around, trying to reach Cheveyo with her hands tied in front of her. Her fingers strained and then touched the fabric of his shirt. She leaned farther in, though Baal was gripping her waist to keep her from falling into the trunk. She was able to touch Cheveyo's face. He was still warm, but that could be because of the hot trunk. His hand was splayed over his wound. His skin was damp with sweat, though, which meant he was alive. Alive!

"Cheveyo," she whispered.

His eyes opened, glassy and unfocused. It took a

moment for them to shift toward her. He was cognizant! She laughed and cried at the same time.

"Time to go," Baal growled.

"I'll give you all the time you want. Just give me a couple more minutes."

Without waiting for his response, she closed her eyes and let her energy flow into Cheveyo. Pain seared her chest, in the same place where he had been shot. It didn't hurt as much as seeing him dying had.

Through the pain she pushed out the words, "Goodbye, sweetheart. I love you. Please forgive me. And don't be mad at me. I love you, I love you, I love you. . . ." She kept whispering the words, buying time.

"That's enough." Baal pulled her back and slammed the trunk lid shut. She stumbled at the sudden movement, but his hands clamped around her waist to keep her steady. He flung her over his shoulder and walked to the house. "Now you do your part."

Had it worked? She felt the pain, and was so tired. Good signs.

"Finally, a smile," he growled when he laid her on the bed.

She *was* smiling, even through the excruciating pain. Her body went limp, melting into the bed. She could see him leaning over her to retie her hands to the headboard, but he was getting fuzzy. Then she couldn't see anything because she couldn't keep her eyes open. His hand grasped her jaw and rocked her head back and forth.

"Hey. You're not going to sleep now, bitch."

She tried to say something but her mouth would barely move. Her words came out a mumble. She wasn't even sure what she was saying. She saw Cheveyo, his image floating in the darkness beyond her eyes.

You're okay now, she told him. *You have a chance to make this right.*

From a long distance she heard shouting, and felt her body being shaken. But it wasn't her body anymore. She floated out of it.

Pope's phone rang. He had just stopped for nourishment and was about to get back on the road. Petra's number showed on the screen. "How did it go?" he answered.

"Not as well as you'd hoped."

Yurek's voice. He let his words, and what they meant, sink in for a horrifying moment.

"The hunter is dead. I have your daughter."

He felt the fluids in his body go cold. "My . . ." Yurek thought Petra was his daughter, probably the reason he'd targeted her. Yurek no doubt had picked up on her Callorian essence, and it was a logical reason for her existence. "I don't believe you."

"I thought you might like proof. I will send you pictures and call back momentarily."

He saw the pictures, and he felt . . . *felt* sadness, devastation. The wound in Cheveyo's chest was mortal. Petra was tied up, Baal leering in the picture with her. The phone rang again. He pressed the button but words failed to come out of his mouth.

"I will take the hunter's body back with me. The girl, though, I could let her go. She means nothing to me. You, however, are an outlaw, Pope. An outlaw with secrets. I suspect your secrets are more than this girl. It is my duty, as a Collaborate Shine, to apprehend you. Of course, you understand this, having been one yourself. Do the right thing and turn yourself in. I will go beyond the right thing and release the girl."

Those words weighed heavily on Pope. It had bothered him to not be part of Cheveyo and Petra's plan. He had never felt so helpless before, not even when he faced the C. "You have told the C about her, though."

"Yes, but she might have fallen into a crevice out in those treacherous mountains. I couldn't retrieve her body and so decimated her remains from a distance. She is no threat to our dimension, so I see no true crime in altering the truth slightly."

His mind sorted through his options as his fingers tightened on the steering wheel. He would not let Petra die. Cheveyo . . . it was too late for him. He closed his eyes, saw that horrible image of him. He recognized the Sinthe's wound pattern. Yurek had brought a weapon with him. He obviously hadn't left his mercenary ways behind.

"How will I know that the girl is free and safe?" he asked.

"Baal will take her near a populated place, and when you arrive at the roadside in the Zion Park area, he will bring her into town. You may speak to her. Then you will come with me with your last scrap of honor." As though there was honor in handing himself over to Yurek. "If you try to fight me, the girl will die anyway. Baal must hear from me once I've delivered you or he will recapture her."

Despair. Yes, he could feel that, too. An Elgin would sacrifice the safety of one to protect others. Petra would opt for that, too. Sentencing her to death, though, sickened him. She felt like a daughter to him, or what he thought a daughter might feel like.

He heard Suza's voice in his head, telling him with

sincerity in her blue eyes that he had a good soul. A man with a good soul would not let his daughter die.

He could save Petra and take care of the biggest threat to the Offspring: himself. Once Petra was safe, he would go willingly with Yurek. Before they reached the finestra, he would bluff Yurek by showing him he could teletransport by moving several yards away. Then he would hold out his hand as though to blast him. Yurek would respond instinctively, using the Sinthe on him. To ensure it was immediately fatal, Pope knew he would have to lunge at Yurek.

"When do I meet you there?"

"In one hour."

"I will need two to get there."

"Oh, that's right. You can't teletransport, can you? A shame to be impotent, isn't it?"

Pope gritted his teeth at the taunt. "I trust that when you joined the C, you promised to uphold its values. Like keeping your word."

"Yes. Attaining your position is something I have wanted for a long time. Bringing in the former Elgin turned Scarlett will be my biggest triumph. But only the first of many."

"I will see you at four."

Pope disconnected. Dying was the only way out, and he should welcome the relief from an existence that included little that meant much to him. He couldn't get involved in the Offsprings' lives, couldn't start a life here. That he was responsible for Cheveyo's death added to his load. Death should be welcoming, but it wasn't. And should he fail and be taken back to Surfacia, he would know that his responsibility for deaths would become much heavier. He would have to succeed in dying here.

* * *

Baal poked at Petra's shoulder. "Do not pretend to sleep. You promised you would cooperate."

He took in her limp body. Before, she'd been stiff, her mouth in a grimace. Now she looked . . . dead. He shoved her sweater up over her head again, but this time he was watching her chest for the rise and fall. He saw the faintest of movement. She could be pretending. He leaned down and licked her neck. No stiffening at all. He put his mouth over her breast, something that had gotten the most response from her. Not even a twitch. He clamped his teeth down on the fleshy part of her breast.

Still nothing, even as red teeth marks formed on her pale skin. He pulled her sweater down, panic rising in his throat. Something had happened when she went out to the hunter. He pushed up from the bed and slammed his fist against the wall, denting the drywall. She had cheated him.

But fear loomed bigger than his anger. Yurek was going to be furious.

Yurek was pleased with the way things were going. He called Baal. "Everything is set for two hours from now. I will find the best place to take the girl. She must not be harmed, as she is to assure Pope that she is free and fine."

"Uh, there's a problem. The girl is dying."

"I hope you are developing, or trying to develop, a sense of humor."

He heard the reluctance in Baal's voice, though. It wasn't a joke.

"I don't know what happened to her," Baal said. "She was fine, and then she pleaded with me to take her out to the hunter."

"You didn't."

"I saw no way she could gain a weapon or escape. She was tied up. I carried her out and stood beside her the few minutes I allowed her to say goodbye to her lover. She touched him for no more than a few seconds, and right after I brought her back into the house, she passed out. She is barely breathing now."

Yurek gritted his teeth. "You idiot!" He held in the other words that threatened to spill out. It was done. "She didn't ingest anything or grab a hidden weapon and stab herself?"

"No. I watched her. She only touched him."

"She has to be faking it."

"I don't think so. I bit her hard, and she had no re-action."

"She's no good to us if she's not awake." He stood next to the hunter's bike, a fine machine. "Pope is going to meet me near the finestra. Once he learns I cannot produce proof of the girl's release, he will resist. But he will be close to the finestra. I will injure him and get him through."

"See, everything will work out after all. What should I do with the girl if she does not revive?"

Yurek considered whether he needed to bring her body back to Surfacia. No, the hunter's body would be enough. "Eat her. Leave no evidence behind." He heard the Glouk's intake of breath. "Is the hunter dead?"

"He was hardly alive."

"Make sure he's dead and bring his body to the finestra. Meet me there in two hours." He disconnected, feeling his human body tighten. As soon as he completed his mission, he would return for the Glouk.

Once back in Surfacia, he would be revered—three beings in addition to his quarry. That it wasn't easy should prove his fortitude. The C would know he was more than capable—and deserving of the accolades Pope had once garnered. He was on his way to becoming an Elgin.

Cheveyo didn't know how long he lay there, feeling the perspiration drip down his sides and the pain thrum through him. He didn't hear the footsteps, but suddenly the lid opened, infusing the trunk with fresh air and light. And the sight of Petra, being carried by the Glouk, her hands bound. It was a struggle to open his eyes. Seeing her was heaven and hell. She reached out with bound hands and placed them on his face. She whispered words of love and apology, and he felt her energy flow into him.

No, dammit! Don't kill yourself. You need all the energy you can get. You can still get out of this alive.

If she heard him, she didn't respond. She stared at him, and everything she'd said glowed in her eyes. She loved him. He couldn't say it back, couldn't will his body to obey him. The pain lessened by degrees, as though she were vacuuming it out of him. Baal said something to her, and the lid shut again.

He flexed his fingers and felt the torn edges of his shirt, the dried blood . . . but no gaping hole in his chest. His body needed to recuperate. It protested when he tried to move in the confining space. No time for rest. He had to get Petra.

He reached up and felt the inside of the lid for a release pull. It glowed slightly, and he pulled at it. Damn, he was so weak. It took two yanks to release it. He was ready for anything, but only baby-blue sky greeted him. He climbed out of the trunk and felt for his knife: gone, along with his keys. All he had was his phone. He needed to be cat. He closed his eyes.

Nothing happened.

Only the tingle, and then it fizzled out. He'd lost his powers because she'd healed him. He had no weapon, no abilities. *You have anger and a fierce hunger to save her.* He peered around the open lid of the trunk, seeing the house. He took the cat position and crept to the front window, becoming one with the brush that grew there.

The living room was pristine, and empty. He moved to the next window, and what he saw seemed to slam his heart right out of his chest. Petra tied to a bed, Baal pulling her sweater up over her head, gazing at her naked chest.

His eyes went black, but that was all he could do. It didn't matter. He backed up and launched himself at the window. In his mind he was cat, crashing through the glass, his murderous glare on Baal. Glass cut him, but he felt nothing beyond his rage. Baal fell back, eyes wide in shock. Cheveyo leapt at him the second he'd gained his balance. His hands clamped around Baal's throat and he rammed his head against the wall. A picture fell, glass shattering. Rage suffused him the way the heat in the trunk had. He kept slamming Baal against the wall, crashing through the dry-wall. He spared a glance at Petra, who lay motionless on the bed, her beautiful boobs—breasts—bared. On the rounded flesh of one . . . a *bite mark*.

That violation surged through him. A growl of rage blew through and out of him. He covered Baal's face with his hand, twisted him to the side, and with every ounce of strength shoved him through the broken window. One of the shards cut into Baal's throat, sending blood spurting over his hand.

Heaving deep breaths, he let go, and Baal slumped to the floor in a heap. The glass hadn't hit an artery,

but he'd bleed out—the same death that Baal and
Yurek would have let him suffer in the trunk.

He turned and ran to the bed. Petra's face looked
so peaceful that for one breath-stealing moment he
thought she was dead. But he could feel the life in her,
barely there. He pulled down her sweater and tore the
ropes from the bed frame, then unwound her hands
and her feet.

"Petra." Agony saturated the word.

God, he'd been here before, holding her and fearing she was dead. Her loose hair spilled over her
shoulders in a golden fall. He slid his hand up her
neck to feel the pulse point at her throat. As shallow as her life force. Everything inside him fell away,
sucked into a giant black hole. She'd given her soul to
save him.

He ran his hands over her face. "Petra."

That time it was a whisper, all he could manage.
She hadn't moved, not a tremor to acknowledge that
she'd heard him. "Come back to me, babe. Don't
leave."

She was no longer the woman he'd loved from afar.
She was inside every cell of his body, the light in his
soul . . . and she was dying in his arms.

He turned to Baal, having forgotten him. A dangerous move. Baal was clutching his wound the way he
himself had not long ago, trying in vain to stanch the
blood, gasping and gurgling.

Cheveyo released Petra for a moment, searching
the room for the keys to the vehicle outside. He found
them on the nightstand and scooped them up. He
pulled out his phone and called Pope.

Pope answered, "What the hell do you want now?"

He blinked in surprise. "Pope? It's Cheveyo."

Silence for a moment. "Is this a trick? Look, Yurek,

you won't get anything more out of me by pretending to be him. Considering that you made sure I knew he was dead, I don't see the point."

"It's not Yurek. You're driving my RV, which I call the Tank, and if you open the glove box, you'll find pictures of Petra and a boy underneath the maps."

A few seconds later Pope said, "How . . . ? I saw a picture of you with a hole in your chest. Was it a fake?"

"Petra healed me, and now she's dying. Healing mortal wounds sucks everything out of her, infusing her with the injuries. She's done this too much in recent months. She's fading fast. Can you heal her?"

"I will try."

Hope surged through him, though it didn't last long. They were running out of time. He realized what Pope had said first. "You've talked to Yurek?"

"I'll explain later. I'll come to you." A few seconds later, he said, "I can't teletransport. Where are you?"

"I've got the keys to the car they used. I'll meet you in the middle to save time."

They coordinated a meeting place and hung up. He hoisted Petra and then turned to Baal on the floor, gasping his dying breath. No way would he survive. Cheveyo tried to remain impartial where his prey was concerned, but he couldn't, not with Baal. Or with Glouks. "Die a long, painful death, you son of a bitch," he said, and walked out.

He set her on the front seat, laying her head on his thigh, then tore out of the driveway. His fingers stroked her cheek as he drove, and he couldn't stop looking down at her.

"Stay with me, babe."

He remembered hearing a similar plea from her after he'd been shot. If he lost her . . . he would have nothing left inside him. It would melt into a black puddle and seep down a drain.

She had said she loved him, over and over, her endearments a light in the dark pain and semiconsciousness he'd been in.

"I love you."

The words felt foreign as they rolled off his tongue. He had only said them to his son, though he'd never heard them from his own father. He had loved Petra for as long as he could remember, but voicing those feelings was far different. He cleared his throat, alternately watching the road and her.

"I love you, Petra."

She had brought his humanity alive. Brought his heart alive. That night in Vegas, he had been a man, a lover. For the first time, he'd been something other than a warrior or monster that killed.

This pain, though, came with being a man. Came with loving. Of all the injuries he'd sustained, this was one he wasn't sure he could overcome. He searched the highway for the turnoff where he would meet Pope. He might be able to heal wounds . . . but Cheveyo doubted he could raise the soul dead.

CHAPTER 20

This was how being human got you killed, Baal thought. Desire had blinded him, swayed him. He would survive because Yurek had Black Lavender, the miracle gel. He grabbed the curtain and shoved it against the cut at his neck. Pain sliced through him at the pressure.

He reached down to his pocket, where he kept the phone. Holding it up so he could see it, he hit the button that would dial Yurek.

"Where are you?" Yurek answered, anger in his voice.

"At the house." His voice was weak. "The hunter stabbed me."

"The hunter? You said he was near dead. What the hell is going on over there? Are you wholly incompetent?"

Yurek would be furious when he found out they were both gone. "I don't know, but . . . whatever she did that drained her, I think it healed him. He cut me. I need the Black Lavender, right away."

"Are the girl and the hunter still there?"

"He took her, drove away in the car. Please, come now."

Silence for a moment. "The hunter's phone was in the car," Yurek said then. "I'm sure Pope won't be meeting me now. I'll be there as soon as I can."

The phone disconnected. Baal was grateful to have a partner, someone who would help him. He had messed up but he would prove himself.

Minutes passed, though he had no idea how many. The edges of his vision closed in, though if he blinked, they widened again. He had no saliva to moisten a throat as dry as the land they'd been traveling over lately. He couldn't hold onto human form any longer. It was too much effort. He felt his body morph to dog. The blood started flowing out again, with the movement and lack of pressure against the cut. He was fading when he heard the bike's engine outside the broken window. A few seconds later Yurek walked in and paused at the sight of him.

"Got yourself into a real mess, didn't you?"

Baal moved his paw, scraping the floor, pleading.

Yurek finally walked over and crouched next to him. But he made no move to pull the vial out of his pocket. "I'd like to know just how she got you to give in. You're in no shape to tell me, though." He stood again and finally dug in his pocket. Not the vial in his hand. The Sinthe. "You have outlived your usefulness, Glouk."

Baal shook his head, wishing for the strength to become human, to beg for his life. He whimpered instead, all he could do.

Yurek pointed the gold weapon at him. The white beam shot out, cutting into him. Not a quick shot like he'd done to the hunter. Yurek held it on him, and it felt as though it were setting him on fire.

"I hate to use up my juice, but I can't leave your body here, and I have no way to get you to the finestra. I'll have to disintegrate you."

He smelled burning flesh. Agony. Smoke. In a blinding flash it was over.

Cheveyo saw the Tank up ahead, pulling behind the closed fruit stand. He looked down at Petra, still out but breathing softly. He parked on the other side of the Tank so that anyone driving past wouldn't see the car. Pope was already out the side door, running toward the car. Cheveyo swore he saw fear and concern in his expression.

"Open the passenger door!" he called as Pope approached.

Pope did, taking in Petra's fetal position. "I can barely feel her Essence. I get no emotions from her at all."

"Pull her out. I'll come around and get her." Pope had her in his arms by the time Cheveyo came around, so he led the way into the Tank. "Here, on the couch."

Pope laid her down gently, his gaze on her, eyebrows furrowed.

Cheveyo crouched next to her, taking her hand in his. "Save her," he whispered, hardly recognizing that raw voice as his own.

He'd never felt so helpless. He was a warrior, not a healer. No doctor could help her. He knelt down beside her, out of the way. Pope's large hand hovered over her as though he were looking for something. His mouth turned to a frown. "I have only healed physical wounds. This is a psychic wound." He met Cheveyo's gaze. "I'll try. I'll do whatever I can."

"Baal bit her. Here." He waved his hand over where

the bite mark was. "The son of a bitch bit her. And I couldn't stop him. Now I can't save her."

"Put your hand here." Pope placed his hand above her upper chest. "I don't know why, but I think it might help to add your energy to mine."

Dried blood lined the crevices of Cheveyo's hand, where he had put it on his wound. He felt . . . something. A sense of peace. Of her. They were connected by blood and by psychic bond. The night they'd sanctified the knife, when he'd cut his hand as well, she'd pressed hers to his, mixing their blood.

Now I'm yours, too.

He sank into the connection, closing his eyes and swimming through the ether of her soul. Always, he felt her, her joy, pain, whatever she was experiencing. Like Pope had said, now there was nothing except remnants of peace. His heart crashed. She was gone.

"Don't give up yet," Pope said, obviously picking up his despair.

Cheveyo sank into her again, pressing his forehead against her side. He floated like a small bubble in a huge pool of water. Searching for signs of life. Of her.

Petra. Where are you?

In the distance, a glow caught his eye. He swam toward it. It seemed to take forever. Finally it came into focus: a golden staircase that curved skyward. Standing midway up was a woman in a long flowing dress.

Petra.

She was faced away from him, her hands on the railing as she lifted her foot to the next step. He moved closer. The atmosphere was like water, making it hard to navigate.

"Petra." The word wasn't audible, not in a normal sense. He didn't think he even opened his mouth.

She turned, and her ethereal beauty stunned him. She was the source of the glow he'd seen. Her hair held a golden sheen, and her eyes were so blue they almost hurt to look at. Her face transformed into a smile. "Cheveyo." Her smile faded. "What are you doing here? You're not . . ."

"Dead? No. And neither are you."

He made it to the base of the staircase, standing several steps below her, leaving her feet at his eye level. He tried to climb higher but his legs wouldn't move. He reached up to her, but it felt as though his body would break apart if he moved too close. "Come here to me."

"I can't. I have to keep going." She gestured to the steps above her.

"They don't lead anywhere. They disappear just above you."

She looked and then nodded, that beatific smile still in place. "It's like those cool puddle mirages on the road, only opposite. As soon as I get to the top of those steps, more appear." She took another step to show him, and one more tread appeared. "See."

His throat tightened. "Don't go any farther." He tried to follow one step up, but the tearing sensation increased. A sense of fear tightened inside him.

She, however, looked at peace. "I have to."

"Who says?"

"I can't explain it, but it's just something I know." She touched the center of her chest. "Here."

He reached as far as he could, gasping at the pain of the tearing, pushing against it, grabbing onto her hand. It felt strange, more like a tingling energy in the shape of a hand. "Why did you save me? You knew you'd put your life on the line."

She tilted her head, looking genuinely puzzled.

"I can't remember what happened down there. It's fading away with every step I take."

"But you know who I am."

Her smile was so angelic, it gripped his chest. "I've always known you, love."

Even though he wasn't in physical form, his reactions felt physical. Those words, and the soft way she'd said them, actually brought tears to his eyes. "Stay with me. Please."

Her smile faded. "I can't."

"I'm not letting you go." He tightened his grip on her hand.

"You have to. It's time."

"I love you, Petra. It's not time, dammit. I was supposed to die, not you." He lifted his face to look beyond her. "I was supposed to die! It was *my* time! Take me. Me!"

Silence throbbed through him. It was no good. He couldn't talk his way out of this. So he would act. He lunged for her, his arms wide.

The tearing . . . it hurt, like his soul being torn from his body. He felt her in his arms for a second. Closed them around her. A blinding light knocked him back, and he fell and fell without landing. He saw nothing but shards of brilliance. Then nothing. Nothing at all.

Petra came to consciousness a little at a time. Being in her body felt strange at first, which was odd in itself, since it was, after all, *her* body. She was hyper-aware of her breathing, and then of the energy flowing through her, the way Cheveyo had shown her. She felt a soft mattress beneath her. The scents she smelled were familiar and comforting. She breathed them in. Sage, before it was burnt. *Cheveyo.* She smiled at the thought of him.

Cheveyo.

His name jolted her heart. He had almost died. Where was he? Where was she? Those questions made her open her eyes. Relief swept through her. He was the first thing she saw, lying on his back, face turned toward her. He was bare-chested, his hair lying on his cheek.

"You're awake."

Not Cheveyo's voice. She lurched up, getting dizzy from the sudden movement, frantically searching for . . . what? Danger.

Pope pushed up from the chair he'd been sitting in, setting aside a magazine as he did so.

She exhaled, releasing the adrenaline surge. "Pope."

He smiled, coming up to the side of the bed. "You're feeling all right?"

"I . . . I don't know exactly. I feel weird." She patted her hands down her body, still in the sweater and pants she'd had on . . . that day? Then she looked around. She was in the cabin, in the master bedroom. "But I'm okay, I think." She turned to look at Cheveyo. He hadn't moved, hadn't sensed her awakening. "Is he . . . ?"

"I don't know. When you died, he—"

She jerked her gaze back to Pope. "When I died? *Died?*"

"You were fading fast. He was connected to you psychically. I felt your life force fade completely. Every muscle in his body contracted. He lunged forward, then collapsed. He's been out ever since; you both have. I brought you here, but I wasn't sure if your souls were even in your bodies." He looked at Cheveyo. "I'm still not, as far as he's concerned."

She turned back to Cheveyo, her chest opening at

what his words meant. "I don't remember anything. No tunnel or white light or anything." Her voice dropped to a whisper. "He brought me back from death's door." Somehow she knew that. She knelt next to him, her hand on the round weal where that horrible hole had been. "Now I'll bring him back." She started kissing his face, his temples, eyes, the bridge of his cheeks.

He didn't come back as gently as she had. He lurched up, his eyes wide and terrified, body stiff. She fell back from his movement. He sucked in great, deep breaths, taking in the room with wild eyes, Pope, and then her.

She put her hand on his leg. "It's okay. You're home. Safe."

He jerked her against him without warning, his hands splayed on her back, crushing her against his chest. His silver jaguar pendant pressed into her skin, but she didn't care. She held him as tightly, her fingers threading into his hair.

Cheveyo held onto her like that for a full minute before letting go. He ran the back of his hand along her cheek, taking her in as though he couldn't quite believe she was real.

She laughed softly. "Are you all right?"

He looked at Pope. "You saved her."

Pope stood there awkwardly crossing his arms and then uncrossing them. "I didn't save her. You did. And I almost lost you both."

That troubled him. She saw the lines on his face, lines she'd never seen before. He always looked ageless, his pale skin smooth. Now, though, he took them in and smiled, a real smile.

"You're beginning to feel, Pope," she said in wonder.

"I think I have always had feelings, but they were deeply buried. Being with you, feeling what you feel, has awakened them. I find it easier not to have them, quite honestly. The last day has been nerve-wracking."

"Last day?" Cheveyo asked, running his hand back through his hair. "When did everything happen? How long was I asleep?"

"You've both been asleep since she died and you went after her. That was yesterday. It is now the next morning."

She died. Those words rolled through her like a wave. She had died, hadn't she? She touched Cheveyo's arm. "You went after me?"

"I remember connecting to you, deeper than I've ever done before. But nothing more. Do you remember anything about it?"

She shook her head. "I wish I did."

"Me, too." He stared beyond her, as though trying to conjure the memory.

Pope walked to the door. "I'll prepare some breakfast." His mouth curved into a slight smile. "Yes, I'll remember to defrost the bread and juice." Then he left, closing the door behind him.

"I need a shower." Cheveyo climbed off the bed and turned to hold out his hand to her.

She let him pull her to her feet, and into him. He kissed her, soft and sweet, and then led her into the bathroom where he turned on the shower.

She took off her clothes and stuffed them into the small garbage pail, remembering how he had done the same thing so long ago. Now she understood why. She felt dirty and grimy in so many ways. He was looking at her in the mirror's reflection. He walked over, running his hands over her breasts, but more in an exploratory than a seductive way.

She looked down. "What?" Her reflection revealed nothing strange.

"You had a scratch here." He ran his finger along the side of her breast. "It's gone. Pope must have healed it."

"Pope saw me naked?"

He chuckled. "No, but I vaguely remember telling him about it." His smile disappeared when he saw the weal on his chest. "Petra . . ."

She came up behind him, her hands going around his waist. "I know, you're mad at me for healing you."

He turned to her. "Mad. *Mad.* You threw your life away to heal me. Something I told you not to do."

"I couldn't let you die." The thought of it, even now, tore through her heart. "But it was more than an impulsive emotional decision. Even without your abilities, which you might lose because I healed you, you still have a much better chance of getting these guys than I do." She crossed her arms over her chest. "It was a practical decision."

He brushed her hair from her face, his expression dark and serious. "You have found your other archetype, the one I hoped you wouldn't discover. You, too, are a warrior, when you're willing to sacrifice your life for others, when you're able to make logical decisions in the face of trauma."

She, a warrior? The word rumbled through her. "It wasn't totally logical. The thought of you dying nearly killed me. And Baal . . . he was going to rape me. In the face of all that, dying wasn't a hard choice."

"Baal's dead." His eyes darkened and his voice grew gruff. "Did it hurt you?"

She shuddered, not wanting to know what he'd seen and what he'd done. "Baal saw us kissing. I think it was after we'd missed Yurek at the first finestra." She wrapped her arms around her chest at the memory. "He . . . he was trying to be a human. He wanted to do everything he saw us do, and he wanted me to like it." Her voice hitched on that last word. She stared past him, back in those horrible moments. "He couldn't understand why I didn't respond like I did with you. He thought . . . I should enjoy him licking me, touching me . . ." She was trembling now, and he held her tighter. "After I healed you, I drifted off. I don't know what he did after that."

"Your clothes were still on, so it didn't do much." He stroked her back.

She closed her eyes, sinking into the feel of his strong body holding hers. "I made him a deal: I'd co-operate if he would let me say goodbye to you. I was so scared that you were already . . . gone."

"Oh, babe."

"I don't want to think about that anymore. I just want to wash myself, twice, three times. I want to wipe away any trace of him." She scrubbed her fingernails up and down her arms.

He stepped into the shower, and she went with him. It was big enough for both of them. He took a washcloth and lathered it up, running it down her back and then over her shoulders, gently around her breasts. The hot water created a cloud of steam around them. He focused on what he was doing, as though performing surgery. Then he squirted shampoo into his palm and scrubbed it through her hair. She lost herself in the feel of his fingers tugging through her hair and rubbing against her scalp.

When he was done, she poured shampoo into her hand and worked it through his thick hair, luxuriating in the feel of it. Damn, washing his hair felt as good as when he'd washed hers. After he rinsed out the lather, she took another washcloth from the shelf and lathered it. She loved the feel of it moving across the planes of his hard body, down his muscular thighs, around the thickness of his erection. He had closed his eyes when she started, sinking into the sensation. She set the cloth down, running her hands across his chest as the water rinsed away the suds.

"Another scar on your beautiful body," she said, not really intending to say it aloud. She ran her fingers across the smooth weal. "I thought maybe your father might have healed you, like he did before."

"I asked him. I couldn't stand the thought of you being captured by them and me being helpless. I would never have asked otherwise."

"And he refused?"

"He said he couldn't alter the physical world anymore."

Those words grated on her, somewhere deep inside. "He was right, about you dying because of me. You almost did. Would have. Which means that's not hanging over our heads anymore."

"You dying is always hanging over my head."

And she hated that. "Can you become cat?" she asked, tucking away the discomfort of that assertion. "Have you tried?"

"Yes, and no, I can't become cat."

"It will probably only last a week or so. I hope."

"Me, too. It's like part of me is missing. We only have one enemy now, but we have no real defense against him, other than my knives. And he has some kind of über-weapon. I've got to ask Pope about that." He faced her. "Petra, I appreciate you saving me, and I understand where you were coming from. But you can't do that again. You have to stop saving me."

"When you stop trying to save the world."

His expression hardened, but before he could say anything, she said, "You told me I was a warrior."

He placed his hands on either side of her face. "You are, but you're motivated by your Healer. So don't get any crazy ideas about fighting my wars with me. I almost lost you once. I can't go through that again."

"I know how you feel. Seeing you with that hole in your chest, it was like the hole was in me, too."

She'd almost lost him, and she would never, ever forget how the sight of him lying in that trunk had made her feel.

Now he was here, she could touch him, and love him. She fell against him, throwing her arms over his shoulders and kissing him. He pulled her tight, their bodies melded, their mouths lost in each other's. She knew he was feeling that same sense of urgency, of near loss, of wanting to absorb each other. He braced her against the smooth stone wall, and the feel of his erection pressing against her stomach sent desire shooting through her.

Water hit his back, sending spray all around them. His hand slid down her hip, thigh, and then around to her intimate places. She was already wet, so ready for him. Dimly she remembered that Pope was fixing them breakfast.

"Fill me," she whispered. "Right here." She wrapped her legs around his waist. "Now."

As soon as she felt the tip of him against her opening, she pushed down, gripping his wet shoulders, arching her head back. His fingers clutched her waist, moving her up and down, long steady strokes. It didn't take long for everything inside her to burst forward. And in that explosion of light and sensation, she saw a golden staircase . . . him reaching for her . . .

I love you, Petra. It's not time, dammit. I was supposed to die, not you.

And then looking beyond her, pleading with God Herself.

I was supposed to die! It was my time! Take me. Me!

Then he'd lunged for her in that surreal space.

Her eyes snapped open at the desperation and pain in his words. He was staring just past her, caught in a memory.

"Did you see a staircase?" she whispered.

He nodded, still struck by the vision.

"You pulled me back. You risked your soul to pull me back, because you love me."

He looked at her now. "I would do anything for you because I love you."

She closed her eyes and breathed in the words. A moment later she looked at him, seeing that love, that devotion, and the pain that went with it. "I love you, Cheveyo. I know you didn't want me to love you, that you wanted to protect me from that, too. But don't you see, we were meant to be together. I want to be with you. I can't not be with you, not now, not anymore. I'm a warrior. I want to be your partner."

She had faced death, and if being with him meant facing death again, she would do it.

His expression hardened, and he pulled out of her and set her on her feet. "No. Get that crazy idea out of your mind." His fingers, still clutching her shoulders, tightened painfully. "You will not be part of my darkness. Or my life. I will protect you from that. Despite what we feel, what we've been through. This ends now."

He cut the shower and stepped out, handing her a towel without looking at her.

She grabbed it, following him out. As he pulled another towel from the pile, she clamped onto his arm. "So brave, my warrior. Except for your heart."

He pulled away from her, drying himself as he walked into the bedroom. It hurt, his walking away, but she knew it was part of his way of protecting her—and himself. She followed him, kneeling down to her bag where she'd left the rest of her clothing. He'd already put on jeans and was yanking a shirt down over his head. His wet hair dampened the blue material on his back and shoulders.

With her clothing clutched in her hand, the towel held together with her other, she stared at his back. "You accused me of not facing my feelings. You were right. I am angry at my father for selling me out, for turning in Eric. And I was jealous that everyone got their happy ending but me. Me, the one who wanted it the most. But I'm not going to deny what I feel for you or that the thought of you being alone your whole life rips my heart out. Not when I'm standing right here . . . loving you." Those last words had come out in a whisper.

He walked to the door, paused and took a deep breath. Without looking at her, he said, "I realized that keeping myself away *was* as much to protect myself as to protect you." He turned to her, and she saw a mask of pain on his face. "You are my greatest weakness, Petra. I lose control when I'm with you. I let my feelings overtake my senses. When I saw Baal touching you, I went blind with rage. Fighting that way will get me killed. And if you're with me, it will get you killed, too. You can't heal me again, and whatever happened in that place, with the staircase . . . I won't be able to keep you here again. You can't stop yourself from healing me. Together, we die. That's the bottom line. I'm not willing to give in to my feelings at that price. Are you?"

She paused, taking in everything he'd said.

He walked out, letting in the scent of toast coming from downstairs. She returned to the bathroom, running a comb through her hair, staring at her reflection and seeing not the princess anymore, but a strong woman. A woman who loved a man so much it ached through every cell, every bone in her body. He was right, of course. They couldn't be together, not unless he gave up fighting evil. He would never do that. The drive was too deep, fueled by loss and revenge and a father who would never let his son go.

She settled into the thought of Wayne Kee. Why couldn't he heal his son? The question bothered her. Even more, something about Wayne himself bothered her. When she had gone to plead for him to release Cheveyo, the man had been cold at the mention of Cheveyo's son dying.

That was indeed regretful. But necessary. The boy child was leading Cheveyo astray. Softening him.

Necessary. An odd word to use. How could a boy's death be necessary?

She put on the rockin' vest she'd bought at Suza's boutique, along with the matching earrings, but her mind was working rather than enjoying the process. She ran eyeliner beneath her lashes but lost interest in the rest of her routine. Something much more important loomed in her mind. It didn't make sense, but she had to check it out.

Cheveyo's cell phone sat on the dresser, probably where Pope had left it. She picked it up and went down the stairs to the china hutch in the dining room.

Pope's voice carried to her. "Human emotions are so hard to understand."

Tell me about it.

"I thought you would be happy that you and Petra

survived. I felt great affection flowing between you earlier. But now . . ."

"Human emotions are our devils," Cheveyo said. "They tease us with things we can't have, torture us with feelings we can't act on. They cause physical pain."

"Yes, I . . . felt pain, here, when I saw the pictures of you and Petra. When my father died, I felt empty. But this pain was new."

She opened the drawer, finding the pictures he kept there. Pictures to keep his pain fresh. Cody's picture was on top, where she'd left it.

"Emotions cause physical symptoms," Cheveyo said. "When your heart is broken, it's called a heartache. When someone annoys you, they're a pain in your ass. Which, of course, goes back to what you were saying about using anatomy in our language."

She turned on the phone camera and took a picture of the picture. She tucked the phone in her pocket and closed the drawer as quietly as possible. Then she walked into the kitchen. "I used to think it was better to bury my feelings," she said. "To deny them. I thought it wouldn't hurt that way." She looked at Cheveyo, sitting at the counter in front of a plate of untouched toast. "But when you suffocate your sad feelings, you also smother the good ones. You have to know sadness to know joy. And once you've felt fear, the relief is so sweet it brings tears to your eyes."

Pope slowly nodded, as though he were trying to understand. "You two are helping me to see how many emotions there are, and what effects they have. It is much less complicated not to have them at all. But I cannot go back."

She released a long sigh. "No, we can't go back.

And we can't undo the damage they've done, or the changes they made."

Pope held out a plate to her. "You are sad. Eat."

Her mouth tugged into a frown as she took the toast. "Very. Because there is only one thing I want, and I can't have it." She flicked a glance to Cheveyo. "Only one person I want to save, and he doesn't want to be saved."

She took a bite of toast, not frozen this time. The raspberry jelly tingled on her tongue.

"There is something else, though, that I feel," Pope said. "Like an opening in the clouds of a stormy sky. I cannot identify that emotion."

It was hope that he'd picked up. She shrugged. "Cheveyo, I need to use your phone for a few minutes. I have to cancel my phone." She hated knowing that Yurek now had the names and numbers of her people. But he would have no reason to contact them. "And I want to make a call."

"Go ahead."

At least he wasn't suggesting she call Greg. She was so beyond Greg, beyond that life right now. As she walked out, she heard Pope say to Cheveyo, "And from you, I feel the opposite of what she was feeling."

Hopeless. She remembered Cheveyo saying that all he could hope for was to stay alive long enough to make a difference. She walked outside, making the necessary calls to cancel her phone. Then she called Eric.

"Hi, bro."

"Petra? I didn't recognize the number."

"This is Cheveyo's phone. I lost mine while we were hiking in the mountains."

"You . . . hiking? No friggin' way."

"You'd be surprised at the things I've been doing."

He laughed, a loud, lusty sound. "Bet I wouldn't."

"Stop that!" Oh, he could get to her. "Can you give me Nicholas's number, please?"

"Nicholas? Sure, hang on a minute." He came back. "Ready?"

She memorized the number, writing it with her finger on her arm. "Thanks."

"You sound . . . I dunno, not like yourself. You okay?"

She smiled at his concern. "A lot has changed. I'll fill you in when I get back."

"You're going to bring this guy with you, right? It's about time we met Mr. Gooey and Dewy."

Her laugh was only halfhearted. "I don't know. He's wrapped up in his job. I'm pretty sure I'll be coming back by myself." Those words leaked sadness.

"I'm sorry, sis," he said, obviously picking up on it. "I hope things work out for you. I really do."

Boy, had Fonda changed him.

"Thanks. Talk to you later."

She hung up, sent the picture via text message to the number Eric had given her, and then dialed it. Nicholas answered, and she said, "It's Petra." She went through the minimum of small talk, just to be polite. "I need a favor. I have a boy I want you to find."

"Psychically, I assume. Is he missing?"

"I'm not exactly sure. You may find him in a grave-yard." She couldn't imagine having to bury a child. The sonogram image of Amy's baby girl flashed into her mind. "But I'd like to know. I just sent you his picture."

"I see it. Cute kid. Looks like Lucas." After a pause, he said, "Eric mentioned that you were out west with Cheveyo. Is this his son?"

"Yes."

"Okay, don't tell me anything else. Too much information sometimes muddies my abilities. Everything okay? You sound down."

She really had to get better at masking her emotions in her voice. Her face, forget it. "I'm okay. This is Cheveyo's phone, so when you call back, just ask for me. Don't say anything to him, 'kay?"

"I'll get right on it."

"You're a doll."

She disconnected. Eric's concern, Nicholas's immediate willingness to help without asking questions . . . the Rogues hadn't abandoned her. She had moved away from them, emotionally at least. Whenever any of them invited her for dinner, she declined, thinking she would be the odd man out. But they *had* invited her. She let out a ragged sigh. When this was over, she was going to reach out to them. She was going to need their support, and they would give it to her. That's how they were, all of them.

She walked back to the house. When she entered the kitchen, the two men looked as though they'd gotten some bad news. Both were standing, facing each other, their expressions wildly different: Pope's was resolute, Cheveyo's not much different than what he'd worn when he told her she couldn't be part of his life.

"What's wrong?" she asked.

Cheveyo said, "Pope wants me to kill him now."

"What? No." She shook her head. "No."

"We've gotten too close," Pope said. "And now Yurek has a Sinthe, something he obviously smuggled through the finestra. We, on the other hand, are temporarily handcuffed in our abilities. Even three against one, we can't hope to keep me from being extracted. It's too big a risk. Think of your people, Petra. That baby."

"No," she said again, looking at Cheveyo. "You don't agree, do you?"

She could see that he didn't, the pain of Pope's request heavy on his expression. "I want one more chance at Yurek before we give in."

She wanted to hug him but held back. Instead, she faced Pope. "You have emotions. That makes you a sentient being and more human than you think. And . . . you mean a lot to me. Like you said, we're family. Family doesn't let family die. We do whatever we can to keep each other alive." She flicked a glance to Cheveyo, knowing she'd just corroborated his argument about them being together. Never mind that. "One more chance, like he said."

He didn't look convinced. "What's the plan?"

Cheveyo pressed his hands against the granite countertop. "We let Yurek find us here. On our turf."

She shook her head, taking in the light, open kitchen. "I don't want to trash this place."

"It's just a place. It can be replaced. People can't." He was looking at her.

It wasn't just a place to him. It was his father's refuge, and now his own. He wanted to believe it meant nothing to protect his heart. Did he do the same with her? "You can't deny what you feel for this place, just like you can't deny what you feel for me."

"I have to separate what I feel with staying alive and accomplishing our goal. They are separate things. Whatever happens to this place, I can fix or rebuild it. I want this over, and this is the best place for that to happen. It's my territory. And we have weapons, which is *all* we have."

Pope said, "I know humans get attached to their possessions. Yurek has your bike. Are you sure—"

"I'm sure. For now, we stay put." He pushed away from the counter and walked down the hall. "Find another weapon, Petra. You and Pope keep working with them. And we get ready."

They were in that strange room gazing at the gleaming knives when the phone in her pocket rang. She yanked it out and saw Nicholas's number on the screen. "Excuse me.

"Hi. Hold on a sec." She walked all the way outside, closing her eyes as the sun warmed her face. "Did you find him?" Her heart was clenched.

"Yes. He's in Phoenix."

"In . . . a graveyard? An urn?"

"Nope. Actually, he was climbing across monkey bars in a school playground."

CHAPTER 21

Yurek spent the balance of the day cleaning the rental house. It wouldn't do for the cleaning crew to find blood, a broken window, and shattered pictures. Leave no trace, one of the Collaborate rules. He'd called a repairman in the next largest town and bribed him to immediately fix the gaping hole in the drywall, as well as the window. Shines were always given plenty of financial resources when on an assignment. The money he'd received on his mercenary jobs had been better than what he would receive as a full-fledged Shine, but that wasn't as important as the prestige, the honor.

By mid-morning the handyman sought him out. "I'm done. Take a look."

Yurek inspected the bedroom. The man had painted the entire wall, and though it wasn't the exact shade of cream as the other walls, it was close enough. The window was in one piece again, the picture repaired. Yurek had to clean up the blood before the repairman came.

Yurek pulled out the amount he still owed the man and handed it to him. "That will be all, thank you."

The man counted the bills. "Thank *you*. My wife's got to have a hysterectomy and we don't have insurance, so—"

"Goodbye."

Stopped short, the man pocketed the money. "Sure, 'bye now."

Yurek followed him out, waiting until the truck was out of view before getting onto the motorcycle and starting it. Shines were trained to operate all vehicles here in the Earth dimension, but this had been his first actual experience riding one. He would procure such a vehicle on every mission from now on.

His destination was the area where he and Baal had tracked the hunter. He was sure the road leading into the woods was his residence, or at least his hiding place. He glanced at his watch. Twenty-four hours before he was to report back to Surfacia. He had no intention of returning without Pope.

Cheveyo didn't know who Petra was talking to. *And you hope it's that guy she was on the date with.*

Yeah, that's what he hoped.

He watched her from the front window as she walked away from the house for privacy. He needed to keep an eye on her, just in case. He looked up to see Pope studying him. "What?" he growled.

Pope actually smiled. "Nothing in particular."

Cheveyo looked at her again, the way the sun reflected gold on her damp hair and made her skin look like honey. The fringes on her suede vest swayed with her movements, and the neckline dipped down to tease him with the creamy vee of her cleavage. Dangling turquoise earrings peered out between the strands of her hair.

"Do you know what she wants to do? She wants

to join me, be my partner. Isn't that the craziest thing you've ever heard?"

The thought of going through this all the time, it *would* drive him crazy. He wasn't about to explore the other things it made him think of.

Pope stepped up beside him. "She's a brave woman."

"Not to mention off her rocker."

"Off . . . ?"

"Nuts. Suicidal." He took a swig of coffee and burned his mouth. He hadn't even put sugar in it. "She went from Princess to Warrior, and now she wants to fight Otherlings with me."

"She loves you. Love, not something I understand, but a powerful motivator."

Cheveyo set his mug on the sill. "I think you do feel it. But understand it? Forget that."

She lowered the phone. Her body stiffened and she stared at the woods for a moment. His senses went alert, his eyes scanning the area. She looked shell-shocked, but not afraid. Her hand went to her mouth, but there was a happy light in her eyes. She turned and walked to the front door, blinking in surprise to see him there.

"Making sure you were all right," he said. He raised an eyebrow. "Are you . . . all right?"

She stood right in front of him, still clutching the phone. "I don't know if this falls into the category of saving you or not . . ." She took a deep breath. "Cody is alive."

The words didn't make sense.

She put her hands on his shoulders, her face inches from his. "Cody is alive. I know it's hard to grasp, but I took his picture on your phone"—she held up his phone, showing him one of Cody's pictures, her hand trembling—"and sent it to Nicholas. He's a finder.

I asked him to find this boy. Nicholas found him in Phoenix in a school playground. He remote-viewed him, saw him playing. He's alive."

His knees wobbled. He took several steps back until his ass rested against the back of the big leather couch. "But I saw him die. Saw his mother dead."

"I know. I saw it, too."

"It can't be right. Nicholas is mistaken."

"Let's find out. The boy he saw was at Grammercy Elementary School. If we leave right now, maybe we can get there before school lets out."

He pushed away and walked to where he usually kept his keys.

Pope jingled them, holding them in his fingers. "Let's go."

Even as Cheveyo's mind filled with irrational hope, he scanned the road and woods as he drove. Yurek would be nearby. Not that he could feel him, but he knew the man would find the house. He made sure no one was following them, taking no chance of leading Yurek to a boy who might be his son. Leaving like this was impulsive, something Cheveyo rarely was. He glanced at Petra. Except where she was concerned.

"We're leaving an opening for Yurek to get in the house while we're gone."

Petra's mouth twisted in a frown. "I know. I should have waited to tell you. But I wanted you to know just in case . . ."

"No, it's all right." Cheveyo's fingers tightened on the wheel. "Let Yurek think he has the advantage. He'll be waiting for us when we get back. Count on it."

Pope said, "We go in pretending we don't suspect he's there."

"*You* go in. Petra and I come in from the back side. Let him think he's ambushing us; we'll ambush him."

They drove for more than two hours, going over the plan. Outside Phoenix, Cheveyo looked up the address for the school and punched it into the GPS. The woman's droll voice led them through the city to a cluster of brick school buildings. His chest was tight, and got tighter the closer they got.

"It can't be him," he said, preparing himself for disappointment.

She sat beside him. "Nicholas has never been wrong, at least as far as I know."

"He's wrong this time. It's a kid who looks like Cody."

Even so, he parked in the lot. He wanted to go inside and ask if a Cody Summers was registered. Like they would tell him anything. He wouldn't be listed on any paperwork. His name was on the birth certificate as father, but it was purposely spelled wrong in case an intelligent Otherling were to track down his records.

So he waited. Cars started lining up, parents ready to pick up their children. He looked over at Petra, sitting stiff and straight in the passenger seat, hands folded tightly on her lap as she watched. Pope stood behind her.

"I know you don't want to put too much hope into this. I know it's not logical. But I feel it." She put her hand on her chest. "He's alive."

Children started spilling out of hallways and doors. He got out of the Tank, his gaze picking through the stream of kids. Each group was escorted to the curb by what he guessed was their teacher. Cody would be nine years old. He'd been tracking his would-be progress, looking for him in every dark-haired boy he saw. What would his son be into now? he wondered in those moments. How tall would he be?

His gaze sorted through them. Petra stood next to him, searching, too. The sun seared them from overhead, rising from the black asphalt, blurring his vision. He kept blinking, staring so hard his eyes were tearing up.

That boy. Something exploded in his chest as his sight locked onto a small boy with hair that was thick and a little too wild and long. He pushed it out of his face as he talked to a boy next to him.

Her fingers clamped around his wrist. "There!"

"I . . . see." And he felt. Felt his son. Cody. Alive. He couldn't breathe.

The other boy playfully punched Cody's arm before dashing over to the car that was waiting for him. Cody waved and continued to wait. An old white car pulled to a stop, and he dragged his feet on the way to it. Cheveyo could barely pull his gaze from the boy, but he forced it to the driver.

Not Darcy, Cody's mother, or her sister Paula.

"Follow them," he said, the words pushing out of a throat so dry they were a mere whisper.

Soon he'd maneuvered his way through the slow crawl of cars onto the road and eventually into an apartment building complex. The place looked tired, the flower beds overgrown, the buildings in need of cleaning.

The woman parked in a spot designated for Apartment C-2. Cody got out, slamming the door shut and slinging his backpack on his back as he headed toward the stairs.

"He's beautiful," Petra said in a soft, reverent voice. "Go, talk to them."

"Not while I'm engaged with Yurek."

His son, standing at the top of the stairs, waiting for the woman to make her way up. His son, healthy, alive, reminding Cheveyo of himself at that age. He watched until they closed the door behind them, and only then could he release the breath he'd been holding.

Petra's hand rested lightly on his arm. "If I'm not enough to stop fighting for . . . if you're not worth it, then maybe they are. You can have a family again."

The thought of approaching the boy paralyzed him in a way that facing monsters never had. "I haven't been part of his life for almost as long as he can remember. What do I tell him about the four years I've been gone?"

If his son had inherited the cat, what then? He would have to monitor him. If he displayed signs of abilities, Cheveyo would teach him how to use them—hide them. But that wouldn't happen until adolescence.

He rubbed his hands over his face. "How? How can this be?"

"You said your father healed you, cleaned up the mess. Could he have lied?"

"I *saw* them die."

"Or thought you saw them die." He turned to her, and she shrugged. "I don't know how. But he didn't want you to have them in your lives. Think about it. They were softening you. Maybe he sensed you were thinking of giving up fighting for them."

Hadn't Wayne accused him of just that? He stood abruptly. "I need to talk to him."

"I want to be there, too." She met his gaze. "Let me come."

He nodded, his mind spinning. He walked back to the bedroom, passing Pope. *Wonder what he's picking up now?*

He climbed up to the loft and fell onto the bed. His body was vibrating so hard, he thought he might turn cat. If he could. He maintained careful control over the roil of feelings inside him. He had to get the facts first.

She reclined on her side beside him, her hand on his chest. "I was able to talk to your father this way before."

He closed his eyes, hands pressing down against the bed.

"Father."

It took several seconds before Wayne's voice said, "Son."

He chafed at the endearment, recognizing the contriteness in the word. It was something he'd never heard in his father's voice before. "My son is alive. Explain to me how that can be."

"I was protecting you. The boy and his mother as well. Getting involved with others, as you know now, is never a good idea. You made a mistake and got the woman pregnant—"

"The boy was not a mistake."

Wayne's voice hardened. "You created an untenable situation. You were softening, and that will get you killed. I could feel your desire for the boy to grow up differently than you had. With a father around, without learning defensive and offensive skills. I wanted to separate you from them so you could focus on your life's mission. I manufactured the memory of their deaths to accomplish this, as well as to fire you against your enemies. I put the idea into the mother's head to hide him away, that you were involved with dangerous people, which was true. So you see, they're safe. Perhaps it will ease your pain, the pain the woman beside you told me about. But now you must focus on your enemy."

"You bastard!" Petra's voice. "How could you take away what he loved and make him think he'd failed to protect them?"

"I do what is necessary."

In life, his father had no emotions, only a cold focus on his goal. He was still that way.

"Son, you do understand, I did what I thought was best. You were born a warrior, and that you must remain."

Cheveyo was so torn between relief and anger, he couldn't speak. "I have nothing to say to you."

He pulled out, coming to a sitting position. Petra sat up beside him, her hand on his knee. Amid the tangle of feelings inside him, he realized she had given him permission to walk away, from his life, from her. She had given him the gift of his son. Now she was willing to sacrifice what they had so he could have his family again. Not with her, but with Darcy, because she thought that's who the woman with Cody was.

"What will you do?" she asked.

He covered her hand with his. "Kill Yurek. That's all I can think about right now. I have to keep my focus."

Anger swept in, shoving the shock and numbness away. He'd lived with the grief and guilt over his son's and Darcy's deaths for four years. And for what? So his father—no, his *teacher*—could keep him focused on killing. That's all Wayne ever was to him, a teacher. Drill sergeant. Never once had Wayne told him that he loved him.

Cheveyo painfully clenched his hands into fists. Heat infused him. His soul vibrated. Petra backed away, watching him with wide eyes. But not fearful eyes.

"I see the cat trying to come through," she whispered. "Use your anger to bring back your abilities."

The morphing process teased him, coming in a quick wave and then receding.

"Your eyes are black," she said. She wanted him to change. Wasn't afraid, wasn't weirded out by it.

He summoned the energy, harder than ever. Morphing came naturally, but he pulled the anger up, like a blanket, and tried to force it. His muscles were clenched so hard they burned with the effort. A growl emanated from deep within him, half human, half jaguar.

On the edge . . .

He fell back to human, sucking in long breaths, his body sagging. "It's not the kind of anger that strengthens me. It cuts me into pieces and makes me weaker."

Her expression fell. "Maybe I should have waited—"

"No. It's all right. Knowing my son is alive, that alone gives me strength. It's the anger I have to control."

He sat on the floor and closed his eyes. The pieces of anger floated in front of him like shards of a broken mirror. If he put them together again . . .

What?

What would he see? The need to do it tugged and grasped at him, like a gaggle of kids. *Pull them together.*

It was the ultimate exercise of his control, something that had always been his pride. Petra, though, had shattered that illusion. He pulled in one deep breath after another, centering himself. In the space of his inner consciousness, he reached for one piece, then another. Each piece felt rubbery, but they fit together, the seams disappearing. One after another, some big, some small, morphing into one large, shimmering black window. When it was finished, when all the pieces were put back together, he looked into the blackness and saw . . . his reflection.

The answer is within you.

Not his father's voice but his own.

The answer to what?

Get beyond the anger and look at the whole picture.

Petra's image appeared behind him, not quite as clear as his own. Their souls were so intertwined, she was here inside him.

"False memories," she said.

At first the anger came, making the whole image shimmer. *Control it.* He was able to maintain it, though Petra was gone. False memories. He had believed, had seen, Cody and Darcy die. You always believe what your senses tell you.

The answer . . .

What if Yurek *saw* him kill Pope, himself, and Petra? If the memory were put into his mind? He would return to Surfacia and report his triumph, minus being able to extract Pope alive. No one would be sent to replace a dead Yurek. The case would be closed.

The hunter inside him reared his head, wanting to kill instead. He pushed that down. Not this time. The ultimate control: not to kill.

He would have to talk to Wayne, though. He summoned him, and Wayne's image appeared in the pseudoreflection.

"You have come to me, son? Even now?"

It was a struggle to hold back the anger, to humble himself to the man who had stolen so much from him. "Teach me how to implant memories."

"The Otherling must die. You cannot allow him to return."

"If I allow him to live, I am saving Pope, and Petra, and myself."

"But—"

"Teach me." Not a request; an order. "You owe me this."

The command hung in the air for a few moments.

Then the window in front of him shimmered, became black. Like watching a scene on a television show, Wayne's image hovered in front of his own. Wayne put his hand on Cheveyo's forehead, sending a green energy into his mind. He watched himself, as though hypnotized, knocking furniture to the floor, setting the scene, and then falling to the floor. The scene faded, leaving only his father's face.

"Do I have this ability?" Cheveyo asked. "And will it be dormant because of my healing?"

"I can give it to you, but you must allow me to go into your mind, your soul."

Cheveyo paused at that. Could he trust this man now? Definitely not. What if he put some memory of Petra dying in his head?

Wayne said, "I'm sorry that you do not trust me."

"Are you sorry that you deceived me? That you caused me such pain? You caused my mother pain, too."

"No. I have done everything for the good of others, and those with a higher calling must often sacrifice their own desires."

Anger made the image shimmer again, and Cheveyo had to once again rein it in. "But shouldn't I have a say in what I sacrifice?"

"Perhaps, but it is done. Will you walk away from your life's purpose because you are angry with me? Anger, love, these are temporary emotions that weaken you, lead you astray. You kept the girl with you, despite my warnings and the fact that you almost died. If she would have died—"

"My soul would have died with her. Give me the power. From now on, I make my own choices. I guide my own destiny."

Wayne said, "Make the right choice. Do not give up what you are."

"I know nothing else."

"Very well." Wayne's hand reached out from the window.

"Only the ability," Cheveyo told him. "Nothing more."

He felt his father's hand reach into his mind, creating a ball of heat and light that burst like fireworks.

Cheveyo's eyes snapped open then, locking on Petra, who hovered nearby. "Yurek will kill all of us in a fiery explosion that will disintegrate our bodies," he told her.

She sat back on the floor next to him, her face frozen in fear. "A precognitive vision?"

"What my father did was unforgivable. I'm going to use it against Yurek."

Her face lit up. "False memories." The exact words she'd said in the vision. She glanced at Pope, sitting on the bed. "Ohmigod, it's perfect."

"The only drawback is, I have to touch his forehead. Getting that close will be dangerous. For us and for him. I get that close, I'm going to want to kill the son of a bitch with every cell of my being." It was a good thing Yurek wasn't the one who'd tried to rape her.

Her face grew sober again. "He's got that weapon that put a hole in you."

"And *he* still has *my* ability." That rankled the most; Yurek could become his cat. He grabbed a dagger that was hidden beneath the mattress. "All I've got are normal, everyday weapons. They'll have to be enough." He manipulated the dagger in his hand. It was likely World War One era, belonging to a Russian Imperial officer. "Let's get back to the house. It's time to finish this."

CHAPTER 22

An hour later they stopped for gas. Petra watched a band of motorcyclists head out of the station's lot as she stood next to Cheveyo pumping gas. "I hope you get your bike back."

He watched them, too, one hand braced against the side of the Tank. "Compared to getting my son back, the bike is nothing."

"Yeah, when you put it that way."

He looked at her. "That was an amazing gift, one I don't know how to thank you for. How did you figure it out?"

"I didn't figure it out, exactly. It was the way your father said it was 'necessary' for your son to die, because he was making you soft. I just latched onto it and acted on a hunch."

"There are no such things as hunches. That was your inner self telling you what you needed to know. It's how I got the idea to use the false memory on Yurek. Your inner self helped in that, too."

"Mine?"

He shifted toward her. "I want to try it, make sure it works before I put my hand on Yurek."

She nodded. "Whatever I have to do."

The moment his warm hand covered her forehead, she closed her eyes. Just his touch could do that to her. A burst of energy shot into her mind, and with it flashes of images: the two of them walking through a vast field of goldenrod, him pulling her close, kissing her surrounded by the lush, tall stalks, everything in fast motion like film speeded up. She felt his hands skimming over her bare shoulders, down her sides and hips. Just when her body began responding, it disappeared.

Her eyes snapped open. "That was beautiful. Especially the last part."

He pulled his hand away, his gaze on hers. "I was going for a nice memory, but as usual with you, I got carried away."

"Not carried away enough, I'd say." She rolled it around in her mind. "Yes, it felt like a memory, as vivid as being in the tub in Vegas." She gave him an impish grin. "Only it went by a little too fast."

He looked at his hand. "It worked, then. I just projected what I wanted you to see, to feel." The triumph on his expression faded.

"Now you'll have to picture us being killed," she said.

"Yeah."

"I noticed I was wearing my vest in my false memory."

He ran his finger down the top edge of the vest, all the way down to the vee at the bottom. "I like it. But I liked it better when it was off."

She cleared her throat, feeling the skin on her chest flush with heat.

The gas nozzle clicked off, and he put it back in the pump. "Where's Pope?"

"In the store."

Pope walked out then, carrying a large plastic bag and a six-pack of soda.

She smiled. "I like him. Really like him."

"Yeah," he said as Pope neared them and pulled out several bags of chips.

"Thought we might like some snacks. There's something pleasurable about buying what you call junk food."

Cheveyo was eyeing the selection. "We should get something more nutritious. We're going to need it."

More nutritious turned out to be a quasi-fast-food burger joint, but at least they had waitresses. Petra kept fiddling with the sheath on a belt that he had fit her with from the Tank's special cabinet. Back in the RV, she worked with it, trying to maneuver it as deftly as Cheveyo had with the dagger earlier. Of course, she knew she would never be as good.

She loved his idea, but hated that he'd have to get close to Yurek to carry it out. They had talked about their plan during the drive back, mostly centering on subduing Yurek while Cheveyo did the memory-plant thing. He was quiet during the last part of the drive, and she had to stop herself twenty times from asking him what he was thinking about.

He had plenty to consider. The upcoming alterca-tion with Yurek. His son. Would he give up his war-rior role to have a normal life? Would he give her up to give his son the family he'd never had? It was more likely that he'd walk away from all of them. Walking away was all he'd ever known, as was being a warrior.

Prepare yourself for that.

She glanced back and saw that Pope was watching her, no doubt feeling her turmoil.

Cheveyo pulled into a parking lot just before they were to reach the road to his house. "Pope, you drive. Petra and I will stay out of sight."

The sun was on its way down by the time they returned to the cabin, sending long shadows across the clearing. She watched him go into full alert mode as they pulled down the road, and she searched their surroundings just as he did.

Cheveyo said, "He's here."

Petra's chest tightened. "How do you know?"

"Power's out. I keep a light on that shines in that window and one around the back. They're both off. Park to the right of the garage, where it's darkest. As you're walking out the door, we'll go out the window on the other side."

Pope's face became a cold mask. "I'll go in the front door, try the switch. That will give him the opportunity to cuff me." His mouth tightened. "Or try. Don't worry, Petra. He doesn't want me dead. Well, he might *want* me dead, but bringing me back alive will garner him the most points. The two of you, though, have to be most careful. Killing you is likely all he wants."

Cheveyo said, "But he might be happy to incapacitate you."

Pope gripped the handle of the door. "I don't feel him nearby. He's probably inside the house." He waited for them to duck down near the window before opening the door.

Cheveyo was already outside by the time Pope closed it. To be so agile. It took her a minute longer than it had taken him. Once on her feet, they crept around the back of the house.

Pope stepped on the first squeaky board, letting them know his position. Cheveyo pointed to an open window, Yurek's point of entry. Cheveyo crept to the window and studied the darkness.

She joined him. *I don't hear anything.*

He pointed at the opening. *We go in this way. Pope will draw Yurek to the front door.*

She nodded, and marveled at how easily he lifted himself through the opening. She would do the same. He watched the doorway as she climbed through and into the room she'd used the first time she came. The second floorboard squeaked.

Pope was almost at the front door. They needed to be in position before he came in. She heard him slide the key in the lock . . . and a shoe shift on the floor.

I heard him. He's in the main area, somewhere in the middle.

Pope let the door slam open, and he would slam it shut, too, giving them a few seconds of sound camouflage.

She followed Cheveyo into the living area. He moved with liquid grace, body poised to react. He rounded the corner of the staircase, ready for attack. The house was dim, the shadows here even longer as they stretched across the wooden floors and leather couch. Cheveyo could see well in the dark. He obviously didn't see Yurek.

Pope flicked the switch several times, muttering. He pulled out a cell phone and punched in some numbers. "Cheveyo, it's Pope. The power's out." The light from the screen glowed against his cheek. "All right. I'll try to find it."

She gripped the handle of her small knife. Damn, her palms kept sweating. She wiped them against her pants. Cheveyo nodded for her to follow. He kept his back to the staircase as he edged toward the arched opening into the dining room. She watched the living area, alert for sound and movement in the deepening shadows. She heard a body bump against something solid.

There! By the china hutch!

The beam shot out of the depth of the dining room inches in front of Cheveyo. He jerked back into her. Pope dove for the floor, and the beam drilled a hole into the wall near the front door. Was Yurek so desperate now that he'd bring Pope back dead?

Cheveyo twisted around the corner, launching his dagger. A grunt of pain came from the dark.

He'd been hit! How bad?

Cheveyo reached up to the bookshelves built into the front of the staircase and pulled another knife from between two books. She ducked around him. She wanted to capitalize on Yurek's shock and further incapacitate him.

He stood right there, ready to blast her with the Sinthe. She dropped, and Cheveyo lunged at his arm. Yurek shifted and the blade missed. The beam shot out again, dropping Pope to the floor as he made his way toward them.

She turned back in time to see Yurek aiming at her. A dead-close shot. She knocked his hand to the right, and the beam seared the edge of the sofa. The smell of burnt leather filled the room. Cheveyo leapt at him. Their bodies collided and the Sinthe flew out of Yurek's hand. It skidded across the wood floor and beneath the couch. Yurek morphed to Cheveyo's cat.

"Son of a bitch," Cheveyo muttered.

Now Yurek could see in the dark. He rammed into Cheveyo, knocking him against the wall, and ran toward the couch. She stuck her knife out, felt him hit the blade as he passed. He didn't falter in his leap over the couch, landing with a soft thud on the other side. She dropped to her knees and felt for the Sinthe. Her fingertips bumped the cold, smooth metal out of reach.

Dammit!

She leaned down, seeing a black paw, claws extended, about to clamp down over it.

Get the weapon, get the weapon.

Cheveyo ran up next to her and shoved the couch toward Yurek. She helped push, and it rolled over onto Yurek. A second later Yurek pushed free. Pope leapt at him. The cat bounded up and met him halfway, throwing them both through the front glass window. The sound of shattering glass made her shiver, but the worst was hearing their bodies thud hard on the front porch. The sound of flesh against flesh sent Cheveyo racing toward the window.

On her hands and knees, she desperately looked for the weapon. Cheveyo hadn't even made it to the window when the cat jumped back in through the gaping hole, throwing Cheveyo to the side. Where was Pope?

Yurek leapt across the overturned couch, landing on her, claws sinking into her back. The force took away her breath, flattening her and banging her head into the wood floor. With a growl, Cheveyo came at them with his knife. Using her as a jumping board, Yurek launched off of her. She curled up in pain, unable to breathe.

Cheveyo jumped over the couch and out of sight. She pushed up. *No time for pain. Catch your breath and go help.*

Footsteps pounded across the floor. She got up in time to see two shadows, cat and man, dash into the kitchen. Cheveyo bounded up onto the island, crouched and ready to leap onto his opponent. He couldn't change to cat, but he was all jaguar in movement and strategy. Yurek jumped up, too, probably aiming to knock him down. Cheveyo leapt to the next counter, slashing his knife midair. The tip of the blade caught Yurek along his leg, making him hiss in pain.

She clutched her knife, but they were moving too fast for her to throw it, especially in the shadows. Yurek spun, sensing her behind him, snarling. He spun again, taking in Cheveyo on his other side. They had him cornered. He growled, spinning in slow circles as they moved in on him.

If she could distract him for just a few seconds . . . "Here, kitty kitty," she said, clicking her tongue.

He did come, leaping at her. She twisted, feeling his furry body bump as he just missed her. She threw herself onto his back, wrapping her arms and legs around him. He shook, trying to throw her off, but she clung harder to his neck so he couldn't turn his head to bite her. He lifted a paw to swipe at her, but she hindered his movement, preventing him from getting in a full swipe.

She felt the tips of his claws cut into her skin before Cheveyo jumped on top of both of them, sending Yurek collapsing to the floor beneath their weight. He morphed back to man and tried to grab at her again. His fingers grabbed her arm, but the angle was too awkward for him to do more than squeeze hard. She was pinned between them, two hot, angry males. She didn't dare try to climb out and loosen the hold they had on Yurek.

Cheveyo reached around and held the knife to his throat, his hand shaking. His eyes were black and she saw the vibration, felt the heat, of the change that wanted to happen. He held on, his teeth gritted with the effort.

Yurek continued to struggle, managing to lift them a few inches before dropping again.

"Don't kill him," she whispered.

"I want to. It's what I am, what I do." He trembled, dragged in a shuddering breath. "I want to so damned bad."

"But you won't."

Silence for a moment. "No, I won't."

Then he slapped his hand on Yurek's forehead with his other hand.

Cheveyo's eyes closed. His veins stood out in his neck, mouth clenched tight.

Yurek went limp. Cheveyo released a ragged sigh and let his head hang. A second later he lifted it and met her gaze. "Pope," they said simultaneously and started to get up.

"I'm here," he said from the doorway, clutching the frame, his clothing disheveled and torn. He looked at the form on the floor. "It worked?"

Cheveyo got to his feet. "It felt the same way it did when I put a memory in Petra's mind, and that worked." He held out his hand to her. "You all right?"

She shrugged, then winced. "Just sore. You?"

"Same. How about you?" he said, directing the question to Pope.

A bruise was beginning to bloom on his cheek. "My head hit the post when we went through the window. It knocked me into unconsciousness for . . . well, I don't know how long." He rubbed his head and grimaced, then held up his hand, a handcuff around his wrist. "Yurek tried to cuff me to the railing."

That's when she noticed the metal was warped and scorched. "You used your ability?"

"It's still weak, but coming back. It worked enough to burn through the chain."

Cheveyo nodded toward Yurek. "I was out for several hours when my father inserted the memory in my head. Let's move him. I don't want to waste a minute."

The two men hoisted Yurek's limp body, and she opened the front door for them. Once he was in the Tank, they tied him up.

"I'll get the Sinthe," she said, running back into the house. Even in the dark she could tell it was in shambles. They'd fix it up again. The important thing was they were all right. It was over.

Over.

Don't think about that right now.

"You're bleeding," Cheveyo said when she stepped back into the RV.

She followed his worried gaze to her shoulder. "Just a few scratches. You have more injuries than I do." Now that he'd pointed it out, though, those scratches started to sting like crazy.

Pope waved his hand over her, and then Cheveyo. The sting went away. The bruises and cuts on Cheveyo's face and arms disappeared. She turned to Pope and lifted her hand.

Pope stilled her hand. "I'll be fine. Save your strength."

"I've got plenty of strength." She saw Cheveyo's stern expression and relented. "Fine."

They drove to the finestra near Zion, a longer drive but better fitted to the memories Yurek would wake up with than the closer one.

She sat in the passenger chair. "So he'll remember fighting us out in the wilderness, and sending us to our deaths into the ravine?"

"We have to account for why he isn't bringing any bodies back," he said. He glanced back at Pope, who was lying on the couch with an ice pack on his head. "He'll remember having to nail you with the Sinthe, and if he's not supposed to have one, he can't really bring your body back anyway."

"I doubt the C has changed their rules in the last three months," Pope said. "We'll use the Sinthe to create scorch marks at the base of the ravine that will coordinate with his memories."

She aimed a hard look at Yurek on the floor, trussed up like a pig. His shirt was crusted with blood, face bruised. "He'll remember the altercation that will account for those injuries."

Cheveyo winked. "And he'll remember a few humiliating moments, too, just for good measure."

Three hours later he'd been deposited, without ropes, on the hard ground. The finestra shimmered, even in the dark.

Cheveyo stared at Yurek, his eyes just as hard as the ground. "I wanted to kill him."

She touched his back. "I know."

"It was hard to stop myself. Other than Pope, I've never let an Otherling live."

Pope was looking at Yurek, too. "He'll be back. Not for us, but for someone else. You can take care of him then."

She looked at Cheveyo. "Will you? Keep fighting, hunting?"

"Who else will fight them?"

She tried to keep her shoulders from slumping. Had she really expected any other answer?

Pope's large feet crunched on the ground as he walked closer to them. "There are other Offspring."

"Are you talking about the Rogues?" Petra said.

Pope gave her a soft smile at her worry. "Not them, though I know any one of them would step up to the fight if necessary. One of the people in the original government program donated sperm to a bank. I have found two of his offspring, though I haven't approached them yet. I don't know what abilities they might have inherited, from their parent or my father." He turned back to Cheveyo. "You aren't the only one who can do this."

"But it's the only thing I know."

She tightened her hand on his back. "There's more to you than being a warrior. You're a lover, too. A father. A man. You can take your need to fight to different levels, like protecting abused children and women. Or becoming a bounty hunter. Take your passion for collecting knives and turn that into a career."

He didn't look convinced. After several long moments he looked at Pope. "These others, are they trained to hunt? Are they able to take a life?"

"The two from the sperm donor could qualify. One is ex-military, and from his records, he's both a skilled killer and an exuberant one. The other is a possibility, too. Then there is Nicholas's sister. And Jerryl's sister."

Petra wrinkled her nose. "That's someone I would not want to meet."

Pope nodded. "Bringing her to the people who killed her brother wouldn't be wise, no matter the circumstances."

Cheveyo nodded. "We should get out of here, in

case Yurek wakes. The last thing we need is for him to see the people he remembers killing."

They made the long walk toward the road where they'd parked the Tank. If she never walked in the wilderness again . . .

Complaining again?

She shot Cheveyo a look of ire. *I deserve to complain.*

Yes, you do. But is it making the trek any easier?

Yes. Though in truth, it wasn't. She wiped the sweat from her forehead and kept on going. For the most part they walked in silence, lost in their thoughts. Probably about the future. She didn't want to hope Cheveyo would come around. Been there, done that.

After what felt like hours she looked into the distance and blinked. The Tank, shimmering in the distance. "Please tell me that's not a mirage."

"It's real," Cheveyo said.

"Thank gawd." She stepped up her pace and nearly stumbled to it, latching onto the door handle. Both men joined her a minute later, looking not the least bit tired but definitely amused at her dramatics.

As soon as Cheveyo unlocked the door, Petra collapsed on the sofa, letting the air conditioner chill her damp skin. Cheveyo handed her a bottle of cold water, and she sat up to drink it.

Cheveyo and Pope stood in the narrow passage of the kitchen chugging down water, too. They had come to mean so much to her, in different ways. Pope with his distinctive looks . . .

"If Yurek comes back on other business and sees Pope, he'll know something is off."

Cheveyo looked Pope up and down. "She's right. You don't exactly blend in. Can you change your appearance?"

"We choose one earth dimension 'suit' and commit to it. I can't morph at will like Yurek. That is his particular energy signature. But I can change my look, if necessary."

Cheveyo nodded. "I think it's necessary."

"If Yurek is close to me, he'll recognize my Essence. That never changes. However, the chances of running into him are skinny."

"And from a distance, he won't recognize you at all," Cheveyo added.

She tilted her head, studying Pope. "You might want to pick something that fits in a little more. You're handsome, very striking, but you stand out. Can you pick, say, a Johnny Depp look?"

"No, it doesn't work that way. I visualize general characteristics and then start the process. It's uncomfortable to change and takes time to get used to." Pope looked at Cheveyo. "Unlike the way you change to your cat, which I suspect is natural for you, changing my suit is not natural at all. Neither is being in the suit to begin with. But I shall have to get used to it, I suppose."

Petra sat up completely. "You never did answer my question earlier: what do you look like as a Callorian?"

"I'll have to revert to my real self before I can change. Are you sure you want to see me? I look even more different."

"I do," she said.

She glanced at Cheveyo, who said, "You can't look worse than a Glouk."

Pope laughed. "No, nothing like that. We're quite beautiful, if I don't say so myself." He sat next to her on the couch and relaxed his body. "It will take some time. Do not wait for me to return to human before heading home."

"Will you be able to talk to us?" she asked.

"Not during the process. Callorians speak to each other psychically and so do not use voices very often. I like the nuances in the human voice. They reveal much of emotions, even if I cannot always tell what those emotions are." He took a breath and closed his eyes. His human suit shimmered, slowly becoming golden static, and then fell away.

"You *are* beautiful," she said on a breath.

His form remained in a human shape, but he was opalescent, the same shade as his eyes. His skin was perfectly smooth, as was his head. He tensed, his body contorting, fingers curling.

"It looks beyond uncomfortable," she said. "It looks painful."

Cheveyo was watching, too. "He wouldn't have done it if he couldn't handle it. I have a feeling Pope can handle a lot." He walked up to the front and started the engine.

Petra remained next to Pope, watching over his transformation. He trembled, and she felt his energy straining. Over the next hour his exterior began to take on a fleshlike consistency. His face took on definition, square chin, full mouth, and a nose that bordered on cute.

"How's he doing?" Cheveyo asked, flicking a glance back at them.

"He's coming along nicely."

They were almost home when Pope's eyes fluttered open. He stretched as though wearing a tight bodysuit, and finally he focused his gaze on her.

"Handsome," she said. "You kept your eye color."

"I can't seem to change it." He ran his fingers through thick hair. "I thought it might be good to not deal with hair since we don't have it in Surfacia, but this will be a nice change."

"I like it."

Pope shrugged. "It'll do. Humans are too preoccupied with appearance."

She had been, not so long ago. "I feel like I've shed my human suit, too. The things that used to matter so much . . . not anymore." She walked over to the passenger seat and sat down. "Everything's different," she said to Cheveyo. But she would go back to her life and try to fit back into it.

His expression was sober. "I see too much of the warrior, not enough of the princess."

"You liked when I was more princess. You don't like seeing me as an equal. But I've changed. I'll never be her again." She tilted her head. "Don't look so sad. I like who I am now. No matter what happens in life, I know I can handle it. I'm not afraid like I used to be. You're different, too."

"Nothing has changed for me."

"Your son is alive. You have the chance to have a normal life. A family. Your father made your choices before. Who you were. Who was in your life. This time you get to choose."

She could see his resolve, in the way his mouth tightened, the way his eyes were shuttered.

"You're not going to see Cody, are you?"

"It's better if I don't. The illusion my father created could easily happen."

She moved closer, her nose almost touching his. "You're going to let us all go, for our own good. But what about your good, Cheveyo? Don't you deserve to be happy? To have love?"

"I deserve to know that I didn't cause the death

of my son and his mother. I deserve to know that I haven't gotten you killed. That's enough."

She wasn't going to give up that easily. Mostly because she could see that boy, his blue-gray eyes shadowed by loneliness, by what was missing in his life. A younger version of Cheveyo, and that alone rubbed her heart raw. "I grew up without my mother, and the loss of her was a hole in my heart my whole life. I was angry at her sometimes, I cried and felt sorry for myself, and occasionally I felt sorry for her. I needed my mom, even if she wasn't normal. Even if she could set fires with her mind."

His gaze hardened as it met hers. "But being with her wouldn't have jeopardized your life."

She sighed. Damned stubborn man. "What if Cody inherited the cat? I'm sure your father prepared you. How old were you when you first turned? What was it like?"

That got him. His eyes darkened in a human way, showing her how scary it had been, even knowing what to expect.

He looked beyond her, sinking back to that time. "I was twelve, almost thirteen. Puberty triggered it. I lost my child's voice and gained a jaguar. Yes, my father did warn me. It was still terrifying. And painful. It is the first several times, like having your body ripped apart and then clumped back together."

He shifted his gaze to Pope. "It's natural now, but not at the beginning. I was overwhelmed with the need to hunt, as though the jaguar had been in hibernation my whole life and was now famished. My father set me loose in the woods and told me to free my cat. I caught and ate a rabbit, and was horrified.

When I came back to myself, I had blood and guts and bits of fur on my face. I threw up. That was my initiation." He pulled his gaze back to her. "I'll watch the boy, of course, and if he shows signs, I'll intercede. I've got a few years."

She looked at Pope, startled at his new appearance. His hair was dark brown, thick and rough cut. And in those eyes she saw the mirror of her pain.

She turned back to Cheveyo, holding onto his words that night after they'd first made love. How would he walk away from her now? How was she supposed to walk away from him?

In a hoarse voice, he said, "I'll make you a flight reservation to go home. My place isn't fit to stay in."

She nodded, though he wasn't looking at her. "Pope, what will you do?"

"Make a life, I suppose. Find a place to live in Annapolis, perhaps."

That made her smile. "Close to your family. We are your family, after all."

He smiled back. "Yes. I have identities that I can use, histories and appropriate paperwork. But I don't have them with me, so I cannot fly. We could rent a car and drive together."

"You'll stay with me until you integrate into a new life," she said with a nod, the matter settled.

"Thank you. I will watch out for anomalies, as you have been doing." He directed that to Cheveyo. "I will keep in touch with you."

"Yes, let me know." That warrior's light shone in his eyes.

It sank her heart.

"But before we go, we shall get your house in order," Pope added. When Cheveyo began to protest, he added, "I'll brook no argument. Petra and I can handle the disarray." She swore he winked at her. "Then we will depart."

Cheveyo didn't look grateful, only resolved. "If you insist."

"I do."

CHAPTER 23

Their car reservation was for the following day. Together with Cheveyo, Petra and Pope had spent the last day repairing the house. Cheveyo worked himself into exhaustion, banging away late into the night until she'd already given up and gone to bed. He fell into his deep sleep the moment his head hit the pillow and woke before she did. Before then, she would have never thought one could avoid someone else when they were sharing a bed. She wore pajamas to sleep, he wore cotton pants. He would not send her from his bed, but he would not let himself be tempted, either.

She paused as she dropped the last of the broken wood from inside the house onto the pile by the steps and watched Pope and Cheveyo set the new window in place. Both men were shirtless, and Cheveyo's chest glistened with sweat. They'd been working all morning.

Pope didn't sweat. It was still odd to see him looking so different. So human. She loved that he was coming back with her, but it didn't assuage the ache that wracked her body and strangled her heart like a vine. Turning away from them, she walked along the front porch to the decrepit garden. Speaking of vines . . . She crouched down and started pulling out weeds, but her gaze kept going to the porch. To Cheveyo.

He was watching her, too, but shifted back to the task at hand. What she felt for him, it was different than the longing she'd once felt for Lucas. Back then she'd thought she needed someone to complete her. She'd seen her friends as halves of a whole, seen herself as a lone half. For a while she'd thought Cheveyo was her other half. Now she knew she was whole by herself, and so was he. She didn't need him to complete her, but she did need him.

She yanked a stubborn weed out with a grunt and tossed it aside. Damn it, she needed him in her life. She was stuck with him in her heart. Her fingers dug into the dry dirt.

"What am I doing? If he doesn't care about this stupid garden, why should I?"

Still, she kept on weeding. It was mindless work that was satisfying. Once she'd amassed a pile of landscape refuse, she turned again to the house. It spoke to her, with its simple lines, front porch with rockers, and the windows that reflected the late afternoon cloudy sky. And Cheveyo, standing on the porch alone watching her, his hand resting against one of the heavy posts. The sight of him made her ache, and she turned and attacked more weeds. It could be a nice garden. Just the right size for some carrots, broccoli, maybe even cucumbers. Definitely herbs. With a border of flowers, just for fun.

She unearthed a tiny tomato hiding beneath the brown vines. "You're a stubborn little thing, aren't

you? Fighting to survive without water, food, or love."
She sighed. "Should I fight? Should I be stubborn?"
She pulled another weed, leaving the tomato in its
place. "He's already made it clear that all he cares
about is his cause. And it's a good cause. Who am I to
tell him, to beg or plead with him, to give it up? I suppose that would be selfish. And frankly, I can't stand
rejection again." She blew a few stray strands of hair
from her face, her hands too dirty to do the job. "I'm
talking to a tomato. Really? *Really?*"

"It appears that you are."

She spun and stood at the same time, her cheeks
going as red as that tomato. Cheveyo had a soft smile
on his face, and sawdust clung to his hair like snow-
flakes on a dark night.

"I guess you heard all that."

He nodded. "The important question is, did you
hear the tomato answer?"

She laughed, grateful for the levity, then clamped
her lower lip between her teeth. "I'm still waiting.
Have any answers?"

He dropped the work gloves he'd been carrying,
tucking the tips of his fingers into his front pockets.
"Should you fight? No, I think you've fought enough.
Should you be stubborn? Yes. Who are you to tell me
to give up my cause? No one can force another to give
up something that's meaningful to him. And yes, you
were talking to a tomato." His mouth quirked. "That
cover it?"

"Pretty much." Without thinking, she flicked away
a strand that was tickling her cheek, probably leaving
a streak of dirt behind.

He stepped closer, brushing away the crumbs of
dirt. "You look good over here, tending my garden."

She met his gaze. "It was lonely and neglected."
Like him. Like her.

He ran his fingers along her hairline. "And you
look good in my bed. And in my home. Except it's not
really a home, is it?" He glanced back at it. "More like
an in-between kind of place, a recovery point."

She felt a thrumming in her chest. She could only
nod, not knowing where he was going.

"What I do, it is worthy. It's been worthy of my sacrifice for a long time. It fulfills me. But not as much
as hearing you laugh. Or making love to you. Or
imagining what it would be like to walk out on my
porch with my morning coffee and see you digging
in the garden, or the joy on your face when you find
one little tomato. It doesn't fulfill me like the thought
of being in my son's life again." He put his hands on
either side of her face. "The thing is, I'm not the warrior my father was. I discovered a fatal flaw: I have
emotions. I love. And I want to be loved. I don't know
what normal is, but I'm ready to embrace being an ordinary—sort of—guy with an extraordinary woman."

When she didn't react, he added, "That would be
you."

She launched herself at him, wrapping her legs
around his waist, burying her fingers in his hair and
kissing him. When she came up for air, she saw Pope
watching from the porch, a smile on his face. Had he
known that giving Cheveyo this extra time with her
would break through the walls he'd built around his
life? Maybe the man knew more about human emotion than they thought.

He hugged her close, as though he would never
let her go. "I want you to come with me to Phoenix.
When I meet my son."

She leaned back and nodded, her throat so tight she couldn't even speak. He carried her back to the front porch. "Petra and I are going to clean up and drive down to see my son. Depending on how things go, maybe I'll bring him up here to meet you."

"That would be nice." Pope gave her a wink, the dog. "Perhaps I'll explore the area more. Maybe go into Flag."

She slid down to her feet, gave Pope a kiss on the cheek, and led Cheveyo into the house by the hand. Before they reached the door, she turned and said, "Maybe you should stop in that boutique, where Suza works. She senses that you have a good soul, after all."

Pope rubbed his chin. "Is that a good idea, considering what I am? And what I look like now."

She shrugged. "I don't know. But sometimes what doesn't seem wise in the beginning turns out to be just perfect."

Petra watched Cheveyo sit down at the driver's seat of the Tank, take a deep breath, and dial the number he'd looked up. It had only given D as an initial, no name.

"Darcy?" he asked when someone apparently answered. He listened. "Oh. I'm sorry. This is Cheveyo, Cody's father. I only just found out where Darcy had taken him and I'm on my way to see him now."

She listened, baffled as to what was going on. When he disconnected, he looked at her with a stunned expression. "Darcy passed from cancer last week. That was her sister, Paula. Right now Cody's staying with her, but she can't raise him. She said my call was a gift from God. The boy needs a home."

She got chills. "Well, let's go bring him home, then."

She held his hand during the entire drive down to Phoenix.

"Our lives are about to totally change," she said, still amazed.

"Oh, yeah." His jaw tensed for a second, but she saw a hint of a smile on his mouth. "Paula said Cody asked Darcy about me a lot. She told him I was a government agent, something like a spy. I remember thinking my father was a super hero. I knew he was off doing important things. But I missed having a dad in my life."

She squeezed his arm, thinking of him as that boy, and knowing his son missed having him around, too.

He looked over at her. "Are you going to be all right with suddenly having a kid? We'll have our own, of course, but being a stepmother to a nine-year-old isn't going to be easy."

She couldn't help the grin that broke out on her face. "You don't know what those words mean to me. Yes, I'm okay with it. I'm excellently awesome with it. My life, my heart, has been empty for a long time. Now it's going to be overfilled." She hugged him, burying her face in his neck and breathing him in. Sage and spice. "Are you going to be all right with suddenly being a dad?"

"Scares the hell out of me." He gave her a smile. "I don't expect it to be easy, especially at first. I'm the jerk who hasn't even come around on his birthday or Christmas. What kind of dad is that? Even a super spy one? How am I going to explain why I've never even sent him a gift?"

"Remember, his mother hid him from you. You

can't send a gift if you don't know where he is. The other part, about hunting alien beings and such—he doesn't need to know that for a while."

He laughed, and she loved the sound of it, the way it crinkled his eyes and showed his perfect white teeth. "Definitely not."

He followed the GPS lady's directions to the park. His expression became more serious as he parked, got out, and opened the side door for her. She paused in front of him. "Are you afraid he's going to reject you? I was worried about that very thing not long ago."

"Maybe I should have talked to the tomato." He grinned when she laughed, but his smile faded. "I wouldn't blame him if he spit in my face."

She kissed him. "It'll be fine."

He took her hand, giving her no doubt that he wanted her by his side. They walked across a grass expanse toward a gazebo. A woman sat on top of one of the bench tables, watching a boy playing on the equipment.

She pushed lanky blond hair from her face and got to her feet when she saw them approach, an unsure smile on her face.

He shook her hand. "Been a long time." He turned toward Petra. "Paula, this is Petra."

Petra shook her hand, but the woman gave her an odd look before saying to Cheveyo, "So this is the woman you used to call out to in your sleep. Darcy told me about that. She was afraid to ask who Petra was. She felt bad about taking the kid, but she believed they were in danger." She met his gaze. "Did you have a dangerous job, or was she lying about that, too?"

Petra tightened her hold on his hand, those words surging through her. He'd called her name. Years ago. He gave her a sheepish grin but looked at Paula again.

"I had a dangerous job, but I've just retired. What do you mean, 'too'?"

Paula's face blanched. "Guess it doesn't matter now. She lied about being on birth control. She wanted out of her situation, wanted someone to take care of her. But she wasn't just using you. She thought she loved you, but when you have parents who don't know how to show love, you just can't be sure what love really is."

His gaze went to the boy, who was mildly interested in the people his aunt was talking to. Did he see his own image in Cheveyo?

"I haven't told him yet," Paula said. "I wanted to talk to you first, make sure you wanted him."

"I want him."

"Thank God. I've got three kids, two jobs, and no father to give me squat to help them. I can't take one more. He's a good kid. I'm sure I'd screw him up anyway. Darcy's best friend's been picking him up from school and taking him to her apartment, to help him with the transition. She loves that boy, but she can't take him either, got some serious health problems. Broke my heart to think about him being put into foster care. When you called, it was like a miracle."

Cheveyo nodded, sliding her a glance. "I've had a few of those myself lately."

Paula waved the boy over. "C'mere, hon!"

Cody ran over but came to an abrupt stop when he neared them. His blue-gray eyes locked onto Cheveyo. He finally pulled away to look at his aunt, his dark eyebrows knitted together.

"This is your father. Your mama always felt bad

that she left without telling him where you went. She was only trying to protect you. But we can make things right."

Petra saw a mixture of wonder, hurt, and confusion pass over the boy's face. Cheveyo tried to mask the emotions she knew were coursing through him, but she saw his chin tremble. He sat down on the bench to put himself at Cody's eye level and held out his hand. "It's great to see you again. I know I haven't been around for a while, and I'm sorry about that. But I can be around now, if you want."

The boy warily nodded. "Do bad guys still hunt you down?"

"No, not anymore. I've retired. I couldn't be without my family anymore." He held out his hand to her, and she sat down beside him. "This is Petra, the woman I'm going to marry. I want to settle down, make a life in a beautiful home I have just north of here. I'd love for you to come visit. If you like it, maybe you can stay for a night or two."

Ease him in, she thought. Good job.

"My mom was really sick," he said, his eyes filled with sadness and uncertainty. "She said she was sorry she couldn't find me a place to live after she went home to God."

Her heart almost broke on those words. Cheveyo said, "You could live with us. We could get a dog. Petra's going to grow us a garden, and if you like tomatoes, you're in luck."

She grinned at that.

"I like cherry tomatoes," he said, curling his finger and thumb to make a circle. "The little ones."

"I can grow those," she said. "A whole bunch of them."

The boy smiled. "Tomatoes *and* a dog?"

She tipped her head toward Cheveyo. "That's what the man said."

"A big dog? I like big ones."

She laughed. "Little tomatoes and big dogs, huh? I think we can manage that."

But his eyes were on Cheveyo. *And a dad. You'll have a dad.*

Cheveyo let out a soft sigh. "God, I've missed you, kid." In those words, she heard such emotion, and saw the way he strained to hold himself back from hugging his son.

Cody took a tentative step forward, and then fell against Cheveyo. He put his arms around the boy and pulled him close, his eyes squeezed shut. Cody's eyes were, too. Her heart filled with the sight of them, with what her life would be like now. She was already thinking about taking him shopping to decorate his room. She hoped he liked *The Wizard of Oz.*

Cody stepped back and turned to his aunt. "Can we go to Dad's house today?"

"We sure can." Paula smiled.

Cheveyo stood. "Right now my house is just that: a house. It needs a garden and a dog. But mostly it needs a family, a dad and a mom and a kid." He glanced at Petra and then looked at Cody. "I think we might be a perfect fit."

Acknowledgments

I'm always grateful for the research help that keeps the book real. Special thanks to the following wonderful peeps:

Lacey Slade for her help in Arizona setting details as well as Hopi information. Lacey wrote me a fan letter and offered to help with my books, little knowing that she lived close to the very area where this book was set.

Nancy Grillo, for a little bit of facial research and a lot of wonderful facials over the years.

Thanks to my critique bud, Marty Ambrose, for encouragement, great input, and friendship.

Thanks to Rachael Wolff. Really.

Coming in June 2012 from Avon Books,
the next thrilling paranormal romance
from Jaime Rush

DARKNESS BECOMES HER

Next month, don't miss these exciting new love stories only from Avon Books

Trouble at the Wedding   by Laura Lee Guhrke

After giving up on true love, Annabel Wheaton settles for a marriage of convenience and a comfortable, if uneventful, future. Determined to save the beauty from an unhappy marriage, the dashing Christian Du Quesne accepts an offer from Annabel's family to stop the wedding. But what happens if he can't resist falling in love on the job?

Bedeviled   by Sable Grace

Under a dangerous spell, Haven is bent on unleashing an evil god upon Earth. Kyana knows she is the only one who can stop it, but with her blood ties to Haven weakening, it's a race against time. With her lover Ryker by her side, they must risk everything to save Haven, and the world, from the hell threatening to consume them all.

The Price of Temptation   by Lecia Cornwall

With her traitor of a husband missing, Lady Evelyn Renshaw's life is in jeopardy and she must hire a capable footman to protect her. Captain Sinjon Rutherford is sure he's the man for the job and can uncover the truth about her suspicious relations. But can he resist the temptations of the lady of the house—or will a new scandal ruin everything?

How the Marquess Was Won   by Julie Anne Long

Julian Spenser, Marquess Dryden, is determined to restore his family's name, and it is no surprise when Julian sets his sights on the beautiful heiress Lisbeth Redmond as the perfect wife to round out his mission. But after one chance encounter with Lisbeth's companion, Phoebe Vale, the two can't deny their irresistible attraction.

REL 1211

978-0-06-184132-3

978-0-06-202719-1

978-0-06-206932-0

978-0-06-204515-7

978-0-06-199968-0

978-0-06-201232-6

At Avon Books, we know your passion for romance—once you finish one of our novels, you find yourself wanting more.

May we tempt you with . . .

- **Excerpts** from our upcoming releases.

- Entertaining **extras**, including authors' personal photo albums and book lists.

- Behind-the-scenes **scoop** on your favorite characters and series.

- **Sweepstakes** for the chance to win free books, romantic getaways, and other fun prizes.

- Writing **tips** from our authors and editors.

- **Blog** with our authors and find out why they love to write romance.

- **Exclusive content** that's not contained within the pages of our novels.

Join us at
www.avonbooks.com

AVON
An Imprint of HarperCollins*Publishers*
www.avonromance.com

Available wherever books are sold or please call 1-800-331-3761 to order.

FTH 0708